Splintered Paddle

Splintered Paddle

A NOVEL ABOUT KAMEHAMEHA THE GREAT

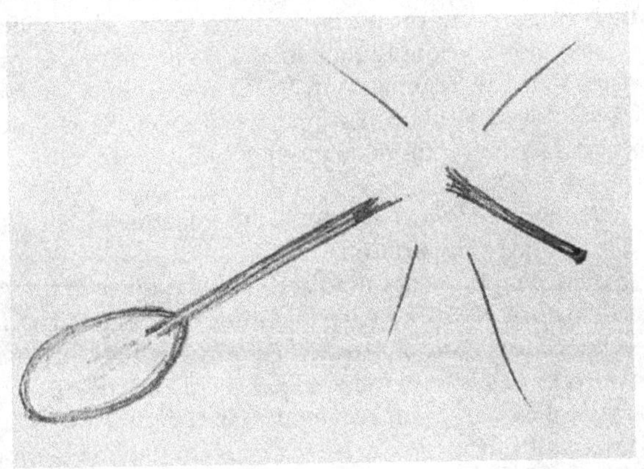

Bill Fernandez

Photographs and sketches by Judith Fernandez.

This is a work of historical fiction based on Hawaiian resources and years of research about Kamehameha the Great's battles as he fought to unite all of the Hawaiian islands. Conversations of the historical characters are the author's creation. Kalani-Moku-Tana is a figment of the author's imagination. The following characters are based on historical information: Kamehameha, Kaahumanu, Captain Cook, John Young, Isaac Davis, Simon and Thomas Metcalf, Keawe, Kiwalao, Kamaka-I-Moku, Kahekili, King Keoua of Kau, Pauli, Kalaniopuu, and Pa ao. Several other historical figures are combined into one or more characters for ease of reading. The gods and heiau are historical.

The *Law of the Splintered Paddle* was decreed by Kamehameha I in 1792 and is included in the Hawaii State Constitution.

The front cover photograph of Hawaiian artifacts was taken at the American Museum of Natural History, New York City, by Judith Fernandez. The three items are: the woven feather cape typical of those worn only by the chiefs and alii (high status), headgear worn by chiefs, and the war god Ku. The cape is typical of intricate featherwork on a base of woven sennit created by Hawaiians using thousands of feathers; no birds were killed for the feathers. The second item is a model for the woven feather headgear worn by the chiefs. The third item, an idol, is the war god Ku, brought to Hawaii by the Tahitians about 1200 AD who introduced taboos and human sacrifice.

The illustration of a splintered canoe paddle was inspired by the University of Hawaii School of Law Library Logo. The cannon sketch was inspired by the artist Brook Kaupuniahi Parker who illustrated K*amehameha, the Rise of a King,* a historical novel by David Kawika Eyre.

ISBN-13: 9780999032671

LOC
Makani Kai Media Publisher Printed in the United States of America
www.kauaibillfernandez.com fcb: Bill Fernandez Hawaiian Author
An Approved Kauai Made Product

Dedication

I lovingly dedicate this book to
my wife,

Judith Fernandez

Acknowledgment

THE HAWAIIAN ETHIC OF FAMILY, *ohana*, means no one accomplishes alone. We are who we are today because of who came before us and who are with us along our path of life.

I particularly want to say *mahalo*, thank you, to my teachers, especially those at Kamehameha Schools who turned this barefoot boy into a serious student. Vernon Trimble, my sophomore class advisor, stands out in my memories as a strong influence on me urging me to attend college.

My editor and friend, Bill Bernhardt, taught me about commas and tries to mold me into a good writer.

Many others have helped me in many ways, encouraging me to continue writing. Mahalo to the Kauai Historical Society, Kauai Museum, and Kauai libraries and local stores for honoring me by including my books in their publication sales and collections, and inviting me to give book talks. Bill Buley of *the Garden Island Newspaper* and his wife, Marianne, encourage me in many ways. Thank you to Hanapepe Bookstore for invaluable advice, carrying my books, and inviting me to do book signings. To all of the readers of my books, I give a loud *mahalo!* (thank you) for your keen interest in my writings and your comments.

Without the encouragement, support and hard work of editing, design, photography and sketches, publication, and promotion of my writings and book talks by my loving and devoted wife, Judith, I could not have written my books. All the credit for what I have written goes to her.

Splintered Paddle, a novel of Kamehameha the Great
Kirkus Review:

"A **historical novel** set during the period of **Kamehameha the Great's battles** to consolidate the Hawaiian Islands stars a **fierce yet tender-hearted young warrior** determined to bring security to his family.

...**1790**, and **17-year-old Kalani** Moku Tana has been sent by his mother... to attend **Kamehameha's Pa lua, a military training academy**. He faces **daunting challenges**... His mother warned him: *"...you cannot show ancestry to the gods...will be tested, humiliated. Be Strong.* ***You must become a koa (warrior)****."* Kalani's father, captured during a battle, was sacrificed to the War god Ku. Gruesome human sacrifice had been brought to Hawaii by the Tahitians...end of the first millennium A.D. On his first day, Kalani makes one fast **friend, Moki**, and **one very dangerous enemy, Hauna**. Kalani becomes skilled in the use of the Hawaiians' primitive weaponry... also...in a **risky romantic liaison** that will cost him dearly...capture of the Western schooner...a new opportunity...**muskets and cannons**. In this **rip-roaring** tale, **Bill Fernandez...has done his research**...narrative is rich in small details of island life before the impact of Western civilization...numerous **battle scenes are graphic, bloody** and **riveting... endless intrigue**...

An action-packed adventure, a wealth of historical and cultural minutiae, and an engaging protagonist."

REVIEWS OF AUTHOR BILL FERNANDEZ
KIRKUS REVIEWS

NOVELS:

The *John Tana* Trilogy

John Tana: An Adventure Novel of Old Hawaii

(Book One of *John Tana* novel trilogy)

"Set in **19th-century Hawaii**, a historical novel stars a **handsome young hero**...the story chronicles a **hatefully racist time and place**...**Fernandez** (***Cult of Ku, a Hawaiian Murder Mystery...***) a **native Hawaiian**, is an **authentic voice** for John and the Pacific archipelago's **turbulent history. Plot twists** come thick and fast...the seductive undercurrent of John's **love** for Leinani...**vivid and intriguing details of Hawaiian daily life in the 19th century ring true**...the striking ending is not tidy, a plus...For the setting and era alone, this **ripping adventure yarn**..." (Emphasis added.)

Gods, Ghosts and Kahuna on Kauai

(Book Two of *John Tana* trilogy)

"...**resourceful Hawaiian John Tana is back**...Hawaii is at a **political tipping point**...is this the beginning of the end for the Kingdom of Hawaii... **racial tensions**...**gods and superstition**...a festering wound on the marriage...As a Hawaiian, **he wants the respect that he feels he deserves**... introduces readers to **Hawaiian history and culture including the mysteries and terrors of the..."old religion"...sketches by Judith Fernandez**... effectively **primitive charm** to the story and bring to mind Antoine de Saint-Exupéry's sketches for ***The Little Prince.***" (Emphasis added.)

Hawaiian Rebellions

(Book Three of the *John Tana* trilogy)

"...wrap-up of a **historical fiction series** starring **a 19th-century Hawaiian freedom fighter**...old loves endure; and familiar hatreds flare**... threats** from the **old native religion...the danger is real**... **kidnapped**...**sugar baron Robert Grant**...**overthrow** of the Hawaiian monarchy and the **annexation...**

by the United States...**raped**...**leper**... **no safety** in this Eden...attempt to **save the Kingdom of Hawaii**...John is a **well-rounded character**...**Action scenes are Fernandez's forte**...tensions between John's **Christianity and the native religion**. He is **trapped between the two worlds**...heading for a **hard choice**...**the realm**...he was **born into**...**will always be pulling at him**...**the whole trilogy—is worth a read.**" (Emphasis added.)

The *Grant Kingsley* Novels

Cult of Ku, a Hawaiian Murder Mystery

(A *Grant Kingsley* novel)

"**Hawaiian history, folklore, and labor struggles**...**a 1920-set mystery packed with violence and murder**...Grant Kingsley...returns to his home in Honolulu...only to find that his **status in his wealthy family**... **is in question**...**A deathbed confession by his mother**...grandmother... wants to **disinherit** him...found dead...**charges Grant with the murder**...Four more...The **depth** of the author's **historical knowledge** is evident...many **fascinating insights** into the era...explores **cultural conflicts in Hawaii**..." (Emphasis added.)

Crime & Punishment in Hawaii

(A *Grant Kingsley* novel)

"**An attorney finds trouble in paradise**...**novel set in Hawaii**...**skin diving** with his friend...come under fire. Keoki is killed, and Kingsley is left with an enemy who vows to **harm his family**...local news...**a different case**...**the Massie Affair**...**racial unrest**...story **combines the factual and the fictional** and seasons them with...**gunfire and Hawaiian history**...a **vivid** picture of discord..." (Emphasis added.)

MEMOIRS

KIRKUS REVIEWS:

Kauai Kids in Peace and WW Two

"**1930s and 40s Hawaii**...**childhood**...Kauai...isolated...**multiracial**... poor families share...large Japanese population...gives **marine life**

glorious coverage...does his best to avoid **sharks**...**Part II: War...Pearl Harbor and its aftermath**...overt **racism**...engaging **tales of innocence and worldly wisdom**...father opens the **Roxy Theater**..." (Emphasis added.)

Hawaii in War and Peace

"...**military school in Honolulu...1944**...**war**...once the war was over, **Hawaii remained at unrest...worker's strike, tsunami**...**toured the mainland** U.S. with his family and found a **nation with unbridled prejudices**...**riveting** account of...a world in disarray...the **grandest impression is the more personal side**...mistake him for a **Mexican**, mistreating him...which of the segregated restrooms he could use...**Engrossing** and identifiable." (Emphasis added.)

Other Reviews

Rainbows Over Kapaa (A Memoir)

"...he spent his **childhood barefoot**, cutting sugar, **diving** for fish and **surfing**...went on to **Stanford University**...the **history** of the Hawaiian Islands from a Kauaian perspective...people from all over the world... **Fernandez family, Kapaa and its Roxy Theater**...popular movie house... because...**World War II troops stationed on Kauai**. **The story of the theater...is intertwined with that of the Fernandez family**...Hawaiian words... mingled with English to give...the **Aloha feeling**, and a **remarkable collection of pictures** traces Kapaa through the years...**a diverse community can live in harmony**..." (Emphasis added.)

San Jose [CA] Mercury News Review

Glossary

Alii	Chief, ruler, noble
Alii Koa	The highest warrior class
Aina	Earth, land (feeds spiritually and physically)
Aloha	Greeting, farewell, love, compassion
Awa	Fermented drink of ceremony
Hale	Home, meeting house of bamboo wood frame and thatch
Haole	Westerner, Caucasian
Heiau	Sacred site of Hawaiians
Hui	Hello
Huhu	Angry, indignant, upset

Imua	Go forward
Ipu	Drum covered with sharkskin
Kahili	Feather staff, symbol of royalty
Kahuna (nui)	Hawaiian priest, or expert in a subject
Kanaloa	Hawaiian god of the sea
Kapa (Tapa)	Cloth from pounded bark of a mulberry or other trees
Kapu	Taboo, forbidden
Kauva (Kaua)	Menial caste selected for sacrifice, slave, servant
Kini	Forty thousand
Koa	Warror; wood used for canoes, paddles, bowls, furniture
Kukae	Excrement
Kulana	Rank, status. position
Leiomanu	Wooden club with shark teeth
Limu	Seaweed
Lokahi	Unity, agreement
Lono	Hawaiian god of agriculture, harvest, fertility, peace
Luau	Party with traditional Hawaiian food
Luakini	A large temple, once a site of human sacrifice
Mai	A direction, such as: "Come here."
Maile	Vine used to make lei
Maikai	Good
Makalii	Seven Sisters Star constellation
Mana	Supernatural or divine power
Mo o	Lizard, reptile, gekko
Nahu	To bite, sting like driving rain, pain
Okole	Rear end
Opala	Garbage, trash
Opu	Stomach, bladder

Pahu	Drum with sharkskin
Palaoa	Whale tooth strung on braided human hair necklace, symbol of high rank
Pa lua	School of military arts
Pa ao	Tahitian priest who brought worship of Ku, human sacrifice
Pele	Fire goddess
Pikoi	Woman warrior

For ease of reading by a diverse audience, I have omitted diacritical marks.

The Law of the Splintered Paddle

"THE LAW OF THE SPLINTERED paddle, *mamala-hoe kanawai,* decreed by Kamehameha I

> - Let every elderly person, woman and child lie by the roadside in safety –
>
> shall be a unique and living symbol of the State's concern for public safety.
> The State shall have the power to provide for the safety of the people from
> crimes against persons and property."

Hawaii State Constitution, Article 9, section 10P

Prologue

In 1758 Haley's Comet sped across the heavens. It was prophesied by the kahuna on Hawaii island that a child of royal blood, born beneath the white streak of a star, would become the "slayer of chiefs".

A son of royalty was birthed on the night that the Comet crossed the skies of Hawaii Island. The ruling king, fearful of the prophecy, ordered the child killed. A servant took the newborn from his mother and fled into the hills. He eventually delivered the baby to the child's uncle, the renowned high chief, Kekuhaupio, who became the infant's military mentor and guardian.

Raised in seclusion, the boy was named Kamehameha, meaning the "lonely one." By the age of fourteen he was tall, eminently strong, and fearless. By that time, he was a proven warrior, skilled in all the Hawaiian weapons: spear, club, shark-toothed dagger, and sling. He was especially talented in martial arts, *lua*.

In Hilo by a sacred temple lay the ponderous Naha Stone. It was claimed by the priests of that temple that whomever moved that giant rock would be: " The greatest king of Hawaii, bringing all the chiefs of the islands under his control".

To prove he was destined to rule, Kamehameha decided to move the Naha Stone. After an epic effort, the fourteen-year old youth toppled it over from its resting place. This feat placed him in the forefront of warrior chiefs that the ruling king, in the years ahead, would call upon in his battles on Hawaii island and Maui.

In 1778, the English captain, James Cook, stumbled onto Kauai and Niihau. It was the first time the Western World became aware of Hawaii. After a short visit he left for the Pacific Northwest to find the mythical passage between two oceans. Unable to uncover a route to the Atlantic, Cook returned to Hawaii, arriving in Kealekakua Bay on Hawaii Island in 1779.

Although treated as god Lono by the Hawaiians, the captain became angered by the theft of one of his small boats. He went ashore with marines to take the ruling king hostage. Cook's attempt to seize the ruler caused Hawaiians to attack him. They killed the captain and four marines. In retaliation, the two English ships, *Discovery and Resolution,* bombarded the villages lining the bay.

Hawaiians were Stone Age people, no metal resources, due to their centuries of isolation from the rest of the world. They fought Cook and his men with wood, rocks, and shark's teeth, but were unable to compete with the English heavy guns that devastated them and their homes from a great distance. Kamehameha was injured by a cannon shot. He would never forget the power of the British guns. He came to realize that they would be what he needed to acquire to win the future battles of conquest.

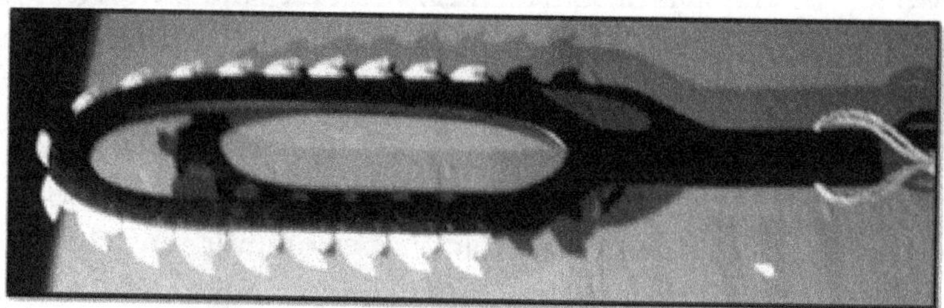

Leiomano shark tooth club

In 1782, the ruling king of Hawaii Island died. He gifted the throne to his son, Kiwalao. To his nephew, Kamehameha, he gave custody of his war god Ku. Several chiefs were upset with the new king for not favoring them in the land division that followed. These disgruntled men enlisted Kamehameha as their leader in a revolt against Kiwalao. In the ensuing battle of Moku-a-hai, Kiwalao was killed. But instead of Kamehameha becoming king of the island, Hawaii split into three parts. The lonely one ruled in Kohala and Kona, the west side of the island. Keawe assumed the leadership of Hilo and part of Puna, east Hawaii. Kamehameha's cousin Keoua of the Red Cloak ruled in Kau, the southern part of the island.

There followed eight years of war. Kamehameha had victories and defeats during this period that he called: "the bitter years." He was unable to defeat his two opposing rulers. Our story begins in 1790. On the slopes of Mauna Loa, Kamehameha had established a school to teach future warriors the military arts and lua.

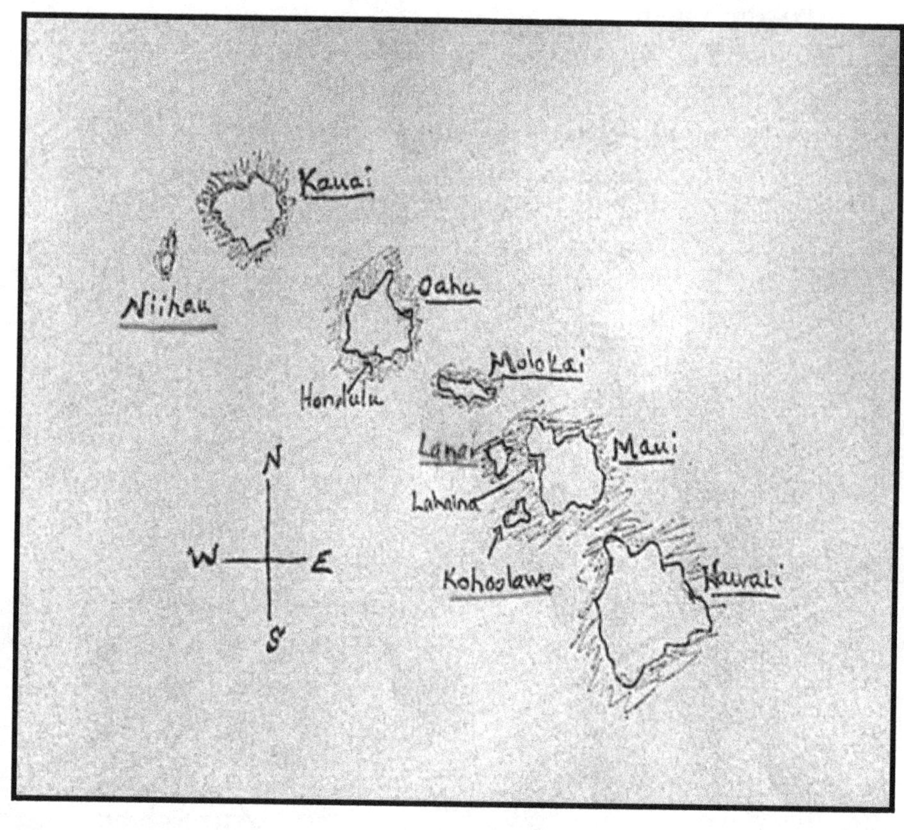
Kauai
Niihau
Oahu
Honolulu
Molokai
Lanai
Maui
Lahaina
Kohoolawe
Hawaii
N
W
E
S

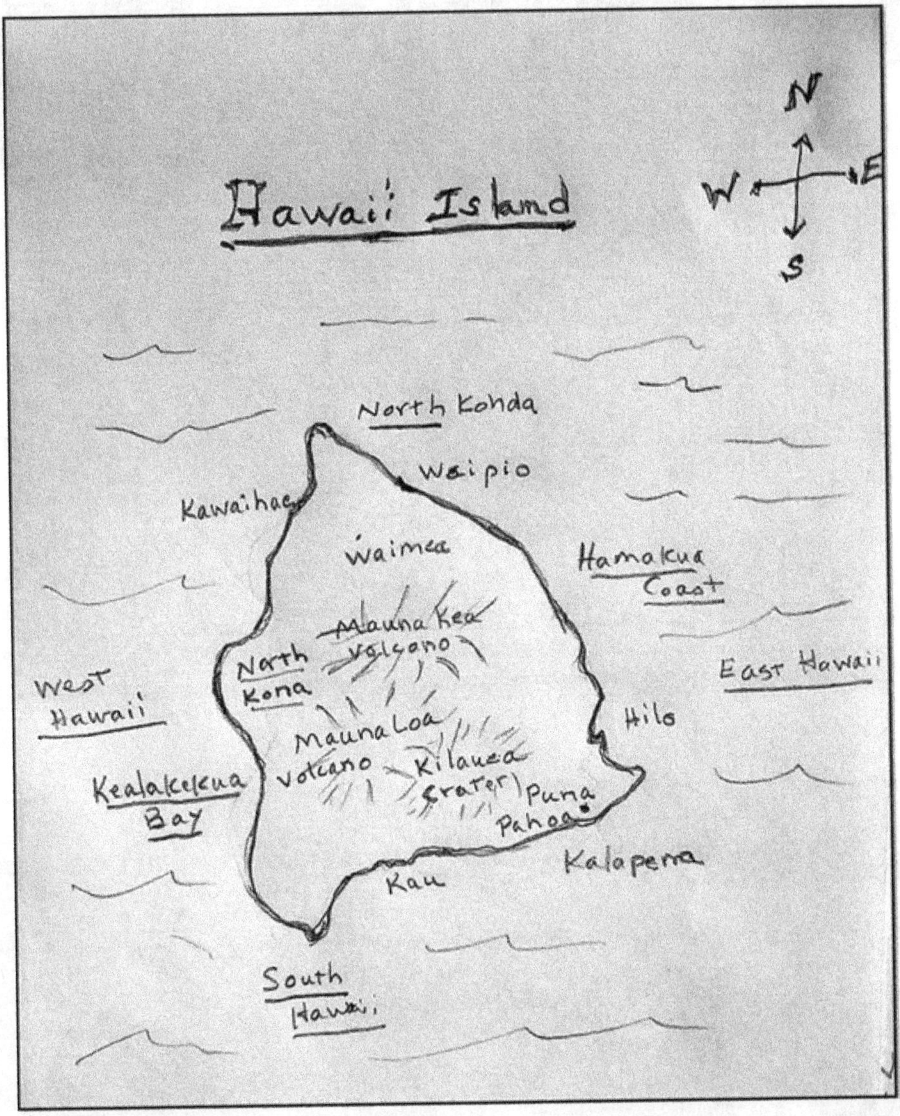

Hawaii Island

N
W
E
S

North Kohda
Waipio
Kawaihae
Waimea
Hamakua Coast
Mauna Kea volcano
North Kona
West Hawaii
East Hawaii
Hilo
Mauna Loa volcano
Kilauea crater
Puna
Pahoa
Kealakekua Bay
Kalapena
Kau
South Hawaii

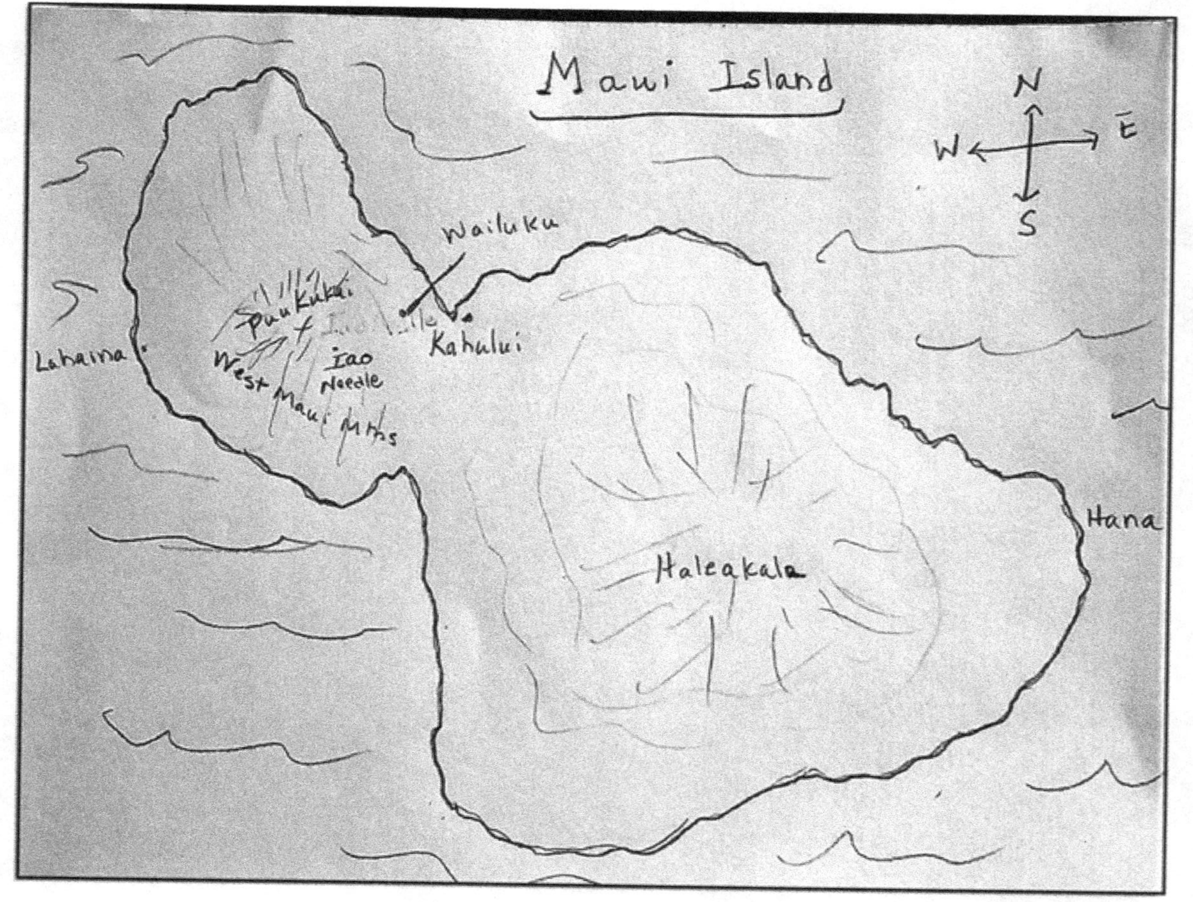
Mawi Island
N
W
E
S
Wailuku
Kahului
Puu Kukui
Iao Needle
West Maui Mtns
Lahaina
Haleakala
Hana

CHAPTER 1

Ku

Kalani's eyes swept over the huge, walled rectangle of the martial arts school. He trembled as he scanned the glaring statues of gods placed in niches along the enclosure. Ferocity marked their faces. Sharp, white teeth ringed gaping jaws. Black, slitted, oyster shell eyes added to the horrifying aspect of the icons of Hawaiian gods.

The unroofed structure lay a thousand feet above the Pacific Ocean. Looming over it towered Mauna Loa, a massive volcano that helped create the island of Hawaii. Cold air flowing from its cloud-shrouded summit added to the misery Kalani felt at his first sight of the frightening interior of his new school. His skin prickled as a mounting fear built within him.

"You, country boy, stop day-dreaming. Get in line with the rest of the *opala* I teach to be warriors for Kamehameha," Hepa the head master of the school yelled. "Over there by Hauna." He pointed toward a burly, six-foot man.

Kalani shivered. At the entry gate that student had threatened him. "My name is Hauna," he had said and thrust his elbow forcefully into Kalani's side. "I am the eldest son of the High Chief of Puna. Who are you? What is your ancestry?"

"Kalani Moku Tana, my father was sacrificed before he could teach me—" "You're nothing but rotten *kauva* rubbish," Hauna yelled, thrusting his broad stomach into the boy's body. "You do not belong here with the sons of chiefs." He emphasized his point by swinging his fist at Kalani's belly. The youth twisted aside, deflecting the blow with an elbow. He escaped further confrontation by scooting through the entranceway of the rock-walled, open-air school. He heard the bully screaming, "I will get you, slave boy."

When he scampered into the paved courtyard of the school Kalani had been hypnotized by the fiendishly carved icons of the gods. It was then that Hepa ordered him to line up next to his nemesis. *Should he disobey? Is the teacher testing his courage?* Kalani reluctantly took his place next to the big man who smiled and whispered, "Today I will beat you until you fall on your knees, beg for mercy, and then I will fling you from the school."

"Pivot on the right foot. Bring your left foot forward. Bend your knees. Clench your fists. Hold them at your side. Remember, Ku is watching," Hepa ordered.

Kalani sensed the war god glaring at him. He looked over his shoulder at the effigy of Ku. The icon's mouth gaped, its pointed teeth protruded from its jaws. It appeared ready to tear him apart. Distracted, he slid into Hauna.

"Fool! You stepped into me." With a sweep of his foot, the Hawaiian tried to trip Kalani to the ground. He dodged the strike, escaping the indignity of falling on his face.

"You," the instructor said and pointed. "Why do you fall out of line? Straighten yourself." He turned to the class. "When I hit the drum again, all pivot on your left foot and face the altar."

The teacher beat the instrument. A dozen men turned. Hauna moved further than necessary and caught Kalani's feet, upending him to the ground.

"You, country boy," Hepa yelled, staring at the youth splayed on the pebbles of the courtyard. "What's the matter? Can't keep your feet? Run into the hills and find me *maile* and be back before the drum beats eight times. Now go."

Kalani picked himself up from the stones thinking to protest, but held his tongue, not wanting to be considered a complainer. He knew he must accept whatever harassment came to him without challenge. But as his eyes met the big Hawaiian who spat at him, Kalani decided to find a way to meet his threats.

He raced through the open gate of the school, past the spearman at the entrance. With a wry grin, the guard yelled after him, "The password is purity." The drum boomed inside the temple and the guard's grin turned into a scowl. "You have one-hundred heart-beats between each strike on the shark skin. Run quick, little man." They both knew that failure to perform the task meant severe punishment, either expulsion or death.

Kalani ran uphill into the lush forest growing at the foot of Mauna Loa. He thought of his mother's parting words, *"The men in the school are chiefs. Unlike them, you cannot show ancestry to the gods. For this you will be tested, humiliated. Be strong. You must survive the training and become a koa."* He had promised her that he would, but he was upset by this first test. *It seems impossible, in an unknown forest, to find maile in eight-hundred heartbeats.*

Massive ferns blocked his way. The youth searched for a path into the jungle. He knew that maile grows deep within the woods, the mother vines roping around trees. Young shoots of the plant grow in the turf below a host tree. The pungency of its leaves smelled like the odor of a dying body and was often placed on the altar of temples to represent the stink of the dead. *Is that to be my fate if I fail?* Kalani shuddered as he thrust himself through the shrubs bordering the forest. The drum beat again.

He raced faster on his bare feet toughened by years of running on the sharp lava rocks of his home district, Kau. Kalani plunged along a narrow moss-covered trail. Giant fern fronds whipped their green fans across his face. Trees with branches covered in swirls of brown filth permeated the air with the smell of decay. Mold filled his lungs, and he was racked with a spasm of coughing. Anxiety increased as three hundred heartbeats passed. The third boom of the drum echoed through the trees.

Wisps of vapor spread through the forest. Kalani shuddered as a cold cloud from the snow-capped volcano enveloped him. Momentarily blinded, he slipped on a smooth rock and fell onto a fungus-covered trunk. His fingers grasped the dank growth. Its fur-like fibers came apart in his hands, and he fell into a mush of wet leaves. He struggled to rise, but sank into mud and could not find secure footing. Despair engulfed him. His heart hammered. His pulse drummed his ears. Panic rose within him.

"Kalani, you are our only hope," his mother said. "*Be strong like Kamehameha. Remember the Naha stone. Powerful forces were against him. Despite all odds 'the lonely one' moved the giant rock and became king. Imua! Go forward without fear.*" Her words eased his racing heart.

He careened against roots and hedges as he forced his body through the slush. To his ears came the sound of running water. He remembered the last time he was with his father. They were before an altar dedicated to the god of fertility. "*Oh Lono, the Heavenly Lord who makes rain which causes all things to grow, accept these offerings of cooked pig, awa juice, and coconuts. I consecrate my son to you on this day when he is taken from his mother's milk and enters into the world of men.*" Rainwater from the god Lono filled the stream somewhere ahead of him. He knew maile would grow by its flowing banks.

He pushed through a bog of rotting things and plunged deeper into the jungle. He had little time to appreciate the wonderland that canopied over him, the olive, emerald, lime-colored greenery that lent a primitive beauty to the forest.

Sharp fronds whipped his body. Broken roots snared his feet and he fell into the peat. He rose, laughing at his clumsiness and the wet earth that smeared him. His spirits lifted as he saw the stream and vines of maile trailing from trees into the bog.

Kalani plodded ahead, then stopped. In the mist he glimpsed the silhouette of something huge. As he stared into the brume, he saw a beast facing him. Its red eyes glared. He searched for a weapon. Found none. He stood little chance against the boar. The wiry hair of the animal could shred a man raw. Its tusks were spears, and with a toss of its head, the beast could rip his bowels and end his life, slow and painful.

"Imua," the word echoed within him. Kalani stood in the spongy mud, his hands at his sides. His fists clenched and unclenched, calming his fear. "Imua," he said. Not to frighten the beast but to give himself courage. He knew if he ran he invited death.

The animal tossed its head. Saliva dripped from its twin fangs. Foam frothed its lips. It grunted then plunged forward, flinging dirty water into the shrubs and sedge bordering the stream.

CHAPTER 2

LIKE A HUGE BLACK BOULDER rolling downhill, the monster smashed forward. Kalani tensed, snuggled his feet onto rocks, and sprung to the side. The charge slowed as the swamp clogged the beast's body. For a moment Kalani lay helpless.

The animal's plunge flung mud in all directions. Filth from the bog smeared the boy's face. The rancid smell of the boar gagged him. Barely able to breathe, he waited for the goring.

Without deviating from its rush, the pig smashed through the mud, up onto solid ground, and veered onto a path leading into the woods. Kalani staggered up, relieved that he had escaped death. He struggled to the stream and the maile plants. He bathed, then tore green-leafed young plants away from the sod, twining his body with the strong-smelling leaves.

The drum boomed for the fifth time. The dense woods muffled its call. Kalani plunged into the bog, then up onto a trail, following the boar's path.

Clarion clear, the sixth boom of the drum struck his ears. Kalani broke through the ferns separating the jungle from the school. He raced for it, happy he would make it to the altar before the eighth blow struck the shark-skinned instrument.

"Halt!" a new guard at the entrance ordered, his spear thrusting at Kalani.

"I bring maile for the teacher—"

"What is the password?"

"Purity!"

"That is not the password. Be gone, you maggot of the forest."

"Please let me pass. I have only a handful of heartbeats before the drum sounds again and I fail in my task."

"You will foul the school if you enter. You are unclean."

Kalani stepped around the man, a weapon slid by him. He darted. The warrior swung his spear. Its blunt end scored a thin furrow along Kalani's back.

The drum boomed a seventh time.

"Stop him," the guard yelled.

The boy raced for the entryway. Pebbles blanketed the entrance and spread into the interior. Above the gateway hung a net filled with small boulders. A second guard released a rope holding the rock-filled mesh closed. A ton of stone plunged down. Kalani dove beyond them. Smashed rocks and splintered pebbles flung sharp shards everywhere. "Ayah, ayah," the two guardians of the gate screamed as slivers peppered their naked bodies.

Untouched by the damage he had wrought, Kalani raced into the inner courtyard and the altar of a small temple. His teacher squatted beyond it, bending over his drum. He struck it for the eighth time. The deep sound died. Hepa withdrew a knife from the folds of his loincloth.

The sharp smell of maile filled the air. The master turned, his face malevolent. Kalani stood next to green fronds of maile flowing over the altar.

The master pointed toward the line of students standing in the courtyard. Bowing low, Kalani scurried to a place among them.

Several students whispered, "Well done!"

The big Hawaiian gave Kalani a hateful look. "You are lucky. But you will not feel so lucky when I finish with you, slave boy."

Before he could answer, the two men from the gate rushed to the altar screaming.

"Go back to your post," the master ordered.

They mouthed obscenities as they left.

Kalani wondered, *How was it possible that at seventeen I could make three enemies on my first day at Kamehameha's lua school?* His thoughts were interrupted by the master's yell, "Each of you grab staves from the armory. Choose your opponent. Prepare for mock combat."

An elbow smashed into his side. Next to him stood the bully. "I am Hauna, and it will be a pleasure to teach you a lesson, son of a kauwa." He swung his fist, but it swept through empty air as Kalani dodged away.

"Save your insults for someone who is afraid of you," Kalani answered. He strode to the stack of staves and selected a long, sleek pole.

Hauna picked a thick rod. "Your mother was a whore who slept with kauwa and produced you, worthless trash who is not descended from the gods." Hauna swung his stick, missed Kalani and smashed into the pebbles of the exercise yard. Rocks flew, hitting other students.

"You should say you're sorry for your clumsiness," Kalani taunted as he pounded his rod into Hauna's back.

The bully bellowed, "I'm going to smash your cocky mouth." Then he charged, swinging his stick to left and right as if swatting at a scurrying insect.

The young boy sidestepped and twisted away from the furious attack, but did not escape the elbow that smashed into his shoulder and sent him sprawling onto the courtyard stones.

"Hey! You two! You're not supposed to hurt each other. Fake your hits," Hepa yelled.

Hauna paused in his attacks and said, "This young puppy insulted me. He called my mother a whore! I am going to teach him a lesson he will not forget."

Kalani picked himself up from the stones, staring in disbelief at Hauna. But he had no time to argue the truth as the bully charged. Kalani danced sideways, avoiding the attack. He bounced on his feet, shifting his body left, right, forward, and around, constantly moving as the brutish man who outweighed him by forty pounds missed him with his wild thrusts and swings.

Hauna paused in his rushes and yelled, "Stop this flitting about like a bee. Stand and fight."

Ignoring the taunts, Kalani danced around the big man.

Hauna swung quickly.

Kalani blocked the blow, but still took a stinging hit to his side.

Hauna started an underhanded sweep.

Kalani struck out with his stave, but the bigger man's strength forced both rods to slam into his thigh.

Students stopped their individual matches to watch the battle. Bets were offered. Someone yelled, "Hauna is older, smarter than the kid, twenty taro on him to win."

There were no acceptances until one student said, "I will take the bets, twenty taro on the kid from Kau."

"Moki, you're crazy," a dozen students chorused. "He is skinny. Hauna is bigger. Will you accept all our bets?"

"Sure, I like the boy from Kau. Look how his feet dance. He is fast like a cockroach."

Moki's belief in Kalani was put to the test as Hauna attacked. Strike, parry, thrust, riposte, two sticks beat against each other in a whirlwind of blows and blocks. Hauna's hard smashes hit Kalani several times. He felt the aches of the bruises on his shoulders, thighs, and chest. But his legs did not get hit. He saw Hauna's body dripping with sweat and his chest heaving.

The big man stopped his attacks. His breath came in great gasps. He held his stave across his chest, nicked in several places as if rats had feasted upon it. Kalani stood at ease studying the lua students who huddled in a semi-circle around them. Most dropped their eyes and looked away. Only one, who he identified as Moki, looked at him, smiling and holding up his fists with thumbs up. Beyond the half-circle of students, he saw the two gate guardians. One of them smiled, crossing his finger over his throat. Hepa stood at the altar, his face set in stone. Kalani knew the master would not stop the fight.

"Hey, piece of *kukae*," Hauna yelled, "admit you are the son of a kauwa. That your mother is opala and sleeps with anybody. That you have no chiefly ancestry. Say that and I will end this beating and just kick your ass out of the school." Hauna started to laugh as he swept his eyes around the hovering students. Most did not join in with his merriment. A few exhibited half-hearted smirks, and Kalani realized that Hauna was the bad man of the class. He used his size to cower the other students.

Kalani remained silent, watching his enemy. A lifetime of training at the lua temple in Kau had taught him to ignore taunts and remain indifferent to insults. But how could he defeat this big man? He thought of his father's advice when they practiced at staves. *"You want your opponent to expose his belly. Ask yourself, why do you curl up when sleeping outside and there is thunder from the god Kane? Because if you face his thunder, its power will strike you in the stomach and blow the air out of you."* Kalani realized that this was the answer. He must entice the bully to expose his belly.

Tired of baiting without a response, Hauna bellowed, "Ku will feast on you now!" He stepped forward, thrusting his rod at Kalani's chest. The boy retreated. Hauna struck wild, chopping blows. Kalani barely blocked them, cushioning the force of the attacks by stepping backwards toward the stone fence of the school. Kalani knew that Hauna intended to force him to the wall. Then, when he could retreat no more, crush him with a final blow.

Kalani dodged, weaved, feinted attacks, then drew back. Hauna met each move with sweeping scythe-like swings, forcing a retreat. Back the boy stepped, twisting his stave to parry bone-breaking blows, each time barely escaping the full power of the strikes by quick rearward movements.

As he neared the wall, Kalani's defense weakened. Blows that he had easily blocked struck his shoulders, arms, sides. He breathed rapidly. His dodging slowed. He backed, until his foot struck the rocks and he could retreat no more. He appeared weak. He barely raised his staff with both hands to ward off a final crushing blow.

Students gasped, their mournful sound fueling a triumphant smirk on Hauna's face. The kid from Kau was doomed. One final blow would finish him. The bully lifted his stave, both hands gripping its end. The muscles of his shoulders and biceps bulged, as he stretched himself to full height. With his rod raised high, his back arched like a bent branch poised to spring forward, Hauna tensed, prepared to crush the insect that cringed below him.

CHAPTER 3

As Hauna's arms swung down in front of his face, they shielded his eyes. His torso was exposed. With all the power in his legs, Kalani pushed away from the wall, ducked under the bully's elbows, and thrust his rod deep into his enemy's belly.

Air bellowed from Hauna's lungs. His stick clattered against the stone wall. The big man sank to his knees and collapsed onto his back. He fought to breathe. His feet pawed the ground.

Kalani stood above him, ready to strike should he attack again. But the bully could do nothing but writhe in agony on the paving stones.

"Enough!" Hepa ordered. "We are done for the day. Go home. Be back early tomorrow for training. There is war coming and soon the great chief Kamehameha will select his fighters." He passed by the beaten warrior, contempt written across his face.

Moki screamed, "Little roach, you were great! Quick moves!"

"Why call me little roach?"

"Because you are fast like the pest we cannot catch. You are also tiny, like the cockroach. Hauna is big. Everybody believed you would lose. I won plenty of taro today. I will share it with you. Come, let's go home and have fun."

"How much did we win?"

"Over three hundred, enough to feed a village for a month."

"Come with me."

Kalani approached the two guardians of the gate. They stared sullenly at him as he approached.

"I apologize for the trouble I caused. I had to get to the altar with the maile or be punished. I won hundreds of taro in the fight. You may have it all. Let's *lokahi* and make peace between us."

Moki began to protest, but Kalani stifled him. The two men looked away, whispering to each other. Kalani waited.

After a long moment, the guard who had released the stones said, "I was very *huhu* with you. I thought Hauna would win. I bet all I had on him. You won. I lost, and my family will go without poi to eat. My friend and I accept your offer of lokahi. There will be peace between us." The guards extended their fists and the three men touched.

CHAPTER 4

"AUNT LEI, I ACHE IN every part of my body," Kalani complained. "Take a look at this bruise."

Squinting through rheumy old eyes, Lei examined the injury. Faint light glowed in the darkness of the shack. A coconut lamp flickered, its perfumed smoke blending with the musty odor of dried grass. "I'm told that the men are calling you 'cockroach'. Maybe you can tell your relatives to get out of the dead leaves of this hut and go bother somebody else." Lei laughed as she made Kalani wince from her probing fingers.

"There's something here. I feel blood when I press. I know a slave who is good with these matters. Maybe he will find an answer for your pain. Besides, a good massage will help." Bending low, Lei crawled through the doorway and disappeared.

Kalani lay back, closing his eyes. This was his second night in Kona and he felt alone. He reflected on how his mother had forced him to leave his home in Kau, insisting that he study at the secret lua school of the high chief Kamehameha.

"Why send me away? I am happy here."

"You must come to the attention of the great man. We are related to him, but this is not enough to give us land and power. Here, we have nothing."

Kalani understood this, with his father and grandfather dead, defeated in battle, and sacrificed to the war god.

"We have no land, no status, in Kau," his mother continued. *"But in Kona, you can help your family regain its power by going to war."*

"But Mother, I've never been a soldier. I don't know how to fight!"

"Silence! Stop whimpering. Your lua teacher tells me that you are the most promising student he has ever had. He tells me that if you hone your skills you could be a great fighter. You must learn one weapon well. Since you are still young, he suggested the sling. It is suited to your size and strength."

"I don't know anyone in Kona."

"You will make friends easily enough. You will stay with your Aunt Lei. I've arranged with my royal connections to have you enrolled in the lua school of the high chief."

His mother's voice softened. "Kalani Moku Tana, you cannot fail your family. Our men have all been killed in the wars of conquest. You are the oldest surviving male. You are our last hope." She stroked her son's face. "Prove yourself in battle and you will regain for us land and power. Fail in war, and there is only slavery for me, your sisters, and their children."

When Kalani took a deep breath, it made his ribs ache where Hauna hit them. It had been a hard week. He had spent his seventeenth birthday trudging the coastal road from Kau to Kona. With difficulty, he had found his Aunt Lei. And today, his first day at the lua school, he had escaped death by finding maile and then fought a grueling battle with a bully.

"*Hui*, we are coming in," Aunt Lei called. She stood, brushing off her tapa garment that twisted around her scrawny waist and hips. Stringy pepper hair flowed in great strands over her shoulders, covering her sagging breasts. She had once been pretty, but at sixty years her face was lined with care reflecting her age. On his knees behind her came a little boy around twelve years old, skinny and appearing starved.

"This is the slave, Minato. His father is sick and sends him to help you. I am told he is very good and knows herbal medicine. I would trust his treatment more than I trust the foolish chanting and praying of the *kahuna*."

Minato examined Kalani's body. His tiny fingers felt soft and silky as they probed the skin. Whenever he winced, Minato begged forgiveness.

"No broken bones, just sore ribs and muscles. I will put ointment on the cuts. It will help. Would you like me to massage your hurt muscles with coconut oil?"

Kalani nodded. Within an hour, he felt re-born.

Lei returned to the hut just as her nephew stretched in pleasure. "Enough of this. Moki said you are to come to the beach. The other men want to meet the new taro chief of Kona."

Kalani got to his feet. "Minato, I must go, but will you come tomorrow and massage again?"

"If the master wishes, I will be here in the evening."

"Good. I'll see you then. I am off to the *luau*, Aunt Lei. You should know I no longer have any taro. Gave it all away."

Lei shook her head, "Give to others. Nothing for us." The older woman smiled. "That's okay. Charity is good. Be careful, nephew. The news of your battle has spread around the village. All the girls are excited to meet you."

Aunt Lei's ribald laughter and broad winks made Kalani's skin prickle. He wondered what new challenges awaited him at the feast.

CHAPTER 5

"A GOOD LUAU, EH, LITTLE roach?" Moki laughed. "Try some awa juice." The wiry young man, two years older, reached over with a full gourd of liquor, his eyes twinkling.

"Do you have to call me 'little roach'? This awa tastes awful." He spat out a mouthful. "Why did Hauna pick on me? Fight me?"

"His father is high chief of Puna. He sneers at anyone of a lower class. He is a bully boy and he knew you could not trace ancestry to the gods. That is why he wanted to hurt you and force you from the school."

"Those aren't reasons."

"To Hauna they are. Even I had trouble with him, for my rank is the lowest in the hierarchy of chiefs."

Kalani moved closer. "Why are those women lined up near the fire?"

"Roach, they are going to dance hula. Listen to the *ipu*, the chanter, the dance begins."

Twenty dark-skinned women posed in the firelight. Its warm glow lit the tropic skies, its sparks pushing to the heavens, burning past the rippling leaves of palm trees high overhead.

The ipu drum boomed and, in rhythmic cadence, the women began their dance. White flowers crowned their hair. Necklaces of dogteeth rattled about their necks as their arms thrust left and right. Around their shoulders and armpits were braided, leafy, green vines intertwined with fragrant flowers. The arrangement accentuated the firm roundness of their breasts. Other than the cloth that covered undulating hips, the dancers were naked.

A steady, monotone chanting filled the air. The women moved their arms, hips, and feet in perfect time to the slapping beat of the ipu drum. Kalani felt a warmth come over him as he watched the sleek, oiled bodies dancing provocatively in front of him.

"Good stuff, eh, little roach? That one in front, with the *palaoa* dangling between her breasts, she is hot for you."

"Which one?"

"Are you blind? See the one with the white whale-tooth bouncing on her chest? She's looking at you." He leaned closer. "That is Hinalea, the head chief's wife. Watch out, little roach."

Kalani saw the dark eyes, delicate nose, and sensuous lips of a beautiful woman dancing with a braided human-hair necklace around her neck. Hinalea thrust her hips toward him, moaning.

The dance ended and the women left. It was time for the men to perform. They moved with vigor and strength. Kalani could barely stay awake. He thanked Moki for inviting him and introducing his friends.

"See you tomorrow. Watch out for what may be waiting in the dark."

Dismissing the jibe, Kalani left the beach and headed through the forest for Aunt Lei's shack.

Suddenly a vine of maile settled around his neck and he was pulled into the ferns bordering the woods. Fragrant perfume from a flower filled his lungs. Hinalea's warm hands drew his face and lips into hers.

Startled by her boldness, Kalani pulled away, but the eager arms of the panting woman drew him back. She whispered, "You are handsome. Strong. I watched you in the firelight. Come. Make love to me."

Her beauty and the lingering effects of her dance excited him. Impelled by a desire he had never experienced, Kalani relented. He held tight the warm hand of the chief's wife, returning her ardent kisses. Nearby, water flowed and tumbled over moss-covered rocks into a shallow pool. Hinalea drew him to the soft grass beneath the waterfall. Her moaning increased. It excited him. He stiffened, as her hands released the folds of his loincloth and stroked his thighs.

CHAPTER 6

MINATO'S LOVING CARE EASED KALANI'S pain and helped him deal with the day-to-day rigors of warrior training. As time passed, he developed a profound admiration for the slave boy's healing skill and gentle nature.

"I can't believe how magical your fingers are. My body no longer aches like a beaten drum. I never thought that the training at the school would be so hard. Tell me, have you always been a slave?"

"Yes, since birth. But my father was once a free man, a chief on Maui Island. His army was defeated in battle when the King of Hawaii invaded. Instead of being sacrificed to the war god, he and his wife were forced into slavery, along with other captured warriors, and brought to Kona. Twelve years ago, their love produced me.

"Tell me master, what are you being taught in the lua temple that causes you such pain?"

"They are preparing my mind and body for war. The high chief Kamehameha plans to attack Maui. As a first step, he will build a great temple to ensure that the war god Ku favors his plan for battle. Minato, why did you stop?"

The slave boy had withdrawn to a corner of the shack, his body cringing, his face marked with fear. A keening sound rose from his lips.

"What did I say that frightened you?" Kalani asked, kneeling by him.

"Pray to your gods, master. Pray for me and my family."

"Pray for what?"

"That my family may be spared. That one of us will not be sacrificed to the war god Ku!"

"You mean that one of you could be killed because Kamehameha wants to win in war? I don't understand why that would happen. Yet, when I think on it, my father and grandfather were sacrificed to some war god to make him happy."

Minato covered his eyes. "Ku must have blood. If he is given enough sacrifices, he will bless a war. How many must die to give joy, only the high priest knows. Even after the battle is won, many of the captured enemy warriors are sacrificed to the god to continue in his favor."

"How did your father and mother escape death?"

The boy looked up, his eyes wide. "Master, women are never sacrificed, they are considered unclean. My father was spared because the head priest believed that the war god was appeased. My parents were taken by the victorious chief as slaves to await sacrifice in the next war."

"You are twelve, Minato. Several wars have occurred since you were born, yet your father has not been sacrificed. Why?"

"Master, my father is an expert builder. He can construct aqueducts and fishponds better than any other stonemason. He is an excellent farmer and knows much of planting and the creation of different varieties of taro. He is too valuable to be sacrificed."

"Then I don't understand your worry. If they will not sacrifice your mother because she is unclean, nor your father because he is too valuable, and you—"

"Master, I have no value. I am just a slave boy, which is why I am afraid. That is why I ask you to pray that I be spared from death by drowning, fire, or knife."

Kalani touched the boy's shoulder. "I will pray for you and do all that I can to prevent your sacrifice. But I fear that I cannot be of much help. Without land or power, I am nobody. If I can be victorious in battle and come to the attention of the great Kamehameha, then I might get land and power."

Minato shook his head. "I have asked you to pray that I not be sacrificed, which means you must pray that there is no war." His brow suddenly creased. "Because of my love for you, I must pray that you become a great warrior, and that can only happen if there is war."

Kalani sighed. "I need status to save my mother from slavery and to find a way to save your life, yet I can only gain status through death and war." He rubbed his hands over his head and groaned. "These ideas are making my brain ache. It is best that I concentrate on gaining power by becoming a koa. Your father was a warrior. A valorous koa, I am sure."

"That is so. He is an excellent spear-catcher."

"A spear-catcher?"

"Yes, and he is also a powerful thrower of spears. My mother told me that he could hurl three in less than six heartbeats."

"Do you think he could teach me to do that?"

"I will ask him. He may be able to teach you if it can be done in secret. You do know that it is forbidden for those of your class to associate with slaves? How good are you at using the sling?"

"Tolerable, I can't hit the target every time. I can throw the stone a good distance, but I miss more often than I hit it."

"What type do you use?"

"Flat ones."

"The kind that sail on you?"

"You know about sling throwing?"

"My father taught me. If you can throw it a fair distance, but can't hit the target every time, it may be your choice of stones. Let me find the right ones and teach you to throw them."

"You two," Aunt Lei interrupted, pushing her way through the door, "time for bed. Kalani has work to do tomorrow."

"Goodnight, Minato. Be sure to ask your father if he will show me how to catch and throw spears."

The slave boy scooted out the door. When they were alone, Lei fixed a disapproving eye on her nephew. "What have you done with Hinalea? Her tongue brags of your powers. Her foolish words have caught the ear of her husband, Chief Makula. Rumor has it that he is angered by her talk. Be careful whom you choose to keep company with. Poor choices can mean trouble for you."

Lei's words shocked him. For several weeks he had enjoyed Hinalea's company. Their love making had been hot, passionate. She had stilled his worries about her husband with soothing words, promising that Makula did not care. But now, he realized that she might not be trustworthy. He vowed to end the affair.

Before he left, he asked, "Under penalty of death, it is forbidden to deal with slaves, the kauwa. When I was hurt, you brought Minato to me, whom you called a slave. Why did you do that?"

Lei stared at her nephew with sharp and piercing eyes. "The kauwa were the first settlers to come to Hawaii from the southern islands. They lived in peace and prospered. Many years after, warrior chiefs came from Tahiti. They brought with them their god Ku. He was thirsty for human sacrifice, thirsty for war. These chiefs destroyed the first civilization and cast the survivors into slavery. These became the kauwa, the untouchables, the despised, fit only to be sacrificed."

"But Minato's father is not descended from the first settlers. He was a Maui warrior, a lesser chief on that island."

"That is true, nephew. But once he lost in battle and was spared, he became a slave, a servant forever to his conquering lord. If your father had not been sacrificed, your family would be slaves today, and you would be in the same position that Minato is in. Women may lose land and power, but they are not killed. Why do you think I live here alone, far away from other people?"

Kalani nodded. "Your husband was sacrificed like my father, and you associate with Minato and his family because their ill fortune is like yours."

"That is one reason. But I also find the family to be helpful and considerate. In their suffering, they are kind to lonely people such as me."

"Minato said that he feared being sacrificed. If the kauwa, the original people, are bred for sacrifice, why is Minato in danger?"

"As I have tried to explain, Minato is in the second class of slave, more a servant than the despised untouchables. But if you were a chief, consecrating a new temple to Ku, would you give him a despicable one, a kauwa, or a grand gift like a defeated chief or his son?"

"Aunt Lei, before I spoke with Minato, I knew nothing about slavery and little of Ku. My mother says I must be a great warrior so that she and my sisters may escape slavery. To be a great warrior I must be a hero in battle and cause death. Is there a more peaceful way to gain rank and power?"

Lei uttered a great sigh. "Before Ku, the original people worshiped Io, a god of peace. People lived without war and human sacrifice. They lived without class differences. As I told you, when the Tahitians came they brought with them the god of war who demanded human offerings. They introduced ancestry tracing to the gods to prove royal descent. The Tahitians said, 'Only royalty can be chiefs and own land.' Remember, when you entered the lua school you could not trace ancestry. This meant that you were not a chief, but a commoner, or a slave."

"Ah, that is why Hauna insulted me. But if I cannot trace ancestry to the gods how do I become a chief?"

"Only one way, you must be heroic in battle. Get Kamehameha obligated to you for your bravery. Get him to confer property to you as a 'black land chief'. It happens rarely, but it happens."

Kalani bedded down outside Lei's shack. He rolled into his cloth covering and stared at the stars twinkling in the firmament above. *The high chiefs are said to descend from these heavenly sentinels. Someday my star will shine, helping those in desperation to have a better life.* Kalani studied the heavens, focusing his eyes on one star. *Arcturus, a happy star,* he thought, *it led my ancestors to this island. It will guide me on my journey to become a great warrior and bring back the peace of Io.* His head ceased its aching as he fell asleep.

CHAPTER 7

"HERE," MINATO CRIED AS HE fished into the water, retrieving a small stone. "See how it is smooth and circular? These are the stones you want."

Kalani fingered an almond-shaped rock, ellipsoidal in form, and oily-sleek to the touch. "This is not like the ones I have used before. I brought some to show you." He withdrew several small stones from the folds of his loincloth.

Minato examined them. "Do they buzz or sing when you throw them?"

"Yes, some do."

"The noise means the rock is wobbling and it will not fly true to its target. This one and the others like them that we will find will hit the target."

The two boys searched the stream bed for more almond-shaped stones. Finally satisfied that they had enough ammunition, they left the water and stepped onto a small, level, practice field.

"Now that we have the right stones," Minato said, "let's talk about the sling and the art of throwing."

"I've already got a sling, let's talk about throwing," Kalan answered.

"You're too impatient. The right equipment makes you a better slinger. Look at your pouch, it does not have a slit to snuggle a stone into. Your knot on one end is too big. You cannot free the release cord easily. Look at the loop on the retention cord. It will slip out of your finger. We had better practice with my sling."

"No, I'll use mine."

"Well, let me show you how to throw."

"I was pretty good at it in Kau. All I need are these new stones. Watch me." Kalani faced a gourd, wound up, and cast his rock. The stone flew high and several feet from the target. "Must be the rock," he mumbled.

Minato shook his head. "It was not the rock that caused you to miss so badly."

"Are you saying it was me, slave boy? Bet you can't do better."

Fear crinkled Minato's face as his body bent in a servile posture. He scurried to the target, retrieved the stone and returned to the firing position.

Minato unwound a sling from his waist. He snuggled the stone into the slit in its fiber pouch and faced the target gourd forty feet away. He pivoted. The loop of the retention cord threaded through the middle finger of his right hand, the knot of the release cord grasped between the thumb and forefinger of the same hand.

He whirled the sling once, stepped forward, and, at the height of his second swing, let free the release cord. The missile smashed into the target, knocking the gourd to the ground. As the pouch of the sling swung around, Minato dropped a second stone into it with his free hand, grasped the release cord, and flung the rock at the target.

"Wow!" Kalani said as the missile struck the gourd on the ground. "I've never seen anything like that. How did you learn to do that?"

"Master," Minato answered, his face stiff, fearful that anything he said would enrage the boy by his side, "my father taught me. It was hard. I could not eat until I did a movement right."

"The lua school is in recess. Teach me."

During the succeeding days the boys practiced with the sling. Minato taught Kalani the techniques of aiming, throwing, and reloading the weapon. Often, he endangered himself by simulating a charging warrior on the battlefield. In the late afternoons, the slave boy's father taught the art of catching, deflecting, and dodging spears. Minato would be at Kalani's side, helping him to learn, encouraging him when he failed to catch a spear. As Kalani became proficient in the warrior arts of sling and spear the two youths bonded. Kalani swore that their friendship would be everlasting.

CHAPTER 8

KALANI AND MOKI EXERCISED IN the inner courtyard of the school. "Practice, practice, practice," Hepa shouted. "Take that whipping cord, twirl the stone thrice, and then cast it around the pole. No," he yelled at a student, "that is wrong! Twirl it like this, then cast it. That's it, you have it."

"This endless practice is not for me," Moki muttered.

"If we want to be good at something, we must do it. The big test comes soon. Our teacher has eyes in the back of his head. Here he comes."

"Enough work with the tripping cords. Kalani, get your sling and stones and show me your skills at the target range. Moki, come with us. I have a role for you to play."

The two students exchanged glances. What did the master intend? Without comment, they moved to the target range, an open field with three bamboo poles driven into the ground and calabashes resting on top.

Hepa stepped off twenty paces and drew a line in the dirt. "All right, Kalani, show me how good you are."

Selecting three almond-shaped stones from his pouch, Kalani pivoted, aimed, and fired his sling. He did it twice more, each time knocking a gourd to the ground.

"That wasn't too bad. But hitting a stationary target is easy. An enemy warrior moves, he does not stand still. Retrieve your stones. Moki, you come with me."

It took several minutes of searching before Kalani found his pebbles. When he returned to the practice range, Moki and Hepa were leaving the school followed by a gaggle of students. A heavy matting with round red circles painted on it draped over Moki's body. On his head he wore a helmet of woven leaves. In his hand he held a six-foot spear.

"Moki, you will walk fifty paces away from us. On my command, you must run at Kalani. When I order you to swerve right or left, do so. When I command you to fire, hurl your spear at him. Throughout this test, he will remain fixed to this spot." Hepa pointed to a line he had drawn in the dirt.

"What do I do?" Kalani asked.

"You see the red circles? One is painted over his heart, a second is around his belly, and the third circles his kidneys. Hit each target once and I will order Moki not to throw his spear."

"But my stone could break through, strike Moki, and kill him."

Hepa scoffed, "The lauhala matting is extra thick and has been soaked in water to strengthen it. It is the same type of protection used by Hawaiian warriors to defeat the bullets of Captain Cook."

Kalani stilled his tongue. He realized further protest would create trouble. He knew that his larger almond-shaped stones were more accurate than the small round ones, but they could penetrate the matting and hurt his friend. He resigned himself to a test that could result in injury to one of them.

"One, two, three-" Moki began pacing fifty steps from the master. The students formed a ragged line away from the danger of flying missiles.

Kalani searched his pouch, selecting several smooth, round stones. He held them in his free hand. He lifted the sling's pocket, aiming it at Moki. He pivoted, sighted over the top of his extended arm at the matted figure marching away.

"Fifty!"

"Turn! Charge!"

Moki ran.

The cradled rock dropped from Kalani's extended hand. His throwing hand circled his body.

At forty paces, Hepa ordered, "Turn left." A round rock struck the red circle on Moki's back.

"One hit," Hepa yelled. "Run straight."

Kalani dropped a stone into the pouch of his sling. In one smooth motion, he swung his arm and stepped into the throw.

A second stone smashed into the red circle at Moki's belly.

"Two hits," Hepa screamed, and, in the same breath added, "turn left!"

At twenty paces, a third stone from his sling skipped off Moki's shoulder, buzzing past his ear. From its sound Kalani knew it was misshapen.

"A miss! Turn right and hurl your spear."

At twelve paces, Moki's spear arm drew back and lunged forward. A rock struck the circle around his heart.

"Hit three," Hepa said as the spear left Moki's hand.

Undisturbed by the light wind, the shark-toothed projectile flew in a graceful arc at the young slinger. "Save yourself! Run away," Moki yelled.

"Move and you are out of the school," Hepa screamed.

CHAPTER 9

WITH THE SPEAR INCHES FROM his body, Kalani plucked it in its downward flight. Pivoting as Minato's father had taught him, Kalani tossed the spear at the feet of his teacher.

"Kamehameha the Great could have caught six of those with ease. All leave," Hepa said, then stalked off the practice field toward the lua school.

Kalani cupped his hand over his mouth to hide a smile. It was not in the nature of a lua master to give praise to a student, but to be compared to Kamehameha showed Hepa's approval of his feat.

"That was an awesome display of skill today, little roach," Moki said with admiration in his voice while the two friends marched home.

"If I had any good fortune today, I must thank two slaves for teaching me the skills that made me successful."

"You mean that kauwa taught you to sling rocks and catch the spear? The despicable ones, the outcasts?"

"They are not the untouchables, the ones with the chevron tattooed above the nose. They are warriors, defeated in battle, and servants of the high chief. My skill is because of their teaching."

Moki remained uncharacteristically silent.

"They are kind and generous people. I will do all I can to save them from being sacrificed. Perhaps I will find a way to give them back their freedom and possession of land."

The two stood together in silence, Kalani believing that he had imparted something important to his friend.

"I don't know if you can accomplish your goals. High Chief Kamehameha's practice when he builds a new temple dedicated to war is to sacrifice defeated chiefs. What are the names of these slaves?"

"Mokihana and his son Minato."

"My friend, you should know that it may be death for you to associate with them. Besides, they have no property. They and everything they have belongs to the high chief, who is their master. At any time, they can be offered to Ku. What is to be gained by dealing with these slaves, other than your own death?"

"I am being taught by them to be a warrior. You saw my skill on the practice field. It is due to their teaching. Without their help, I would have failed the tests, been disgraced and banished from the school. They are kind and generous people. Minato is like a brother to me, thoughtful and caring. I will do what I can to save him and his family."

Moki nodded. When he spoke, his words came as a surprise. "When you speak of disgrace, you should know that Hauna has been bragging. He says you will be punished for playing with Chief Makula's wife, Hinalea. Have you been delving into places where you should not go?"

Kalani grimaced, "I knew she would get me into trouble. That's why, for the past weeks, I have avoided every luau I have been invited to."

"Yes, you have acted like a hermit. I have heard that you have made quite an impression on Hinalea. But Chief Makula is a jealous man, big ego. He believes any woman he loves should rave only about him. Be careful, little roach. Even though you may try to avoid trouble, it will still find you."

Darkness shrouded the village as the two friends picked their way along a rock-strewn path bisecting two large fields of taro. Pillars of flame from bonfires burning among the scattered thatched huts guided them towards the hearty laughter of men eating.

In an open area between the huts, leaf mats covered with calabashes of food fanned across the ground. Several friends from the lua school motioned Kalani to sit by them. After a few mouthfuls, he received a message and rose to leave.

"Where you going, little roach?" Moki asked.

"Aunt Lei wants me to come to her. For what reason I do not know. See you in the morning."

"Get to bed early. Big things are happening in the coming days."

Another feasting man rose from the food mats when Kalani passed by him. He picked his way through a crowd of warriors until several drunken men blocked him as they boxed and wrestled. Kalani dodged around them. He heard someone yell, "Let me pass." He saw a man struggling to get through a mass of naked bodies.

Serves him right for trying to push into that unruly mob. He wondered why the man had not avoided the drunks as he did. He crossed through the village and entered the jungle trail leading to Aunt Lei's shack. Behind him he heard the noise of someone running.

A bonfire blazed, throwing flickering light into a maze of ferns and trees. At the feast an ipu drum boomed. Kalani knew there soon would be dancing. Should he have stayed? Had fun?

He walked with his head bent, his eyes adjusting to the darkness. He stumbled into logs blocking the path, forcing him to step into clumps of giant ferns. Soft hands reached out, tugging him down. He resisted for a moment, but Hinalea's warm body pressed into him. The curve at her thighs thrust against his loincloth.

"I have missed you. Wanted you so much," she moaned. "Come and make me happy."

As he fell onto soft grasses, he thought he heard footsteps on the trail. But Hinalea's cries as she forced herself upon him blotted out sounds. He surrendered to her passion.

CHAPTER 10

Chief Makula picked up a gourd and offered it to the warrior squatting beside him. "Hauna, how do you like the *limu kohu* mixed with raw *opihi*?"

"Excellent. Better than any I have had in Puna."

"Drink this awa. My slaves fermented it perfectly. Isn't it the finest you have ever tasted?"

Hauna took the offered gourd, drank, and said, "That is so."

"How are you feeling since your unfortunate accident many weeks ago?"

"My insides have sorted themselves out. I can function without pain."

"Ah, that is good. I believe you told my servant that a new student from Kau tripped you into a workout pole at the lua temple." Makula studied Hauna, wondering if the man would be truthful or deceptive.

Hauna licked his lips several times. "Yes, that is true. The man claimed it was an accident, but I believe it was intentional."

"How so?" Makula asked, feigning surprise at the answer.

Hauna spoke with vehemence. "When the man tripped me, he whispered that my mother is a whore."

Makula smiled, knowing that Hauna is a liar and thus could be bought. "Ah, you are right. I did hear that the man may have acted intentionally." Before he said more, a warrior came to the royal thatched hale seeking entry. The chief signaled him in.

The soldier crawled on his stomach, came to Makula, and whispered what he had seen in the forest.

"Damn, may the gods smite him," Makula hissed.

"Bad news?"

"Your enemy is seducing my wife. This makes him my enemy. Tell me, are you accepting this man's arrogance without seeking revenge?"

"The trash from Kau has many friends in the lua school. I dare not challenge him."

"Do you fear him?"

Hauna scowled. "Are you accusing me of being a coward? That boy from Kau is nothing. I can squeeze the life from him at any time I want."

"No, no I didn't mean to challenge your power. But he has become my enemy and I must find a way to end his life without fastening blame upon myself. After all, he is a favorite of the master of the lua school."

"You are wrong. Why would he choose to befriend a child who has no royal blood in his veins? No, Hepa is not a fool. He knows that I am the future king of Puna when my father dies. He has everything to gain by choosing me over that cockroach. For the evil that the scum did to me I also want to end his life."

"Many unfortunate calamities occur by accident or by the gods."

"You would help me destroy him?"

Makula smiled, Hauna was in his trap. Using him, he would eliminate the upstart who had soiled his wife and enlist an ally in his great plan to betray Kamehameha. More awa juice was poured, and as the two men drank, a bond formed. Soon, Hauna joined in a plot designed to bring about Kalani's death and doom the great high chief.

CHAPTER 11

RAYS OF THE MORNING SUN flared upward into a halo of gold, igniting the dark clouds brooding above a fiery red sea. Twelve nearly-naked men stood shivering on the grass field outside the lua school, waiting for Hepa to speak.

The lua master stared at his students. "Attention. Today, we test your abilities in war: running, climbing, swimming, and canoe handling. Some of you will fail, others will succeed. The first six who pass the tests will join Kamehameha's camp. From these six, he will select his warriors."

This promise dispelled the gloom Kalani felt. The day had started with trouble. Earlier that morning he approached Hauna and offered to make peace. The big man refused, snapping at him. "You have offended Chief Makula; I will not befriend someone who plays with another man's wife."

Kalani sighed as his wandering thoughts returned to what the teacher instructed.

Hepa gave his orders. "Your first task will be to run to the mountain where the iwa'iwa fern grows, secure a frond, and place it into the bag at your waist. Return to the beach and swim to the islet a hundred canoe lengths from shore. Gather from the rocks three pink opihi, then swim back to the beach and head for Kealakekua Bay, where a canoe awaits you. Cross the bay to the temple of Hikiau."

"But teacher," a student interrupted. "We are naked, without tools to cut the ferns or pry free the opihi."

"You have your wits. Improvise, as a warrior would when separated from his army. You are to use only nature's implements to sever the fern and pry loose the opihi. Now go!"

Twelve students charged toward the forest fringing the lua school. Hauna disappeared into the woods, the other eleven contestants followed him.

When Kalani broke through the scrub of trees marking the end of the forest, he saw three students ahead of him, but not Hauna. He paused for breath, searching the hills.

Rock-strewn ground rose toward tall peaks cloaked in cushions of billowing clouds. Saw-toothed ridges faded in and out of view. Vapor wisps descended toward the sea. Silvery slivers of rain-fed waterfalls rushed down the mountain. They burst into fans of spray and bounced against rocks in their free fall to an unseen pool. Sunlight crowned the falling water with glowing rainbows, adding color to a drab landscape of short flaxen-colored grass that clung to the side of the volcano.

"Stop dreaming," Moki said, coming to Kalani's side. "We go or lose the race."

Roused by the challenge he began to run along the thin trail that wound up the slope of the mountain. At one point the path narrowed, curving around a huge crescent-shaped mound. He looked over the edge to the ocean hundreds of feet below. A few shrubs and a tenacious hala tree grew from the sheer rock face of the cliff.

Kalani searched for a sharp, thin rock to use as a knife. He saw his lua mates spread out over the mountainside. He did not see Hauna. Upward he hiked, then sideways, moving for the waterfalls.

Spray soaked him. Fifty feet away Kalani spied a patch of iwa'iwa clinging to wet rocks. The narrow path he followed ended in clumps of grass fighting for the sun through tiny cracks in the hardened lava.

He hugged the side of the mountain and felt with his toes for the thin ledge that provided a precarious track to the green ferns. He did not look down, willing himself to believe he walked on firm ground. The crevice he clung to with his fingers scored his skin. He ignored the shooting pain as he inched toward the iwa'iwa.

He reached for a fern and grasped a frond. Its roots refused to budge. He dared not use his other hand for it held him close to the cliffside. His toes had run out of shelf to stand on. His calves stiffened. If they cramped he would be doomed.

Iwa' iwa fern

He pressed his body against the eroded rock. He bent the fiber stalk of the plant until the fern came free. He inched back along the thin ledge until he reached level ground. He thrust the plant into his pouch and trotted toward the beach. Several of his friends called for directions to the ferns. Kalani showed them and continued on his way.

When he reached the rock mound that caused the trail to narrow, he slowed his pace. Suddenly, he heard a 'whoop' and a stone attached to a tripping cord wrapped around his leg. Several yards away, Hauna and another man held onto an end.

Kalani reached to the snare. A sudden pull flung him backward. Like a hooked fish, he jerked his foot several times. His struggles caused the thin rope to slacken and come free. He felt his body slide over the cliff's edge.

Hauna cursed, "Damnation!"

CHAPTER 12

DESPERATE, KALANI REACHED FOR THE branches of the hala tree clinging to the side of the hill. Thorny leaves sliced his hands. Despite searing pain, he managed to grasp a limb that halted his fall. Below, huge waves pounded onto the black rocks at the mountain's base. Above, he heard men talking as they approached the cliff's edge.

He spied a shallow cave beneath the fiber roots of the tree. Hand-over-hand, he swung into it, disturbing a bird from its nest. It cawed, leaped, and soared out, gliding over a roiling sea filled with white foam.

Tropicbird

Hidden, Kalani listened to his attackers.

"Don't see anything in the ocean. Waves must have dragged him away," Hauna said. A man answered, "He is gone. My master Makula will not like this. He wanted to torture the boy. Take the iwa'iwa I got for you. There is a knife in the pouch to pry out the opihi. I go. Hurry on and win the test."

Kalani crouched in the cave. He seethed, angered by the treachery. But trapped in the small crevice, there was nothing he could do.

He took in shallow breaths to still his racing heart. The wind sighed, rattling leaves of the lonely tree. The tropicbird soared nearby, screeching at the boy in her nest. He tested the cylindrical roots of the plant. Satisfied they were imbedded firmly into the rocks, Kalani pulled himself from the cave, searching for a way up the cliffside.

Footsteps and voices forced him back into his hiding place. He feared the noise he made would give away his presence.

"Good thing your friend pointed out where the ferns were."

"Yeah," a voice, muffled by the wind, answered. "He showed them to us, but those ferns were hard to get out of the rock."

"Moki, is that you?" Kalani called.

"Who is that? Who called my name? Show yourself or I will bust you up."

"Is Hauna still around?"

"Hey, what's going on? Hauna not here. Who is this talking? A ghost?"

"Moki, help me. I'm right below your feet. Look over the edge."

Kalani nearly laughed as he saw his friend cautiously peering over the cliff. He edged along the trunk of the tree.

"What you want us to do?"

"Get me out of here."

"How?"

"Both of you, undo your malos. Tie them together like a rope. Throw an end to me and pull me up."

"You want us be naked in the sun?"

"Just do it, please."

"Hey, brah, you going owe us one," Moki grumbled as he removed his garment, tied it to his friend's malo then tossed the rope over the cliff.

Kalani grasped an end and yelled, "Pull."

The effort nearly ended in disaster when his lua mates got too close to the cliff's edge which began to crumble. The rescue team moved backward, and Kalani pulled himself onto firm ground.

"What happened?" Moki asked.

"Hauna and a servant of Chief Makula knocked me over the cliff. Hauna is a cheater. His crony picked the iwa'iwa for him earlier this morning and gave him an iron knife to gather opihi. Come, we must catch him before he wins."

The three young men raced down the mountain trail. At the seashore, Kalani passed a warrior who uttered a curse and yelled, "Stop."

The three boys ignored him, dove into the sea, and swam toward a small islet four hundred yards from shore.

CHAPTER 13

"YOU HAVE NOT BEEN LOYAL to me, Hinalea!" Chief Makula snarled, seated cross-legged on an elevated platform covered by a large mat. A white cloth was draped across his loins. Behind him, two slaves held tall feather kahili, symbols of royalty. Hinalea faced him, her eyes wide.

Next to Makula sat a huge woman, a garland of leaves wound in her hair. Behind the chiefess lounged two other females, each wearing a crown of flowers. Loose white cloths covered their shoulders, draping to their knees.

"Your lover is dead!" the chief yelled. "No more can you bluster and brag." He emphasized his words with a vicious slap across Hinalea's face.

She fell, tears welling in her eyes.

Makula turned to his other wives. "What should we do with such a faithless woman?"

They cringed. Any answer from them was muted by the loud voice of a guard calling from the threshold of the royal hale. "Great chief, your sentinel at the beach seeks entry, he has important news."

Makula grunted and a warrior crawled through a low, rectangular door into the palace.

"Why do you come?" Makula demanded of the prostrate man.

The sentinel rose from his submissive posture while keeping his head below that of the chief, and answered, "I bring bad news, your majesty. Kalani lives."

Makula's cloth covering slid from his hips as he jumped to his feet. "You lie! He fell into the sea!"

On his knees, his back arched in a servile posture, the warrior spoke to the earth. "I report what I saw, your enemy came running onto the beach with two others. They dove into the sea and swam toward the islet."

Makula stomped his foot on the platform. "Order my canoe prepared for voyage. Have eight men fully armed and ready to sail." He spat on Hinalea, lying face down on the floor. "I will deal with you later." He aimed a kick at her side, then crawled from his hale.

Makula failed to see the smile that lit Hinalea's face.

CHAPTER 14

Opihi

KALANI PERCHED ON CORAL SWEPT by surf washing over the small islet. He pondered the solution to the second task, prying loose from the rocks three seaweed-covered limpets. He knew that these prizes were hidden under the pink sides of the boulders being smashed by the waves. Men had died trying to capture these shell-covered snails, pounded into oblivion by the roiling sea.

The other two lua students shivered near him. "What are we going to do?" Moki asked, a wave washing over his legs.

Kalani remembered what worked in the past. He searched for a large conical shell shaped like a pyramid. In a crevice he spotted one and worked it free from the coral that held it. He retrieved a sliver of stone from the pouch at his side and slid toward the water.

Waves pounded the small island, pluming white foam over his body. Kalani searched for rocks washed pink by the sea. The foam receded into the ocean. Clamped to red stones, he saw a forest of weeds sprouting from pyramid-shaped shells. The opihi clustered together. He watched the sea curl into a massive wall of white, higher than his eyes. It drew back revealing moss-covered boulders descending into the deep. A split-second pause, then the long block of water swept forward.

Kalani crouched, clinging to a rock. The massive surge smashed over the islet and drew back. He scrambled to the pink rocks momentarily uncovered. An opihi bubbled, exhausting air from its shell. Kalani shoveled his sliver into the bubbles, levered, and the limpet came free.

He glanced at the ocean. A curling wave, mirror smooth, monster high, rolled toward him. Kalani plunged his primitive tools into another limpet, pushed, and the shell came into his hand, the creature inside clamping onto his open palm. A powerful mass of water shoved him into the pink boulders, pushed him higher onto dark rocks, paused, and then drew him back toward the maw of the sea.

Kalani tried braking his slide. The rocks were slick. His feet failed to slow his plunge. He reached for crevices with his fingers. The force of the sea fumbled his arms over the stones.

A moment before plunging into the deep, he hooked a hand around a boulder. His feet slipped into cracks between stones. He held tight to the rock. He inhaled as a wave buried him. For what seemed like an eternity he waited for the foam to pass. When he heard the popping sounds of receding water, Kalani rose from the swirl and scrambled to higher ground.

To his surprise, he saw a grandfather-sized limpet near the high-water mark. He pried it loose before leaping to a higher stone as another wave smashed into the rocks.

Bleeding from bruises on his body, he called to Moki, describing how to pry loose the opihi. He handed his tools to his friend and skipped over the rocks to the submerged fringing coral of the islet.

"There he is, Chief Makula," a voice yelled. Startled, Kalani saw a hundred yards away eight warriors flinging their paddles forward in one smooth motion, propelling a double canoe toward the islet. Chief Makula stood on its prow, a feather war cape flowing behind him.

Kalani dove toward the shore. Curving his body underwater, he angled toward a wave-smashed headland fifty yards away.

CHAPTER 15

"HEAD FOR THE BEACH," MAKULA ordered. Eight warriors thrust their wooden paddles into the sea, shooting the war canoe over the water toward shore.

"Pull harder. The boy must be just ahead of us."

But the chief saw no one swimming to the beach.

Puzzled, Makula looked to the islet. Tossed by a wave, his vessel rose. He saw dark hair moving toward the headland. "Turn for the open sea!"

A hundred-and-fifty yards ahead of the craft, Kalani broke the surface. Makula smiled in triumph. "Pull, pull."

The war canoe neared the swimming boy. "Give me a spear," the chief demanded. At the curved prow of his vessel, he raised his spear, aimed at Kalani's back, and whipped his arm forward just as a wave smashed into the side of the canoe, spoiling Makula's aim. The spear slithered into the sea.

"May the gods destroy him! When we are near, two of you jump in and rope him."

Kalani heard the command. He glanced at the coastline ahead. With a wash of waves, two submerged rocks rose above the surface. A narrow cut into the fringing reef lay beyond them. Kalani aimed for the passage.

Makula yelled, "You two jump in and grab him." Before anyone in the craft could act, the canoe crunched into stones.

Kalani surfed through the narrow cut, reached the base of the headland and climbed from the water. Two paddlers slid into the sea. In his stranded vessel Makula seized a spear and hurled it.

"Thank you," Kalani taunted as he caught it. He brandished the weapon over his head, stepped around the point of the promontory, found a path, and scampered up the cliff. He did not need to look back to know that Makula's henchmen came after him.

He followed the ridgeline and when it tapered down, he slid to a beach at Kealakekua Bay. In the distance, he saw the three-tiered temple of Hikiau looming above the shore. Even this magnificent stone structure was dwarfed by the hills that ringed the bay. At the water's edge stood a teacher from the lua school. "You are a little slow. Hauna is well on his way to victory."

"Any other students ahead of him?"

"No."

Behind him, Kalani heard the distant shouts of his pursuers. "Which canoe can I take?"

The man made a sweeping gesture and Kalani selected a sleek craft. He shoved off from shore, paddling into the heart of the bay, heading for the temple a mile away. He heard loud voices behind him: "We are warriors of Chief Makula. We demand one of these canoes."

The teacher answered, "You have no authority here! Chief Kamehameha controls this bay. These are canoes for the students of lua. Go to the village to borrow one."

Kalani looked back and saw two men by the teacher. One man made a move to take a canoe and the lua instructor raised a cudgel. The other warrior called to his companion, "Stop, we will go to the village."

He did not have time to watch what they did. A hundred yards ahead, Hauna paddled toward the temple. Despite this overwhelming advantage, Kalani vowed to overtake his enemy.

CHAPTER 16

"MAY THE GODS LAY THEIR curse on that evil boy," Makula ranted as his war canoe traveled around the promontory that splayed out into the ocean like the thumb of a giant. More black rocks, thick with moss, blocked his passage, forcing him to sail into deeper water.

Far ahead, he saw the end point of Kealakekua Bay where the High Chief Kamehameha lived. "The man has not favored me with land and power. Soon he leaves to conquer Maui. Then I will join Keoua and we will seize this island," Makula muttered.

He searched for his quarry. In front of him many canoes skimmed the sea fishing, traveling, or surfing. He thought back to a time ten years earlier when Captain James Cook had come to this bay. He remembered the white sails of his ships, *Discovery* and *Resolution*, bulging like billowing clouds carrying the god Lono across the water.

Cook proved that he was not a god when he died in this very bay, struck down by Hawaiian warriors angered by his attempt to capture the King of Hawaii. After the captain's death, the two British ships bombarded the village, killing many and destroying buildings.

Makula remembered these events, wondering if the white sails would return. If they did, he believed they would bring weapons that belched fire and killed from afar. He knew that with such armament, a warrior chief would be victorious over his enemies.

Makula broke from his thoughts, his eyes searching the bay. "Where among all these vessels is that terrible boy?" he said. In the distance, he

saw the towering stone pile of the sacred temple. "If he has escaped my warriors, he will head to it."

"Pull towards Hikiau," Makula ordered.

Kalani saw Hepa standing on shore. Beside him stood a tall man, a red and gold cloak over his shoulders. Ahead, Hauna paddled leisurely toward them.

Kalani felt disappointed. His enemy would win, meet the High Chief, and, with the aid of Makula, gain Kamehameha's favor. Glory and land would follow. But he had a slim chance: Hauna appeared unaware of pursuit. With all the energy he could muster, Kalani flung his paddle into the water, and pulled, first to one side and then to the other. His craft narrowed the gap. Soon they were less than twenty yards apart.

Shouts swept across the water. Hauna paused and glanced back. Their eyes locked. The bully reared back, his voice rose to a screech, a sound filled with disbelief. "You are dead. I saw you fall, how—"

"I am a ghost," Kalani interrupted. "I have been sent to take you to the world of the dead where you are to live in eternal darkness for your crimes."

Hauna shook his head. "How you survived, I do not know. But you are real and I will beat you and then end your life." The big man turned, thrust his wide blade into the sea, and pulled with the enormous power of his muscular arms.

During the momentary pause of screams and yells, Kalani had not ceased paddling. The gap between canoes narrowed significantly.

More voices called and the boy knew that Makula and his goons were bearing down upon him. He did not dare look back, for Hauna's powerful, rhythmic strokes were sending his canoe flying across the water. Kalani's heart sank. His enemy would reach the finish point ahead of him and claim victory.

A canoe length separated the competitors, the beach lay fifty feet away. His head spun. His breath came in great gasps. Despair crept over him. *I will not win. Hauna will meet the High Chief, and I will lose my chance to be a warrior.*

Kalani felt water bunching into a swell beneath his canoe. People on shore screamed. The two crafts paralleled each other with Hauna ahead by half a canoe. With powerful strokes Kalani caught the peak of the wave before it crested. The prow of his boat lifted and rushed like a speeding arrow toward the beach.

The surging water engulfed Hauna in bubbles of white foam, slowing his canoe. Before he could regain control, Kalani shot past and washed onto shore. He leaped from his craft and raced for Hepa and the chief by his side.

A frustrated Hauna beached his canoe and plodded up the sand to the finish point. Behind him, two tattooed warriors landed their vessel and watched the approaching war canoe of Chief Makula.

"Very good," Hepa praised. "You deserve to be first. The youngest student in my class continues to show his great ability. Let me present to you High Chief Alapai-nui, a cousin of Kamehameha the Great and one of his closest advisors."

Kalani prostrated himself. Alapai-nui smiled and said, "You have good manners, young man. My cousin will be happy to meet you."

Alapai-nui paused as a war canoe surfed onto the beach. Makula leapt from his craft and stormed toward the finish point. "Ah, you have come to pay honor to the winner of this contest."

Makula fumbled for an answer. Kalani sensed that the man could not admit that he was chasing after him for seducing his wife.

"Yes, I came to see the six finalists. But how is it that Hauna is not the winner? When I last saw him, he had a comfortable lead."

"Kalani cheated," Hauna yelled. "He could not have collected the iwa'iwa fern, the three opihi from the islet, and beat me to the finish line. I demand that his bag be examined."

With a stern look, Hepa untied the pouch around Kalani's waist, reached in, and pulled out wet, beautiful fronds of iwa'iwa fern. He rummaged in the sack and withdrew one, two, and, finally, a third large opihi, their conical tops sprouting with the seaweed found only on the little island. With a smile, Hepa raised the limpets and the ferns so that all could see the trophies of victory.

Chief Alapai-nui grinned and placed a wreath on Kalani's head and a necklace of shark's teeth around his neck. Then he turned, motioning to an attendant to bring a glinting neckpiece of mother-of-pearl. As he held it in his hand, he called to Hauna to come forward. "To the runner-up in this contest I award—"

"Wait," chorused several voices from the beach. Everyone turned and saw five lua students, Moki leading them.

"What is the meaning of this intrusion?" Makula blustered.

Moki rushed to Hepa. "Kalani would not tell, but I will. Hauna tripped him over a cliff and left him for dead. Someone helped pick the iwa'iwa for him and gave him a knife to get the opihi."

"Those are serious accusations," Alapai-nui spoke sternly. "The students were not to receive help from anyone. They were to use their wits and nature's implements to secure their prizes."

Alapai-nui turned to Kalani. "How did you get the iwa'iwa and the opihi?"

Kalani explained what he had done.

"You, Hauna, how did you get the iwa'iwa and the opihi?"

"I bent and broke the fern stalks and pried the opihi from the rocks with a sharp stone."

"Let me check Hauna's bag to see if he accomplished his tasks," Hepa interjected, untying Hauna's sack.

Hepa reached in and pulled out a full-leafed iwa'iwa. A second time, he thrust his hand into the sack, only to withdraw it with blood on his fingers. "There is sharp iron in this bag!" Hepa howled, sucking a cut finger.

The lua master fumbled in the tapa container a third time and withdrew an iron knife. Pointing it at Hauna, Hepa hissed, "You used this to pry the opihi from the rocks. Get out of my sight. You are a disgrace to the school."

Kalani watched Hauna's face dissolve into misery. He saw him looking at Makula, but the chief turned away, finding a sudden interest in the grimacing statues that lined the wall of the temple above his head. Hauna slunk from the beach, disappearing into the throngs of villagers lining the shore.

Hepa turned to his other students. "Empty your bags. Show me that you have finished the tests. If you have, all of you will be presented to High Chief Kamehameha."

Food and intoxicating awa juice flowed in abundance at the victory party that night. All eleven young men laughed, joked, and swapped stories of the day's adventures. As the bonfires raged on the shore, Moki came to Kalani. "There are several girls at the women's compound who are dying to entertain you tonight."

Kalani gave Moki a frigid stare. "Just make sure that no one's married to royalty. I've had enough of jealous chiefs."

CHAPTER 17

TALL COCONUT TREES SHADED A stone checkerboard. Kalani studied the game pieces. He picked up a white pebble, jumped it over a black one, and removed it from the board. "Your move." He smiled at his opponent, certain that he had placed Lehua in a hopeless position.

He recalled the time he first met her. For three days after the test, he awaited a signal to come to High Chief Kamehameha, but none came. Hepa remained in Kealakekua Bay to sharpen the skills of his students. He promised more trials would occur before they graduated from lua training.

It was on his second night that he met the princess. He, along with his lua mates, feasted in the men's area of the village. Bonfires cast flickering light upon the mats where men thrust fingers into vessels of poi, pork, and baked fish.

In the stillness of the evening a rhythmic chanting came from the women's compound, their words praising the beautiful moon, the sweetness of the air, and the pleasures of love. Soon, an ipu drum sounded and Kalani heard the rustle of swishing leaves.

From the darkness, slaves rushed to the mats to gather the wooden plates. After they disappeared beyond the firelight, twelve women came into the compound with oil- sleeked gourds in their hands. They sat and began a rhythmic beating on the gourd instruments, moving their chests from side-to-side.

Soon the striking of palms on ipus stopped and the women sat cross-legged upon the mats. A nose flute whistled a weird, plaintive tune.

Moki pulled Kalani onto the matting and the men began to dance. They stomped around the women, circling them as the drums pounded a new.

As he stepped, Kalani's eyes locked onto those of a young woman. She did not drop her gaze. Instead, she stared at him, thrusting her breasts right and left in time to the beat. Her boldness and sensuous beauty jolted his heart. He felt heat rise within him and forced his eyes away. When he gazed back, she would not look at him.

The music ceased and Kalani returned to his place on the mat. He stole a glance in the direction of the young beauty. The women moved into the darkness, male dancers following them. Kalani saw legs, saucy hips, and flowing black hair go past the glowing beach fires. In the grey shadows beyond the light, a young woman looked back, searching, and found his eyes. A momentary connection, and he felt sure she beckoned to him before disappearing into the darkness.

His heart tripping, Kalani leapt from the mat and raced into the shadows. His eyes blinked in the night and for a time he could not see. A soft voice called, "Over here." He stumbled toward the sound.

When he came to the place where he had heard the enticing whisper, no one was there. "Where are you? Who are you?"

"My name is Lehua," a voice tremored seductively. "Meet me tomorrow in the village, before the sun falls."

"Wait," Kalani said. There came no answer.

The next day, he worked at lua practice, his anxiety building while the earth moved in the heavens. Just before twilight, he entered the village and found Lehua waiting for him near the men's compound. She laughed. "Come to the home of my mother. We will play a game and get to know each other."

Kalani sighed, his eyes wandering from the board. He could not believe that he played such a boring contest. He had expected more excitement on their first meeting.

A dark stone jumped three times over his white pieces. "I win again," Lehua teased, rising from her squat.

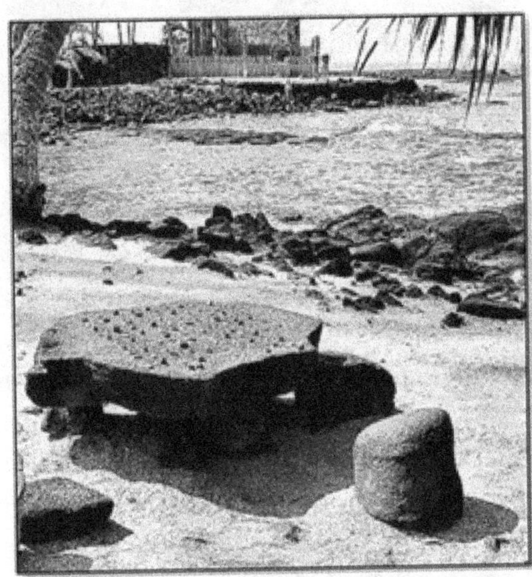

Kalani shot back, "You win because I let you."

"I win because I am a woman and of higher class than you," she challenged, pointing a finger at him, a coy smile on her face.

Kalani pounded the mat with the flat of his palm, scattering the black and white stones. He lunged for her accusing finger, but Lehua turned and ran, her feet flinging pebbles over the ground. Her flight aroused his desire to conquer her, and he leaped after the girl.

When she looked back, her face was lit by a saucy smile with a sparkling challenge in her eyes. Kalani charged, grasping for her body. Lehua's feet churned sand into his face and she fled for the protection of coconut trees growing along the beach.

"Aha! This is the game you intended to play. I will win it, for I am stronger and better than you. And when I catch you—"

"All you will catch will be the wind," Lehua teased, dashing behind a coco palm.

He ran toward her hiding place. A pebble struck him on the back. He pivoted and saw Lehua teasing him. He reached for her, but she sped to a raised earthen walkway bordering two taro patches. She picked her way along the path, cleared the obstacles, and fled into the jungle.

Not far behind, Kalani ran on the dirt berm. Heavier than Lehua, his foot slipped, sending him into a muddy field of leafy taro.

From the jungle, Lehua laughed. Angry shouts came from laborers working among the plants in the field.

Kalani pulled himself from the mud and resumed his pursuit. "Where are you, Lehua?" he called as he brushed aside branches of koa. Other than the hum of insects and the rustling noise of leaves disturbed by the wind, no answer came.

His head throbbed with mounting desire. He wanted this elusive young woman, but he realized from the night before, and her skill in eluding him today, that she was good at this game. He breathed deeply, forcing his heart to stop racing. When his pulse ceased pounding, he listened to the sounds of the forest.

Noise came from his left. Thinking it a ruse, he plunged into the ferns on his right. He saw a fleeing foot and lunged at it, grasping an ankle. Lehua escaped from his wet hand, running through the shrubbery onto a hard earth trail.

He followed, the game of pursuit increasing his hunger for the woman. The path led upwards into a small glade. At its edge, Lehua stumbled. Kalani reached for her, but the young woman recovered her balance, eluding his grasp. "No, no," she said, "you won't catch me." With a throaty laugh, Lehua sped into the forest and headed for the beach.

When he emerged from the brush, Kalani saw people hurrying toward the center of the village. Ahead of him, Lehua raced to her home. An imposing woman called to her, "Where have you been? Everyone is going to the square. A *kahuna nui* will be singing out his last prophecy. Hurry, we must go to hear him. Who is this young man chasing you?"

Lehua laughed. "His name is Kalani Moku Tana. He won the lua contest. I met him last night at the village luau."

He slowed to a walk. Lehua smiled and said, "Meet my mother."

He prostrated himself before the royal woman, but she waved a dismissive hand. "Good to meet you, young man, but we must go to hear the wizard's prophecy."

"Who is this prophet?"

"The man is the wisest of all the great seers. When he chants, everyone listens, for he speaks words that become true. He sees the future and knows what will be. He travels among warring tribes, spreading his wisdom. No one harms him."

Lehua swayed into Kalani's side, rubbing her hips against his.

"Stop it, you can play later."

Approaching the village center, the trio spied a large fire burning near a hut, the flames providing light and warmth to the crowd seated outside. A white cloth covered the door. Only the crackling of the flames broke the silence. The throng prostrated themselves while Lehua, her mother, and Kalani moved to the front of the meeting place. A handsome man sat on a large mat.

"Aloha," Chief Haewa whispered. The royal couple rubbed noses. Lehua and Kalani flopped behind them and servants crawled up to the newcomers, carrying bowls of food.

"Has anything happened?" Lehua asked.

"No. The kahuna nui has been in his hut for some time," Haewa answered. "He has not stirred since sending word that he is creating his last prophesies. But tell me, who is this man? What is his ancestry?"

"He is Kalani Moku Tana," Lehua answered, "and the winner of the lua competition."

"Yes, I heard of it. Disgraceful that there should have been cheating. I understand that the wrongdoer has left for his family home in Puna. Tana, state your royal lineage."

Kalani shuddered. *I knew that this day must come.* He recalled Hauna's insults that were partly true. Steeling himself, he recited his family history. "My mother is a great-granddaughter of Kamaka-I-Moku, the mother of Keoua, father of High Chief Kamehameha. My grandfather and father were defeated in battle and sacrificed—"

Before he could finish, a hush enveloped the audience. Through the cloth-covered door of the hut crawled an ancient man, little more than bones covered by skin. He squatted before the crowd and looked upon the villagers. The wizard's hair was pure white, hanging in long strings that nearly touched the ground. Sunk deep into his skull were glaring eyes. A razor nose with small openings divided the center of his face.

In a thin voice, the old man chanted:

The first who come to Hawaii find paradise,
They live in peace and prosperity,
Until Pa ao arrives with his God Ku.

"Who is Pa ao?" Kalani whispered.

With a frown, Lehua answered, "A high priest from Tahiti. He came to Hawaii many years ago with his war god. Pa ao demanded that temples be built to him and that the people make human sacrifice to Ku."

War comes, blood covers the ground;
Who can save this land from its despair?
A warrior is born on a stormy night,
Stolen from his mother's arms as war drums beat,
The warrior will fight many battles,
He will have victories and defeats;
Until one day white clouds will come again,
They will bring weapons of great power,
With these weapons the warrior will be victorious,
He will rule supreme over all the islands of Hawaii.

With this last phrase, the old wizard rose, looked about him, then said, "With weapons of great power, he will rule supreme." He raised his sallow face, thin hands and arms toward the night sky, then collapsed before the fire.

Kalani saw that Haewa was shaken by the prophecy. The warrior that the seer foretold was Kamehameha. But since the killing of Captain Cook, the foreign ships with billowing white sails had not returned.

"What shall we do?" a puzzled Haewa asked.

"It is clear what must be done," Lehua answered. "We must go to Kamehameha and tell him of the prophecy. We must tell him that the foreign ships with the great sails will be returning. To be victorious, he must make friends with the foreigners and acquire their fire weapons."

"I am to meet with the great Kamehameha tomorrow," Kalani interrupted. "I can tell him of the prophecy." On uttering these words, Kalani knew that he had made a serious blunder.

Haewa glared at him. "Your ancestors were defeated in battle and sacrificed," he snarled. "You have no land, no power. You are not of the upper class. It is I, Chief Haewa, who will speak to Kamehameha of the prophecy. Be gone: I forbid you to remain with us or visit my daughter."

Kalani prostrated himself before the chief. "Forgive me, your majesty. I was foolish, presumptuous, and forgot my low caste. It is you alone who can speak to the great Kamehameha of the prophecy."

Staring at the back of the boy humbling himself below him, Haewa snarled, "Those of lesser rank must know their place. I will not forgive this breach of protocol. Leave us."

CHAPTER 18

HEPA AND SIX STUDENTS CANOED to the village on the north end of Kealakekua Bay, where the lua teacher and the shore guards chanted a landing protocol. Once the warriors were satisfied, the students came ashore and entered the royal compound.

Seated on a platform, Kamehameha watched young men wrestle. Nearby, women worked at making cloth by pounding mulberry bark, while several men mashed taro to produce poi.

When the students came closer to the throne, Moki nudged Kalani. "The woman sitting next to Kamehameha is wife number four, Kaahumanu, his favorite. See that tall guy over there, the one wearing the red cloak? His name is Akaka. He travelled all over the world, and just came back to Hawaii. The gossip is that Kaahumanu is sweet on him. They better watch out, Kamehameha is a jealous man, and you know what jealous husbands do?" Moki dodged aside, escaping Kalani's kick. Hepa frowned and the two young men settled down.

A conch shell blew and Kalani saw a splendid war canoe skimming over the water, approaching the village. A herald from the craft announced, "Chief Haewa wishes an audience with High Chief Kamehameha."

After concluding the ritual preliminaries, permission to land was granted. Haewa trudged up to the royal compound, his retinue following him. He and his party prostrated themselves before the ruler.

"Come forward," Kamehameha said. "What news do you bring me?"

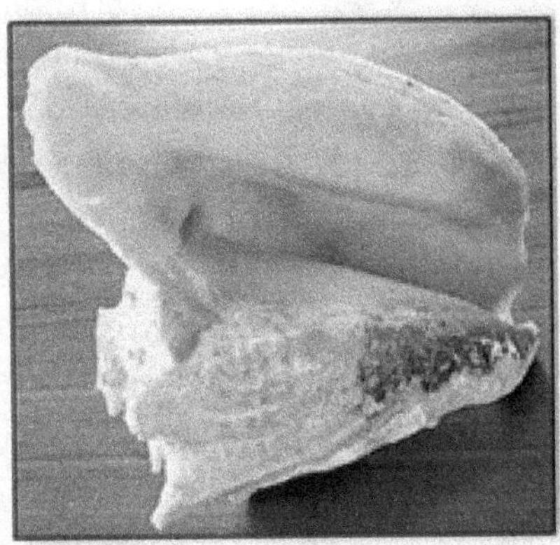

The chief approached and, with many words and gestures, embellished on the prophecy of the wizard. When Haewa finished, Kamehameha sat silent, eyes fixed on the man.

Another conch shell called across the waters and a second war canoe surfed onto the beach. A tall, muscular warrior leaped from it, racing toward Kamehameha. The guards recognized an ally of their king and let him pass without challenge.

The newcomer prostrated himself. "Kamehameha, the white sails have come again to Hawaii. Other chiefs are already seeking guns and powder from the returning foreigners. If we—"

"We can trade for these armaments," Queen Kaahumanu interrupted. "Give the white men food and sandalwood and you will get the weapons you need."

Suspicion in his voice, Kamehameha asked, "How do you know this?"

Kaahumanu spoke slowly, choosing her words with care. "I have it from a visitor to the ship of the American, Captain Russell. This white captain said he would trade iron, guns, and powder for food and sandalwood."

"Who is this visitor?" Kamehameha demanded.

Evading his question, Kaahumanu said, "There are more ships coming to Hawaii from foreign lands. Other chiefs are trading with these foreigners for weapons. You must act, my Lord, and get these fire sticks before your enemies possess them and defeat you in battle."

"Did you go on Russell's ship?" Kamehameha persisted.

Kaahumanu retorted, "You let your other wives go where they want to go, sleep with whomever they wish, but you treat me like a child, always restricting my freedom. I am Kaahumanu, and I will do as I please."

Kalani was shocked by the queen's words. He knew that it was not uncommon for royalty and commoners to have several partners. The coupling of a man and a woman is a natural and healthy act, not a despicable or evil one. While casual sex was not a reason for punishment, direct disobedience of the high chief, even from his favorite wife, meant swift and certain death.

For some moments, Kamehameha and his fourth wife glared at each other. Then Kaahumanu relented, saying, "I did not go aboard Russell's ship. I learned the news from a friend of the captain."

The normal business of pounding mulberry bark, mashing poi, and wrestling contests resumed. Kamehameha's eyes fell away from his wife. Kalani saw the queen glance at Akaka, who returned her look with a smile.

"For too many years we have tasted the bitter waters of defeat," Kamehameha declared. "I know the power of the white man's weapons. We must get them."

"What good are guns and powder if we do not know how to use them?" a chief protested.

"We will kidnap foreign sailors and force them to teach us," Kamehameha answered, looking around him. When he spied Hepa with his six students, he stood and motioned for the lua master to approach his platform.

Hepa prostrated himself. "At your request, I have brought with me the six finalists who passed the tests of bravery and skill."

"You have come from my lua school, let me see what your students can do." He ordered servants to bring spears, while he directed the six men to stand fifty feet away. Suddenly he flung the weapons in rapid succession.

Kalani and Moki caught the missles tossed at them, but the remaining four did not, dodging away from them. One student was nicked in the thigh and blood gushed lfrom his wound.

Kamehameha shouted, "If you wish to succeed as warriors, you must learn to catch spears. You two," he pointed at Kalani and Moki, "catch these." The monarch threw two pointed sticks at Kalani and two at Moki. Then he hurled one more at each of them.

Kalani caught the first two in his right hand and the third in his left. Moki caught the first, but missed the second, escaping impalement by dodging away. The third weapon fell to the ground.

"Let me show you how to catch spears," Kamehameha pointed at Moki. "Throw your three at me."

With a frown, Moki threw the first spear in his hand at the high chief. He picked up the remaining two and hurled them as well.

Kamehameha easily caught the first, then darted to his right to gather up the others, both badly thrown. He looked at Hepa, standing nearby. "Is this the best you have?"

Hepa pointed at Kalani.

Turning to him, Kamehameha challenged, "Let's see if you can do better."

Spear throwing

Kalani threw his three in six heartbeats. His throws were powerful, his aim accurate. The missiles flew at Kamehameha, yet somehow the high chief managed to catch two of them and deflect the third.

Kamehameha grunted his approval. He ordered Kalani to approach him.

He went to the ground, remembering protocol. In this servile position Kalani crawled to the high chief.

"Rise up and tell me your name," Kamehameha said. "Who is your family and what is your age?"

"My name is Kalani Moku Tana and I am seventeen years old."

"And your family?"

"My grandfather and father were sacrificed, defeated in battle fighting for your cause. My mother is Umi-ula Moku, a relative of yours."

"Ah, yes, your mother is related on my father's side. She came to me some time ago to speak on your behalf. At her request you were placed in my lua school to train as a warrior. Your teachers have taught you well; you will join my army. Go to Alapai-nui, you will serve under him."

On his knees, Kalani said, "Thank you, High Chief Kamehameha." He almost added that his teachers had been slaves, but he held his tongue, remembering how his foolishness had angered Haewa.

Kamehameha issued orders. "Alapai-nui, take some men and head north along the coastline. Warn every chief not to harm the foreigners. Instead, they are to trade for weapons. Tell them that if the opportunity presents itself, they are to kidnap foreign sailors. They are to obey this command or die.

"Haewa," he continued, "go south to the border of Kau and give the chiefs loyal to me the same message.

"High Priest of Ku, attend to me. Before we attack Maui, we must plan a new temple. We will give the god sacrifices to gain his favor in the coming war."

CHAPTER 19

ALAPAI-NUI AND KALANI TRAVELED NORTH spreading Kamehameha's order not to kill but to capture white men. As they paddled along the coast the two became friends. Alapai-nui admired Kalani's strength, good humor, and intelligence. The youth learned politics and the protocol of dealing with chiefs.

News came of a horrible massacre at Olowalo village on Maui. An American captain, Simon Metcalfe, angry because Hawaiians had stolen a cutter from his square-rigger, had enticed Hawaiians to his ship, the *Eleanora,* to trade. More than fifty canoes came. When they had assembled on the starboard side, a dozen cannon destroyed the small fleet. Hundreds were killed.

There was more. Metcalfe had come to north Kona, beaten its chief, and kicked him from his ship. The insulted ruler vowed to kill white men who visited his shores. Alarmed, Alapai-nui and Kalani hurried north. Both men knew that despite all insults, Kamehameha needed the white men's knowledge.

Within a day, they sailed into north Kona. Anchored in a small bay was a schooner. "Look," Kalani pointed, "the ship is surrounded. White men are being thrown overboard."

Across the still waters came a chilling command, "Kill the haoles." Warriors jumped into canoes pursuing floundering sailors. Alapai-nui screamed, "Stop, in the name of Kamehameha."

The warriors ignored the command and began smashing paddles into the helpless men. Blood colored the water. Kalani worried that sharks would come to finish what was left.

One sailor swam away from the clumped mass of boats and men. He neared shore when a canoe shot away from the melee and raced after him.

"We must save him," Alapai-nui yelled.

Kalani began a rhythmic beat, "One, two, three on the left. Switch. One, two, three on the right. Switch." Their canoe shot forward, passing dead men floating in the water. Several war craft hovered around them. "Pray to the gods that we can save that one," Alapai-nui muttered.

The paddlers ahead were experts. Kalani's vessel could not close the gap. The foreign canoe slowed as it came alongside the swimming sailor. Paddles were raised and slammed into the sea. Water splashed in geysers around the defenseless man.

Alapai-nui screamed, "Stop." But the attackers ignored his call. A paddle struck the man's head. Other paddles rained down onto his face, ears, neck, back.

The canoe of vengeful warriors stopped their beating. Several hands reached down, pulling the sailor in. A warrior grabbed the seaman's neck and squeezed.

Alapai-nui's canoe slammed into the craft and the chief yelled, "In the name of Kamehameha, I order you to stop or die." Kalani raised a spear, pointing it at the warrior's heart. He wondered if the man would obey. He did not want to kill him.

Slowly, the strangling hands opened, releasing the seaman. The two canoes bumped onto the shore. Kalani reached in and manhandled a half-blind, bruised, and bloodied white man out of the canoe. He carried him up the beach, Alapai-nui following.

The north Kona chief came to shore and strode to the injured sailor.

"Why did you attack these men?" Alapai-nui demanded.

"Because Metcalfe hurt me, I vowed to kill all haoles. When his son Thomas came in that ship," the chief pointed to the *Fair American*, "I took revenge."

"Kamehameha issued an order not to kill white men. He needs their knowledge. How many dead?"

"Six, maybe seven, if this one dies."

"Then you must die, for breaking the order."

"I did not know of it, but—" the north Kona chief waved toward the *Fair American,* "won't our leader be happy with that ship, the cannon and muskets in it?"

Alapai-nui smiled. "Yes, that may be so."

In the succeeding days, weapons were off-loaded from the *Fair American,* including a brass cannon. Kalani helped hide the cache of armament and the ship. Alapai-nui was eager to tell Kamehameha the news. He waited for the rescued sailor, Isaac Davis, to mend. When he could travel they left for Kealakekua Bay.

As they paddled south, word came that Captain Metcalfe had anchored in Kealakekua Bay. Villages were ordered abandoned and all canoes to remain away from the *Eleanora.*

When they were near the bay, Kalani heard thunder. It was not like the god Kane's loud, rolling blast, but a clap, then a whining in the air. The vessels beached, and they were met on shore by warriors who guided the party to Kamehameha.

In the high chief's compound, Kalani learned that a sailor from Metcalfe's ship, John Young, had been captured. Since then, Metcalfe had been firing upon the deserted villages for two days.

At the cooking fires that evening, Alapai-nui made his report. Kamehameha listened with a stone face. Once finished, he rose. "Metcalfe will be gone soon. The weapons of fire will be brought to me. The two haole sailors will teach us. When all is ready, we invade Maui. Alapai-nui, return to the north and warn the chiefs not to kill white men."

CHAPTER 20

Pu u kohola Heiau

"WHERE HAVE YOU BEEN?" MOKI demanded when Kalani joined him in a line of men passing rocks. Below them, a human chain of ten thousand warriors and slaves stretched from a stone quarry, miles away, to the top of the hill and a temple under construction.

"With Alapai-nui meeting with the sub-chiefs along the coast, we needed to convince them to trade with foreign ships for weapons of fire and encourage them to kidnap, but not kill, the foreign sailors."

"Kill foreign sailors? Why kill them?"

"They have been evil to our people." Kalani related how Captain Cook and his men had been treated like gods, yet the British attacked and blew up villages. "When the white sails returned to Hawaii they killed and destroyed. A little while ago, an American named Metcalfe fired his cannon, killing hundreds of Hawaiians."

"I heard about that massacre. The deaths must have made your job impossible," Moki said, passing a massive rock to his friend.

Kalani cradled the large stone in his arms and handed it to the next man in line. "Kamehameha wanted fire weapons so much that he spread word that anyone who harmed foreigners would be sacrificed to Ku."

"Did this work?"

"Not in the way you might think." Kalani went on to explain the seizure of the *Fair American*, the killing of sailors, and the capture of Isaac Davis.

Moki shook his head. "Did Kamehameha sacrifice the north Kona chief?"

"No, because he gave our leader cannon, muskets, powder and the surviving crewman, Davis. He is grateful since he needs those weapons to start a war against the king of Maui."

Passing a stone to the man above him, Kalani looked to the top of the hill. The sun rolled into the western horizon, its dying rays burnishing the sparse grass of the hillside to a rich orange. Above him, men hoisted stones onto a three-stepped pile of rocks. The almost-finished open-air temple to Ku glowed red in the sunset. Despite it being a warm day, he shivered thinking of the horror to come.

"Quit time," Moki gasped.

Thousands of men ceased working and trudged to the beach. At the compound of the warriors the two friends ate hastily and went to bed.

The next day, eight men marched down the hillside, bearing a heavy platform on their shoulders. Swathed in brown tapa, the high priest of Ku sat on it, surveying the workers as they moved rocks to the new temple.

"Don't stare at that evil man," Moki warned. "He might choose you for sacrifice." He passed another stone to his friend. "Look at that temple. Everything up, altar finished, luakini pit dug."

"Luakini pit?" Kalani asked. "I thought 'Luakini' was the name of the temple we are building."

"Ku priests call it a luakini temple, because at its altar is a deep well, the lua. That is where the bodies are tossed after sacrifice."

"And *kini* means forty thousand!" Kalani whispered. *Is that the number of bodies that might be tossed in?* He shuddered as he reached for the rock in Moki's hand. *The nightmare of his sacrificed father and grandfather flashed before him and his hands faltered.*

"Watch it. Don't let it fall, or the high priest will choose you to sacrifice to the tree."

"Ayah," Kalani answered, saving the rock from dropping to the ground. He handed the stone to the next person and then asked, "What do you mean 'sacrificed to the tree'?"

Moki grunted and heaved another stone into Kalani's hands. "Before sacrifices are made, the temple needs a new statue to Ku. In the forest, they find a perfect ohia tree. The high priest blesses it and makes a human sacrifice. The man is buried in the roots. The trunk is cut down. Ku is carved from it."

Kalani glared at the departing priest. *He thought of his dead father, the fear that was in the heart of his friend, the slave Minato. Anger swept reason away. This cruel practice must stop.* He moved to pursue the cleric.

A rock struck his belly, blowing air from his lungs.

"Don't be a fool," Moki said in a low voice.

Kalani faltered, clutching his stomach, struggling for breath. He stared at his friend and then his eyes lost their anger. "Thank you for saving my life."

Moki nodded, "Be smart, brother. The priest has got the power, we obey or die. Maybe tomorrow you will become a chief and we obey you." Moki laughed. He laid his rock onto the orange dirt of the hill, his body shaking with suppressed mirth.

"That is not funny. Someday I will be a chief and end this senseless killing."

A drum beat sounded from the pile of stones above them.

"Ha! End of work," Moki said. He draped an arm over Kalani's shoulder. Arm in arm, the two boys descended to the workers' village. Once there, a laughing Moki asked, "Roach, are you coming to the awa feast?"

"Who wants to drink with a crazy man like you?"

"Don't take it so hard. What chance do we have of being a big chief? Stop crying and come with me."

The two boys huddled at an eating mat, Kalani picking at a chicken. As he munched on a sweet potato, Moki nudged him. "They brought women to the camp."

"Is that so," Kalani said, faking disinterest. Yet his body tensed; it had been weeks since he had been satisfied by a woman.

"Well, if you're not interested," Moki's voice trailed off to a whisper, then he added, "check out the big shack past the coco trees."

Kalani stood and stretched away stiffness in his back. He took a sip of awa. The fiery liquid warmed his throat and raised a fire in his belly. "I think I'll take a swim, then rest."

Moki smirked, heading for containers of awa juice. "Don't let the sharks eat you. Me, I'm going to drink, then maybe I'll join you."

Kalani sucked cool, crisp night air into his lungs, trying to control his trembling. In the dim light of kukui torches the entrance to the large shack loomed ahead. Several women stood by it, their bodies oiled, hair flowing over their shoulders, draping over full breasts. Inside the building Kalani saw bodies writhing, heard people jesting. A woman lounging at the entrance stared at him. He dropped his eyes to the ground.

She sidled up to him, smiled, caressed his face, stroked his thigh. He felt a hardness coming. He knew she could be his.

Kalani drew back. This was not what he wanted, public love making. The woman spat, "Not good enough for you?"

Confused, he ran. He wanted relief from the burning in his loins but felt shame at the wanton love making. He had heard the ribald jests of gawking onlookers expressing praise for male sexual prowess. He had been taught that the joining between a man and woman should give each pleasure, and that privacy was important for it showed respect. Only a braggart strutted about like a peacock displaying his rigid equipment for all to see.

He ran along the sand, then splashed into waves that washed over his feet and dashed him with water. At a stream he removed his loincloth and dipped. The cool flow swirled around him, releasing tension in his body. A breeze puckered his skin, he swam into the sea.

Apprehension of what would come remained. He ducked underwater. The enveloping ocean calmed him as he crab-crawled beneath the surface.

Kalani's chest brushed sand. He planted his feet into it, pushing above the surface. Sunlight had shaded into evening. Water splashed into his face and a voice said, "You got some kind of body, but are you any good at making love?"

He saw his loincloth flowing past and lunged at it, but the woman who held it escaped his grasp. He followed her onto the beach, where she stood with his covering draped over her shoulder. "Come and get your cloth."

Not far from the shore the woman crawled into a low shed lounging seductively on soft mats. "Come inside and we will see how good you are."

Kalani paused, staring. "I will not take you against your will."

The woman returned his naïve look. "It is true, that we were brought here for one purpose, to give men pleasure before the sacrifices start. But in your shyness, I find you exciting. Come and make me happy."

For two nights, they enjoyed love. On the third evening, the large shack and the beach hut were empty. Kalani knew that on the morrow the temple would be ready and the rituals would begin.

CHAPTER 21

PLAGUED BY BOREDOM, KALANI STRUGGLED to stay awake as the mass of worshipers responded to the priest's prayers. Above him rose three long tiers of stone that led to a raised platform on which a bloody altar stood. To each side lay ceremonial buildings used by priests. In a row behind the altar stood statues of various gods, their ugly wide-mouthed grimaces glowering at the audience below.

He shook his head to drive away the dizziness that threatened to make him sleep on this second day of worship. The first had been spent in prayer to purify the new temple. The blood on the altar came from a pig sacrificed on the opening day. Kalani hoped this would be the only gift to Ku, yet he sensed otherwise. All the chiefs and warriors allied with Kamehameha were assembled before the altar and aligned according to their rank. He had been placed in the fourth row. Behind him sat the commoners, answering the prayers of a white-robed priest standing on the raised platform of the temple.

His mind wandered from the droning rituals to the woman he had met on the beach. She had excited him. Their love making had relieved his anxiety. But today tension rebuilt within him, a fear for what would come.

As the setting sun flamed from yellow to bright orange, a naked man stepped from a hut next to the altar and stood before the crowd. His oiled, bronze body gleamed in the dying sunlight. The priest ceased his incantations and left. The naked man, a living representative of the god, cried out, "Stand for Ku, Hail Ku." The multitude stood, yelling several times, "Hail! Hail, O Ku!" When the audience went silent, men bearing effigies of gods lined up on each side of the naked man. When they were in a straight line, the representative of the deity led them in a circuit around the platform, around the glowering statues of gods, and around the worshipers. Once the circuits were completed, the bearers of gods and the naked man lined up on a rock tier below the altar.

A drum boomed three times. The audience fell silent. The high priest walked from a hut, his body swathed in a white cloth. In his hand, he held stalks of ferns. Beside him came a second priest holding a skull containing seawater. They stood in front of the altar, crimson from the dying sun's rays. Dipping his ferns into the skull, the high priest sprinkled seawater on those below him, and called out, "To whom does the earth belong?"

"The earth belongs to Ku," the naked man said.

A second time the high priest called out, "To whom does the earth and all who live therein belong?"

"The earth belongs to Ku," the audience answered. Once these words were uttered, a fire bearer ran along the back wall of the temple, lighting torches. Drums boomed. Two priests emerged from the hut, striding to the altar. They held a newly carved statue of Ku. Worshipers fell to the ground, prostrating. The priests placed the effigy into a posthole by the altar. Its mother-of-pearl eyes glared. Its pouting mouth gaped wide, revealing jagged teeth protruding above its lips.

The naked man cried out, "The earth belongs to Ku! All who live therein belong to Ku!"

"All belong to Ku," the worshipers repeated.

Kalani mumbled the words.

"Ku! Ku!" chanted the crowd. They began to shout the name as two priests dragged a slender boy toward the altar.

Kalani woke from his listlessness and stared in horror at the child struggling against the priests. Who is it? He could not see clearly. The youth fought to escape.

"Blood for Ku," the high priest screamed.

"Blood for Ku," other priests repeated.

"Blood for Ku," the audience answered.

The victim twisted, pulled, kicked until a club smashed his head.

Men raised the child onto the altar. The high priest retrieved a knife. He yelled, "Blood for Ku."

Light from the blazing torches glinted off the shark teeth ringing the ceremonial weapon. The high priest plunged the dagger into the boy, then sliced it down his body.

The sacrifice screamed. Blood spouted over the hands of the priest spurting onto the altar.

"No! No!" Kalani cried as he recognized Minato. His words were drowned by a thousand voices yelling, "All belong to Ku."

He fought to approach the altar and stop this insanity, even if it meant he would die. But the yelling masses surrounded him, pressed against him, and held him in place.

"Minato!" he cried out. *How could they do this to the sweet boy? Memories flooded over him. He felt gentle hands massaging his aches. He heard the slave's frightened voice asking forgiveness when his rubbing caused pain. His laughter when they found the right stones in the stream. Minato's happiness when he caught the spears.*

Kalani wept. His chest heaved. His legs felt weak. Only the press of the mob kept him from falling. *All those happy times with the slave boy were gone forever.* As *Minato's dead body slid into the pit he vowed that their shared dream of the end of sacrifice and freedom for slaves would be fulfilled.* More victims were dragged to the altar. Kalani did not hear their wails as sorrow overcame him.

CHAPTER 22

August 1790

A messenger ran to the threshold of the hale of Kahekili, King of Maui and Oahu. He crawled in and wormed his way into the presence of the tattooed ruler. Below the throne of the king, three chiefs squatted. They watched the messenger inching to the platform.

"What news?" Kahekili demanded.

"My Lord, sacrifices have been made at Kamehameha's new temple. In the night sky, his priests have read signs. They say Ku favors war and Kamehameha will defeat you. Take your land from you."

The king snarled, "That upstart is trying to seize Maui again! He and his uncle tried to beat me years ago. But I crushed them."

Kahekili pointed to a chief. "Go to our capitol and gather faithful allies. Kamehameha will land at Hana. Once he is mired in a siege of our fort, destroy him!"

To another, he said, "Go to Lahaina. Gather warriors from our allied chiefs. Kamehameha may repeat the serious blunder of his uncle and invade there. If he attacks in the west, fall back and join the army of my son. With your combined forces, crush him!"

To the third, he said, "Leave for Kauai and get war canoes and men. Return with them to Oahu and await further orders. I remain here to defeat chiefs who rebel against my rule. Go."

Stretched across the sea, six hundred war canoes raced for Maui. Kalani forced his paddle into the water, willing the pain in his heart to die. In his craft, a dozen musketeers heaved their leaf-shaped sticks in unison, pushing their vessel to Hana. A large double-hulled craft sliced through the waves toward them, a gleaming brass cannon lashed to a platform in the center. Gunners Isaac Davis and John Young rested in a shelter beside it.

"Kalani, did you waterproof the muskets and ammunition we unloaded from the *Fair American?*" Davis yelled.

His senses dulled by the tragedy that gripped him, Kalani pushed harder into the sea, the strength of his effort leaping his canoe ahead of the gunner's craft.

"Brother, Davis wants you," Moki said. "Slow it down. We don't want to get to the Hana fort before the cannon."

Kalani shipped his paddle, eased the soreness in his shoulders, and glanced toward the double canoe that moved abreast.

"The equipment, is it water tight?" Davis hollered.

"Yes."

"Don't get ahead of us. When we land, stay close. Guard the cannon. The fort on the eastern tip is a tough nut to crack. Kamehameha failed to take it in the past."

He acknowledged Davis' orders and resumed his paddling. *His bitter thoughts turned to the coming fight. He would prove himself. He had trained with the musket. Loaded and fired the brass cannon. He would charge the fort and take it.*

The fleet landed, and Kamehameha forced the defenders to retreat into their Hana stronghold. To Kalani's surprise, instead of laying siege, the army embarked and sailed northwest. There followed a bewildering series of landings and embarkations. Each time Kalani noted Kamehameha conferring with a local chief. When the canoes moved on they had food and more fighting men.

Moki slapped the water. "Why aren't we stopping in Lahaina? Good looking women there. I need some loving."

"Who would want to love you? You're so ugly."

Moki nudged Kalani with his paddle. "Yeah, well I'm more handsome than miserable you. Stop being a pain in the okole. Why aren't we stopping on that beautiful sand beach and—"

"Davis told me that Kamehameha doesn't want to repeat the same mistake his uncle made many years ago when he invaded Maui. His army landed in Lahaina, then marched overland to take Wailuku."

"Yeah, I heard that story. The king sent his Alapa division ahead, eight hundred of the finest chiefs in Hawaii. They came across the neck of the island, bragging how they were going to beat Kahekili. But the man was smart. Waited until he had them trapped in the sand hills. Wiped them out."

For a time, the friends did not speak, paddling north with a steady rhythm. Six miles ahead loomed the long, four-thousand-foot high wall of Molokai Island. Equally far away, and to Kalani's left, lay Lanai Island, a huge, barren, orange lump of rock. Peaceful, Kalani thought. The three islands blocked the wind and made the ocean calm. The water stood so still that the bright sun sparkled from an aqua green mirror of sea. Within the channels between the islands, he knew that massive creatures came to calve and mate in the spring. The whale could not be caught, they were too huge. But sometimes one would beach. Hawaiians would pry loose its teeth, braid human hair, and create the palaoa, an ivory whale tooth necklace, the crown jewel of Hawaiian royalty.

Kalani's thoughts dwelt on those powerful warriors who had landed on the hot beaches of Lahaina a long time ago. Experts at war. Brave men. They believed themselves invincible. By themselves, they would destroy Kahekili. How foolish they were, marching to Wailuku for all to see, then ambushed by the wily king of Maui. Maybe the Alapa should have stopped at the sacred springs of Lahaina. Made offerings to the lizard god Moo. Then they might have been saved from destruction.

Kalani shook himself from his dreaming. "Kamehameha learned from that beating. He has re-built the Alapa Division, choosing the best of his army. Davis says he plans to land at Halehaku Bay. March over the mountains to Iao Valley and hit Wailuku from the rear. The Maui king won't expect it."

"Eh, brother," Moki said. "You say the best! How come he didn't choose me?"

"Because you're opala, worthless."

CHAPTER 23

WITHIN HIS ROYAL HALE, THE regent of Maui spoke to his generals. "That upstart Kamehameha has fooled me. He lands at Hana, as my father predicted, but instead of laying siege, leaves! He sails along the coast sowing dissension wherever he goes. I believed he would come to Lahaina and march overland to Wailuku. I prepare my plan. Instead, he heads north."

"He has learned from the failures of the past," one general said. "Hana proved the undoing of his uncle many years ago, when the king of Hawaii attacked us. He laid siege to the fort too long. It gave your father time to prepare his defenses."

"Yes, he told me of his ambush of the Alapa at Wailuku. All were killed. But Kamehameha is devious. He avoids battle. Creates discord among my people. But now we have him! My spies tell me that he has split his army and has come ashore at Halehaku Bay. With a few men, Kamehameha is rushing to hit us from the backside. You will take three thousand of my warriors. March into the mountains and crush him."

"What are my orders?" a second general asked.

"Kamehameha has acquired fire weapons, tubes of metal, golden like aged bamboo. They hurl iron balls heavier than stones. These weapons will land at Halehaku. Take a thousand men. Wait until Kamehameha is on the march. When his vanguard arrives, attack, seize the wonder weapons. Do not fail me."

With one voice both generals answered, "We will not fail. Surprise and overwhelming force are on our side." The men prostrated and left.

"I never thanked you for saving my life," Isaac Davis said as he and Kalani trudged along a hillside trail leading a hundred warriors dragging a shining brass cannon. Davis and his men were in the rear of Kamehameha's army. Ahead of them, warriors rushed to join the high chief and his Alapa division.

"I didn't do anything. Alapai-nui had full authority to save foreign sailors. The chief and I just happened to come upon angry warriors beating you. We stopped it before you were killed." Kalani paused for some moments thinking carefully over what he would next ask. "Why do you fight for Kamehameha?"

Davis slowed his pace. "At first, John Young and I did not want to. We tried to escape to a British ship but were caught. Your High Chief did a remarkable thing: he made us royalty, gave us land and slaves, all the women we could want. Let me tell you, that's how you buy friends."

Kalani sighed. "I hope I can be that lucky and get Kamehameha to give me some land. But I don't want slaves. I don't want women, either, just land." There was sadness in his voice.

"One way is to prove yourself in battle."

"I haven't had a chance to fight. Just sail, land, then sail again." He fell silent for a time. *His thoughts wandered to the sacrifices at the temple to Ku. He remembered seeing Davis there in the first line of worshipers.* He asked, "What do you think of our god Ku?"

Davis grasped Kalani's arm. "I guess I can speak freely, since I am royalty and protected by Kamehameha. That ceremony was the most awful thing I ever saw. Standing and sitting for hours while a priest recites prayers and other priests pass through the audience, saying, 'Death if you leave. Death if you make noise.' Then there was that crazy man who ran around naked, leading those others carrying idols. But worst of all were the deaths." Davis closed his eyes. "I saw some poor man with a hook in his mouth. He was dragged to the altar because the priest had not caught a certain kind of fish to sacrifice to Ku." He shook his head at the memory. "You people had better stop this insane killing. If you rule the masses by fear and kill without reason, your society will never progress beyond the Stone Age."

Kalani agreed with Davis. I have lost three that I loved to the war god. The man had it right: sacrifice suppresses people through fear of death. I must find a way to end it. Eliminate slavery. How I will do this, I do not know.

A warrior came up the hill screaming, "The enemy has landed in the bay and they are marching to attack the village."

"You!" Davis said, pointing at Kalani and the other men moving the cannon. "Go. Stop the enemy. Musketeers, stay with me."

With a hundred warriors at his heels, Kalani ran for Halehaku. He heard thunderous sounds of the pahu drums coming from the village. *Would they get there in time to save the base? Save Kaahumanu?*

Kalani ran past thatched hales. He saw the feather cylinders of kahili thrust into the sky. Kamehameha's queen stood beneath the royal symbols. He raced toward them, warriors following.

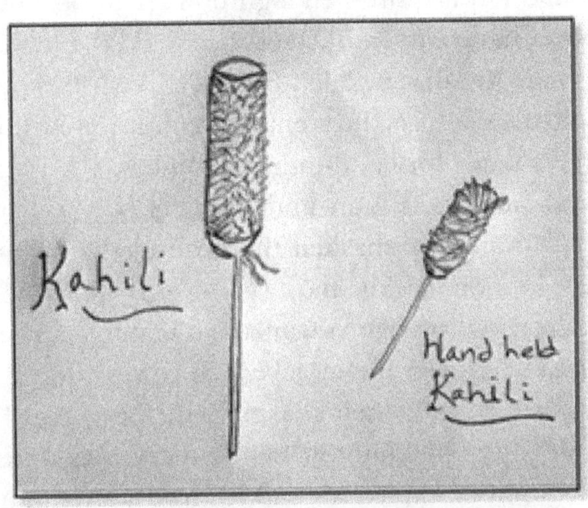

He came to a line of men. Within the center Kaahumanu stood. Beyond the queen, Kalani heard the din of booming drums. Maui warriors were attacking.

He prostrated himself before the beautiful woman. Kalani gasped, "Oh, great one, we are here to aid you. What shall we do?"

Kaahumanu studied the muscular back, trim hips, and thighs of the youth. She flicked the feather kahili in her hand onto Kalani's shoulder.

"You men abandoned the cannon to help us? These scavengers of Maui are not after this camp, they want the gun you were guarding!"

Kalani raised himself without permission.

The queen ignored his breach of protocol and pointed her kahili. "You hear the thunderous drums? They are bluff and bluster. Behind those drums are hostile warriors marching towards the cannon." She pointed to a chief in charge of guarding the wonder weapon. "Take your men. Return to the gun. Save it for Kamehameha!"

Kalani raced to Isaac Davis and the musketeers. He saw a column of enemy warriors charging uphill at them. On the opposite slope, the cannon's guards were coming to help, but were many yards away.

"Steady," Davis said. "Hold your fire until I give the order."

Kalani worried that the musketeers were not properly trained. Kamehameha had not acquired enough powder to permit target practice. On the other hand, the musketeers occupied the high ground.

This advantage became evident. Spears thrown by enemy warriors fell short. Despite this failure, the menacing column continued to attack, clubs and daggers ready for hand-to-hand combat.

"Fire!" Davis yelled. Cannon and muskets belched smoke at the oncoming men. Grapeshot smashed the head of the column. A few of the musket balls hit home, while most flew over the enemy.

The noise, the shooting flames from the metal tubes, the destruction by the iron missiles caused the attackers to retreat downhill. Feather-caped chiefs rushed to rally their shaken men. Davis and Kalani struggled to ram powder and ball into the brass cannon. Musketeers fumbled with paper envelopes of explosives and ramrods, attempting to reload their weapons.

With the respite from gunfire, Maui warriors rallied and charged again. A crescent red and gold helmet loomed over Davis as he loaded the canon. The Maui chief swung his cudgel. Kalani's stone smashed his temple and the man sagged to the ground. In rapid succession, he flung his almond-shaped stones at onrushing warriors. Davis lit the fuse. The blast of grapeshot ended the charge.

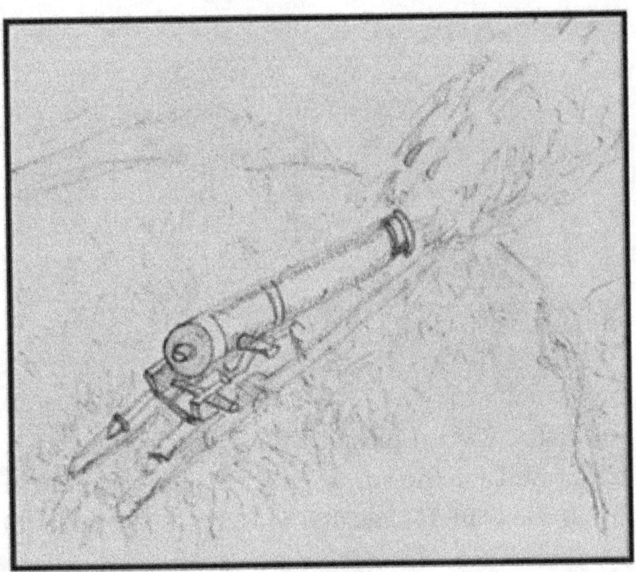

A hundred warriors came to their aid and smashed into the Maui raiders. Broken by the charge, they fled.

Davis yelled, "Kalani, help me pull this dead chief away and move the gun."

They repositioned the weapon, the two men loaded it with ball shot, and fired at the retreating warriors. The round smashed into them, tipping the balance. The raiders were finished. They ran, taking with them the other Maui men that opposed Kaahumanu.

Kalani, Davis, and the survivors watched the enemy flee, laughing and bragging as each man recounted how he fought and won the battle. Kalani slumped to the ground, exhausted, thanking the gods that he saved the cannon. If it had been lost, he would have squandered his chance to gain status as a warrior.

A messenger arrived. "Kamehameha needs all his warriors. March faster. A Maui army is approaching."

Kalani looked at Davis, his eyes pleading.

The gunner smiled, "Go and win glory. We'll catch up."

CHAPTER 24

In the pre-dawn grey, Kalani picked his way along the trail to Pii-Holo Mountain. He prayed for the sun to end its slumber and rise over the horizon, lighting the trail. He needed to run. Get to the battle before it ended.

Soldiers slept along the path. Some woke, complaining at the noise of his passage. He ignored their mutterings. He must find Kamehameha. Show his valor.

Sunlight spread across the ocean, sweeping up and over the land. Men stirred ahead of him. Kalani neared the point of contact between two armies. His eyes darted about, searching for Moki and his lua mates. The trail became thick with warriors marching forward. He slowed his pace, dodging between naked men.

Up ahead he heard loud drumming, signaling a battle. He shoved his way through dawdling men. He wanted to fight. When he broke through the brush, the trail dipped into a valley opening onto the sea. Warriors lined its ridges. Across from him stood the tall high chief, with his helmet on almost seven feet tall. He held a long thrusting spear in his hand. The golden feather cape clasped to his throat wound around the weapon, whipped by the breezes flowing up the valley.

Kamehameha yelled at the Maui general standing below him. "Almost Royal, you are a terror to women, only able to win battles with children and youths who do not know how to fight. I challenge you to single combat."

Two hundred feet downhill, another muscular man stared at the giant. He rested a foot upon a rock, flung back his shoulders, and screamed, "It is true that my name means 'Almost Royal' and my lineage is not perfect. But you parade about as noble born. You are not. Your mother mated with a kauwa and you are their secret child."

Kalani gasped. This was the same accusation Hauna had made of him, slave boy. A child conceived in the dark of night by his mother and an untouchable. He knew that insults before mortal combat were common, but this was the ultimate smear. What would his chief do?

Kamehameha stiffened. His arm drew back, the golden cape slipped from his ten-foot weapon. With a powerful heave, he threw it.

The Maui general stood still, insolent. He did not lift a hand to catch or ward off the descending missile. Kalani thought him brave, but foolish. He knew how far Kamehameha could hurl a spear.

The weapon struck. It sliced into shrubs, stopping several feet from the rock on which the general stood. The Maui army, trapped in the valley by the forces of Kamehameha, cheered. Kalani heard a familiar voice hooting in derision and saw Moki and his lua mates.

He forced his way through the brush, and embraced his friend who said, "We have the Maui army hemmed in. Their general is desperate. He is baiting Kamehameha into single combat. Winner takes all."

"Almost Royal is a smart man. He won the battle of insults, raised the morale of his army, and enraged Kamehameha. Look, our chief is charging downhill flinging stones."

Kamehameha had shed his cape and helmet. Except for a loincloth, he ran naked. His hand whirled around flinging a barrage of rocks. The Maui general leaped ahead, slinging his stones.

Kamehameha was not hit but the Maui general's head was scored by one of Kamehameha's rocks. The high chief grasped a cudgel and swung it with powerful sweeps.

The Maui leader countered with a short spear, deflecting the club, and stabbing at Kamehameha. His spear thrust missed.

Kamehameha's cudgel splintered on a rock. Undeterred, the high chief moved in for the kill, swinging the remains of his stick. The general stabbed with his shark-toothed knife.

Kalani heard a gasp. Kamehameha's club smashed into the general's chest. The man staggered. A blood-covered knife fell from his hand. Another blow brought him to the ground.

Moki and his mates cheered. Kalani's face froze. His eyes stared at Kamehameha's belly. Blood spurted from it, dripping down and onto his loincloth. He saw the high chief clap his hands over the wound. Akaka rushed to him. Together they stumbled up the hill.

Before Kamehameha disappeared over the ridge, he raised his fist, red with blood. The yells stopped. "*Imua*! Go forward!" he cried. His voice rang out strong. His command clear. Kalani and thousands of warriors attacked the dispirited army of Maui.

CHAPTER 25

KAHEKILI'S SON LISTENED TO THE wailing outside his palace. He knew his people were frightened, convinced that Kamehameha is unstoppable. With a frown, he motioned his senior advisor to approach. He detested that the older man did not consider him the equal of his father.

"My king, Kamehameha's wound has given us time to prepare for his attack on Wailuku. But the few survivors of our defeat at Pii-Holo Mountain have sown fear among our people."

Seated on mounds of tapa, the regent studied the grizzled face of the advisor. His voice trembled as he said, "Yes, I know. It is unfortunate that my cousin lost the fight to the death. Although cut in the stomach Kamehameha lived. My general proved to be a fool. He had to fight a duel, winner takes all. Kamehameha had slipped around his army in the night with his elite division. When dawn broke, the general's army was trapped in a valley between the Alapa and the rest of Kamehameha's warriors."

With disgust in his voice, the advisor said, "His forces were already beaten when your cousin made his challenge. But if he won he would have saved them. The man had fought many desperate combats before and been victorious."

"Kamehameha's bowels should have covered the ground with their slime. Instead my general's chest was crushed, his face broken."

"It is unfortunate that your cousin did not win. Majesty, Kamehameha has landed in Kahului. We must prepare for the coming battle."

"You are right. Combat cannot be avoided. But morale is poor, and I am told that Kamehameha's foreign weapons of fire are invincible. You will gather the women, children, and old people, and take them into Iao Valley. They can watch the fighting from the heights. If we lose they can hide in caves or try to cross over the mountains and flee to Oahu."

The advisor grimaced. "Your majesty, the people I take with me into Iao cannot make it over the steep mountains, nor can they survive for long in caves without food or water."

"Then they should die, rather than become slaves of Kamehameha. Go and fulfill your task."

CHAPTER 26

KALANI AND MOKI MARCHED TOGETHER. Other musketeers straggled behind them. "Halt. Right face," John Young ordered. "Present arms."

Men stumbled. Moki dropped his musket. Its clatter drew a sharp look from Young. "Pick up that weapon. Hold it steady in your hands."

"This is making me sick," Moki complained.

"Come on," Kalani whispered. "I was on a hill at Halehaku and saw men die because they were slow. Tomorrow, our lives may depend on how fast we can shoot."

"Throwing spears is easier," Moki groused.

Kalani lowered his weapon. "Kamehameha has been fighting with spears and clubs for eight years and controls only a third of Hawaii Island. Today he has cannons and muskets. He will win, if we know how to use them."

"Maybe I should thank you for getting us a job with the musketeers. I still think that throwing a spear is easier than fighting with this fire stick."

John Young looked at Moki, his voice harsh. "Four musketeers died on a hill because they weren't fast enough. A well-trained soldier can load and fire the Brown Bess in fifteen seconds. Even a mediocre soldier can load and fire two shots every minute. Right now, you men take longer than a minute to load. More than thirty seconds to aim and fire. Most of the time you miss!"

Young paused in his tirade, shifting his anger from Moki to the rest of the musketeers. "Present arms. Fire."

The musketeers drilled until darkness forced Young to dismiss them. The two friends went to the resting place where mats were laid out and fish roasted on hot coals. They sat and ate with hundreds of other warriors who worried about the coming battle.

Many fires flamed along the beach. The ocean whispered as slow waves washed the sand. Kalani gazed toward the distant outlines of the mountains of Iao Valley. Below their crests, burning wood twinkled in the night. *He wondered if the Maui soldiers were shivering before the flames, anxious over what the dawn would bring.*

"Oh," Moki interrupted his thoughts, "I would give everything I own for a woman."

Kalani laughed. "You don't own anything, so why would a woman want you? Besides, there are none to buy. All the women have been spirited into the hills to save them from men like you."

"Oh, you're an innocent boy?" Moki answered loudly, disturbing the men around them. There were growls of "stop yelling."

"Sorry," Moki apologized.

The two friends relaxed against rolled-up tapa cloth. Kalani studied the heavens as if he could read the stars like the priests. *Would they tell me if I will survive tomorrow's battle? I know one message that they pulse: you will be brave.*

From their vantage point on the heights above the left wing of Kamehameha's army, Alapai-nui and Kalani surveyed the battlefield. Warriors with fourteen-foot spears formed a ragged line extending the length of Iao Valley. Some distance beyond Kamehameha's men stood a similar line of Maui soldiers.

Priests between the opposing armies were withdrawing. They held aloft effigies of gods and screamed that death would come to the loser of the battle. In this confrontation of deities, Kalani believed that Ku, Kamehameha's god of war, would be victorious.

On a mound a good distance from the two men stood the regent of Maui, his shoulders draped in a brilliant feather cape of red and gold. A tall, feathered war helmet crowned his head. Feather kahili towered over him. Around the regent were chiefs clothed in less brilliant capes, helmets, and loincloths. Messengers ran from a central hillock where Kamehameha's sub-chiefs were clustered, some dressed in cloaks of brilliant yellow and red. Thousands of feathers plucked from captured birds had been stitched into the webbing of coconut sennit to create these glorious capes.

Kalani wore only a narrow loincloth. His hair was cut in a crest. Only men of rank could wear the distinctive feather capes and helmets. He knew that the colorful clothing had little defensive value. It seemed that their only purpose was to attract the attention of friend and foe alike. But he yearned to wear the majestic capes, the ornate helmets. *Maybe I will prove himself today. Become alii koa, a warrior chief.*

The priests now withdrawn, the enemy skirmishers moved forward to throw stones at the battle line. "Where is Kamehameha?" Alapai-nui muttered.

Blaring conch shells filled the air, relieving the tension of the two men as Kamehameha marched toward battle under kahili and adorned in a magnificent golden feather cape and an equally glorious feather helmet on his head. Behind him rolled the brass cannon hauled by scores of warriors. Alongside the gleaming weapon marched a dozen musketeers, their hair cut into a midline crest, tufts sprouting upward like feathers stuck into hats. Their white loincloths were encircled by bands of red and edged with white feathers.

Alapai-nui grunted in satisfaction. He ordered Kalani to join the musketeers and hurried to greet the king.

As he relieved his shoulder of the weight of the Brown Bess, Kalani stared ahead. In the distance rose the green slopes of Puu Kukui Mountain, the long-dead volcano that had created west Maui and the islands of Kahoolawe and Lanai. Masses of billowing clouds hid its peak. Rain flooded down its sides, flowing into a deep cut in the valley and streaming in a cold rush to the sea.

A rock pelted the ground in front of the musketeers. Kalani turned to his commander. "Permission to engage the enemy."

"Permission granted," John Young replied.

He raced past the hillock filled with chiefs and burst into the open space between the two armies where he saw an enemy slinger dancing about hurling stones. With an underhand throw, Kalani whipped a rock that struck the man on his shoulder. The enemy skirmisher howled and ran away.

Three stones flew through the air in rapid succession. Kalani dodged them.

"Hold on, we're coming," lua mates yelled.

Stones zipped by.

He sheltered behind two large boulders.

Missiles smashed into the rocks. One ricocheting stone hit a friend. Kalani stood, pointed a pebble-filled hand at the enemy, and whipped three almond-shaped stones in rapid succession. Two missed, but the third sliced into the face of a warrior who stumbled away from the fight.

John Young yelled, "Come back."

He returned to the line of musketeers and aligned himself with his companions. Isaac Davis rammed powder and shot into the muzzle of the brass cannon. Next to it, John Young loaded a swivel gun.

In front of the cannon and muskets were Maui chiefs, their feather capes and helmets ruffled by a rising wind. Around them, soldiers assembled. They shouted threats and insults. The chiefs urged their men to charge the guns.

The warriors formed themselves into a massive block. Fourteen-foot spears dropped level to the ground. Caped leaders pranced around, yelling commands. The enemy phalanx lurched forward.

"Steady lads, hold your fire until I give the command," Young ordered.

Kalani glanced to his side and saw the faces of the musketeers gripped with fear. The enemy spearmen outnumbered them.

Attackers screamed fierce war cries and charged. The distance between the forces narrowed.

"The enemy will hit us before we shoot," Kalani complained.

"Fire cannon!" Davis yelled.

The brass gun erupted. Dark smoke and flame burst from its mouth. Grapeshot shredded Maui men. A dozen fell, still the enemy ran toward them.

At fifty yards, John Young gave the order, "Fire." The swivel gun and musketeers let loose, scything down a swath of soldiers. Seconds after, another blast from the cannon stopped the enemy charge.

Most of the Maui chiefs lay dead or writhing on the ground. The warriors still standing seemed dazed, as if uncertain whether to move forward or retreat. A hail of spears ended their uncertainty as the Alapa division struck the confused enemy. Those who survived fled.

"Take enemy chiefs prisoner. They will be sacrificed to Ku," Akaka yelled. "Kill the rest of the wounded."

"Hey, what do you think?" Moki boasted. "Not bad? I fired and loaded and fired again."

Kalani rested on his musket, ignoring his friend, a frown wrinkling his forehead. The order to kill the wounded shocked him.

"Hey, little roach. Wake up," Moki scolded as he strutted about, a huge grin on his face. "You didn't answer my question. I was good. Yes? I shot faster than the Maui men could throw their spears."

Kalani ignored his friend's boasting. The screams of the wounded enemy filled his ears. The victory proved to be a horror for him. *I can picture my father and grandfather wounded and sacrificed on the battlefield. There had to be a better way to end a war than this wanton human destruction. I do not know what I can do to stop it. Deadly retaliation on a defeated enemy was expected.*

CHAPTER 27

Iao Valley, Maui

KAMEHAMEHA ORDERED HIS ARMY TO advance, pushing the enemy into Iao valley. Kalani marched with the cannon and muskets under the high chief's personal command. The victorious forces pressured the Maui warriors into the narrowing funnel between tall hills. Once hemmed in, the bunched mass was cut down by cannon and musket fire. Water that once flowed swiftly to the sea slowed. Corpses filled Iao stream creating a lake, dammed by the dead.

The last rays of sunlight glimmered golden upon the topmost ridges of the west Maui mountains. Long shadows spread upward and over the many fissures that rifted the sides of the dead volcano like dozens of wrinkled fingers. Milky clouds swept past a tall stone peak claimed to be the erect phallus of the god of the underworld, Kanaloa. The white vapors swirled low to the ground, filling the gullies around the eight-hundred-foot up-thrust rock with billowing, twisting strings of white.

Kalani rested under the shadow of the towering pillar watching a handful of enemy soldiers scramble deeper into the west Maui mountains. "I think the fighting is over. I don't hear yelling anymore and all I see are men running away."

At his side, Moki whispered, "Yeah, but listen, don't you feel something creeping toward us in the clouds? It wants to pounce and take us into Kanaloa's dark land?"

"No, I don't. Are you seeing phantoms in these hills?"

Moki shivered, then stuttered, "I-I'm not saying that there are any spirits of the dead coming for us. But in ancient times, they buried kings and royalty in these hills. With all these bodies lying around, maybe the Night Marchers will be coming to pick up souls."

Feet splashed the water of Iao stream. "The ghosts!" Moki panicked, turning to flee.

Kalani seized his loincloth. "It's not the dead that are marching."

Alapai-nui came into view with warriors and a crowd of frightened women, children, and old men. When the high chief spied the two musketeers, he called, "Kahekili's son fled to Oahu. He left women and children hiding in caves. They will die. Search for them. Bring whomever you find to Wailuku. Promise no harm will come to those who surrender."

"Are there other search parties?" Kalani asked.

"Yes. Be careful."

With a wave, Alapai-nui motioned his troops and captives to move. Single file, they crossed over the bodies in the stream and proceeded toward Wailuku.

"Of all the rotten luck," Moki groused. "We got to spend the night in these hills looking for fugitives."

They searched upland for a time, but soon day lost its struggle with night and the young men could not see ahead of them. "Let's work our way back to the stream. Find a good place to bed down for the night," Kalani said.

"Okay by me, but let's not fall asleep by any dead bodies," Moki stuttered.

CHAPTER 28

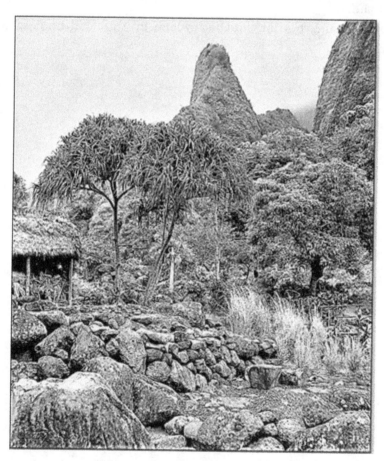

Iao Valley

Morning dew chilled the valley as first light spread over the hills. Birds flitted among the trees. Water splashed against rocks. Awakened by the sounds, Kalani picked his way over a jumble of boulders to Iao stream. He checked for bodies. There were none. He unwound his loincloth, splashed into the water, gulping its coolness. He scrubbed away the grime of battle, happy to be alive, wondering how many warriors were asleep forever. Chilled, he stumbled to the bank, rubbing his hands over his body.

"Nani, no one is near. We can gather water without being seen," a female voice whispered.

Kalani ducked beneath the branches of a tree. He parted its leaves and saw two young women. He watched them fill their vessels and trudge up the rock face of the mountain.

He drew his cloth around his waist and splashed back into the stream, heading in the direction of the women. They had reached the crest of a talus pile when he called to them. "Hello, my name is Kalani. I am here to help you. Are there others with you?"

His words startled the women. They stared at him. Fear cloaked their faces. Without answering, they disappeared over the crest.

"Wait!" he called, struggling up the pile of loose rocks. "I'm not going to hurt you. I want to take you home to Wailuku."

Rocks flew. He slid sideways, stones clattered to the valley floor. He escaped to the safety of boulders bordering Iao stream. "I'm not going to hurt you. I'm here to help." Rocks ceased falling. An old man appeared, a spear in his hand.

"Hey, little roach, what's all the yelling about?" Moki called from across the stream.

The old man disappeared, followed by more rocks skipping over the crest.

"A bunch of Wailuku people are up there."

He yelled, "We are warriors of Kamehameha. Your king is defeated. He has abandoned you. You will die in that cave. Let us help you return home. We promise not to harm you."

Except for the crash of water careening off rocks, there was silence. Moki crossed the stream. "What's going on?"

Kalani rolled his eyes uphill. "I think they're discussing what to do."

A pretty face peered above him. Her dark eyes stared at Kalani. His heart pounded when the young woman asked, "Do you promise that you will not harm us? Do you promise to take us safely to Wailuku?"

"Yes, to both questions," Kalani answered, anxious to see the rest of the radiant beauty hidden by the rocks.

A dozen women, children, and old men slid down the talus pile. When they reached the stream bed, one of them asserted authority. "My name is Nani." She pointed at Moki. "You! What is your *kulana*?"

Moki stammered, "I, I got none."

She turned to Kalani. "And you?"

"My mother is a distant relative of Kamehameha."

With a dismissive wave of her hand, Nani said, "I am of the Wohi class, the same rank as Kamehameha. I am superior to both of you, so I will take charge."

She ordered Moki and Kalani to create a litter for her mother, who lay injured beside the stream. Once done, Nani led the group to Wailuku.

The journey proved difficult. Corpses fouled the water, raising a stench that filled the valley with horrible smells. They entered the capitol city and continued on as Nani led them to her family compound in Kahului. She dismissed Moki with a curt wave, saying, "I will call you when there is need of you." Then she demanded that Kalani help find her father.

After hours of searching, he complained, "We have been seeking your father for a long time. Maybe he is among the dead or has run away to Oahu."

The young girl eyed Kalani, an imperious look upon her face. "My father would never do such a thing, run away and abandon his family. We will continue the search."

Controlling his anger, he answered, "Your wish is my command, princess."

After more hours of searching, a spent Nani sighed. "Maybe he is among the dead?"

"We haven't checked the area where the wounded chiefs are waiting to be given to Ku."

Nani shuddered. "I have avoided looking there, fearing what I might find. Let's go."

Only a priest and a lounging guard stood watch over the sacrificial captives. They studied the two young people entering the prisoner compound but did not challenge their presence.

Nani searched the wounded lying in the open, mostly men of rank, some still wearing their shredded feather capes. "My father is not here."

Kalani touched her arm and pointed to a low shack in the corner of the compound. She shuddered, walked to the threshold of the building, and crawled inside. "Oh, Father—"

He entered and found her weeping beside a man who lay wounded in the hut. "We will take you home," Nani said.

"They will kill us," her father answered. "Leave, before you arouse suspicion. Bring water and food when you return."

Tears streamed down the young girl's cheeks. Kalani placed his arm around her shoulder. With a violent twist, she pulled away. "You are lower class! You may not touch me without permission!" Then she sobbed, her body shaking. Puzzled, he kept his distance, yet her rejection excited him. Her snobbery made her desirable.

They walked in silence to the family compound. When they arrived, Nani wiped her tears away, haughtiness returned to her face. "If you could save my father, my mother would be grateful." Then she disappeared into her home.

CHAPTER 29

KALANI PROSTRATED. "GREAT CHIEF ALAPAI-NUI, wise and powerful ruler. Your loyal warrior comes to you in humility and begs of you a boon."

Alapai-nui smiled at the boy. "Stand up, my brave koa, and tell me what you request."

Kalani's heart jumped. Alapai-nui called him *koa,* the highest rank in the warrior class. His voice quavering, he said, "I seek the life of a captured Maui chief."

Alapai-nui studied the youth for a moment before he spoke. "You must know that Kamehameha is displeased. He did not capture Kahekili's son. He has not decided who should be sacrificed in his place. But I will speak to him on your behalf. Go. Attend to me when I call."

For a week Kalani waited to hear from Alapai-nui. In the daytime, he practiced with Moki and the other musketeers. Evenings found him visiting Nani. She was the most beautiful woman he had ever met, surpassing even Kaahumanu. Each night he tried to convince her to walk with him, but each time she refused.

Every day Moki asked, "How are you making out with that nasty woman? Has she fallen in love with you?"

Kalani answered, "No. She is Wohi, of higher rank than you and me. You have to respect the upper class. Give me time. I'll turn her around, you'll see."

Days passed. Kalani noted on his evening visits that Nani became less reserved, less imperious. On the seventh evening, she said, "I have not been able to see my father. Have you spoken with anyone in power to save his life?"

A light wind rattled the coconut leaves. The air was warm. The moon shone a silver path across the sea. Waves swished across the sand. "Come walk with me in the moonlight," Kalani begged.

Nani nodded.

Their eyes met. He saw within them despair, grief, the barrier of her pride gone. Worry drove her to walk with him, find an answer to her question. He felt a tingle, the beginning of an urge. Should he lie? Tell her that he saw Alapai-nui and her father would be saved? With the right words, he believed that she would be his.

Kalani reached to her hand. Their fingers touched and twined together. The warmth of her skin fired his heart. "Like you, the night is beautiful. The coco leaves are making music in the wind. The surf is washing gently over the sand. Walk to the water with me."

Nani did not answer. Instead, she stepped toward the sound of the waves, drawing Kalani with her. In the moonlight, he saw the smoothness of her shoulders, the silky skin of her back, and the swing of her slender hips. He thought to pull her into him. Take her. The moment passed as Nani released his hand and ran into the water swooping over the beach.

She splashed through the surging sea then raced toward a group of coco trees. He chased her, following footprints sunk in the wet sand. Beneath the branches of the small woods, he thought that what he wanted would be his. But Nani did not stop.

Puzzled, Kalani followed her home. She lifted her head. In low tones she said, "You have not answered my question."

"Princess, I have tried—"

Nani put a finger to his lips. "But failed. Know this: the differences in our rank will always be a barrier. It is my duty to remain a virgin and marry someone of higher class. My children must be of a caste greater than mine. You cannot help me. Go! Do not return."

The next day, shaken by the disillusionment of the evening, Kalani received word to meet with Alapai-nui. He dreaded what the chief might say. After they greeted, Alapai-nui appraised Kalani for some moments before saying, "It appears that you have friends in high places, besides me, of course." He grinned, then placed a friendly hand on Kalani's shoulder. "Come, let us walk."

Two servants carried a litter bearing Nani's father into the family compound. Heralds announced their arrival. Nani and her mother, Napua, rushed to the litter, weeping. Household servants prostrated themselves before their master.

Napua gasped. "You are still hurting from your injuries. Let me call the kahuna to help you."

"No, don't call him. He will only make my wounds worse. I am healing."

"Father, how is it that you have left the sacrificial center? Are you still under threat of death?" Nani asked. Wonder and fear were in her voice.

"My release is the strangest thing. I expected to be sacrificed, since I am one of the highest Maui chiefs in captivity. This morning, his majesty Alapai-nui came into the prison with that young man." He pointed to Kalani, standing just outside the compound.

"Oh no!" Nani gasped, her eyes flicked toward Kalani.

With a puzzled frown, the chief asked, "You know this man, Lord Tana?"

Nani gasped again. "Lord Tana! His name is Kalani, but—"

Her father interrupted. "Alapai-nui called him Lord Tana."

"I know the young man," Napua said. "He helped us leave our hiding place in Iao Valley and brought us here." She looked at her daughter with a little smile. "And he has been visiting every evening. But tell me, how did you escape from the prison?"

"I did not escape. Alapai-nui told me that Lord Tana had pleaded for my life. Kamehameha has spared me and ordered my return to the family."

"Oh, that is wonderful," Napua and Nani cried in unison.

The chief quieted their celebration. He held them away from him. He searched their faces. "You must know that you and all I possess are now subservient to Lord Tana. He holds my parole."

Nani stared at her father. The happiness that had filled her face moments before dissolved. She stood in silence.

Kalani watched Nani, tears welling in her eyes. She looked at him, shrieked with an animal agony, and ran crying into the family home. Bewildered, he left the compound.

CHAPTER 30

SLAVES LIT KUKUI LANTERNS IN the hale of the High Chief of Puna. The light drew shadows onto the pili grass covering its bamboo frame. "King Keoua, I will help you conquer Hawaii Island while Kamehameha is away," Chief Makula promised the ruler of Kau. He pointed to the man squatting by his side and added, "And so will the new High Chief of Puna."

Hauna raised a cup of fermented awa to his lips. "I drink to the new alliance of Kau, Puna, and Kona."

Keoua, his hand unsteady, lifted his gourd to his lips and said, "To the new alliance. I will conquer Hawaii, with your help." He waved his container of awa juice at the two men.

"I am sure you will reward us when you are supreme," Makula answered. "Now that my father is dead, and I am High Chief of Puna, I can give you the men and weapons you need to beat the bastard Kamehameha," Hauna boasted.

"Bastard you say! I have been fighting my cousin for eight years. All that time I did not know he is a bastard!" Keoua emphasized his words.

Hauna winked. "It is said that Kahekili, King of Oahu and Maui, seduced Kamehameha's mother and is the father of your cousin."

"Legitimate or not, he is one tough man to fight. We cannot take him lightly. What is your plan, Keoua?" Makula slapped his palm on the mat upon which the men sat.

"The turncoat High Chief of Hilo claimed to be my friend. He gave Kamehameha troops for his invasion of Maui, thereby allying himself with the upstart. Hauna and I will attack Hilo where the traitor rules. We will take that district, then I will march west, into Hamakua and Kohala. That will leave only Kona in Kamehameha's hands. Makula, prepare your forces. After Hilo is taken, Hauna will join you. Together you will conquer Kona. Before Kamehameha returns, we will control all of Hawaii and the upstart will be no more."

Hauna snarled, "Yes! And then will come the division of the land and revenge against my enemies." His eyes glazed over, his voice turned sinister. "And those who challenged my honesty will be tortured and sacrificed."

Oil lamps burned, their points of flame puffing smoke that created a shadowy haze within the room. Hauna's face became rigid, his eyes barely focusing. He stared upward.

"When will you strike?" Makula asked, breaking the heavy silence.

"In a month, the Seven Sister stars we call Makalii will rise in the eastern sky and the New Year will begin. That marks the festivities of Lono, when peace fills the land. I will attack before the Seven stars rise and destroy the High Chief of Hilo. Kamehameha will be in a dilemma. Does he act against me, or observe the peace of Lono? If he returns to Hawaii to fight me, he risks the anger of the god. If he fails to return, we will occupy the remainder of his lands."

"A brilliant strategy. When will you come with your army?"

"My men are already on the march, they will be here in a week. Are you ready to act when they arrive, Hauna?"

"Yes!"

"Good! Makula, return to Kona and prepare your forces. After Hauna and I capture Hilo, I will move west into Hamakua and Kohala. Hauna will join you. Depending on Kamehameha's actions, be prepared to attack in Kona."

When the men finished with their planning, Hauna announced, "I have a feast prepared and six beautiful dancers to entertain us."

"Hauna, times have changed since your father died two months ago. Now that you are the ruler of Puna, how many of these women are the wives of your chiefs?" Makula asked.

"Three. You must tell me after the evening's fun whom you enjoyed most, the wife or the virgin."

CHAPTER 31

KALANI STOOD WITH AKAKA, DAVIS, Young, and several high-ranking chiefs inside Kamehameha's residence in Wailuku. He wondered why he had been invited. What new plans did the supreme ruler have since his conquest of Maui?

"Within a month, the seven stars will return in the heavens and the festivals honoring god Lono will begin," Kamehameha said. "My spies tell me that Keoua is planning to attack Hilo before the New Year begins."

"If he strikes, do you have enough forces to stop him?" Akaka asked.

Kamehameha nodded. "The High Chief of Hilo gave me warriors and war canoes to fight in Maui. Yet I believe he has enough men to stop Keoua."

Akaka looked away, as if not convinced. His gaze returned to his leader. "I have heard that Puna has a new high chief, Hauna. He could join Keoua and they will take Hilo from our ally."

A gasp escaped Kalani's lips. *How had his enemy become so powerful?*

Kamehameha looked with disapproval in the direction of the sound, then returned to his conversation with Akaka. "Yes, they could join forces while I am occupied elsewhere."

Isaac Davis stepped forward. "I think you should return to Kohala and prepare for Keoua's attack."

"I must go to Molokai first."

"Molokai, my Lord?" Akaka interjected. "Whatever for? If your possessions on Hawaii are in danger, you should go there to protect them."

"I must ensure the royal succession by having children of the highest rank."

"You go to Molokai to secure a higher-class wife than you already have?" Akaka said, his voice incredulous.

"Yes. And I expect that you will leave for Kona immediately. Prepare my forces there. Take what warriors you need from Maui."

"May I have your cannon, Isaac Davis, and John Young?"

"No. They will come with me to Molokai, but Kalani Tana is constable of a section of my muskets. You may take him and his men."

"So, you are the new constable," Akaka said, inspecting the six-foot-two-inch musketeer. Kalani had grown a light beard and moustache. His body had become hard and well-muscled. Hair covered his head, making him very handsome.

Akaka motioned to squat. "How many men do you command?" he asked, settling himself beside the young warrior.

"With myself, there are four."

"Be prepared to leave for Kona tomorrow. Now go."

Kalani rose, disappointed that he did not have more time on Maui to persuade Nani to consider him as a suitable candidate for marriage. But as he thought on it, *her rejection had been clear: I do not have enough rank to be her husband. Should I use my parole power to cajole her into submission?* He dismissed the thought. *If I cannot have her willingly, then I will not have her at all.* These conflicts swirled in his mind as Akaka walked with him to the front entry and called to his guard, "After Lord Tana leaves, no one is to enter."

Kalani crawled out through the low entrance. Akaka sealed the door with a heavy leaf mat. The guard leaned on his spear and, for a few minutes, the two comrades exchanged stories. He said goodnight and headed for his sleeping hale. A movement at the rear of Akaka's quarters caught his eye. Moonlight lit the face of Queen Kaahumanu. Kalani ducked into the shadows.

"Dear heart," the queen sighed as she stood at a back entry. "Let me in."

"Come through the covering," Akaka answered.

Kaahumanu pushed aside the flap of tapa and slipped into the hale. Kalani heard her say, "My love, my husband is sending you from me."

"I will only be gone for a short time."

"If I could find an excuse, I would go with you. But Kamehameha insists that his wives come with him to meet the royal bitch that will sire his dynasty."

"But aren't you able to give him children?"

"No. More important, I do not have enough rank. The one he seeks has the greatest in all Hawaii. She has the burning power upon her."

Kalani smiled. *So, Kamehameha seeks the highest-ranking female in all the islands. It means that he will have to crawl into her presence every time he wants her. He can never be above his queen but instead must lie on his back as they make love.* Kalani scowled. *If I marry Nani, will she require that I do the same? Obey the traditions of class differences?*

He stepped away from Akaka's hale, thinking over the ridiculous rules associated with royalty. His thoughts wandered to Kaahumanu. *Despite the loose morality among the high-born, everyone knew of Kamehameha's infatuation with his fourth wife, and his burning jealousy. Akaka was younger, handsomer than the older man. I think the affair between these lovers will not end well.*

CHAPTER 32

"EH, BROTHER, ARE YOU TELLING me that you are the lord of that nasty woman? That is good. Maybe you can teach her not to push people around," Moki said, squinting through a sight attached to his musket.

"Darn it," Kalani said, "I think that bird glue won't work. It will burn off with the heat of the gun's explosion and the sight will fall off."

"Did you hear what I asked?"

"Don't call Nani a nasty woman!"

"Okay. I'm sorry. I guess you're soft on her. If you want her take the woman since you are her lord."

"You're dumb. You can't just order these special people around."

"Don't call me dumb. Maybe you're the dumb one. When you lose a war, the winner gets to take the other guy's property and make him and his family slaves."

Kalani winced. He thought of his mother and sisters in poverty, facing slavery because they had no property. He eyed Moki, a fierce anger boiling within him. "While I am alive, Nani and her family will not be slaves!"

Moki backed away. "Okay. I apologize. I won't talk about her anymore."

"Make sure you don't."

Moki dashed away yelling, "I just thought you might get that high-class woman to kiss your—"

Kalani threw a rock at his friend.

The next day Kamehameha left for Molokai and the woman with the burning kapu. Kalani set sail for Kona.

Three weeks later, Akaka assembled chiefs at Kealakekua Bay. The men were uneasy, evident by the buzz of excited conversation. In a corner of the building, Makula stood apart, a sly smile on his face. Kalani pointed to him and whispered, "I don't trust that man. He is going to make trouble for Kamehameha."

"Maybe trouble for you because you're playing with Hinalea again," Moki answered.

"Yeah! If he were less brutal to her, she would not need my love." Kalani paused for a moment, thinking of Nani. "I need someone to ease my pain."

"Suit yourself. You have been lucky the last few weeks since Makula has been away. Now that he is back, watch it. He is big and mean."

"The mean part I know about. Hinalea told me about what he does to her. He may have huge muscles, but a pig's heart. Too bad we need the man in the coming fight."

A hush settled in the building as Akaka rose to speak. "I came to Kona to organize the defenses of the district. Kamehameha is on Molokai contracting a marriage, and most of his army is on Maui, mopping up resistance to his rule. The New Year celebrations have started. With everyone in a party mood, warriors refuse to think of war. And what has happened? Our enemy Keoua has conquered Hilo and sacrificed the High Chief." Akaka paused to let his words sink in. "We must prepare for an attack."

Men grumbled, and one voice spoke out. "This is festival time. We will offend the god Lono if we go to war."

A second chief shouted, "Why is Kamehameha away pursuing a royal marriage? He should be here, fighting with us!"

Akaka pointed at the first speaker. "It does not offend Lono if we prepare to guard ourselves against aggression." He glared at the second and said, "Kamehameha has sent me to fight for him. I have never lost in battle. I have warriors from Maui and fire weapons to defend us." The shuffling stopped. A buzz of chatter filled the room. Several voices chorused, "We have heard of these wonder weapons. They caused the stream of Iao to be dammed with the dead. We are with you, Akaka. With such weapons, we cannot lose."

"These men are like children," Kalani whispered. "One moment frightened and confused, believing they cannot win. The next shouting and acting like supermen. Little do they know how few muskets we have."

"Yeah," Moki answered. "I have to go. See you at the beach."

Kalani nodded.

The meeting continued and plans for defense were discussed. Kalani noted that Makula probed to learn the number of men Akaka had brought to fight and the firearms he had available. Akaka did not tell him. The gathering ended with the chiefs told to levy their commoners and report with them at Kealakekua Bay in a week.

Kalani left the gathering deep in thought. He had been unable to see Nani before he departed Maui. *I wonder if we will ever meet again.* He walked to the beach. Thrust into the sand stood a towering standard, its upper crosspiece decorated with leaves. Attached to it, a white tapa cloth, with yellow tassels flapping in the wind. Along the coastline, bonfires provided warmth and light, dispelling the cool breezes and the shadows of evening. Someone grasped his arm. Kalani raised a fist to strike, lowering it when he saw Moki.

"Come to the ocean. We are going to have fun tonight."

Although he knew that the New Year is festival time, Kalani had never been at Kealakekua Bay during the annual fertility rite. He was stunned to see thousands of people flocking to the sea. Moki dragged him to one of the bonfires, where men and women were throwing off clothes and dashing into the water. Drums throbbed. The fires warmed his blood. Kalani felt aroused by the wild activity around him.

Moki tore off his loincloth. He screamed in excitement, "Take off that thing. Show you're a man. It will be fun tonight. First, we swim, to purify ourselves. After that—" Moki leered as he headed into the waves brimming with white foam as they swept over the sand.

Kalani removed his cloth. He would swim, then meet Hinalea.

Rays of sunlight flowed over the eastern mountains. Thousands of bronzed bodies lay along the shoreline. Kalani propped himself onto an elbow. He studied the clumps of naked people around him. By his side lay a pretty woman, an arm thrust over her eyes. Nearby, Moki slept, sprawled over the bodies of two females. "Hey, get up." He pulled at Moki's leg.

His friend raised his head. "Go away, pest, I'm in heaven." He fell back onto two bare breasts.

"Get up. We have to go to work."

"Okay, little roach, I'm coming," he yawned, shoving away from the women. His awkward movements woke them.

"Where are you going, sweetheart?" a dark-haired beauty asked.

He bent his back and stretched, "My boss, this guy," gesturing toward Kalani, "he's telling me, 'Go to work.' Sorry to leave you."

The woman smiled. "Can we come with you? My friend and I can make you both very happy."

"No," Kalani spat. "What we do does not involve women."

"We won't be in the way," they begged. "We can clean, pound poi, make cloth, and then—"

"Kalani, don't be a stick in the mud," Moki protested. "The girls are willing to take care of us. Why do you say no?"

"Have it your way," Kalani answered, trudging towards the training ground.

Moki clapped and laughed, "Hey, little roach, I'm going to show the women our hale. Maybe stir up a little fun. Then I will come."

When Kalani entered the training area, a messenger requested that he attend upon Akaka. He headed for headquarters where he found the chief exercising. Between lua moves the man said, "You have done an excellent job with your three men. But we need more musketeers."

Kalani nodded. “We also need guns and ammunition, to practice firing.”

Akaka smiled. “Then we will get more of both.”

“From the gods?”

“No, word has come that Captain Russell has returned to Hawaii and he’s trading along the coastline. He promised to meet me where the *Fair American* was captured. We’ll go there to see what my friend is selling.”

CHAPTER 33

AKAKA AND KALANI HURRIED NORTH searching for Russell but failed to find him. Rumors drove them to a small bay where they stopped their quest and waited. The next day, a small flotilla of double canoes entered the bay, conch shells announcing the coming of Alapai-nui. He brought news that Keoua had taken the north coast of Hawaii, and was heading west to capture Kohala, the birth district of Kamehameha.

"Where is the high chief? What is he doing?" Akaka asked, alarm in his voice. Alapai-nui looked grim. "He has succeeded in arranging a marriage to a ten-year-old high-born princess. Now he is negotiating peace with Kahekili."

"Is peace possible?" Akaka asked. "Kahekili cannot be happy with Kamehameha since he seized Maui and almost killed his son."

Alapai-nui nodded. "Even worse are Kamehameha's terms: Kahekili is to surrender Oahu and acknowledge him as his sovereign."

Akaka shook his head. "Those demands make it impossible to achieve peace. Kahekili would be wise to stall negotiations while Keoua sweeps Hawaii Island into his kingdom. Then he could invade Maui and take it from Kamehameha."

"Our leader is aware of this," Alapai-nui replied. "While negotiating with Kahekili, he is planning a return to Hawaii. You are to join him on Molokai. From there, you will sail with his army to Kohala, where you will attack and defeat Keoua."

"But what about the soldiers I am gathering? What about Captain Russell?"

"That is another reason that I am here. Captain Russell is due tomorrow. Conclude your business with him and be off to Molokai. I will take charge of the defenses of Kona and send whatever soldiers you gathered to Kawaihae."

Russell arrived the next day and heavy bargaining began. Since Kalani was the only trained musketeer he became an essential part of negotiations. The captain was a tall, lanky man, with a nose over-long, and a bony chin. His hair was dark brown, his eyebrows bushy, and with the stubble of a beard he appeared as swarthy as a pirate. Yet his eyes were kindly and he took an immediate liking to Kalani. "You remind me of my son," Russell said, clapping his hand on his shoulder. "How about shipping out with me? See the world."

Akaka laughed at the suggestion and said, "Thank you for trying to steal the best we have, my friend. We need him in Kona. There are very few with his knowledge of musketry."

Kalani sighed. "I really know very little. Davis and Young, two British seamen, taught me, which isn't much. I have a lot to learn." He cast his wistful eyes onto the deck of Russell's ship. The timber was well oiled, rigging secure, sails wrapped tight around their poles, the brass cannon at the gun ports gleamed in the sun, and sailors busied themselves about the ship. He knew from what he saw that Russell was a man that could teach him much of the great world that lay far beyond Hawaii.

The captain pursed his thin lips and lifted the tricorn from his head, smoothing the felt. He took his sleeve and slowly polished the silver emblem fixed to the front of the hat. "Seeing as how we will be laid up here for a few days waiting for the sandalwood, throw in an extra cord and I'll teach this boy how the Americans fought in their Revolution and beat the British."

Akaka laughed. "We haven't agreed on how much sandalwood you want for muskets and ammunition."

"A mere technicality, whatever we agree on for the firearms, plus a cord. Deal?" Russell thrust out his hand. Kalani held his breath, fixed his eyes on a narrow crack on the deck, fearful that if he said anything, Akaka would refuse the offer.

Alapai-nui interjected himself. "It's a deal. He is the best we have and will only get better with your training. Come, name your price for the weapons."

An agreement on sixteen muskets and plenty of powder and ball was reached that day. Akaka left for Molokai with half of what was bargained for. It took five days for the sandalwood and food to be brought and loaded onto Russell's ship. True to his word, the captain, a Boston seaman who had fought in the American Revolution, taught Kalani the tactics of skirmishing, fighting behind walls, trees, and fences that had made American militia so formidable against the clockwork soldiering of the British army. "You want to harass the bigger force. Don't stand and fight. Hit them and run. Then hit 'em again."

Russell drilled Kalani in the proper loading, aiming, and firing of muskets, and how to dismantle and care for the Brown Bess. He regaled the young boy with stories of battles fought. When his ship was loaded and ready to sail, he gave Kalani a book of illustrations with soldiers in action. "Study these," Russell said, pointing to the pictures. "You might not understand all the words, but remember what I have taught you, look at the pictures and you will get the idea. Someday you will sail with me to see the world."

Kalani nodded, shoved the book into a water-tight packet, shook the captain's hand, and dove overboard. Russell weighed anchor, and Kalani watched the sailing vessel slip out of the bay, heading for China.

"Where have you been?" Moki complained. "The festivals are ending. You missed all the fun." He winked at the two women pounding poi and tapa. They giggled, glancing at Kalani.

He ignored their inviting looks, strode into the shack, yawned and collapsed onto a mat. "I am tired. Alapai-nui pushed us so hard that we canoed here in one day."

"What's the big rush?"

Kalani repeated the war plans he had heard.

Moki's eyes danced with excitement. "We will fight for Kamehameha and become heroes?" He laughed and strutted about with a wooden stick against his shoulder, pausing in front of the women. "We will blow that Keoua away, with our cannon and muskets!"

The girls mocked fright. Moki dropped his stick. He gathered them into his arms. "We will squeeze Keoua's warriors like this and wipe them out." He kissed the young women several times.

Kalani clapped his hands. "A great performance, oh mighty hero, but you and I are stuck in Kona."

"Damn!" Moki cried, sitting down. "You mean four musketeers are going to defend Kona?"

Kalani laughed. "Alapai-nui has five hundred warriors and will attempt to enlist more. I've brought eight muskets with me, which gives us twelve guns."

"Where will you find eight men that are smart like me to fire these weapons?"

"The same place I found you, worthless bag of wind, our lua school."

Moki quit his prancing and leaped onto Kalani, wrestling him to the floor. They laughed and rolled around for some minutes, until Moki gasped, "Enough!" He stood and asked, "When do you leave?"

"Tomorrow, after I recruit our men, I will send them to you. Then I'll visit my aunt and spend the night with her."

CHAPTER 34

THAT EVENING, AFTER EVERYONE HAD left for their sleeping quarters, a woman slipped away from the camp. She traveled south, climbing over a ridge and entered the next valley, picking her way through the village to the hale of Makula. Challenged by the guard, she said, "Wake our master. I have news."

Makula heard a voice at the threshold of his room: "Lord, wake. Your spy has returned." Curious, Makula slid away from a sleeping Hinalea, stepped past the prostrate guard and to the doorway of his royal hale.

"Great Lord, I have news," the woman whispered. "Kamehameha returns to Kohala to fight Keoua. Alapai-nui is sending soldiers from Kona to help him. Your enemy Kalani Tana is coming to the lua school near your village to recruit warriors."

"Good. Return before your absence is discovered." After the spy left, Makula pondered the report. "Kamehameha is stripping Kona of its warriors. He is leaving it defenseless. I will send word to Hauna to come at once. We will seize Kona. When that filthy boy comes here, I will capture him for Hauna to sacrifice."

The next morning, Kalani hiked over the mountains to the lua school. He found Hepa and requested eight men to serve as musketeers. Hepa made his selections and Kalani instructed them to join Moki.

He left his teacher for the home of Aunt Lei. Kalani walked into the forest near the lua school. Though the clouds shadowed the woods it did not seem as fearful a place as the first day he had arrived in Kona. The forest felt cool, peaceful. Birds sang. Butterflies flitted, disturbed from their leaf perches by his passage. How pretty they are, he thought.

A flash of movement. A man leaped onto the trail. "We meet again, Kalani Moku Tana. This time, you will not escape."

Startled, Kalani studied the henchman for a moment. "You are Hauna's friend, the one who tripped me over the cliff. Is Hauna your master or Makula?"

"Makula! Come with me to your death."

"Take me if you can," Kalani answered, his voice low. He settled into a fighting stance, fists clenched, arms at his side, knees bent.

Two men rose from the brush, staves in their hands. They charged. Kalani stepped sideways. He grasped the rod of the leading warrior and rolled backwards with a foot placed into the man's belly and, using his momentum, flipped the warrior into a tree.

The second man struck. Unable to escape the blow, Kalani raised the staff he had wrested from the first attacker and blocked the hit. The force of the blow splintered both rods. Kalani smashed a broken end into the man's face. Blood spurted from his nose. Dazed by the shock of the blow, the warrior stood, bewildered. Kalani struck a fist into his belly. The man faltered, and Kalani crashed an open palm into his jaw. The warrior fell like an axed tree.

A cudgel smashed into Kalani's head. He went to his knees. Another blow hit him. Dazed, he pitched forward into blackness.

CHAPTER 35

"GET UP!" A VOICE YELLED as a foot struck his ribs. The pain forced him awake. His head throbbed and threatened to burst. "Get up," the voice snarled again. Kalani strained to focus on Makulu standing over him.

"You are pitiful," the chief sneered. "A worm. Whatever made you think that you are a better lover than I? It would be a pleasure to kill you, but Hauna wants you alive for sacrifice. He will be here after he completes the conquest of Hilo. Before your death, you will admit that I am the better man. After you die, Hauna and I will strike Alapai-nui, take Kona, and Kamehameha will be finished. Farewell Tana, we will meet again when Hauna comes." Makula left.

Kalani watched him walk to the entryway of the prison cave, where two sentries stood watch. "Guard him well. I would not want to lose him before Hauna arrives."

A burning thirst parched his throat. Kalani called to the guards. "Water."

One of them stood, seized a vessel, and threw its contents over him. "This is all you get."

Urine slid over Kalani's head, dripping to the floor. The smell acrid, like fermented poi, but the bland taste soothed his blistered lips.

Hours passed. His bound arms and legs ached. His mind whirled. He sank into unconsciousness. A voice woke him. "I have water and food. He must be kept alive by Makula's orders until Hauna comes."

Rough hands forced drink into his mouth. "There is food by your side. I will free you to eat but make no sudden moves or I will kill you."

Kalani hurt too much to fight. His head throbbed like the beating sounds of pahu drums. His ribs felt on fire. Hands free, he shoveled in food, then submitted to being bound. Soon, he fell into a deep sleep.

Sunlight streamed into the cave. Kalani raised himself from his stone bed. A terrible aching in his head blurred his vision. He sensed a lump on his skull and knew it caused his suffering.

Food and water lay near him. He studied the prison cave while he ate. The ceiling loomed eight feet above him. Its surface mottled with streaks of blue. The rock tube widened in a crescent shape until it opened to a cloud filled sky. There were no trees that he could see. Birds flitted about the entry. The familiar sound of waves did not come to his ears. Kalani realized he lay in a lava tube far above the sea.

What were his chances of escape? Two guards lounged at the entrance, clubs and spears leaning against a side of the cave. He searched but could not see anything he could use as a weapon.

He hunted for a sharp stone with his fingers to cut his bindings, he felt none. Dejected, Kalani realized he could not get free. He shook his head to dispel the gloom overwhelming him. He resolved to die like a warrior. He would spit in the face of his enemies, no matter their cruelty.

At mid-afternoon, a shrill voice aroused him. "I bring food and drink."

"You are early. What do you have for us?" a guard demanded.

"Good awa. The finest made, a vessel for each of you to enjoy."

An old person swathed from head to foot in a brown cloth stood at the cave entrance offering a gourd to each man. They seized the vessels, downing their drink in rapid gulps.

"Very good," one man said. "Do you have more?"

"I have one for the prisoner, but he won't need it where he is going," cackled the shrouded figure.

A guard took the offered cup and drained it. The servant approached Kalani. The second man stood. "He's going to die. Don't waste food on him. Give it to—"

His words slurred, and he crumpled to the floor.

The remaining warrior tried to rise, but he staggered and sagged to the stones.

Puzzled, Kalani watched the shrouded figure rush to him, pull out a knife and sever his bonds. His hands were stiff. He rubbed his palms together as he came to his feet. He studied his savior. "There's something familiar about you."

Hinalea shed her garment. She stood naked, her bronzed body sharply contrasted by the grey dust in her hair, face, and hands. Makula's wife brushed the soot away, raised herself and kissed Kalani. "I have come to save the one I love," she murmured, pressing her body against his.

Kalani winced.

"I'm sorry," she said, pulling away.

"It just hurts where your husband kicked me. How did you find me? What about the guards?"

Her eyes danced with mischief. "Such a flood of questions, my darling. The guards are asleep and may never awaken. I poisoned their awa juice, but you must make sure that they are dead before we go. If not, Makula might suspect me."

"I can't kill defenseless men," Kalani objected.

"Well, I can," Hinalea scowled, plunging her knife into the heart of one of the sleeping guards. She grabbed a cudgel from the other and smashed his head. "Come, sweetheart, let us go before someone comes."

Kalani shuddered. *If she could kill for a person she loved, what would Hinalea do if I make her jealous*? He shook off the morbid thought and followed her.

During their escape, Hinalea told him that Makula had boasted of his capture. As he strutted about, he revealed where Kalani was hidden and the plans for sacrifice. "He even said that he would make me watch you die and take me as you perished. Oh, how I hate him. You are different, kind and gentle. There is none better than you."

Kalani smiled and kissed her. "Thank you for saving me. What has happened since I have been trapped in the cave?"

Hinalea pouted. "Don't you want to tell me how much you love me? Desire me above all others?"

"Yes, I love you and desire you, but tell me the news."

Hinalea sighed. "Since you won't make love to me until I tell you, this is what I know. Several nights ago, Makula left our bed. I followed and overheard him speaking to a woman named Ilima. She gave him information of the weakness of your forces. I heard Makula making plans to capture you, join with Hauna, and conquer Kona. It is only today that I discovered where you were hidden." Hinalea concluded her report by pulling Kalani onto the grass.

Despite his aches, he felt his body grow hot. Hinalea thrust herself against him. Jolts of pain stabbed his ribs. He writhed in agony.

Hinalea withdrew, tears in her eyes. "I am sorry I hurt you. I want you, but only when you are well."

"Come with me to Kealakekua, where I can protect you," he begged.

"If I come with you, Makula will know I am a traitor. If I return to him, I have a chance to help you. In the battles to come, who knows who will win? If you are victorious, come to me." Her eyes brimming with tears, Hinalea said, "Go! Remember that I love you."

CHAPTER 36

AIDED BY EARLY MORNING LIGHT, Kalani stumbled along the path leading into Kealakekua. Dogs barked, warning of his coming. A cur trotted about, tail standing rigid, face taut with menace. The animal growled until the injured man left his territory.

Kalani came to the threshold of the shack he shared with his friend. "Moki, are you there?" he whispered, his voice wavering with exhaustion.

"Who is that?" Moki answered.

"It's me, Kalani."

"Go away," Moki said. "You are dead. I don't want ghosts in this house."

"I'm not dead. Come outside, bring some water, and help me."

"You are dead, I saw the body. It was all broken. Go away before I call the kahuna."

"Look, this body is going to come in there and break your body if you don't help me."

"Okay, I'm coming, but if you're not real, I will get the kahuna to blow you away."

Moki stuck his head through the threshold and grabbed Kalani's leg. "This is solid. Maybe you're not a ghost." Satisfied, he came out and searched every aspect of his friend's face.

"Cut the clowning, I'm not a ghost."

"Makula sent a body two days ago. He said it was you. He claimed a fisherman found you at the bottom of a cliff. The face was smashed."

"That's all part of his plan. He doesn't want anyone poking around his village looking for me. He's gathering men to attack Alapai-nui and take over Kona. Your girlfriend is one of his spies and maybe the other girl is a spy, too."

"What do you mean spies? They are both sweethearts. She is always taking care of me, even when we are training." Moki gave Kalani a wink.

"Yeah, well, your sweetheart almost cost me my life. Let's find Ilima and take her to Alapai-nui. Grab some rope."

The two men walked to the women's sleeping hale. Moki called Ilima out. When she came through the threshold, she shrieked, "You're supposed to be dead."

Kalani roped her, saying, "I'm very much alive, no thanks to you. We're taking you to Alapai-nui."

Ilima resisted, forcing Moki to drag her by the hair through the village. With the struggling woman in their hands, they came to the home of the chief. Kalani told Alapai-nui of his capture, escape, and the plans of Makula and Hauna to conquer Kona.

"Is this true? Are you a spy?" Alapai-nui spoke sternly to Ilima.

"Not true, not a spy," the girl whimpered.

"Moki, place her in the shed. I will send men to force the truth from her. Kalani, come and tell me what you know of the coming attack."

Several days later Alapai-nui paced in his quarters, then stopped his fretful striding and faced Kalani. "It's been several days since you escaped. My scouts tell me there's no sign of Hauna by land or sea. Are you sure he's coming to join Makula?"

"Yes, the man gloated how he and Hauna would take Kona away from Kamehameha. Didn't Ilima confirm any of what I've said?"

Alapai-nui rubbed his chin. "Only after torture, but she knows nothing about the timing of Hauna's coming or how many men he will bring. How have you progressed with your training of the new musketeers?"

"The men from the lua school are raw. They do not have the discipline required for standing in a straight line, loading, and firing a musket. But they are eager to learn the white man's way of fighting. Thanks to you, we have enough powder and ball to do target practice."

"A white sail entered the bay while you were a prisoner. They were reluctant to trade guns, but willing to sell me plenty of ammunition. I understand you developed some new battle techniques."

Kalani decided to impress Alapai-nui. "I learned from Captain Russell how Americans fought in their revolution. He told me they hid behind trees. Used rock walls for defense. Placed their muskets on logs to steady aiming. Isaac Davis taught me the British way of fighting. Stand in a straight line. Kneel to aim. Fire together. These lessons helped me create some simple tactics for combat."

Alapai-nui smiled, as if he understood this young man's need to make an impact. "Good. If we are going to win, we must use the military knowledge of the foreigners. I have news that Kamehameha has landed at Kawaihae. Keoua of the Red Cloak, who entered Waimea with his advance guard, is retreating. The high chief seeks reinforcements from us, especially your musketeers. I fear I can only keep you for a few days before I must send you to him."

At that moment, a messenger arrived: Hauna was coming north along the coast. Only a two-or-three-day paddle from Makula's village.

"How many canoes and men?" Alapai-nui asked.

"No more than fifteen war canoes, maybe three hundred men."

"I would have expected Hauna to bring more. With Makula's four hundred warriors against my five hundred men and your muskets, there is a chance to win before the Puna king arrives. We attack now!"

CHAPTER 37

An annoyed Makula shouted, "Alapai-nui, why have you come to my village with your army? You arrive without a declaration of war. Is it your intention to fight me? Why so? I am your friend, Kamehameha's friend."

"You are not my friend. Nor are you Kamehameha's friend. You plot with Hauna and Keoua to seize Kona and make it your kingdom."

Makula waved away the allegation. "Not true. Not true. I am loyal to the great chief."

"Do you deny that Hauna is sailing with three hundred warriors to join you and seize Kealakekua Bay?"

"I know nothing of that. Who told you such lies?"

"Your spy, Ilima."

"You would believe a woman?"

"My loyal warrior, Kalani Tana, told me the same."

"You would believe a boy? A nobody who is not a chief?"

"Tell me, if you are loyal to Kamehameha, why do you refuse to send your warriors to aid him in his fight against Keoua?"

Makula smiled condescendingly. "It is festival time. My men have been busy."

"Yes. Busy preparing for war against Kamehameha! You and your chiefs will surrender now. Disband your army or there will be war."

Makula sneered. "Hauna is near and our combined forces will crush you. I will hold you until he lands. Then you will all die."

The chiefs retired to their battle lines. The two armies stretched from the ocean to the low hills. Wide, level terrain lay between them, with sparse vegetation separating the forces.The battlefield tumbled from the hills to the sea, bisected by a stream filled with rocks. Makula had chosen the site for its defensive value, knowing that crossing a rock-filled, running steam with steep banks is deadly for an attacker.

Kalani weighed the odds of winning as he and a dozen musketeers marched toward the rivulet. Though outnumbered, Makula held all the defensive advantages. He need only wait - force Alapai-nui to come across the water and be beaten. By the time Hauna arrives, the Kona army would be crushed.

Fifteen yards from the bank, four coconut logs were embedded. Kalani, Moki, and two veteran musketeers knelt, rested their muskets on the trees, and fired at enemy warriors massed in a block across the stream. They exchanged muskets with the raw recruits behind them holding four loaded weapons, and shot again. This unanswered fire continued until twenty warriors lay dead.

Kalani heard men screaming for action. He saw two chiefs in red and yellow capes run to Makula. They pointed at the musketeers. The continuous volleys brought down more enemy. With gestures and yells, the words swallowed up in the din of battle, the chiefs returned to their soldiers. They proceeded to kick their men, forcing them to attack.

Kalani ordered his men to retire behind rows of pointed stakes buried into the ground. "Thread your way through the sticks. Form a line behind them."

Moki pranced alongside, bubbling with excitement. "See my shots? I killed a dozen of them. Wahoo!" he yelled.

"Did any of our men get hurt?" Kalani asked, stepping around rows of stakes.

"No. We were too far away for spears and stones to get us." Moki looked toward the stream. "See, the enemy charge is slowed by the rocks and water. Our slingers are dancing around. Whacking them!"

Kalani worked his way through the stakes. "Moki, go to the right and I will be on the left. Musketeers, form a straight line between us."

A group of women rested in a coconut grove. He called to them, "Ammunition bearers, bring the extra powder and ball!" They rushed up, handing out ammunition. Kalani turned to Alapai-nui's command post forty yards to his left and gave a hand signal.

Alapai-nui shouted orders, and warriors led by three chiefs came to each side of the musketeers. Messengers ran to the slingers, ordering them to clear the area.

Thirty yards beyond the stakes, the first of Makula's warriors crossed the stream, two chiefs in the lead. More men climbed the bank, bunching together. "Level spears," a chief ordered. The mass of men surged forward.

"Musketeers, present arms!" Kalani said. He waited until the attackers were slowed by the embedded stakes. "Fire!" Men fell into the pointed wood, blocking others from threading through. From his center position, Alapa-nui yelled, "Hurl spears."

A swarm of missiles struck Makula's milling men. The combination of the stream, musket fire, stakes, and spears halted the enemy charge. Alapai-nui pointed, and a second detachment of spearmen struck the flank of Makula's warriors.

"We're beating them," Moki pranced about.

"Maybe, but I still see warriors trying to cross the stream. Reload and wait. I think our chief is ready to finish them."

"Attack," Alapai-nui screamed. A concealed reserve force charged. The power of their strike swept away demoralized troops at the stakes and forced the survivors to flee across the stream.

"Forward," Kalani ordered, and his musketeers returned to the coconut rests. Without pausing to kneel, Moki fired. "I got that guy." He jiggled about like a crazed man. "Oh, am I good." A stone crashed into his side and he doubled over in pain.

"It's not fun when the enemy strikes back." Kalani grimaced.

Conch shells blared and Makula's remaining warriors retreated. Strewn across the battleground were the bodies of three chiefs and more than a hundred men. Alapai-nui's losses were negligible. His soldiers stood at the stream, yelling taunts and challenges at Makula's demoralized men.

"Ready!" Kalani yelled. At his order, twelve muskets smoked. A dozen iron balls flew. Six of Makula's men fell and those who remained across the stream fled.

Makula raised his spear. "Alapai-nui, I challenge you to a duel! Winner take—"

An iron ball blew the helmet from his head. Kalani stood holding his smoking gun. He reached for another musket.

"Someone you love is dead," Makula snarled, disappearing into the mob of retreating warriors.

Alapai-nui sent men to pursue the fugitives, instructing them to offer amnesty to those willing to surrender. He ordered the rest to the beach.

Kalani rushed to him. "My lord, I need to find out who Makula has killed."

"I cannot spare you. Come. Bring your musketeers to the shore and await the arrival of Hauna."

Frantic, Kalani sought Moki. "You must do something for me. Find Makula's palace and his wife, Hinalea. I must know if she is dead or alive."

"The chief will miss me."

"If I leave, my absence will be noticed. I can explain why you are gone, if anyone asks. Now go."

For hours, Kalani stood guard and worried at the lack of news. Toward late afternoon, scouts reported that Hauna's fleet was in sight, prompting Alapai-nui to form up his forces with Kalani and his musketeers next to him.

Hauna's flotilla approached the beach, stopping fifty yards from shore. The Puna chief stood in the lead war canoe. He shouted over the water, "Where is Makula? What is the meaning of this army?"

"Your friend has fled into the hills, hunted by my warriors," Alapai-nui hollered. "I have unmasked your evil conspiracy to steal Kona from Kamehameha, and I challenge you to fight us to the death or surrender."

"We will not fight when you have the advantage," Hauna screamed. "We go to join Keoua in Waimea."

"Yes, run away like the slimy slug that you are," Kalani yelled, raising his musket to attempt a long-range shot.

Hauna stood defiant at the prow, his brilliantly colored royal cape cupped around his back by the wind. A red helmet with a yellow crescent of feathers towered above his head. He pointed his shark-toothed dagger at Kalani and yelled, "Shoot, you filthy cockroach."

Kalani's gun wavered, then went to the ground. He knew that their mutual hatred could only end with personal combat.

Hauna screamed, "Paddlers, pull for Kohala." With his canoe skimming over tossing whitecaps, he thrust his dagger into the air several times and called out words lost in the wind.

Kalani shuffled in the sand, tormented by all that transpired. A hand pulled at his arm. "Come with me," Moki said.

Darkness forced the two men to use hand torches as they followed the path to the home of Aunt Lei. Moki assured Kalani that Hinalea had fled to the mountains with other members of Makula's family.

With his torch held high, Kalani forced his way through tall ferns, pushing into the compound of Aunt Lei. The silence surprised him. Absent were happy sounds and warm fires.

The fire stick Kalani held wrapped light around burnt bamboo frames, the thatch covering only embers. Both shacks were gone. A cry arose from his lips: "Moki! Search the ruins."

The two men sifted through the charred remnants of the structures. Moki called, pointing, "Look in the corner." Kalani followed his finger to a long lump on the floor. He knew the burnt heap was his beloved Aunt Lei.

He knelt by her remains, tears dripping from his eyes, pitting the corpse like raindrops falling into mud. "Why did you have to kill her, Makula?" Kalani wailed.

CHAPTER 38

After the victory, a feast was held. Kalani picked at his food, watching the roaring drunken men around him. Moki jostled him saying, "Eat. Make love." He pulled a woman into him, kissing her lips, stroking her thigh.

"You still trust her, even though she was a friend of that spy?"

"She is okay! Besides, we leave for Kawaihae tomorrow. I have no time to find a woman who will give me loving like this one." Moki grinned, rubbing the girl's bare leg. She purred, nuzzling into his chest.

"Suit yourself," Kalani said, pushing away his food. "I'm still mourning for my aunt."

A warm hand folded over his chest. Kalani's lungs filled with the sweet smell of perfumed oil that only royal ladies wore. A soft voice whispered, "Chief Alapai-nui sent me to lighten your sadness." The woman's breath filled his ear. Her lips played over it, her tongue stabbing in and out. Then her kissing moved to sensitive areas around his neck, and a hand slid along his side.

Excitement came as Kalani felt the softness of her breasts pressing against him. He stood, the woman helped him into the shadows. Men hooted. Moki called, "Kalani, watch out for the ghosts that eat people in the night."

"Pay no attention to your friend. I will not devour you. I have come to give you happiness." The woman's hand twined about Kalani's neck, pulling his mouth into her lips. Her tongue darted in, their breath mixing.

Kalani heard a thump. His companion howled, pulling away from him.

"Get away from my man," Hinalea hissed, wielding a paddle above her head and smacking it into the buttocks of the lady.

"Oh, that hurts," she gasped, raising her hands to protect herself.

Kalani grabbed Hinalea, wrestling with her.

"Let me hit her."

While they struggled, the woman stumbled into the shadows and fled.

Hinalea tossed the paddle, reached up and drew Kalani in. Her hands groped, seeking to excite him.

He pushed Hinalea away. "Why did you hit her? She was told to make me happy."

"I'm the only one that can give you happiness."

"What did you expect of me? Go without? You fled into the hills with your husband."

"He is no longer my husband. I have escaped from that awful man and come back to you. I am the only one you need to cure your pain." Hinalea snuggled into him. Her breathing grew deeper.

Later that night, Kalani gazed at the dying bonfires in the village. Hinalea lay contented by his side. "What are you thinking, sweetheart?"

"Tomorrow I must leave to join Kamehameha and his army."

Hinalea reared up. "You must take me with you."

"No, we will be fighting Keoua. It's too dangerous."

"I can take care of all your needs. Tend to your desires. I will make you happy," she promised, emphasizing her words by rubbing against him.

"You would be an excellent camp follower. But I need someone to find my mother in Kau and bring her back to Kona."

"Isn't there anyone else to do that?"

"Hinalea, you are the daughter of a chief and chiefess living in Kau. It would be easy for you to find my mother and two sisters and bring them here. Once they are in Kona, I'm sure you have connections that will help them."

Hinalea pouted, bit her lip, and sighed, "If I do this for you, will you promise to be true to me while we are apart? Will you promise not to love anyone else?"

Kalani had been thinking of his mother since Aunt Lei's death. *Makula was out there, still a threat. He might kill her and my sisters. Hinalea had come at an opportune time.* His thoughts flashed to Nani, imperious, haughty, desirable. With a sigh he said, "Yes, I promise to love only you."

In the morning, Kalani, Moki, and the other musketeers set sail for the north shore of Hawaii. Hinalea and four servants headed south for Kau.

CHAPTER 39

TWO DAYS LATER HINALEA SAILED past Kona, entering the forbidding shoreline of Kau. The land looked bleak, marred by ages of molten lava pouring from the great earth funnel of Mauna Loa. When the streams of lava cooled they left massive mounds of ugly dark rock studding the end of the island. Hinalea gazed at the massive volcano swelling from the sea. Like a woman's breast in passion, she thought, cupped and firm. The nipple, covered with snow, was partially hidden by clouds swirling around it.

Waves smashed into the rugged promontory of South Point, forcing the canoe toward the rocks. Hinalea knew it was touch-and-go when you moved from a sea calmed by a shielding mountain into waters whipped by winds driving west. She urged her paddlers to sail into the swells, to avoid the pitching or rolling motions that could force the canoe broadside to the waves and swamp it.

Weaned in the sea, Hinalea guided the canoe through the roiling waters at the island's end. The hostile black face of the coastal cliff became more forgiving. Strong trade winds brought heavy clouds filled with rain. The deluge added to the misery of the travelers. Hinalea stopped paddling and bailed. After several hours, she pointed toward a fishing village niched into the rock landscape. Once landed, she left her servants and traveled upland to the home of her parents.

"Hui, daughter, you have returned. Has your husband beat you again? Threatened your life?" her mother asked.

"He is a bastard. I have left him and am seeking a woman by the name of Umi-ula Tana. Do you know her?"

"She's a poor widow living with her daughters over the next ridgeline. What do you want with such worthless scum?"

"Mother, how can you say that? They were once people of class like you and me. In fact, Umi-ula is related to Kamehameha."

"Don't mention that upstart's name in this house! Your father has joined Keoua, fighting to take control of this island from that evil man. To think that the people of Kau saved his life when he was a baby, reared him and educated him. How does he repay us?" Without waiting for an answer, she continued, "With endless wars of conquest. But enough of that upstart. What is your business with Umi-ula?"

"She is the mother of the man I care for."

"Daughter, you are married to a great chief, why do you sleep with trash?"

"He is not trash. He is a warrior, a leader of Kamehameha's musketeers."

"I know it is not sinful for a chiefess like you to sleep around. I had a little fun myself, but to have relations with a common warrior while you are married to a man like Makula—that is an abomination." Her eyes narrowed, "Tell me, how old is this person?"

"Eighteen." Before her mother could speak, Hinalea rushed ahead, "I know what you will say, but he is a mature man."

"Mature man! He is two years younger than you. Did he still have fuzz on his cheeks when he seduced you?" Pausing in her tirade, the chiefess studied her daughter. After many moments of silence, she said, "I see. You were the one that snatched him from the cradle and taught him to be a man. Oh, that is so wicked."

Hinalea raised her eyes and stared defiantly at her mother. "Tell me, how many boys have you seduced? More than the fingers and toes on my hands and feet, I'm sure. Don't criticize me when you have allowed many to enjoy your favors. All you need to know is that he pleases me when we make love."

"Ah, it is true that I should not criticize since I have led life to the fullest. But I ask you, can a boy of eighteen love only one? Or does he leap from one passion to another and another? Does he even love you?"

Under the glare of her mother's eyes, Hinalea hid her face in her hands. "I know he loves me. He said it. He loves me."

"For your sake, daughter, I hope this child does not destroy you. Your husband is a jealous man. Remember how you came to us for protection when he beat you once before? I fear he will come seeking you. Enough of this. Umi-ula lives over the next ridge line, near the village."

Hinalea pondered her mother's parting words as she hiked up the hill. From the very first night, she had been intrigued by the women's gossip of the victorious boy from the lua school. When she saw him in the firelight, she felt a yearning within. Beardless, hair trim, neatly fitting over his head like a warrior's helmet. His eyes sharp, questing, shining through dark brows. His nose, royal, his lips, sensuous. Oh, how sensuous they were.

She paused at the top, catching her breath. Below lay a small settlement. People worked on the hillside beneath tall stalks of mountain taro. Hinalea marveled at such plants. They grew without constant water. Lowland taro needed flowing streams and ponds to survive.

Makula is a pig, she thought. He abused her from the first time they mated. He forced her into unnatural acts. When he finished, he rolled over and slept. The pain in her bottom became so severe, it took hours to subside. The horror of his rutting continued whenever they coupled.

Kalani was not like that. When she first pulled him to her, he was gentle. She showed him where best to touch. Find the places that pleased her. That first week with him was glorious. Sweet in his lovemaking. Kind to her when they finished. His massages were heavenly. When she asked him where he learned the art, he said, "from a slave". She laughed. That is how it was, pleasure and laughter. That's the way it continued for many nights thereafter.

Hinalea ran. The breeze smoothed her skin, cooling it. The exhilaration of exercise erased her doubts. Kalani loved her. She loved him. That was all that mattered.

She found someone who directed her to Umi-ula. When she came to the lean-to, Hinalea was shocked. Open to the air on three sides, it was nothing but an elevated platform of leaves thrust into the side of a hill.

Outside the hovel, a woman worked, weaving a basket. She looked up as Hinalea approached. "Aloha," she said.

"Are you Umi-ula?"

"Yes."

Before Hinalea could speak Umi-ula said, "Come inside. You're sweating. We have water. Not much food, but you are welcome to what we have."

Hinalea felt embarrassed. She had brought nothing. Kalani's mother would share everything she had. The old woman was beautiful in her kindness.

Umi-ula wobbled when she stood. Hinalea reached to her. The sunlight shone on white hair. It glinted from wrinkled bronzed skin. Umi-ula smiled, "I can do it. Don't worry. Come from the sun." Hinalea followed her into the shed. Its height low, a little more than five feet, but Umi-ula stepped in without a pause.

Hinalea stooped as she entered. Umi-ula reached for a gourd and offered it to her before she squatted on the dirt. Her face drooped as she did so. Hinalea sensed her embarrassment at the shabbiness of her shed.

"Why do you come?"

"Your son sent me. I will bring you to Kona."

"How is he?"

Over the next few minutes Hinalea recounted all she knew of Kalani, finishing by saying, "He is a hero. With his muskets he defeated my husband and drove him into the hills."

"Your husband!" Umi-ula gasped.

"Yes. But you need not know that story. It is enough to say, Kalani is worried. Makula will seek revenge upon you. He killed your sister. You may be next."

Umi-ula wrung her hands, looking about at the bareness of her hovel. "We have nothing. My husband and his father were sacrificed.

Whatever we had was taken away from us by the chiefs of Kau. My daughter and I live as you see us." She bowed her head, weeping.

"A daughter? I thought there were two."

"My oldest and her child died from disease. The other has gone to fetch water. Ah, there is Ane. Hui, we have a visitor."

A young woman strode up, a jug fastened to her hip. She was attractive, taller than her mother, and slender. Hinalea suspected that Ane gave what little they had to eat to her parent. She explained her mission to Ane and the danger.

The young girl looked away, tears welling in her eyes.

"What is the matter?" Umi-ula asked.

"My lover will never find me if I go to Kona."

"Who is he?" Hinalea asked.

"He is a warrior fighting with Keoua. He is my husband to be. I think I bear his child."

CHAPTER 40

MAKULA YELLED FOR ENTRY INTO the compound. "What do you want?" Hinalea's mother answered, coming through the open door of her hale. "Oh! It is you."

"Where is Hinalea? She ran away from me again. I was told she came here to find Umi-ula."

"Did you beat her?"

"Kalani, that boy, is the cause of my troubles. I think he may have something to do with what Hinalea is up to here. Where is my wife?"

Makula saw the chiefess hesitating. His fists clenched as he remembered the crunching blow he had delivered to Hinalea's belly. He saw fright in the woman's eyes.

"My daughter has gone over the hill to the next village to find Umi-ula."

"If you are lying, I will return."

Makula called to two warriors and trotted with them from the compound.

"My husband is fighting with Keoua. If he were here you would not be so mighty," the chiefess yelled, then rushed into her home and gave orders to a servant.

"Mother, why must we go?" Ane begged. "We should wait for my man to return."

Umi-ula wrung her hands. She knew how much her daughter was in love. "There is great danger. Your brother has made a deadly enemy and he is coming to kill us."

Ane hung her head, weeping. She shifted the dirt inside the lean-to with her foot.

A man ran past a small garden of sweet potatoes. Hinalea recognized him as a servant of her family. "Hui, what is it?"

Breathing hard, he stopped at the shed. "Makula is coming. He has two warriors with him. Your mother thinks he intends to kill you all!"

"Then we must go," Hinalea said. "Take nothing but your clothes and water. We leave for the ocean, now!"

The women grasped gourds. Umi-ula seized a palaoa, placing the whale-toothed necklace around her neck. "I cannot leave this," she smiled at Hinalea. "I once was royalty."

"Follow me," the servant said. "I know a path through the lava fields."

For hours they walked past ugly mounds of rock, blackened by the fire from within the earth. The cooled lava lay in heaps along the trail. The travelers avoided areas of the sharpest stone. As the rocks cut into her feet, Hinalea wondered if they needed to go so fast, or even if her husband knew the route they had taken.

At a rise in the ground she looked back. Three men were running toward them. She recognized the six-foot-four giant among them. Kukae, she thought, why is Makula so jealous? He has three other wives. Yet she knew that he believed his penis to be glorious. No man could be a better lover than he. She realized that her bragging tongue had set Makula aflame with jealousy.

"Hurry," the servant wailed. "We need to get to that other hill." He pointed. "There is a ravine. A bridge. Maybe we can stop them."

How, wondered Hinalea, but she followed the others. Umi-ula slowed. Faltered. Hinalea came to her side, placed an arm around her. Together they stumbled forward. The older woman smiled. "Thank you."

Her words warmed Hinalea's heart. She knew at that moment that she loved Umi-ula.

"Climb up. Climb up," the family servant begged.

Hinalea gasped. At the crest she saw a long narrow ravine. Twenty feet below, a stream ran to the sea. She looked back at the approaching men. "We're trapped."

"No, no. Come a little way. There is a bamboo bridge."

"What good is that? They can cross over it too."

"We will cross and hurl it into the stream."

"With what?"

"This knife. Our hands. Find loose logs and tip the bridge over."

Hinalea shook her head. She realized there was no better plan and hustled everyone over. The women scurried about looking for logs while the servant sawed at the bindings that held the bridge on their end to a coconut piling sunk into the crest of the hill.

As she hunted, Hinalea glanced below. The warriors were climbing. Their imminence hurried her search. She found a tapered coconut log and two long sticks of bamboo. "All of you, come help. Umi-ula, Ane, pick up the bamboo."

The coconut log was heavy. It took the strength of two people to drag it. Hooting sounds came from below. Ane panicked, her eyes darting.

"Please don't run. We need you," Hinalea begged. Umi-ula stroked her daughter's hair, whispered to her. Ane calmed, picked up the bamboo and dragged it to the edge, returning to help move the log.

The warriors were halfway up the hill, continuing to yell as they came.

"I've cut the bindings. When I lift, shove the bamboo in. Good. Now push."

A stick cracked. Beyond the ridge, there were shouts. "Kukae," Hinalea swore.

"Push the other bamboo further in, then down. I will shove this coconut log into the gap."

The servant rolled the log in just before the second bamboo splintered.

"All together, heave."

Hinalea heard rocks rolling into the stream. Makula's voice boomed, "Where are they?" Fighting her panic, she prayed they would be delayed hunting for them.

The bamboo bridge creaked. The far end held fast to the ridge.

"Lever up and down. Then roll it to the right," the servant whispered.

Makula came above the hill crest. Two men followed. They paused.

Hinalea stifled a scream. The two women whimpered. The bamboo bridge screeched, the sound drawing the men.

"There!" Makula yelled. "Get them."

"Heave!" screamed the servant.

Four desperate people shoved together. The far end of the bridge groaned.

The warriors were steps away.

With another effort that collapsed the women to the ground, the bridge came free, plunging into the ravine.

Makula raged, "Hinalea! Stay there. You are mine. Warriors! Find stones."

"Quick," the family servant said. "Follow me. Bend low."

They scuttled from the ridge. A hail of rocks chased after them.

Ane screamed, stumbling into jagged stones.

Hinalea pulled her up and helped her away from the falling missiles. Both women were soon smeared with Ane's blood.

The servant whooped, "We did it. They will never catch us."

It was mid-day when they reached the fishing village and found Hinalea's four servants who collectively shook their heads. "The canoe we have cannot take two more."

A tired Hinalea said, "Can we find one or—"

A servant interrupted. "I know a fisherman who has a magnificent double canoe."

The party trudged toward several vessels pulled onto the sand. One man carried a weary Umi-ula. At the shore they found the fisherman who owned the craft.

He was reluctant. "It is a special canoe. I designed and built it to catch the tiger shark."

"Oh!" a servant said. "That is unusual. How do you catch it?"

The man began to explain, but Hinalea interrupted. "We are desperate. We need a canoe like yours."

CHAPTER 41

Makula shook his fists at the escaping fugitives. He looked along the ravine, seeking a way down or around. To the right, about a mile or more away, the cut in the earth ended and he ran toward it.

His anger mounted, thinking of the evil done to him. He would kill the mother and daughter. Take back Hinalea. Play with her. Make her suffer. Then, but…

After rounding the shallow taper of the ridge, the warriors regained the path. Makula knew the fugitives headed for the sea. A fishing village was not far away. He urged his men to hurry.

"What do you want?" Hinalea begged. "I've offered you my canoe. I have promised to have my men return yours. Share what you have with us. Please."

The fisherman shook his head. "I need the vessel to fish, to feed my family. Your craft is not big enough for my crew."

"I can get ten baskets of mountain taro for you. It would feed your family for a month."

The fisherman stroked his chin, shaking his head.

A loud cry came from the hillside that sloped into the sea.

All five looked up. Hinalea saw Makula thrusting a spear into the air.

"Twenty baskets of mountain taro. Come." Hinalea seized the wale of the double canoe and began to push it into the sea. Her servants helped. Soon the craft crested the waves heading for deep water.

Hinalea looked back and saw Makula at the shore screaming at the fisherman. She smiled. Then she frowned as Makula pushed the obstinate man, seized a canoe, and thrust it into the sea. Soon two canoes rushed for Kona.

"They have seven paddles to our three," grumbled one of Makula's warriors.

"Several are women. Their craft is heavier. We will catch them. Raise the sail." Makula strained to keep the fleeing double canoe in sight. After hours of pursuit, darkness came, and he could barely make out the outline of a pole. "They will not escape," he muttered, shoving his paddle into the sea, urging his men to do the same.

A three-quarter moon rose to the east, and he saw his quarry. He felt the tightness of his sling around his waist. Stones bulged in the sack at his side. If he got close enough he would sink them. For years he had trained in hurling dense rocks at canoes. His high arch and accuracy had holed many. At a hundred yards he could score a hit. At fifty yards he would not miss.

The wind died as they sailed in the lee of the fourteen-thousand-foot volcano. He saw his sail luffing, slowing their progress. He reached to a rope and secured it. Ahead, Hinalea's vessel slowed. Whether because of dying wind or fatigue he did not know.

Through the night the chase continued. Makula's canoe crept closer as the hours passed. At this speed they would reach Alapai-nui's village before noon. He had to catch them before then.

At dawn there was a gap of a hundred-and-fifty yards. Makula urged his worn men to pull harder. He dug his stick into the sea, skimming the boat forward. The gap narrowed. Within an hour, the distance had closed. Makula loosened his sling. He selected a stone and stood for a long shot.

Hinalea watched the growing light with apprehension. Her crew was exhausted. Umi-ula lay on the platform between canoes, weeping. Ane vomited over the side. Hinalea judged she was pregnant, not seasick. She worried that her heaving could abort the baby. "Go on the platform. Rest with your mother."

"No. I must help." She raised her paddle and pushed it into the water.

A splash occurred behind them. Hinalea looked back. Makula stood at the prow of his vessel, his hand whirling. She had heard stories of warriors slinging stones three hundred yards and hitting canoes. But that was from a hill at a massed flotilla. She judged the distance between vessels to be half that range. Makula's canoe rolled in the waves. They were a small target. It seemed impossible to hit them.

She watched Makula fling his second stone. The missile rose high, arcing gracefully. "Kukae," she swore. "However brutal the man is, he is a great athlete. Ane, you're slowing us. Stop. Everyone else pull hard." Hinalea flung her paddle into the sea, her arms and shoulders screaming with the effort. She knew if they were unlucky, the stones would reach them.

Makula saw his rock splash short of his quarry. They were not in killing range yet. He settled back to paddle. The wind was freshening, but he judged that Hinalea would not raise her sail. The westerly breeze would push her vessel away from land. He thought she might try for the beach. He directed his men to work to the inside of her fleeing canoe. He intended to cut them off if she turned in.

An hour passed. The gap narrowed. Makula's paddling became frenetic. He would get them, he vowed. When within seventy-five yards, he yelled, "Pull, pull." He stood, his balance sure. He whirled his sling, every part of his body moving - legs, waist, shoulders, arms, elbows, wrist. On release, he knew the stone would not miss. It slammed into the platform of Hinalea's canoe. A woman screamed.

"The next one will be a paddler," Makula muttered. "Pick them off. Save Hinalea for last." He flung his rock. The canoe veered. The missile smashed into the side of the boat, splintering wood. Makula smiled. They were in killing range. He could not miss.

"We're all going to die," Ane wailed.

"No, we are not," Hinalea said emphatically. "We are coming around a point. I recognize it. Paddle."

Ane seized her stick and plunged it into the water. She screamed when a stone hit and broke part of it. She shoved what was left into the sea.

Another rock struck a servant. The man slumped over, slowing the boat.

Hinalea thought their position hopeless. Makula was picking them off one by one. The man was awesome with his weapon, she thought.

They cleared the point of the bay. Canoes sped toward them. Hinalea recognized Makula's village that Alapai-nui now controlled. She screamed at the approaching vessels, "Makula the traitor is coming."

A rock scored the back of a paddler, drawing blood. Hinalea heard a yell, "I will get you." She did not look back, lest her boat slowed. They moved into the pack of vessels as another stone smashed into a canoe.

When she felt safe, she looked back. Makula was running away.

After landing, Hinalea took the women to property under her control, near a City of Refuge. "You will be safe here. If in danger, flee to the City. The gods protect it. No one will dare harm you."

She had a thatched hut built and provided servants to care for Umiula and her daughter. Satisfied that she had fulfilled her part of the bargain, Hinalea sailed for Kawaihae.

CHAPTER 42

LATE AFTERNOON SUNLIGHT GLOWED ON a calm sea. A light wind sent low combers flecked with white foam swooping onto a beach. With a great effort, Kalani and his musketeers paddled ahead of a building wave. Like the cupped hand of a giant, the cresting water lifted the canoe and hurled it toward shore.

To his left, Kalani caught a fleeting glimpse of a woman surfing, strands of dark hair hiding her face. Before the wave touched shore, he saw her crash into the water.

His double canoe crunched into the sand. Musketeers leaped from their craft and a second wave lifted the vessel, flinging it further onto the beach. Kalani joined his team in pulling the vessel higher onto the shore. His glimpse of the surfer annoyed him. *I know her from somewhere in the past.*

Chief Akaka strode to Kalani. "Good, you are here. Kamehameha needs all the warriors he can get: Keoua is on the march. Have your men unload, then report to the musketeer shack."

Akaka ordered a slave to spread a mat, bring juice, and food. Kalani studied the water in search of the elusive surfer. He spotted her at the point where waves crested. He gestured toward the woman. "Who is that?"

"Princess Lehua, one of the attendants of Queen Kaahumanu. Do you know her?"

"I did once, long ago." He watched the girl catch a wave. "Beautiful," he muttered.

"Yes, my niece is an excellent surfer," Akaka agreed. "Sit down, we need to talk. Great events have happened since we fought on Maui. Keoua controls most of this island and at the moment is advancing toward us. The king of Oahu has allied with the ruler of Kauai, intent on recapturing Maui. Kamehameha has his back to the wall."

Lehua crossed the beach in front of them. Distracted, Kalani fumbled for words before saying, "With our muskets and cannon, we can defeat Keoua and any other enemy who challenges us."

Akaka slapped him on the back. "Good! In the coming tests of power, only the strongest will win, and we have the foreign weapons and Keoua does not."

Kalani watched Lehua moving to the village then begged permission to leave. When Akaka ordered him to stay, he reluctantly settled onto the mat.

"All of us must march forward and defeat Keoua. But we might not annihilate him, only weaken his army. Once Keoua is on the run, we need a lightning force of raiders to attack his rear in Puna and his homeland, Kau."

Startled, Kalani said, "What you propose has not been done before. What does Kamehameha say?"

"I have not suggested it to him, but I know he loves bold moves. That is how he won on Maui, catching the enemy by surprise using daring and aggressive maneuvers." Akaka paused, looking at Kalani. "The raiders would be taking a chance," he added. "They could all be killed. But if they brought Keoua to his knees, the rewards would be great."

His heart thumping, Kalani forgot his interest in Lehua. He studied Akaka, hope building within him.

"I have heard of your brilliant tactics in battle," the chief continued. "Your muskets defeated a very powerful foe. I want you to be the core of my raiding force. Once Keoua is retreating, if we defeat the remnants of his army, Kamehameha will rule this island."

Kalani cast his eyes onto the sand. He felt overwhelmed by the offer. *It might lead to death, since raiders would be driving into the heart of Keoua's country. If we are successful, it could mean promotion to the status of "a black land chief," a feat rarely achieved by a common warrior.*

Puzzled by his silence, Akaka said, "Of course, if you are afraid, I can seek the help of others."

"I will do it!"

They struck fists to seal the bargain. Kalani excused himself and threaded his way through the mass of warriors readying for war. Moki called to him, but Kalani waved him off. His appetite aroused, he sought more interesting fun.

Near the women's compound, he glimpsed the lustrous dark hair, rounded hips, and shapely legs of Lehua disappearing into the eating house. He recalled her father's threats and weighed the punishment for entering the women's area. He restrained his desire. Servants were bringing food to the men's section, so he decided to return to it.

He grabbed a large platter and filled it with shredded pork, sweet potatoes, cooked vegetables, dried salted fish, and poi. He strode to a felled coconut log where he laid the plate onto the grass. Moki joined him, his own platter filled with aromatic food.

Servants bustled about in the open area near the eating-house, clearing the ground, smoothing it out, and laying a large mat in a prominent position. A constable shooed away any warriors who tried to sit on it, and Kalani congratulated himself for picking a good spot to see whatever unfolded that evening.

Two large fires attracted spectators to the festival arena. Men appeared with sharkskin-covered gourds, nose flutes, feather covered rattles, and small whistles. From a distance, a booming drum echoed, blending its sound with the rustling leaves of the palm trees. It boomed again, followed by the haunting call of the conch shell trumpet.

The dense throngs parted, forming a tunnel for the conch shell blower, announcing the arrival of Kamehameha dressed in a golden cape, helmet, and white loincloth. Beside him walked Akaka, tall as the king and similarly dressed. A third man strode with them, the high priest clothed in a white toga and carrying an effigy of the war god Ku.

On each side of the trio came bearers of the royal symbols, the feathered kahili, and behind them other chiefs.

Kalani grimaced when he espied Chief Haewa marching with Kamehameha's entourage. He wondered if Lehua's father continued to reject him as a suitor for his daughter. Deep into these thoughts, he did not see one of the chiefs approaching until Isaac Davis stood beside him. He looked up into the smiling face of his friend.

"I'm glad you have come," the gunner said, embracing the young man. "I've heard wondrous things about your abilities with the musket. Meet me early tomorrow at the royal compound." With many eyes watching, Davis embraced Kalani again and returned to Kamehameha's side.

A nose flute played a haunting tune, joined in by the slapping beat of calabash drums and rhythmic sticks striking coconut shells. Dark male figures clad in white tapa cloth danced into the clearing. They stomped on feet girdled with dog tooth anklets. Their arms, circled with boars' teeth, moved in time to the beat. They swung their hands back and then together. They jumped in unison, stepped to the right, then to the left. They faced each other, mimicking combat. They slapped their hands against their chests, boars' teeth clashing together. Nose flutes reached a high crescendo then wailed away. The men finished their dance and left.

A hush settled over the crowd, disturbed only by the sounds of a crackling fire and the rustle of palm leaves. Barely audible, there came the clicking of rock castanets followed by the loud rattle of pebbles in a gourd. A musician began slapping his hands against a hollow wooden drum, emitting a deep bass sound. A chanter sang. Dozens of women came into view, some with their hands held high, castanets snapping, others holding onto feathered gourds, rattling them in time to the chant.

Kalani became excited at the sight of the scantily clad women, their slim garments barely covering their loins. Then he saw Lehua, the most beautiful of the performers. She twisted her torso in emphatic movements that flung her bodice up and back against her firm breasts, her hips gyrating with provocative movements.

Moki had to restrain him from jumping into the arena and joining in the dance. Lehua swayed her hips with pronounced thrusts and twists. He half rose, but she moved away, disappearing into the midst of the other dancers. Out of the corner of his eye, Kalani saw Haewa scowling. He would have risked incurring his wrath and pursued her except for the presence of Kamehameha. To interrupt the dance would have been a serious breach of protocol.

Excited, Kalani stood and stepped into the darkness, seeking cooler breezes coming from the sea. The dance ended with a thunderous beating of the drums, the arena fell silent, a conch shell blew. Kamehameha stood. "Warriors, Keoua of the Red Cloak has attacked our lands. He has devastated the taro fields, laid waste to the farms, and now he dares to invade the place of my birth, Kohala. The coward has made his conquests over the bodies of old men and children. Keoua has not felt the mighty strength of you, the bravest of the brave. He has not felt the power of our cannon, nor death from our muskets. I say to you that Ku, god of war, is with us. Tomorrow, we go forward to defeat this godless man! Go forward, and win!" Kamehameha took his seat as loud shouts broke loose.

Kalani skirted the crowd, searching where he thought women would be waiting in the shadows for lovers to come. Though several of the dancers played their soft hands over his arms, he ignored their caresses. Someone called his name. His heart tripping, he ran toward waves washing the sand.

Slender footprints led to the water, skirting the edge of the breaking surf. His heart pounded as he followed the steps. In the dim silvery light of the rising moon, a lithe figure raced along the shore. Kalani broke into a lunging run.

The young girl glanced back, teasing him. She raced onto the rocks of a promontory and crawled to the edge. She stood on the end, in a maelstrom of water that blew up, around, and onto her. A path of silver flowed across the sea and Lehua entered it, swimming toward a rising moon.

Kalani slipped over the rocks and into the sea. He fought the bruising surge, the forceful ebb and flow of the ocean until he gained open water. He turned about, searching for the elusive girl. A hand lifted above the sea. Lehua waved and swam around the promontory.

He followed, intent on seizing his prize. Though he searched, he could not find her. After frustrating minutes, he gave up and returned to shore, wondering if what he had seen was only a dream.

With first light, Kalani picked his way between hundreds of sleeping men. In the distance, towering clouds shrouded the massive height of Mauna Kea, portending a coming storm. At the beach, he began his morning exercises. Near him men unloaded nets from canoes and removed fish trapped in the mesh. His workout complete, he selected a half dozen fish and returned to the shack of the musketeers.

While he cooked for his companions, Moki sidled up to him, a slow-breaking smile on his face. "You get her last night?"

"Eat your breakfast," Kalani scowled, shoveling cooked fish onto a platter.

"I did well," Moki jabbed his friend in the shoulder. "You remember the nice round one that gave me the sweet eye?"

"No, I don't," Kalani answered, turning sputtering fish in the fire.

"After the dance, she grabbed me—"

"I don't want to hear your story of last night!" He aimed a weak punch at Moki's shoulder.

His friend scooted away, teasing, "Eh, I know where the girl is."

"Eat!"

Moki sighed, sat down, and bent to his fish. Kalani reached an arm around his neck, "Where is she?"

"Lehua? You will find her at the royal compound."

CHAPTER 43

UNDER A HALA TREE, KALANI stood outside the royal enclosure. He considered his options. Based on the information he had forced from Moki, he had rushed to the area without any clear plan of action. Now that he was here, what should he do?

An answer came when Isaac Davis marched to the compound and walked past two guards at the entrance. Kalani dashed after him, calling his name. Davis motioned to him and ducked into a hale. When Kalani entered the building, a conference was underway.

Akaka stood in the center of a circle of a half-dozen chiefs, his imposing height dominating the room. "Kamehameha is determined to push forward, despite the advice from the high priest to build a temple to Ku." He paused, waiting for his words to sink in.

With a hostile look at Kalani, Haewa said, "Before I speak, I ask: why do we have a person here who is not a chief?"

Nettled by this challenge, Isaac Davis stammered, "I invited—"

"Kalani Moku Tana is here at my request," Akaka interrupted. "He and Chief Davis have an important role to play in the coming battles. Do any of you have objections?" Akaka glared at Haewa, who shook his head.

"However," Haewa said, "I did want to ask why Kamehameha is rushing to attack Keoua, instead of first pleasing the war god by building a temple to him and making proper sacrifices. Failing to please Ku is inviting defeat!"

A long silence ensued. Kalani felt a rippling apprehension building in the room. Unlike the others, he was happy that a place to worship the war god would not be built. Even if it meant his death, he would never attend the consecration of a new temple and watch innocent men sacrificed to an ugly wooden statue.

In a commanding voice, Akaka swept away the tension. "Kamehameha has promised the high priest to build the largest stone structure ever constructed to any god. To make the greatest sacrifices to Ku once it is built. But for now, he must act against the forces of Keoua. His advanced guard is near us. If Kamehameha does not defeat Keoua soon, he will lose *mana.* Those who are undecided might waver and move over to Keoua's side. Kohala will fall, followed by Kona. Kamehameha will be finished."

Before anyone could question him, Akaka continued in a voice rising in pitch. "We outnumber Keoua's approaching soldiers. With the cannon of Isaac Davis and the musketeers of Kalani Moku Tana, we have a decisive edge. Armed with these foreign weapons that deliver death from afar, we will defeat Keoua!" Perspiration streamed down his face, the heat of his emotions permeating the room. As one man, the chiefs vowed to attack. Akaka smiled and asked them to gather their warriors and follow Kamehameha to Waimea.

Haewa walked out with the other chiefs. As he brushed past Kalani, he whispered, "Stay away from my daughter. Your life depends on it!"

Kalani's eyes flashed with anger, but he did not respond to the threat. Silently, he vowed to seduce the princess.

Akaka detained Kalani and Davis. "When will you be ready to leave?"

Kalani answered that he and his men were ready to go at any time. Davis explained that a carriage for the cannon had not been completed. The bad weather would destroy the gunpowder, which must be waterproofed. He did not have sufficient men to move the big guns.

"We need your cannon to win," Akaka said, his normally forceful voice shaky. "A hundred men will report to you. They will carry the cannon on their shoulders, if necessary. We must get the weapons to Waimea."

"Let's not be hasty. Give me time to complete my arrangements. We can leave in two days, maybe sooner."

"All right," Akaka conceded. "I will abide by your timetable, but get to Kamehameha as soon as you can.

"Kalani, you and your musketeers will stay and protect Davis and the cannon. Keoua does not have such weapons. There may be an attempt to capture them." Akaka left.

Alone, Kalani wondered what to do. *Return to the musketeers, give them the news, and resume their training for the coming war? Chief Haewa had threatened me with death. But his daughter Lehua drives me wild with desire. To conquer her would be a dangerous, exciting game.* Hooked by his passion, he decided to try.

Hale and shacks were scattered about. There were so many that he thought his search for her would be fruitless. A few servants scurried among the thatched grass structures, the steady rain hastening their movements. He guessed that those who made their home in the compound were either sheltering from the storm or off to war with Kamehameha.

The rain grew heavier, adding to his misery, cooling his heat. Hunger drove him to search for food. In an empty hut, he discovered yams and bananas. He ate and fell asleep.

"Master, why are you resting in the house of the servants?" a voice prodded him awake. Drowsy, Kalani shoved himself up. A man cringed by his side, eyes fastened to the floor of the shack. He decided to bluster like a high chief. "It is impudent to question me. I seek the Princess Lehua. Where is she?"

The servant stammered, "The princess lives at the hale of Queen Kaahumanu." "Bring me fresh clothes, then take me to her."

With a clean white malo girdling his loins and a toga flung over his shoulder, Kalani followed the servant onto a stone path. It no longer rained, the dark clouds had moved beyond the land and out to sea. Above him, the sky was blue, flecked with streaks of white clouds moving lazily to the west. The late afternoon air felt crisp and cool with a light breeze shimmering the coconut trees in an enclosure ahead of the two men.

The servant travelled along a massive stone wall, its edges softened by tall, slender ti plants, their broad green and yellow leaves adding color to the bleakness of the lava rock. The path brought them to an opening in the wall that led to a glade of coconut trees. Among the trees sat two large buildings, sides open to the air. A pond lay next to the structures. Kalani knew that it stored fresh fish for the use of those who lived in this royal enclosure. Beyond the pond, ocean waves pounded against a wall of stone designed to keep the fish sealed in while allowing fresh seawater and nutrients to sweep into the pond though an intricately designed passageway.

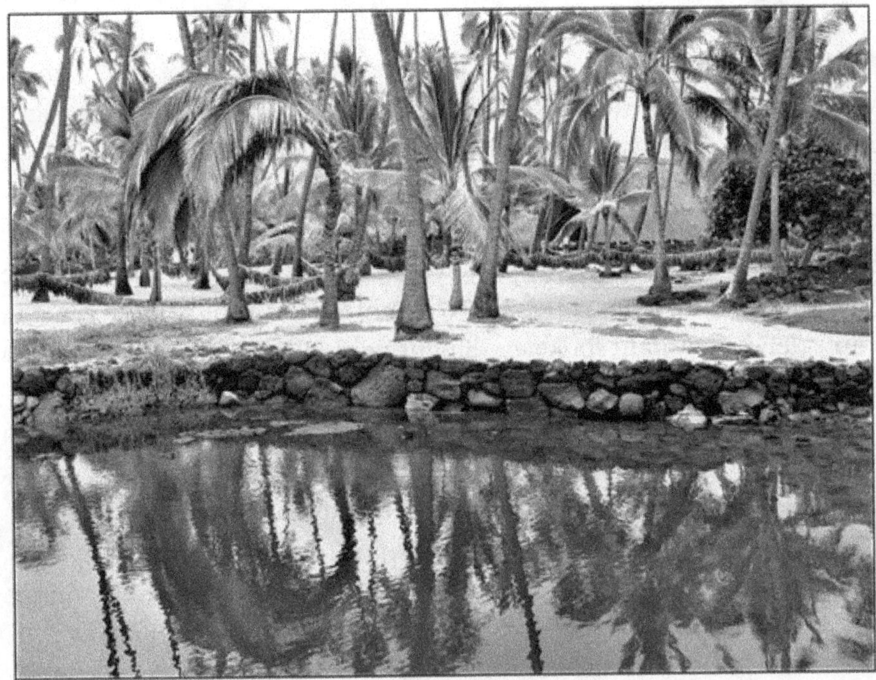

Fishpond

He dismissed the servant, and strode to the largest of the buildings, its front marked by the royal kahili set into stanchions fixed in the dirt. Women worked within it, some beating mulberry into cloth, others dyeing the beaten cloth yellow with juice from the olena plant. An old woman with a wreath of green leaves girdling her hair sat by a long board overlaid by a yellow cloth. She printed a carved pattern on it, using a wooden block smeared with black ink brewed from the soot of kukui nuts.

A younger woman, with a whale-toothed necklace resting between her breasts, supervised the workers. A garment of red-and-yellow-patterned cloth covered her body, enhancing her beauty. Kalani recognized Kaahumanu, the favorite wife of Kamehameha, and walked to her. He lowered himself to the ground, lest his shadow touch her. "Oh, revered Queen, we met when we fought together to defeat the warriors of the king of Maui."

"Raise yourself so I may see your face. You need not worry about taboo in my presence." Recognizing him, Kaahumanu exchanged breath in the traditional way before demanding an explanation for his presence.

"Revered Queen, I and my musketeers are assigned to guard the cannon. The movement of the gun to Waimea is delayed. Would you be traveling to join Kamehameha? We can offer you protection to ensure your safety." As Kalani spoke, he caught sight of Lehua scraping strips of bark from a mulberry sapling.

"Your offer is most welcome," Kaahumanu smiled, taking his arm and dragging him away from the area where Lehua worked. "I was planning to leave tomorrow. Will Davis be ready to go then?"

He saw Lehua rise and vanish into a grove of mulberry saplings. Distracted by her hurried departure, he did not answer. Kaahumanu switched a royal kahili against his shoulder. "Can you go tomorrow?"

"Maybe. I need to check with Isaac Davis."

"Do so and advise me of your plans in the morning." Kaahumanu dismissed him and disappeared behind a red tapa cloth hanging over a long pole. Kalani rushed to the grove of mulberry plants, forcing his way into them. Laughter goaded him. He thrashed through the thicket, emerging by a low stone wall. Beyond it was a hard-packed sand area filled with statues of grimacing gods. A wooden structure with two platforms dominated a City of Refuge.

City of Refuge

Set in the midst of the statues stood an altar covered with cloth. He felt the oppressive, sinister atmosphere of the place that reminded him of the many sacrifices made to the god Ku. He rubbed his eyes, as if this would erase memories from the past.

An evening breeze rustled the leaves, chilling his body, damping the heat that had driven him to pursue Lehua. He knew she hid among the icons to test his courage, challenging him to overcome his fear of the gods. Then he saw her kneeling, her face lifted towards the altar of Kane, her lips murmuring prayers.

Lehua was easy prey for his passion. Yet Kalani knew that the gods and the bones of long dead chiefs buried beneath the sand threw a protective mantle about her.

The temple was blessed with the power of their collective mana. To trespass with the intent of seducing the woman seeking refuge within would be a sacrilege warranting death. He slipped back into the bush, angered that, once again, Lehua eluded him.

CHAPTER 44

WAVES SPREAD WIDE ONTO THE shore, white foam flecking the edges of the footprints made by Kalani's musketeers. An hour before first light, the frustrated young man had roused his troops and ordered them to drill.

Moki ran alongside him, grousing, "What's the matter? No loving last night?"

He ignored the jibe. Instead he picked up the pace, commanding the stumbling men to run faster. After another hour of drilling, they returned to the compound where he ordered the musketeers to eat and prepare to march.

While his soldiers prepared to leave, he sought Isaac Davis. When he found him fussing over his cannon, Kalani said, "Kaahumanu wants our protection on the road to Waimea."

"If the queen is going to join us, best tell her majesty that we leave no later than mid-morning. To tell the truth, I'm not keen on shepherding womenfolk when we're heading for war. But she asked for our protection, so I can't deny her."

Kalani bit his tongue, not wanting Davis to know that it was he, not Kaahumanu, who had come up with the idea of protection. He raced to the royal compound, where he found the queen supervising slaves as they packed.

"It will be mid-afternoon before we can leave," Kaahumanu said. "Will you wait?"

"Davis is anxious to go, but our progress will be slow. Come when you can. If you do not catch up with the wagons by evening, I will fall back and find you."

Though he searched for Lehua, he did not see her. He left the royal compound downhearted, hoping she would be part of the queen's traveling party.

Mauna Kea

It is all ugly, Kalani thought as he trudged beside the wagons containing gunpowder and cannons. The ground around him lay covered with water-starved shrubs struggling to reach for the sun. Their roots clung to cracks or crevices in a massive old lava field beneath Mauna Kea. Weather-beaten black rocks lay scattered in mounds and ridges across the land. Spiky tufts of yellow pili grass flattened by the wind poked through sand-colored dirt. These were hardy plants, deep rooted, turning green on the first rainfall after long, dry days. Kalani missed the sounds of the sea: crashing waves, screeching birds, howling wind. The ocean lay to the north, hidden by the low Kohala Mountains.

The ground sloped upward. The air became thinner. The yoked humans pulling the wagons gasped and stumbled as they strained to climb the dirt trail leading to Waimea.

Davis walked at Kalani's side. "This is the easy part," he panted, sucking in and blowing out breath like a bellows. "There are twelve miles of good ground between Kawaihae and Waimea. But should Keoua retreat into Hamakua, we will face gullies, valleys, and streams making it almost impossible for our men to haul the guns overland. Kamehameha believes these wonder weapons will win him battles, but they take time to set up and are vulnerable to surprise attacks."

"With my twelve muskets and John Young's men, we can destroy any attackers before they damage your big guns," Kalani boasted.

"I pray that will be so. Let's move on before the wagons get too far ahead."

Kalani stood transfixed, searching the roadway to the west.

"Looking for Kaahumanu?" Davis asked. "You can depend on queens never to show up on time. They travel with a lot of complaints." He gave a knowing wink. "Come on, let's hurry and catch up."

Blazing fire red, the sun descended over the horizon. Kalani spotted a group of travelers a mile to the rear. While Davis's warriors and wagons went into bivouac, he grabbed a cake of dried poi and a stick of fish, and raced back along the road. Within minutes, he found Lehua walking with the queen, chatting about hair and the right combs to use. When she saw him, she flashed a momentary smile, teasing him by pursing her lips in a kiss. He stepped to her side, taking hold of her arm while acknowledging the queen's greeting with a deferential nod.

It was dark when Kaahumanu's group finally reached the bonfires of Davis's soldiers. Mats were laid out and temporary shelters built. The women were curious about Kamehameha's weapons that could destroy an enemy from afar. "You defeated the traitor in Kona," Kaahumanu said. "Tell us how."

Kalani saw Lehua join a circle of women. He decided to enthrall her. "Makula plotted with Keoua and Hauna to seize Kona. He gathered an army. Hauna sailed from Puna with a thousand warriors. Alapai-nui came to me, worried. 'What shall we do?'"

Lehua was transfixed. Her eyes widened. "I said to our chief, 'Let us attack before Hauna comes. With my fire weapons and my plan, we might defeat the overwhelming forces of Makula.'" There was silence at the bonfires. Kalani saw Lehua, her mouth gaping wide.

"We came to the enemy village, outnumbered two to one." Women gasped. "Makula thought himself safe across a stream, impossible to cross. His warriors lined the banks, boasting, insulting us with their taunts, daring us to come over. Their spears leveled to kill us as we entered the stream." Kalani paused, watching the effect of his words. The queen leaned forward, an intent look on her face. Beside her, Lehua swayed back and forth on her knees.

"I showed them how Americans fought in their Revolution. Behind shelters, we fired our muskets. Rows of Makula's warriors fell. We fired again and again. The stream ran red. Corpses lined the bank. I hit Makula's head with a bullet. He ran. His army ran with him."

Lehua clapped her hands. "You're my hero," she shouted.

"What of Hauna?" Kaahumanu asked.

"When he came with his thousand, I challenged him to combat. He saw Makula's army destroyed and fled to Keoua."

With an intensity he had never seen, Lehua came to him. "You should have killed that evil man for rebelling against Kamehameha." She took a feather lei nestled in her hair and placed it on Kalani's head. Their bodies touched. She whispered, "You are my hero." Then she stepped back, studying him as if seeing him for the first time.

He finished his story with a flourish. "With these new weapons, we will destroy Keoua and his army!" Women clucked their agreement, their faces wreathed with smiles. Kaahumanu screamed, "Keoua is doomed!" The others picked up her cry, "Keoua is doomed!"

Lehua whispered, "Keoua is doomed." She swayed her body into his, her breasts heaving. She raised her face, eyes shining, lips murmuring, "I want you."

For only a moment, Kalani thought of her father's warning. His yearning for the elusive girl blew caution way. Excited by the perfume of her hair, the sensuous movements of her hands, he edged her toward the shadows, seeking a comfortable place to fulfill their love.

CHAPTER 45

THEY CAME AT DAWN, RAIDERS moving along the Waimea Road. Their whispers and pounding feet roused Kalani. Disturbed by his movements, Lehua stirred, reaching her hand over his chest, and snuggling her bare flesh closer to his.

In a depression of soft grasses next to a low rock ridge which concealed him from casual view, Kalani peered over scrub-filled rock. He saw men silhouetted by the weak light of a rising sun, moving in the direction of Davis' campsite.

He yelled, "Wake up! Wake up! Death is coming!" He whirled his sling, flinging stones at the raiders. The attackers slowed their rush, searching. A missile struck a man, bringing him down, another one screamed in pain. Kalani pulled Lehua up and said, "Let's get out of here!"

A detachment pursued the naked couple. The rest of the raiders struck Davis' camp, which was unprepared for the onslaught.

Over rock-strewn ground the lovers ran, a trio of Keoua's men close behind. Though Kalani was swift, Lehua ran faster and reached Kaahumanu's sleeping area before him. She rushed about, rousing people.

Kalani heard a yell, "Hit him." A warrior threw a spear. He snatched it and faced his opponents. Two men stopped, leveling weapons. A third pulled a knife from his loincloth and circled.

"Here is death," Kalani shouted, thrusting his weapon at the two opponents. They stepped back, avoiding his feint. He pivoted and charged the third warrior, hurling his sharp stick into his belly. The man gasped, dropped his knife, and wobbled as he sank to the ground. Kalani jerked at the haft of the embedded spear, pulling the dying man toward him, then swung him stumbling into the remaining warriors.

Without pausing, Kalani ran into Kaahumanu's camp, searching for another weapon. Guardians of the queen came to him, spears poised, ready to strike the enemy. In their midst, he watched his pursuers run, leaving their companion to thrash about, the spear in his body furrowing the ground around him.

Kaahumanu walked to her guards, glanced at the dying man. Then she studied the lean youth, appraising his rippling muscles. Kalani thought he saw a glint of lust in her eyes, but she suggested nothing. Instead, she said to one of her women, "Bring this boy some clothes. When you are dressed, go with my men and help Davis."

Once he received cloth to wear, Kalani ordered the queen's guard into a wedge, and hurried to the main camp. He found chaos, wounded and dead warriors littered the ground, friend and foe intermixed.

Loud shouts came from the bivouac area of the cannon. Kalani urged his small force toward it. Three men loomed ahead. Kalani ordered a charge. The sudden attack brought the enemy soldiers down.

"Help!" Davis screamed.

"Go toward the voice," Kalani ordered.

A grotesquely painted warrior barred his way, swinging a knotted club. Kalani dodged. His spear slashed the man's arm. An elbow smashed Kalani's jaw, knocking him to the ground. Blood blinded him. He glimpsed a cudgel descending. A scream. A body fell onto him. Moki peered, "Brother, are you okay?"

A loud voice yelled, "Retreat! Retreat!"

Dazed, Kalani saw warriors running away. Moki kneeled by him and said, "Stay still while I pull this body away."

When Kalani stood, he spied Isaac Davis standing near his men. He hobbled to him. The white chief gripped his arm. "If someone hadn't sounded the alarm, we would all be dead. Was it you?"

Kalani nodded.

It took most of the morning to sort out the camp. Dozens of men on both sides were dead or wounded. After burials were completed, Davis called a council of war.

"We need to get word to Kamehameha to come to our aid."

"I say we push on and try to make it to Waimea before nightfall," a warrior said.

"An unwise move," Kaahumanu objected.

"Why so, my Queen?" Davis asked. He had tried to keep the headstrong royal away from the discussion.

"Because you do not have enough men to move the guns and still defend it from attack."

"But if we remain here and help does not come, we will be overwhelmed in the night," Kalani said.

"If we stay, we die, if we go, we die." Davis shook his head in despair.

"We cannot sit here and do nothing!" the queen exploded. "Davis, send two of your fastest runners to Waimea. Assign the men you need to move the guns and powder. Kamehameha must have them. Those not necessary to drag the cannon will arm themselves for defense. We march for Waimea."

Kaahumanu closed the meeting with a flourish, ordering Davis and Young to take the point with four musketeers. She and her women would be in support. Three dozen men hauled the cannon, powder, and the wagons of Davis's wounded soldiers. Injured enemies were killed.

Kalani and a half-dozen musketeers became the rear guard. He watched Moki and Lehua race for Waimea. They had no weapons, relying on speed to accomplish their mission. "If anyone can make it, she will," he muttered.

The column trudged uphill. Kaahumanu and her women, their hair knotted, loins girded with layers of cloth containing knives, small clubs, tripping cords, slings, pouches of stones and other weapons, marched in two columns on each side of the wagons.

By noon, the small army straggled, heavy guns slowed by the rutted, rock-strewn road. Kalani trotted to the queen. "Majesty, what can I do to help?"

Kaahumanu stared at him, a hint of anger in her voice. "Do not repeat the same mistake you made at Halehaku. Back to your post, now! Women," she bellowed, "yoke to the guns and pull."

"A true *pikoi*," Kalani said as he returned to the van.

The terrain for miles was featureless except for shallow depressions where small forces could hide. In disarray, the train inched closer to the safety of Waimea. Fearful of attack, Kalani hurried to Davis. "Should we stop and close up?" he asked.

"No, I think if the enemy comes, it will be either from front, rear, or both. Go back."

Davis proved wrong. Enemy warriors came over a low ridge, heading straight for the disorganized center of the column and the guns. Women stopped pulling. Armed with spears and stones, they hurled their missiles. Davis, Young, and some musketeers formed up and fired.

"Shall we help?" one of Kalani's men asked.

"It may be a feint. This is our army's only reserve. All of you stand fast."

As quick as they came, the enemy withdrew. Kaahumanu yelled, "Move the wagons."

Kalani slowed his musketeers, placing them into a fire line. He loosened his sling, removed several stones from his pouch, dropped back, and scanned the tufts of low scrub and thin ridges of rock. From hidden positions, enemy soldiers leaped out. He flung three missiles in rapid succession. A warrior screamed, flinging his hands to his face. A dozen more continued their charge.

Kalani ran to his men, seized his musket, and yelled, "Fire!"

The volley brought down four of the attackers. The charge faltered, the remaining enemy staring at their fallen companions. The afternoon sun burnt hot, birds wheeled in the sky cawing. "Evil birds," Kalani said, "preparing to feast on the dead." The line of musketeers stood silent.

A tattooed man pulled back his spear. Kalani shot him. The surviving enemy fled.

Davis ordered the column to form up and keep moving. Then he saw a cloud of dust descending the Waimea road. Kalani studied the advancing men. He cheered, "It's Moki and Akaka."

By late afternoon, the group entered Waimea. Akaka urged Davis and Young to keep moving and catch up with Kamehameha. Kalani asked about Lehua. Akaka smiled. "She was the first to run into Waimea and raise the alarm. At the moment, she is resting in the royal compound."

Desperate to see her, Kalani sought to delay his departure, begging Davis for time to rest and heal his wounds. "Let me wait until tomorrow. Moki and I can easily catch up with you."

Grudgingly, the gunner agreed. He and Young began trekking east with a reconstituted force of warriors.

As Kalani watched them go, a servant came, delivering a message: "Come when dark." Beaming with anticipation, he strutted towards the men's sector, noticing Kaahumanu near its entrance, her eyes fastened on the handsome Akaka. They made visual contact. Akaka nodded, and entered the eating house.

Kalani watched the chief wolf down his meal and leave. Kalani finished his supper and rose. Moki grabbed him, insisting that he remain to drink and swap stories of the battles just fought. He tarried for some moments to please his friend. Kalani worried that Lehua would not wait for him. Impatient, he ended the conversation and rose again. "I need to check supplies."

Moki wagged a finger at him. "I think you should know something before you go."

"Keep it until tomorrow," Kalani grumbled.

"No, you must hear it tonight, before you see the princess. Your life depends on it."

Assuming a nonchalance betrayed by a tremor in his hand, Kalani answered, "What makes you think I'm off to see the princess?"

"You think that no one watched you last night? You tell those hero stories. You think that nobody saw you take Lehua into the dark? You are playing with forbidden stuff."

"What do you mean, forbidden?"

"You are my friend, so I will tell you. Lehua's father has promised her to Kamehameha. She is to be wife number six."

Kalani's legs buckled, and he fell onto the eating mat. "How do you know this?" "Isaac Davis told me. He watched you last night. He knew you are in big trouble."

"What does Davis want me to do?"

"Break it off, while you are still alive."

Hanging above the great volcano, the moon shone on the drab landscape of Waimea. Filled with gloomy thoughts, Kalani debated what to do. His youthful eagerness had caused him to throw caution away to win the elusive princess. He hovered outside the royal enclosure, undecided. *Should he seek the forbidden woman or slink away and save his life?*

Torn by indecision, he was startled when he saw Kaahumanu leave the compound, walking toward a copse of trees. Curious, Kalani followed her until she reached its edge. Akaka stepped out into the moonlight. He took the queen into his arms. They clung together for many moments, until Akaka broke their embrace and drew Kaahumanu into the woods.

Their actions decided him. "If Kamehameha's favorite wife can enjoy forbidden love, why shouldn't I?"

CHAPTER 46

RAIN POURED FROM LOW-HANGING CLOUDS, filling the pock-marked ground with pools of water that flowed over sharp lava rock into a stream roaring downhill. Cold wind swooped around Kalani's head adding to his misery.

He wiped water from his face. His men huddled naked under the slight protection of a koa forest. Nearby, teams of men yoked to wagons of guns and ammunition stood waiting. Although layers of cloth covered the ordinance, he worried whether they would remain dry. The downpour showed no sign of weakening.

Isaac Davis scurried through the falling drops, his eyes darting. He slithered into a mud pond and pointed to the stream, "Kamehameha wants the guns moved across. Keoua and his army have stopped their retreat and are assembling ahead of us about a mile to the east."

"It is impossible to cross while it is raging toward the sea," Kalani objected.

"Kamehameha needs a victory. He has been battling Keoua for eight years and only controls a third of this island. Keoua has stopped. He faces defeat if we can get the guns across."

"Is it worth the risk?"

"You are wise for a beardless young man," Davis smiled. "Young and I agree that it would be foolish to cross while the stream is running like a rogue river. Be prepared to move when we judge it safe."

Kalani nodded in agreement. *We have come too far over harsh terrain to throw away our great advantage in battle.* He prayed that Keoua would wait and not continue his flight.

Within minutes the torrential rain stopped. Within an hour the rapidly flowing stream moderated its flow. Davis ordered the cannon across it. After a huge effort the ordinance and wagons crossed on a makeshift bridge. Once assembled Young directed the artillery train to bivouac within some woods adjacent to open terrain that sloped toward the sea.

On top of a mound, Kalani studied an ideal battlefield, a broad flat plain that descended from a grove of coconut trees to the edge of cliffs that fell hundreds of feet into the sea. Keoua had concentrated his army at the lowest part of the grade.

By Kalani's side Davis giggled, "Kamehameha will be attacking from higher ground. Our cannon will have the advantage of plunging fire. We'll shred them tomorrow."

Campfire smoke whirled into a blue sky. The storm that had slowed the advance of the army moved west, leaving clean, crisp air with a promise of good weather. "Tomorrow will be a great day," Kalani said, surveying his men munching an evening meal of fish and poi cakes mixed with water. "These warriors are raw, without experience in battle. Despite this, you and Young have trained them well."

"We have tried," Davis sighed, "but it is hard to teach naked, barefoot farmers." The gunner shrugged and limped away.

"The men are brave," Kalani called after him.

Troubled by Davis' words, he did not hear Moki's footsteps until his wiry friend nudged him with his shoulder. "What are you thinking about, lover boy? The sweetheart you left in Waimea? Was her loving worth your life?"

"What are you talking about?" Kalani demanded, shaken by the threat.

"You are like a kid. You think everyone is blind. No one sees what you do? You think Chief Haewa doesn't have spies in Waimea?" When Kalani did not answer, Moki looked at his friend, a great sadness on his face. "I knew you were hard-headed, but I didn't think you stupid—"

"Don't call me stupid!" Kalani jabbed a finger into Moki's chest.

"What do you call it," Moki yelled, "when I tell you to stay away from a girl promised to Kamehameha. You ignore my warning. You satisfy your body instead of using your head, which you are going to lose."

Sobered by the threat, Kalani scolded himself for trysting with Lehua in Waimea. He had taken advantage of her naiveté, her hero worship, enjoying what her father had forbidden. She had proved to be wild, exciting, kindling a spark within him that demanded satisfaction. Now he must pay for his surrender to passion.

"Who will order my death? Kamehameha? Haewa?" Kalani choked on the names, his dreams of glory erased, his mother forced into servitude, all because of a foolish act that had provided him brief moments of happiness.

Moki shook his head. "I don't know who will kill you."

Kalani croaked, "When?"

"The guy who told me didn't know. Maybe it will come during the battle. Every wound looks the same, enemy or friend. Watch the back, little roach. It would be sad if our friendship ends tomorrow."

Moki's news was not the only shock Kalani received that evening. The next one came when he finished his dinner of half-cooked sweet potatoes, washed down by gulps of water. Wiping his palm across his lips, a shadow created by a bonfire crossed his face. He leaped into a fighting stance, startled by the apparition.

"My, you are a jumpy young man," Akaka scolded. "Have you already heard the news I bring you?"

"I didn't mean to offend you," Kalani stammered. "Are you here to punish me for my foolish act that has angered Kamehameha?"

"You have angered Kamehameha?"

The guilt-ridden youth did not hear the question in Akaka's voice. Without thinking, he confessed to his romantic adventures with Lehua. When he finished his garbled version of his love affair, he begged Akaka to seek Kamehameha's forgiveness.

The man and the boy studied each other for many moments. Akaka stood impassive, his face revealing nothing. Contrite, Kalani dropped his eyes, accepting what he perceived to be the older man's condemnation.

Akaka tousled his hair. "I knew when you watched my niece surf at Kawaihae that you wanted her. Could I have stopped you? Yes, by sending you away, but then I would have lost a great warrior. Will Kamehameha condemn you? No, he will not. He wants his wives to have experience in love before they marry him, so they are more exciting. Only his number one wife must be unsullied by any man. She must be a virgin, having a higher caste than all others, for it is she who will produce the royal children when he is king. That young girl has been selected and is now safe in Kona, waiting until she is old enough to marry him. No, it is not Kamehameha that you must fear, but Haewa, who has high aspirations for his daughter."

"Are you angry with me for making love to Lehua?"

Akaka smiled, "Why should I be? You did not force her, she wanted you. No, making love is a normal act to be enjoyed by all those who desire each other."

Confused by this approval of his actions, and chagrined that he had revealed so much, he said, "If you did not come to punish me for what I did with your niece, why do you seek me out?"

Akaka paused, studying the handsome boy. He noted the dark hair that spread around the sides of his face, the peach fuzz of youth turning to black whiskers. The young man's body was well proportioned, the muscles supple, rippling with hidden strength. At eighteen years of age, Kalani looked like a grown man. Yet from his defiance of Haewa and his foolish confession, Akaka knew the youth to be governed by emotions and prone to foolish mistakes.

"You must not take what I say as a reflection on your bravery, or that Kamehameha and I think you a coward."

"A coward! Why would you think of me as a coward?"

Akaka sighed and said, "I know you are not a coward. But it is Kamehameha's intention to go into battle tomorrow, without all the preliminary boasting, insults, and challenges to individual combat. He wants to hit Keoua hard with the cannon and muskets."

Puzzled, Kalani asked, "What has that preliminary stuff got to do with thinking me a coward?"

"Your nemesis, Hauna, chief of Puna, is with Keoua's army. He has challenged you to individual combat tomorrow, claiming that you are a coward. He says that if you do not fight him, then it proves to everyone that you cheated in the test of honor."

Agitated by the challenge, Kalani paced about, shaking his fists in the air, shouting, "Coward! Hauna is the coward. He is the cheater. I beat him once and I will beat him again." Blinded by his emotions, he failed to note Akaka's disapproval until the chief seized him by the shoulders, arresting his wild ravings.

Akaka shook the high-strung young man. "You will not fight Hauna. Your duty is to protect the guns and obey Isaac Davis."

Wrestling away from Akaka's grasp, Kalani kicked the ground, raising a cloud of dust. "I'm not a coward."

"Now you understand why I am here. I had to find you before you heard of Hauna's challenge from someone else. The high chief and I know that you are unafraid and would fight Hauna, but your personal vendetta could ruin Kamehameha's plans for victory. Will you obey my command and ignore Hauna's challenge?"

Kalani sulked, his pride hurt that he could not fight his enemy. He realized that if he permitted his ego to control him, he would never achieve his goal: to be recognized by Kamehameha as worthy of the status of chief. "I promise to do what you ask."

"Good." A broad smile broke across Akaka's face. "I'll see you in the morning."

When he bedded down for the night, Kalani thought*: Nothing worse could happen to his life besides Haewa and Hauna wanting him dead.*

"You filthy pig," a harsh voice hissed in his ear, forcing him awake. Kalani tried to lift his head, but a sharp knife scored his throat.

"Don't move, you bastard, or you're a dead man," the grim voice warned.

Kalani froze. Was it an assassin sent by Haewa or Hauna? But that was not the code of the warrior, resolving vendettas in the dark. Real warriors fought in the openness of day, for all to see. Only a coward struck at night. He peered into the dark, trying to conjure the face of the cloaked figure hovering over him. The knife pressed harder into his flesh, causing blood to seep from a shallow wound at his throat. If he moved, he knew his life would be sliced away.

"Who are you?"

"Someone who hates you," the figure hissed. "I, who have given you so much, look how you repay me."

Despite the harshness in the voice, he knew that a woman held a knife to his throat. But who? Was it Lehua seeking vengeance for stealing her innocence? No, it could not be her. "Who are you?"

"You see, I knew it," came the answer. "All men are the same, forgetting so soon the woman who loves you. Tasks were given for me to perform. I did them. I saved your mother and sister from poverty. Brought them safely to Kona. How do you repay me? By making love to another! You are wicked and shall die for your sins."

"Hinalea," he whispered earnestly. "Why are you doing this? I am not guilty of any wrongdoing."

She seized his hair, stretching his neck back like a chicken about to be sliced. "Are you saying the stories I heard in Waimea are untrue? You did not seduce the princess? Oh, I listened to the horrid tales of your wickedness."

"All untrue, I love only you." Kalani lied, desperation in his voice.

"Only me," Hinalea purred.

"Yes, I love only you," Kalani lied again.

"Good, because I also love only you," Hinalea whispered, releasing his hair and removing the knife from his neck. She kissed away the blood from his throat, smothering his face, his body with her passion. He allowed her desire to consume him, relieved that it was a jealous woman who had threatened his life and not his enemies.

Morning came and Hinalea refused to leave the battlefield. "I will stay with you. Help you in the fight. Fetch water, food, supplies."

Keoua's army formed at the low end of the sloping plain. Chiefs resplendent in capes and feathered helmets swaggered from the main body to taunt and insult the men of Kamehameha. Prominent among them was Hauna, who bellowed, "Kalani is a coward. A cheat. The son of a kauwa. He is afraid to face me in individual combat."

Kalani ignored the ranting, joining his musketeers with Young and his men. The combined group marched forward, deploying in two ragged lines ahead of Kamehameha's army. Isaac Davis pushed a brass cannon and a culverin to the edge of a coconut grove.

"Present arms. Fire!" Young ordered. The volley felled several enemy warriors.

"Fall back!"

In good order, the musketeers retreated, aligning themselves alongside the cannon. Isaac Davis fired his two guns. Grape-shot shredded the enemy ranks, ripping holes in Keoua's crescent-shaped line. Davis reloaded and fired again. With his second round of grape, the enemy ran, large gaps appearing in what had once been a battle line packed with warriors.

Davis howled, "We got them! Look at them go." His glee faded as he saw his gunners standing by the cannon. "What's going on?"

"We need powder," Kalani answered.

"I'll run and get powder," Hinalea said, racing uphill toward a distant line of men marching to the battle.

A phalanx of soldiers, led by Hauna, broke through Keoua's disintegrating front line. Young's musketeers fired a volley, but it did not stop the new attackers. They kept coming.

"I'm out of ammunition," Moki cried. "This gun is useless."

"What stupidity! We're winning the battle and somebody forgot the powder for our weapons. Moki, grab spears!" Kalani ordered.

He seized a weapon and, with his friend, moved forward to meet the enemy attack. To his disgust, the remaining musketeers retreated, refusing to fight the enemy swarming into the coco grove.

On the other side of the trees, Kamehameha and Akaka battled hand-to-hand with three enemy chiefs. Other warriors, Haewa among them, rushed to help Davis, who had abandoned the cannon.

"They're taking the brass gun," Moki screamed.

"Get 'em," Kalani yelled, charging into a knot of men harnessing the cannon. Two warriors met his attack. One was brought down by Moki while Kalani sidestepped and ripped open the second man with the point of his spear.

Beyond the melee swirling around the cannon, Hauna screamed, "You are mine, coward."

Warned, Kalani struck away the missile that Hauna threw. But failure did not discourage his enemy who charged, a knife in his hand. A warrior stepped in and Hauna slashed at him. He did not score a hit. The two men grappled, wrestling each other to the ground.

"My God! Oh my God!" Davis screamed. "They're hauling my guns away."

Setting aside his personal vendetta, Kalani attacked the raiders. Other warriors of Kamehameha came to his aid, Haewa in their midst. It was close combat, clubs and knives striking and stabbing. Friend and foe blended together, standing toe-to-toe as they dodged, parried, seeking in any way to kill each other.

A hand snaked out of the melee, thrusting a knife. Unaware of the sneak attack, Kalani stepped away to avoid a blow from an opponent's club.

"Behind you!" someone shrieked.

Kalani twisted and saw Haewa.

"Die," the chief snarled, jabbing his dagger at Kalani's heart.

"No!" Hinalea cried, throwing herself into Lehua's father, swinging her knife into his gut. They fell against each other, mortally wounded.

Kalani choked, shocked by Hinalea's sacrifice. He pulled her from Haewa's grasp, a dagger sticking in her belly. When he drew the weapon out, Hinalea gasped. She looked at him, lips quivering, eyes shining.

Kalani leaned, trying to capture her words. "I love you," Hinalea whispered. Her eyes shone for a moment, glazed, then closed forever.

Kalani wanted to shout, but words would not come. His chest heaved. Guilt wracked him. His mind raced, pounding his skull. *I had lied. I repaid her love with lies. I caused these deaths by my lust for Lehua.*

Hauna screamed. Kalani saw him coming. He held Hinalea to his heart, her blood flowing over him. Death would end his pain.

A club struck the berserk man. Hauna staggered, falling to the ground. Kalani watched warriors pick up his enemy and drag him to Keoua's battle line. Raiders turned the great brass cannon. Akaka yelled, "Musketeers, we have gunpowder. Load your weapons."

Moki came. "Plenty danger, brother."

"Let me be," Kalani said.

"Brother, we have to get out of here. Those guys are aiming the cannon at us."

Moki pulled Kalani up, Hinalea cradled in his arms. Kalani's tears washed away the grime on her cheeks as he nuzzled her flesh. Thirty yards away, the muzzle of the cannon gaped. Keoua's men pranced around it. One of them lit a fire and put it to the touch hole.

"Shoot!" Young screamed. Muskets barked. Warriors fell. Moki laughed. "A stupid man. No powder in the gun."

Kamehameha attacked, recaptured his cannon, and drove the raiders from the coconut grove. Keoua withdrew from the battlefield.

Exhausted by many days of marching and the rigors of battle, Kamehameha's army was unable to complete the victory by pursuing a defeated enemy. Dead were buried, the wounded enemy sacrificed. Kamehameha returned to Kawaihae, vowing to build the most awesome temple ever dedicated to the god Ku.

Moki gave Hinalea's knife to Kalani, muttering, "Best thing is to let everyone think Haewa died a hero, fighting to save the gun." Kalani accepted his wisdom. He carried Hinalea from the battlefield.

He would bury her in the Hawaiian way.

CHAPTER 47

THIN SLIVERS OF LIGHT PIERCED the darkness of the hale. Kalani stared at the pili grass covering the bamboo frame of the building. He thanked the gods for the builders who made this house leak-free. Rain had pelted Waipio Valley during the night, adding to the miserable evening he spent with the two surviving sons of the high chief of Hilo.

Hot heads. They wanted to charge into the city and kill Keoua. An argument raged into the late hours of the night. "We are too few," Kalani protested. "Blind attacks mean defeat. We must get allies before we challenge the King of Kau."

Reasonable proposals had fallen on ears unable to hear due to the brain-numbing news of death by mutilation. Revenge burned in the innards of the sons of the high chief, knowing their father's heart, kidneys, and liver had been torn from his body, eaten by Keoua and his minions for their mana.

Hours of argument failed to still the passions of the young men. Only Kalani's threat to pull out his musketeers quieted their anger.

Relieved that his desperate arm-twisting had convinced the hot heads to make a stealthy entry into Hilo, they struck Kalani's heart with their final request. Pain deadlier than the vicious bite of the brown eel jolted him when they demanded sacrifice to Ku.

"Impossible!" Kalani said, *the memory of Minato's death blazing in his voice, his eyes.*

"Why impossible?" Eleele, the elder son of the dead chief, demanded. "Kamehameha ignored the warning that he must make human sacrifices to Ku before fighting Keoua and what happened? He did not defeat him. Now he has sixteen thousand men building the greatest temple ever dedicated to the war god. Plenty of sacrifices will be made before he fights the King of Kau again."

"That may be, but we don't have thousands of slaves here in Waipio to sacrifice," Kalani answered, suppressing his anger, trying to reason with the older man.

"Why not take some of the farmers living here in this valley?"

"That's foolishness. Keoua killed many when he invaded Waipio. If we kill more, the survivors will hate us. It will cost us a supply base when we fight in Hilo."

"I think you are a coward," Eleele challenged. "You can't stand the sight of blood."

"You are stupid. All you want is to kill, and stomp anyone who stands in your way. Your mouth is bigger than your courage."

Eleele stared at Kalani, his eyes knifing into him. "You think I have no courage? Let us see who the coward is. Tomorrow morning, an hour after sunup, we fight knuckle to knuckle. The winner will choose who will be sacrificed."

Fighting to control himself, Kalani held his tongue. *My foolish words had already destroyed any chance to succeed in the venture to attack Hilo. Without the help of the sons of the dead high chief, how could I find allies?* His thoughts were interrupted by renewed challenges.

"Scared, huh? You can always say you're a coward and let me choose those to sacrifice. Maybe even you?"

"I will be at the water's edge an hour after sunup."

Kalani's skin glimmered in the early morning, sleek from the coconut oil he had rubbed over his body. "What are you going to do, little roach? Escape by climbing a tree?" Moki said, nudging Kalani with his elbow, then dodging a halfhearted punch. "Looks like plenty of people are coming to see you get beat up by the best boxer in Hilo."

"Moki, you don't have to make it any tougher than it is."

"Eleele has a big punch. How did you get into a fight with him? We're supposed to be friends, working together, not beating each other."

Kalani sighed. "I don't know how I got into this. If I win, we could lose an ally. If I lose, he gets to sacrifice whoever he wants, including me."

"Yeah, I heard about it. Word is spreading about the fight. I don't know what's going to happen, but either way it ends, it is not good."

The day was warm, yet coldness gripped him. He searched the skies, studied the distant dormant volcano of Mauna Kea, darkened a deep blue by the shadow of clouds hovering overhead. He prayed to the gods for a storm to come sweeping from the mountains into Waipio and end this fight. All he saw were bright clouds floating in the sky.

Kalani's musketeers came to him jabbering, "If Eleele wins, he chooses who will be sacrificed. Let us fight the Hilo boys now."

Kalani's heart sank. Akaka had trusted him, given him the pick of six musketeers and promised that Kalani would be a leader in the lightning strike to take Hilo for Kamehameha. He knew that his obstinate refusal to sacrifice the natives of Waipio to Ku threatened the fragile alliance between the followers of the dead Hilo chief and the forces of Kamehameha. Without allies, an attack on Keoua's heartland would be defeated.

Staring at Mauna Kea, Kalani begged, "*God Lono, I am dedicated to you. Give me wisdom, I am bewildered, help me.*"

One of his musketeers muttered, "None of us wants to die. Let Eleele sacrifice whoever he wishes of the natives living in Waipio."

"No!" Kalani cried, the bile in his stomach erupting, rushing into his throat, souring his mouth. *He could see Minato, blood spurting from his chest like a wave pounding against the rocks. The red fluid from the slave boy's heart flooded over the knife hand of the high priest, covered the sacrificial altar, then dripped to the floor of the temple. Near the altar the slanted mouth of god Ku drank in the sanctified offering of the high priest. Its pebble eyes bulged, demanding to be fed more human sacrifice.*

Kalani shook like a wet dog shedding water. His throat shut tight from the vomit that threatened to spew out. He whispered, "None of you will die. None of the people in this valley will die. If I am defeated, I will sacrifice myself to Ku. Moki will be your leader in the coming battles."

Shock disfigured Moki's face. He slapped his chest, then placed the palm of his hand against Kalani's heart. "What do you think? You are my brother. You will not die. No way. I will fight Eleele, his brother, all those Hilo guys."

A wan smile lit Kalani's face, dispelling the horror that had just visited him. He reached his hand around Moki's head, pulling their foreheads together. "I love you like a brother, but should I lose, let me be sacrificed. Let no one else die to appease Ku. Then take our warriors, conquer Hilo and kill Hauna. Promise to do this for me."

Moki tried to wrench his head away, but Kalani held him fast, two men bound by friendship. Kalani's vow to end slavery, to end sacrifices to the god Ku, coursed between them, penetrating the deepest recesses of their memories and leaving indelible scars that would only disappear when the vow had been fulfilled.

For many moments they stood welded together. After a time, Kalani relaxed his grip and Moki stood away, eyes welling with tears. He turned from the gaping musketeers. "Yes, I promise."

On the headland at the ocean end of Waipio valley, waves dashed, flinging sprays of seawater over black stones. There was no sand beach. Kalani searched for the place where he had buried Hinalea. Days before he had cut her open, removed the organs that corrupt, salted the cavity of the body, and let the dead woman dry in the sun. After a time, he wrapped the shriveled corpse in tapa, and buried it beneath a mound of stone.

His thoughts turned inward, blotting out the sounds around him. *Would this be my last day of life? If so, would I be granted a burial in the Hawaiian way, or be cast into the pit beneath god Ku to rot, melt, and mix with the other offerings until the flesh of human and animal were jelled together into one stinking pool?*

A muffled pounding roused him. Fifty Hilo men, the followers of the dead high chief, marched to the shoreline, Eleele in their midst.

Some beat drums, creating a chaotic racket, others chanted insulting songs.

Kamehameha's twenty-five warriors were already at the beach, standing in a semi-circle around Kalani. They watched the raucous men in silence, their quiet demeanor rare at a sporting event. Frustrated, the Hilo men changed from yelling sarcastic challenges to making bets, offering ridiculous amounts of taro, food, and canoes, badgering the men of Kamehameha to wager on their champion. No bets were taken.

Eleele stepped from the midst of his followers, glowering at the silent men. He did not taunt. Instead, he yelled, "Are you ready to be beaten?"

Kalani wondered how he should answer. With an insult? With surrender? With silence? He stared at Eleele, a bigger, older man, a premier boxer with a punisher reputation. A fighter, who, once he had the advantage, would pound his opponent into the ground. The crowd grew silent, waiting for his response.

"So long as the light of the sun shall brighten my eyes, Eleele, I will not let the blood of slaves or freemen flow from the altar of sacrifice. Instead, let us join, mingling our mana, join our spears, driving our shafts into our common enemy, Keoua."

Eleele sneered. "It is too late for pretty speeches. It is time to test your power against mine." Despite Eleele's bravado, Kalani sensed that his words struck home with the men of Hilo. Even Eleele's younger brother nodded in agreement, while others whispered to each other.

Unmoved by the dissent behind him, Eleele directed one of his men to create a rope rectangle in the grass. This done, he stepped inside it, "Whoever falls beyond the rope is the loser, unless you surrender before then. Come within the box, youngster, to be mangled."

Discouraged that his words had not brought peace, Kalani glanced at the field around him. Hilo men and the men of Kamehameha stood in a ragged circle to witness this senseless combat. *It was not like festival time, he thought, when boxing and other sports were welcomed with colorful dress and gaiety.* Today, none of the people of Waipio had come to learn their fate.

Kalani entered the rope box and assumed the fighter's stance, fists clenched, arms held to the side, knees bent ready to spring. Eleele mirrored his posture several feet away, eyes glaring, trying to intimidate his foe.

Kalani felt the training by the slaves flow into him like the morning tide washing onto the shore behind him. Words from Minato's father buzzed in his head: "Do not block the punch with your fist, as is the custom. It only leads to broken hands and arms. It is not dishonorable to deflect a blow with your forearm. When you have the chance, use this strike that I show you." Kalani had practiced the six-inch hit every day since he had learned it.

Eleele began the bout. He feinted with one hand, then threw a roundhouse punch at Kalani's face. Blocking the powerful swing with his arm, Kalani felt the shock of the blow racing along his forearm as Eleele's fist pounded into his shoulder and glanced from his jaw. Eleele's other hand slammed at his belly. Kalani twisted away, the blow sliding along the ridged muscles of his stomach.

Relentless in his aggression, Eleele rained blows, many of them blocked, but some striking home. Then a solid punch to the ribs jarred Kalani, bringing him to the ground. Eleele came in for the kill, striking a hammer blow. His punch hit into the grass inches from Kalani's face, Eleele's balance was upset by Kalani's twisting feet.

Eleele lay on the ground for a moment, rubbing dirt from his hands. Kalani scrambled up, wincing from the pain in his side. he noted the silence of the spectators, the failure of Eleele to taunt him, while deeper in the valley he saw villagers clumping together.

The Hilo chief came at him again swinging wild blows, driving Kalani to the edge of the rope marker. He ducked under a swooping arm and slid past Eleele. He did not strike his opponent's exposed side.

A puzzled look crossed Eleele's face. "Why don't you hit me? You had an advantage, but you failed to strike."

"Listen to me, think of what I say. You are not my enemy, our enemy is Keoua."

"Bah!" Eleele spat, and swung into Kalani, his punches hammering into the boy's body. Then, opening his arms, the man grasped for

Kalani's back, seeking to break him in a crushing embrace. Eleele's stomach loomed inches away. Kalani's fingers, toughened by months of breaking through planks, struck deep into the belly.

Eleele howled. He staggered backward, gasping. His feet wobbled and he collapsed over the line.

Kalani stepped across the rope and pleaded with Eleele's younger brother, a look of wide-eyed surprise on his face. "Eleele and I are both over the line. Beg him to accept a draw in this combat. Like you, I mourn the death of your father. Keoua, who ate your father's heart, is your enemy. Hauna, who ate your father's liver, is my enemy. We must fight together to destroy our mutual enemies. If this argument does not persuade you, look behind you at what is descending upon us."

Marching toward them were hundreds of hostile Waipio residents armed with sticks and clubs.

Eleele's brother winced. "To save ourselves, it appears that we must join together. I still think my brother would want some kind of sacrifice to the gods."

"Then let me choose the sacrifice."

"Agreed."

A restless crowd stood by the stone mound of the open-air temple, warriors of Hilo and Kamehameha mixed together with the people of Waipio. Alapai-nui, who had come with additional fighting men and gunpowder stood with Eleele and his brother.

Busy voices melted into silence. A white-robed priest walked to the altar where three carved statues hovered over the sacrificial slab. The priest searched their grim faces, muttering prayers to the deities. He turned to the worshipers, dipping fronds of wild fern into a vessel, and then showering them with droplets of water. Finished with his ministrations, he stepped to the side, signaling.

Kalani walked onto the rocks of the holy place. He was followed by two litters borne by Moki and the musketeers. These were placed below the icons.

"Oh, Lono, god of nature," Kalani chanted. "Oh, Kane, god of the heavens. Oh, Kanaloa, god of the world below. Oh, great gods of our people, accept these sacrifices that we offer you."

The priest handed him a knife. Kalani raised it to the statue of Lono, saying, "Great lord, take this gift, bless your people, aid us in our war against Keoua." He sliced the knife into the body in the first litter, Kalani cut off the ear of a baked pig. He took the severed flesh and placed it into a gourd dangling from the neck of Lono.

Before each statue, he made a similar incantation, then his offerings. For Kane, he filled his gourd with fermented liquor; Kanaloa received baked taro.

The gifts completed, the priest came to the center saying, "Oh, Lono, eat of the sacrificed swine. Oh, Kane, drink of the nectar of the awa root. Oh, Kanaloa, fill yourself from the fruits of the land. Proclaim your blessings upon your people, upon the warriors of Hilo and Kamehameha. Consecrate what we place before you to those who partake of it."

The prayer finished, the priest signaled, and men removed the food to woven mats set out in a field beyond the temple. Late into the night, the worshipers ate the pork, the poi, and drank the liquor until they were gorged.

Next morning, the warriors of Hilo and Kamehameha paddled east, ready to do battle with Keoua.

CHAPTER 48

ONE HUNDRED MEN SPED ALONG the cliffs of the Hamakua coast. All day they paddled against a surging sea roiled by powerful winds blowing toward the setting sun. Darkness shrouded their advance as they pushed through the night. Despite their efforts, dawn found the war party miles from Hilo Bay. Too deep into enemy territory to risk a daylight entry, the small strike force rested in a shallow, rock-strewn bay, and waited for the sun to finish its voyage across the sky. Toward dusk, the warriors left their haven and paddled into the sea, fighting against great waves whipped by an angry wind.

In the early morning of the third day, the small fleet entered Hilo Bay. Canoes were concealed in brush near the beach. Eleele, his brother, and Alapai-nui headed inland in search of a friendly chief.

The sun sat high when Alapai-nui returned and gathered the strike force, leading them inland. A mile from shore, they entered a walled compound active with men. An elder, his beard wiry white, motioned the warriors to an open area covered with mats. Servants brought food and water.

"Come with me," Alapai-nui said, leading Kalani to a large building that served as a palace. Within moments, Eleele limped in and sat next to Kalani. The two men stared at each other. "You landed one hit, but that won the fight. One day, teach me your secret." Eleele smiled, offering his fist to Kalani.

Kalani touched it. "I'm sorry I had to hit you, but you're stronger than any man I know. If you had crushed me in your grip, it would have ended my life."

Eleele nodded. "There is no anger in my heart, my brother."

"I am undeserving to be your brother."

"You fought a fair fight, and you will be my brother when we join in blood."

Kalani waited a moment before answering. "Agreed. Why are we here?"

"We await others," Eleele replied. "Hilo men are angry. When Keoua returned after his defeat by Kamehameha, he divided the best lands of this district among his followers."

"The custom of the conqueror," Kalani answered.

Eleele scowled. "True, but putting foreign chiefs in power over this district angered the people. Once he made this division of land, he left with his army for Kau. It is time to strike. With your warriors and chiefs loyal to my father, we will reclaim his domain and defeat these foreigners from Kau."

With Alapai-nui's strike force and three hundred Hilo men, Eleele swept the forces of Keoua into the mountains. On the verge of victory, when the Hilo army reached the border of Puna, a chief refused to go deeper into enemy territory.

Eleele protested, "You cannot abandon this venture. We must strike into Puna, hit hard at the retreating Keoua, the eater of my father's heart."

"I have no quarrel with Hauna, the chief of Puna. For me, it is enough that Keoua is gone from Hilo. More important, my land is not secure. We have only pushed the enemy into the hills. If we venture into Puna and then Kau, these men will return and take my land."

"I hate Keoua," Eleele seethed. "My brother Kalani, who sits beside me, has a quarrel with Hauna. These cannibals ate the flesh of my father. We want them dead and I command you to help us."

The chief fixed rheumy eyes upon the younger man. "Your father was killed before he could name his heir. The Hilo chiefs have not accepted you as high chief. That title could be given to your younger brother, or someone else. Until that decision is made, I refuse to obey."

Shaken, Eleele humbled himself, begging, "If you will not follow me, what of your men? Will you take them from me?"

The old chief's eyes flickered for a moment, then a slight smile creased his lips. "No, those who wish to follow you into Puna may do so."

After the meeting Kalani sat with Eleele, discussing the older man's motives. "The chief is not foolish. He is letting you plunge into Puna and maybe Kau. If you win, he remains in your favor. If you lose—"

"I think that is what he wants," Eleele said. "Give us just enough men to try, but not enough to be victorious. Should my brother and I be killed, he will be ruler of Hilo."

"That is typical of our chiefs, they play the power game. Switch from side to side, wherever they can find an advantage." Kalani sighed. "A warrior like me can't do that."

"That's because you're not a chief, with followers who owe allegiance to you, and commoners who belong to you," Eleele interjected.

"I'm trying. At least I am considered koa, a professional soldier. If I can beat Hauna, defeat Keoua, I'm sure Kamehameha will recognize me."

"Yeah, or maybe he'll use you and give you nothing. Let's get ready to fight in Puna."

Alapai-nui, who had brought gunpowder to Kalani, left with twenty-five warriors for Kawaihae. In command of twenty musketeers, Kalani plunged into Puna with his blood brother, Eleele, and two hundred Hilo men, pursuing the superior armies of Hauna and Keoua.

Above the village of Pahoa, Kalani, Eleele, and Moki peered over a ridge. Below them the land was grim, nothing but dark rocks and patches of dying weeds. Behind them warriors were eating dried poi and sticks of salted fish. The men joked, laughed, slapped each other as they ate their meal.

"Morale is good," Kalani said.

"They haven't fought yet. They haven't seen how many warriors Hauna has. My scouts say we are outnumbered."

A chief asked, "My lord, would it be cowardice to suggest retreat?"

Eleele stared at him. "We have not fought in a single battle. Are you afraid?"

The soldier looked away. "No, but can our small force stand up to the mighty power of Keoua and Hauna?"

"Do not be afraid of Keoua. See, in the far distance, the smoke from Kilauea? His army is beneath the volcano, heading for Kau. Keoua is not aware of our presence. We can strike down Hauna before he can return to help him."

"But Hauna has four hundred Puna warriors poised to defeat us."

"Don't worry about that," Kalani joined the conversation. "Most of his men are commoners, tillers of the soil, untrained in war. Rumor has it that Hauna taxes them heavily and takes the women he wants for himself and his cronies. He does not respect the elders. If we deal his army a crushing blow, Puna will fall into our hands."

Eleele nodded. "Wisely said, my brother. We need only tear out the heart, and the rotten structure will fall. What should be our plan? Charge into Pahoa and wreak havoc among the enemy?"

"An unwise move," Kalani answered. "Let us rest on this higher ground. In prior battles, when the enemy attacked uphill against our muskets and cannon, they were at a disadvantage. Let Hauna come to us. This is what we should do: build a low wall twenty feet below this ridgeline."

"A wall! Whatever for?"

"To hide. Use it to defend."

"Warriors do not hide," Eleele said, disgust written on his face. "We stand for the enemy to see. We insult. Challenge duels to the death." Eleele rose flexing his muscles, clenching his fists he punched the air.

"We will not win using words. To win we have to fight like Americans."

"Americans? Who are they?" Eleele demanded.

"They live far away. In a land thousands of times bigger than our island. They fought a powerful enemy and won."

"Hum. How do you know this? How did they win?" Eleele asked, intrigued by Kalani's boasting.

"Months ago, I met an American, Captain Russell. He came from a city called Boston. He liked me. Said I reminded him of his son. We spent many hours together. He told me how American farmers fought people like Captain Cook, Isaac Davis, John Young. They hid behind walls, trees, fought from hills. They beat the English koa!" Kalani's voice resonated with excitement.

"They beat the English koa," Eleele said, shaking his head, "Farmers beat professional soldiers?"

"Yes, and we can do the same."

"Explain your plan."

"On this side of the ridge we build a low wall twenty feet below the crest. Musketeers will hide behind it. All along the ridge we line the rest of our warriors, heavy in the center and to the right. I want this left side to look thin, induce Hauna to attack here."

Throughout the day, the small army prepared for battle. Below them, scores of Puna soldiers marched into Pahoa. Late in the afternoon, a richly-cloaked group of chiefs stalked in, Hauna in the lead. Kalani knew an attack would come the next day. Into the night two hundred warriors worked, building a wall.

At dawn, Kalani watched the dark clouds that had obscured the stars drifting west. The horizon blazed red, only heavy smoke from the distant crater of Kilauea marred the perfect sky.

Kalani mixed with the men, praising their valor, sharing their food. Moki sidled up to him, saying: "Brother, what are we going to do?"

With a wink of his eye, Kalani said, "Same tactics we used to beat Makula."

"Yeah, I know that routine," Moki laughed.

Above them, sentinels on the ridge overlooking the village sounded the alarm. Hauna's army began forming up, preparing for battle.

"Where are you, Kalani?" the High Chief of Puna yelled. "I challenge you to combat, coward! Show yourself! Or are you too frightened to fight?"

Twenty feet below the ridgeline, Kalani crouched at a low rock wall. Anger seized him as Hauna kept up his taunts. "I'm going to fight the bastard," he said, rising to leap over the wall.

Moki pulled him away from the low parapet. "Stop. Follow your plan. You fight him, we lose."

"I don't care. I hid the last time he challenged me. He's calling me a coward. Everybody will think that I'm afraid."

Moki wrestled with Kalani, holding him back. "It was your idea to make the left side weak. It was your idea to build this wall. Your idea to put the muskets here. What are you going to do, throw it all away to fight Hauna?"

Kalani gave up the struggle. "I suppose you're right," he conceded, rubbing his arm where Moki had gripped him. "But I'll get that bastard. One day, I'll fight him to the death."

Moki nodded. "But for now, cool head main thing."

Slingers skirmished below the ridgeline. Calabash drums boomed. Puna warriors yelled insults, clashed their spears together, and stomped their feet, making a cacophony of sound. On the ridgeline Hilo warriors taunted, screamed their defiance.

Hauna massed his soldiers. Pumping his spear into the sky, he lowered it and pointed at the middle of the Hilo men strung along the ridgeline. In one sweeping motion, four hundred spears came level to the ground. A massive phalanx of Puna men marched uphill.

"Musketeers kneel," Kalani said. "Steady your guns on the wall. Pick an enemy. Fire!" Warriors fell. The attack faltered, giving time to reload and fire once more.

More attackers were hit. The Puna charge on their right flank slowed. "Reload and fire." Kalani ordered.

Hit a third time by small iron balls, the enemy warriors stopped. A few Puna men began to run away, but red-caped chiefs screamed at their stunned soldiers. With kicks and fists they reorganized the dispirited line of troops who then continued their march uphill.

"Retire to the ridge. Follow the plan," Kalani directed his men.

The musketeers withdrew. Puna soldiers on their right flank of the attack slowed as they came to the wall that had just been abandoned.

"Shoot." A fourth volley, supplemented by spears thrown by Hilo men on the ridge, crashed into the milling soldiers, struggling to get over the stone wall. A second set of spears rained down upon them. Stones followed, smashing the right side of the enemy attack.

"They're running," Moki cried, jigging in a circle. "They are leaving their wounded and flying home to Pahoa."

"Yeah, but our center is in trouble. Hauna is hitting it with everything he has. Come. Eleele and his brother need our help." Kalani gathered his musketeers and charged, aiming his attack for Hauna, who stood in the midst of warriors swinging a war club.

"Give it to them," yelled Moki as he struck his spear into the side of a Puna soldier. "They don't know how to fight like real men."

"They're just farmers." Kalani gasped, smashing his cudgel into an opponent who dropped his weapons and fled. "Hauna forced them to fight.

"Run! Run!" he yelled.

Surprised by the flank attack, frightened by the shouting, the peasant soldiers panicked. Fear spread. Morale fell. The rabble screamed, "Run! Save yourself."

They ran, escaping death. In the press of fleeing warriors, Hauna was shoved downhill, trapped by his men. Kalani pursued, intent on fighting his enemy.

Eleele yelled, "Kalani, come back. We need you!"

His emotions overwhelming him, Kalani ignored the command, stepping over and around bodies in his pursuit. A hand grabbed his arm, pulling him. "Eleele needs you. There is trouble. Come."

With a scowl, Kalani followed Moki, gathering warriors as he went. His group attacked Puna forces still fighting on the hill. Assailed from front and side, the enemy retreated.

Despite Kalani's desire to go forward and continue to fight Hauna, Eleele refused to counter-attack. "Let the enemy disintegrate. Do not ruin our victory by being impetuous."

As Eleele predicted, the Puna army vanished. From a few frightened captives, Kalani learned that Hauna was fleeing to Kau, intent on catching up with Keoua's army.

CHAPTER 49

THE SUN'S RAYS FOUGHT THROUGH a grass roof and sprinkled light over Kalani's face. He lay in an uneasy doze. Tremors in the night had shaken the ground, building into a terrific blast. Kilauea volcano erupted at midnight, spewing flame high into the sky. Pele's display of power put fear into the small army of Hilo.

Shrill voices brought him awake. Annoyed that his slumber had ended, he stretched, yawned and stooped through the threshold of his shelter. The morning was cool, crisp, threatening. The sky roiled with ash clouds piling high in towers of dirty smoke. Men who had slept outside were jabbering, pointing to the smoldering volcano.

Moki strode up, a wry smile on his face. "Little roach, did you feel that volcano doing the hula? Swinging the ground? Rumbling around? Then bursting with a whoosh of fire?"

Kalani laughed at Moki's lame attempt to find humor in a dreadful night.

Moki's smile faded. "We have a problem. Nobody slept. The men are saying, 'Pele is angry'. Maybe we should give up chasing Hauna. Go back to Hilo, where it is safer."

"And let Hauna escape to Kau? Give him a chance to fight us again? We are not going back."

"Maybe you better rethink this," Eleele said, striding to them, his head shaking. "Kilauea is blowing up. The closer we get, the worse it is. The men fear Pele's wrath. They are near to panic. I think we should return home while we still can."

Sweat beaded on Kalani's forehead, trickling into his eyes. He rubbed the sting away with the back of his hand, weighing his words. He did not want to make demands of frightened men, yet Hauna had to be stopped from reaching Keoua. The army could not turn back with an enemy still out there, able to join forces with the formidable king of Kau. Kalani said, "Brother, we pursue men who ate your father." Eleele's face stiffened. "If we do not catch Hauna, Keoua, and kill them, they will come back to feast on you and me."

Eleele's fists clenched. He cracked his knuckles. The stolid expression on his face changed. "We go forward, my brother."

Shaken Hilo men shuffled toward sparking cinders shooting up from Kilauea. The path they followed skirted below and around the raging volcano. Suddenly, ash-filled clouds burst from the caldera like a monstrous dark mushroom springing from the earth. Sunlight dimmed.

The ground darkened. Men were dusted with a layer of grey. *"Pele, still your wrath,"* Kalani prayed as he saw wild fear in the soldiers' faces. The army was in panic.

At mid-morning, Kilauea rumbled with renewed violence. The ground waved. Men tumbled, clung to boulders, trees, shrubs, anything to hold onto and remain upright. Thunder roared from the smoking caldera. Giant rocks hurled into the sky. The air became electric with flashes of lightning, as alternating streams of red and blue light flared from the summit of the mountain.

Eleele gripped Kalani's arm. "Pele is going to kill us. She has never been so wild. We must run from her anger."

"We can't stop. I caught a glimpse of Hauna up ahead. If he reaches the King of Kau, all that we have won will be lost."

Eleele shook his head. "The men will go no further into this alternating fire and darkness. Forget Hauna, Keoua. Pele will destroy them. We must save ourselves." Adding emphasis to his words, the volcano roared, throwing towers of hot mud into the darkened sky. Rifts opened in the earth, releasing geysers of steam, spewing fountains of fire. The ground convulsed. The once-hard rock came alive. Men screamed, "Pele angry! Pele angry!"

Kalani realized that he could no longer force these warriors into the terrifying unknown. They were cowed by the fury of the volcano goddess. Pele had obliterated their courage. The Hilo army, reeling from the shocks of the explosions, began to disintegrate.

An eerie silence came over the land, broken only by the whimpers of men and the word "Pele," muttered over and over again. Kalani watched black smoke billow in giant swirls and descend over them. The warriors who muttered "Pele" shouted, "The night marchers are coming!"

Kalani yelled, "Return to Pahoa." Detonations blasted the air. Powerful waves of sound clapped the warriors. They fled.

He crouched, covering his ears. Eleele, Moki, and several musketeers came, begging that he turn away. "Someone must stop Hauna!" Kalani said over the din. "Eleele, take your men and mine back to Puna. Wait for me. If I do not return in two days, you'll know I'm dead."

"You're not leaving me out of this fight," Moki said. "I'm coming with you."

An avalanche of boulders tumbled and bounced in a blizzard of stone. The sky canopied with thick smoke. "Hide," Moki screamed. The friends stumbled beneath a ledge as scraps of stone showered the trail, splintering into stinging shards. Kalani flung his arms around his face, covered his ears, shutting off the resonating blasts aching his head. "Pele, stop your anger," he begged.

"Shall we give up?" Moki asked.

The day was a horror. Where they hid was a brutal place. They were squeezed into a shallow shelter, cowering from flying slivers of stone, bleeding from small cuts. Finding Hauna in this maelstrom of fury seemed impossible. Kalani hunched toward Moki, feeling his warmth. His breathing was steady, his friend unafraid. "We shall not stop," Kalani said.

The two men climbed higher, threading through tall grass sprouting from crevices bordering the trail. Kilauea brooded above them, smoke puffing from its mouth. With a blast the volcano came alive. Dark clouds pealed from its innards spreading out, obscuring the path. Wind whipped among the rocks, flipping aside the momentary gloom. In the clearing smoke were three men. "Hauna!" Kalani warned. "Moki, loosen your spear!"

Volumes of sulfur gas plumed from Kilauea, displacing the clean air with a pungent smell. "I'm blinded," Moki gasped, stumbling to the ground.

Confused, Kalani knew he should not breathe. The stifling air would dull his senses, kill him. He searched the ground and touched water. Moki choked. He released his *malo.* He soaked it, covering his cloth over his friend's face. His lungs screamed for air. He thrust his mouth close to the small stream.

At the water's surface he inhaled pure air. He lay on his side breathing its coolness. Unwrapping Moki's cloth, he dampened it, tying the wet garment around his friend's face. The smell around him became less pungent so he stood, pulling Moki up. "Our enemies are ahead. Ready your spear, loosen your club. Come."

Fog billowed, slowing their advance. A flash of lightning, its thunder momentarily shattered the mist. Huge figures were silhouetted in the shifting light. "Kill them," Hauna yelled. Three spears thrust toward them, forcing the two friends back into the gloom. Voices shouted, "Die, maggots! Feast no more on the warriors of Puna."

Sharp sticks jabbed the murk, like needles poked by blind men seeking to puncture a squash. Kalani heard Moki yelp. A warrior appeared in the fog driving a spear toward the sound. "Got him," Moki said, his sharp stick stabbing into the man's chest. The wounded warrior thrashed in the dirty clouds, like a harpooned whale smiting the sea. "Watch out," Kalani warned, swinging his club at a second man thrusting his spear through the murk and into Moki's side. The heavy stick crushed the attacker's skull. He fell onto the lava rocks, blood spurting over him from Moki's wound.

"Kauwa, die." A spear plunged through the clouds. Kalani leaped away, losing his weapons. They clattered onto stones and, disappeared into the murk. He crouched and listened. A giant slipped by, Hauna's face swiveling from side to side, eyes searching the fog. He thought to jump upon him, but the man had an advantage, his spear thrust out, jabbing. He felt for something to fight with, clutched loose dirt and rocks. Moki groaned. Hauna swiveled, his spear stretching to the sound. Kalani flung what he held.

Hauna bellowed. His stick missed its mark, his hand swept to his face, wiping dirt from his eyes.

Kalani rolled upright ready to fight, but his enemy disappeared into the murk. Moki lay groaning on his back, blood seeping from his side. Kalani whispered, "Try to lay quiet, my brother, Hauna is out there, blinded, but dangerous." Moving his hand along the ground, he sought enemy warriors that had fallen. He felt a head, found a depression and knew the man was finished. He heard labored breathing, saw an upright spear trembling in front of him.

Muscles tensed, Kalani raised himself, balancing on his toes waiting for Hauna to come. Another explosion thundered. Overhead a glowing red ring of fire grew until a fiery mass spilled over the ridge heading in a flood down the sloping side of the caldera.

Rain pelted, sizzling into steam when it hit the lava river. Sunlight shafted through the clouds, mixing with the red glow of liquid rock. A westward wind whipped away the dense smoke. In the boulders and rents marring the Kau trail, Hauna stood.

With a savage roar, the big man threw his spear, the weapon arching at Kalani's heart. Swift though it flew, Kalani's grimy hand moved faster, seizing the missile. Hauna roared again, preparing to throw a second weapon. As if answering his challenge, the earth convulsed, flinging both men to the ground. High above, more hot mud spewed from Kilauea, hurtling in burning streams toward them.

Kalani feared for Moki. He darted to him, lifted the wounded man and scurried up a hillside. He looked back. He saw the lava spill onto the path to Kau, covering the bodies of Hauna's cronies. Beyond rising fingers of steam, the dim figure of Hauna retreated from a molten river.

In a hollow, Kalani spread his cloth. Laying Moki on it, he checked the wound. "Not deep," he said. He cradled his friend in his arms, hesitating as to what to do. In the distance he heard Hauna scream, "Come fight, slave boy."

The challenge decided him. "You'll be all right. Rest. I go to Hauna."

Moki twitched and closed his eyes.

He struggled around lava burning red, flowing unchecked as it swept the land. Hauna waited, taunting. Though the air was warm, Kalani shivered. His enemy was big, biceps the size of hogs, shoulders as wide as the limbs of the ohia tree. He loosened his club, a pitiful weapon, no match for Hauna's eight-foot spear.

A stream of lava snaked between them, its long thin finger separating the men. Hauna waved his weapon in a mocking salute, its point girdled by shark's teeth, the butt knobbed and heavy. "Cheater. Eater of opala. You will die slow," he hissed.

A gusting wind blew dust into Kalani's eyes. It made him blink. Sweat from the heat of the lava stream trickled down his face. He reached for a rock to smash the sneer from his enemy's face.

"Only a girl child throws stones. Run away, little one, before I skewer you like a pig on a spit," Hauna sneered.

Kalani straightened, stepped onto warmed rocks, advancing toward Hauna. "Raper of dogs and worms, fit only to rut with pigs," he shouted, a year of frustrations welling up, bursting out. His club hand whirled, the restraining thong biting into his wrist.

Enraged, Hauna leaped over the flowing fire, thrusting his spear. Kalani parried the strike with his club, kicking with his foot. It missed by inches as Hauna turned away, levering the haft of his spear up and into Kalani's jaw. Blood spurted from a cut on his throat and Kalani drew back feeling the wound's sting constricting his breath. Hauna smiled. "Only trickery and your friends saved you at the lua school. As I promised, you will die slow." Hauna feinted, charged, sweeping his spear in wide swings in front of him.

Kalani retreated, deflecting the weapon as best he could, but the sharp, tiger shark teeth at its tip sawed into his chest, ripping his skin. Desperate, Kalani leaped onto higher ground, stumbling into a jumble of dead bodies covered with ash. Fine grains of pumice filled the air, rising from the corpses like souls leaving their hosts. Frozen hands reached for him. Contorted faces with sightless eyes, covered by grey grime, stared at him. For yards beyond the point of his fall, Kalani saw hundreds of bodies strewn on the ground. Many in awkward positions, some with faces touching in one last kiss, some clutching children to bosoms smothered with volcanic dust. The only thing that moved was a pig feeding on the corpses. Hauna came up, staring at the field of death. Both men knew that a furious Pele had struck down the men and women of Keoua.

Hauna raged, "Kau's army may be gone, but you will die, then I will retake what is mine!" He flung his spear. Kalani brushed it aside. Hauna seized a club from the grip of a corpse, stepped across the body, wildly swinging his cudgel.

The two men battled among the dead. Hauna used the advantage of the higher ground, forcing Kalani down the sloping mountainside toward the pools of lava. Their weapons smashed into bodies. Their feet slipped on corpses as they dodged killing blows. Lava flowed into the field of death, frying decaying tissue, adding the stinking smell of burning flesh to the fetid air.

Hauna's furious attack proved to be too much to withstand. Kalani retreated, searching for an advantage, but Hauna gave him none. The bully's club glanced from Kalani's head. Dazed, he tripped over a corpse. With a triumphant scream, Hauna yelled, "Die, kauwa." He raised his cudgel, his mouth gaping like Ku, his teeth white.

As he strode forward to deal the killing blow, Hauna's foot slipped on the ooze of crushed flesh. He teetered, danced for a moment among the slime of broken bodies, and fell, his face and arms crashing into a pool of hot mud. He tried to shove himself from the molten rock, then screamed a terrible scream. He stumbled, falling further into the fiery lava.

Blinded by blood flowing over his face, Kalani barely saw his enemy. "Here!" he yelled, trying to attract Hauna back to a wall of corpses. "I'm coming to help you." He choked on blood trickling into his mouth. Kalani hurried over the dead attempting to reach his enemy to help him escape the horrible burning death.

Hauna staggered further, thrashed in the lava stream, then pitched forward into the fiery mud. His body twitched for some moments, then lay still at the edge of Keoua's dead army.

Kalani limped away from the horror. His head pounded with every step, his throat dry, rasping as the gas from the volcano filled his lungs. He searched for Moki. Exhausted, his body racked with pain, Kalani fell. Unable to move, his eyes closed.

CHAPTER 50

HAUNA'S HANDS, COLD WITH DEATH, wrapped around his throat. Kalani tried to fight the shadow, speak to it, but words failed to come. His fists flayed air. He struggled from his dream. Sweat covered his body and pain throbbed in his head.

A voice said, "Drink. Eat." Water and food, shoved into his mouth, choked him. He fell back, dizzy. He heard a voice say, "I think he is dying." Then the shadow world returned. Grey, everything grey.

Kalani opened his eyes, sunlight poured into the hut through its low doorway. Someone moved next to him. He heard a voice, saw the figure of a woman coming to his side. "Drink this," she said, pouring water into his mouth. For a moment the liquid soothed him, then the choking came and he was not able to drink. Thirst overwhelmed him and he seized the vessel, drinking until the woman took it from him.

He lay back, exhausted. His stomach rumbled and he begged for food. The woman brought a small bowl filled with poi and he ate it, asking for more. She refused, saying, "Priest tells me not to give you too much. Later, when you are stronger, I will give you more."

"What is your name?" Kalani asked.

"Nohea."

"Where am I?"

"At a beach near Hilo Village."

"Nohea, forget what the priest said, I want more to eat."

"No, I cannot disobey. I would be punished. Rest for a time and then I will give you more."

Exhausted, Kalani fell back onto his blanket.

"Now that you are awake, I will find the priest," Nohea said.

Several days later, the local shaman, a man named Mauloa, treated Kalani with a regimen of herbs and prayer. "This weed is horrible," Kalani complained, hating the foul taste of the crushed roots that the white-haired priest forced into him.

"They are not weeds. It is olena, the finest herbal medicine. It will cure coughs, earaches, all ailments. Your lungs are corrupted, scored by Pele's smoke. I will pray to Lono and ask him to heal you.

"Oh Lono, god of peace and bounty, help this poor boy to health. Free his body of the wrath of Pele." Mauloa went on for several minutes making his requests. When finished he told Kalani to mind Nohea, take his medicine, and he would return. The prayers of Mauloa, recited in a gentle chant, had hypnotized him and made the foul drink easier to accept. Over time, the wizened priest's words and his soothing massages relieved Kalani of the pain in his head and the coughing that wracked his lungs.

The day was sodden. Heavy rain had fallen during the night and when the sun rose, the air became doughy from evaporating moisture. "Hey in there, are you up? It's going to be a sunny day, but muggy."

Kalani sat upright, his movement so fast that his head spun, but he was desperate to see his adopted brother, learn what had happened since the fight with Hauna. "Come in. Why haven't you come to see me sooner? What has happened?"

Moki scooted through the door. "Whoa, one question at a time. First, how are you?"

"I'm fine," Kalani said, wanting to hear news and not dwell on his illness. "The last I remembered before I found myself in Hilo was collapsing by the volcano."

Moki rubbed his side. His spear wound had healed, leaving an angry scar. His face became serious. "Thank you for saving my life. I owe you."

Kalani felt his *aloha* and knew he had *aloha* for Moki. This man was his brother as if whelped from the same womb and suckled at the same mother's breasts. "You have done much for me, you owe me nothing. Please, the news."

"The crackling in the air had gone away when I got up. I could still see lava flowing, but there was only a wisp of smoke from Kilauea." Moki rubbed his hand over his hair, cleared the sweat from his face. "Didn't see you, I thought you were dead. Fell asleep and got woken by a shout."

"Eleele?"

"Yeah, he had come back. We started looking for you, found you in a heap. You were out of it. Eleele and his men made a litter and we hauled you back to Hilo."

Kalani suspected there was more to the story than Moki told. "I vaguely remember a lot of noise, men shouting."

"Not much more to tell except..." Moki looked at the ceiling, his hands fidgeting.

"Tell me."

"Puna was blowing up like a volcano, our Hilo army was gone. Word had spread that Hauna was dead and you were the killer."

"I did not!" Kalani spat. "Sure, I meant to kill him, but he slipped in lava and died. I tried to save him..." His voice trailed to a whisper as he remembered the ragged heaps of bodies lying frozen grey. Their deaths must have been sudden. "What happened in Puna?" Kalani asked, shaking himself from his morbid thoughts.

Sweat dripped from Moki's brow, stinging his eyes. He grabbed a cloth and wiped his face, then continued. "Eleele had a handful of men and I could barely walk, useless in a fight. We knew Hauna was a mean chief, but he had friends. About a dozen hit us when we got to Pahoa. Eleele went berserk. They ran. That's it."

He knew there was more to the event than Moki related. But he felt it unwise to question his friend. He would find out what really happened later. The two men discussed Kalani's illness and Moki left.

Shortly after, Eleele came into the hale and squatted beside him, offering his wrist and scar where their blood had mixed. Once they touched he said, "I see you've been eating that olena root, your tongue is yellow with stain. Hate the stuff. I'd rather munch on sugar stalks, sweeter. Have some awa, fresh chewed." Eleele laughed, spitting into a gourd and handing it to Kalani.

He took the alcoholic beverage and pretended to drink. It was a breach of etiquette not to do so. Awa drinking is a sign of respect; by sharing saliva, you share your mana. But the juices of the olena were rumbling in his stomach and Kalani felt that drinking awa would make it worse.

Eleele appeared worried. He had fallen silent and had moved into the shadows of the hut. "What is it, my brother?"

"I have not been selected to replace my father. My younger brother has deferred to me as the oldest son, but the few remaining chiefs still alive in Hilo are vying for the position of high chief. I fear that the selected winner will be the one who gives away the most land. While the chiefs squabble Keoua's men are creeping into Hilo threatening to retake it."

"What of Alapai-nui, Kamehameha, my musketeers? You must have followers. How many men can you muster?"

"Your soldiers are here, but they have no gunpowder. Alapai-nui left a dozen warriors, and I have twenty, maybe thirty, men loyal to me." Eleele became agitated and he slammed a clenched fist into the thatch wall, poking a hole through the grass.

"Calm yourself. I understand your anger. Such an undermanned force cannot seize power, but with Keoua dead, and his army destroyed by Pele, we could overcome these perils."

Eleele frowned. "Keoua is not dead, he escaped Pele's wrath and is in Kau recruiting another army. That is why I'm upset. 'The eater of flesh' is coming back and I can't stop him."

"Then Kamehameha must strike while Keoua is weak. He must seize Hilo and Kau."

"I have sent him the news, but he is immersed in building his temple to Ku. I pray to the gods that he acts. You must get well, my brother. If Kamehameha does not come, I will need your help."

Eleele left, and Kalani walked from his hale, contemplating what his blood brother had said. As he wandered, he noted differences between Hilo and his home, lava-strewn, barren Kau. *Here the land lay green with tall trees, ferns, and flowers all growing wild. Constant rain, dropping from clouds seeking to rise above the great volcanoes of Mauna Loa and Mauna Kea watered the area and made everything grow.*

He thought of his escape from the power of Pele, *reliving the horrors of the explosions, the burning death of Hauna. Had I been dealt a warning to mind the gods and make sacrifices to them? Yet those who had been covered with ashes had pursued the way of the warrior and worshiped the gods. Instead of glory, death was their reward for war.*

Why continue to pursue it? Was it the promise to Minato to gain power, help those who were enslaved cheat sacrifice? Was it the urgings of my mother to become a koa, rise to the rank of chief, and free my family from poverty? An even greater torment festers within, guilt for my deception of Hinalea.

What should I do? Give up the profane life and embrace the sacred? Become a priest in a temple of refuge, saving persecuted people from death?

His head bursting with inner turmoil, exhausted by his illness, Kalani returned to his hut and fell asleep outside. He dreamed that Hinalea held a knife to his heart. Pursing her lips, she mouthed the words, "Join me in death."

Rain forced him awake. He crawled into his grass home. In a corner, a fire had been lit, its low burning coals casting a glow onto an altar. Pearl-shell eyes reflected the flames, three small carved images of gods stared at offerings of food and water resting on the mantelpiece. Kalani knew that Nohea had placed these gifts to be blessed by the deities. Before he ate, he prayed to them for help in solving his turmoil.

Deep in meditation, he did not hear Mauloa enter until the priest woke him from his trance. "Sorry, it is time to take your herbal juice."

He took the offered cup and drank the evil beverage in a gulp. The sour taste gagged him for a moment, but before he could vomit, he forced the drink to remain in his stomach.

"How many more times?"

"Twice more before your lungs will be healed."

"Tell me, how I can become a priest?"

"That is a surprising question. I thought you are a warrior."

"I am, but I would like to know how to become a holy person."

"You must be born to serve the gods. There is no school to teach you. Nor is there a way for a common person to become one through war. But you can always apply to the High Priest of Ku in Kohala. He may need holy men to help in the hundreds of human sacrifices that will be made before the next round of fighting for Hawaii resumes."

Kalani shook his head. "I cannot be a part of human sacrifice. Is there any way to find a peaceable solution to gaining power?"

"Ah, I wish it were so. I am a priest of Lono, and we do not practice human sacrifice. In these unsettled times, I fear that the only way to status and power is through warfare. Ask yourself this: how else could high chiefs make commoners fight for them if they did not fear death? The high priest will tell you that sacrifices of enemies and slaves are necessary to appease Ku, yet I know that the priests of the war god conspire with the ruling chiefs. Human offerings are made to increase their power over the common people."

Bewildered, Kalani gripped Mauloa's arm. "Then I have no choice. I cannot prove my bloodline as a chief and no birthright as a priest. To gain power, I am doomed to join Kamehameha in endless war."

Mauloa took Kalani's hands. "For a man without royal ancestors, your only path to power is to become a 'black dirt chief'. If you wish to avoid warfare and its pain, seek refuge in our temple to Lono. The warring chiefs have not begun to kill us. I don't think they will do so since the common folk believe in our peaceful god."

Exhausted by this jumble of ideas, Kalani slept.

For two days, he wrestled with his emotions. While he felt weakness from the turmoil, his physical strength improved. The coughing left. He could stand and walk for brief periods. On the second evening, Moki visited and suggested they go to the common house. "I think you need a woman, to make you better."

"No. I'm too weak. There is too much on my mind, I don't want to fail in my performance."

"Nonsense, little roach, you must come. Nohea has taken a fancy to you. She will take care of everything. Make it easy for you. More important, Eleele needs to talk to you of his trouble."

Startled by this statement, Kalani agreed to go. He insisted that Moki trim his hair and beard. Washing, he rubbed sweet coconut oil over his skin. When he was ready, he shuffled to the common house.

Men he recognized were there: musketeers, a handful of Kamehameha's warriors, and several followers of Eleele. Women came to the waiting men. With unusual gusto, Nohea pushed away those who attempted to take Kalani. She led him to a curtained area where she relieved him of his stress.

While he lay on a blanket enjoying the afterglow of love, Moki nudged him. "Come." Kalani followed him to a secluded room lit by a single lamp. Its eerie light fell on Eleele, squatting on a mat with his brother and two other men. "I hope you are better after some moments of pleasure?" He slapped Kalani on the buttocks, emphasizing his point.

"Is it you I must thank for the sweetness of Nohea?"

"Thank Nohea. She has wanted you ever since you arrived in Hilo."

"She has helped cure my illness inside and out. Tell me, why have you summoned a wounded man to this quiet spot?"

"Tomorrow, the Hilo chiefs gather to give their loyalty to a new high chief. It is uncertain whether I will be the one selected. There are rivals to what should be my right as the eldest son of the high chief of Hilo. These men are making lavish promises of land and slaves. I need someone from Kamehameha's army to tip the scales in my favor." Eleele paused.

Kalani turned from Eleele's stare, studying the side of the hut. He noted the fine workmanship of the house builder who had notched, then lashed, the upright poles to the support beams and rafters. Thatches of lauhala leaves had been spread over the framework, giving the room a watertight seal.

During the long pause, he sensed the eyes of the five men boring into him, waiting for his answer. *What should I do? I do not want to go back into the fray of war or the intrigues of politics.* Rest, heal, his mind screamed. Kalani gave up his inspection of the construction. "I thought you had sent for help from Kamehameha?" he asked, seeking to avoid commitment.

"There has been no direct answer from the high chief to my request. It is rumored that a fleet of canoes is heading for Hilo. Whether this is true, I don't know. Will help arrive tomorrow? This, I also do not know, but I must prepare in case it does not. Before he left, Alapai-nui placed you in charge of the warriors of Kamehameha. I must look to you, my brother, to stand by my side."

Eleele's demand shriveled Kalani's heart. *The struggle for supremacy of the islands had resulted in war that did not cease. Farms in Waipio Valley had been destroyed. Men had died in battle or been sacrificed to the war god. Many more would perish. Should I end my journey without achieving a single goal that I had set? Could I use illness for an excuse and deny my help to the man who called him brother?*

In the hush, one of Eleele's henchmen sneered. "If you are afraid, then we will seek another to assist us in our cause."

The man's harsh words shook Kalani from his lethargy. Shame blew away the clouds of uncertainty. "I will help you, my brother. When and where is this meeting tomorrow?" He turned to Moki. "Rouse our musketeers and have them meet me at my hale at first light."

Men gathered at a large building set within a grove of coconut trees on a thumb-shaped peninsula jutting into Hilo Bay. Inside the open-air house, mats were spread with food and water. During the morning, warriors and chiefs arrived from different fiefdoms in the Hilo district.

Kalani studied them as they entered the meeting place. Rumor favored the oldest chief in Hilo to become the ruler. He had a telling argument: when their former high chief had sided with Kamehameha, it had brought the wrath of Keoua upon them. He had remained neutral in the battles fought for control over the district. When Keoua won, all those who had supported Kamehameha were sacrificed. The neutral chiefs had survived Keoua's wrath.

By midday, seven candidates were assembled, and the rounds of heraldry began, each man tracing his royal ancestry to some undisputed ancestor of the noble class. Kalani winced as he listened to the recitations of genealogy. *I know that the sacrifices of my father and grandfather ended my hope of showing chiefly status by tracing my lineage to the gods.*

It took a seemingly interminable time for the qualifications of the seven to be concluded. There followed a series of prayers to Lono uttered by Mauloa, in which he begged the god's help in providing wisdom to the assembly.

It was mid-afternoon before the speeches began. By evening, when the torches were lit, it was clear that there were only two candidates who qualified for the position of ruler: Eleele and the eldest Hilo chief. Stepping into the center of the conclave, the priest Mauloa called for silence. "We are in turbulent times. Keoua and Kamehameha, two cousins, have been fighting for dominance of Hawaii Island but neither has prevailed. All of you have suffered from this rivalry and tonight you must decide who will lead us. Let us hear what each man has to say."

Chosen to speak first, the older man deferred to his primary supporter. The spokesman reminded everyone that the elder of the two candidates had shown exemplary wisdom by refusing to join Kamehameha in his conquest of Maui. Eleele's father had done so, breaking his neutrality to Keoua, and the result had been warfare visited upon Hilo by the King of Kau. The chiefs who had sided with Kamehameha were defeated and sacrificed to the war god. Those who had remained neutral in the conflict, had survived. There were murmurs of approval when the man finished.

It came time for Eleele to speak. He rose, nominating Kalani to be his spokesman. Disagreeable buzzing ran through the audience. Several voices called out, "Who is he? He did not announce his lineage. What is his rank?"

Eleele waited for the protesting to subside. When the meeting place became silent, he said, "He is Kamehameha's representative in Hilo. That is why I chose him to speak for me." Murmurs of "Kamehameha" rippled through the audience.

Kalani stood studying the men. He noted hostility on the faces of several chiefs and hoped there could be some who might be persuaded by what he had to say. He shook the dizziness from his head. "It's true that you still live after Keoua defeated Eleele's father. How were you rewarded for your neutrality? All of you were forced into hiding. Your land and your servants were taken from you by Keoua and given to his followers. You were restored to your fiefs when Eleele returned to Hilo with warriors of Kamehameha and his new weapons of fire. But your enemies will return to power if Keoua comes again."

Kalani paused for some moments to measure the effect of his words. He knew that control of land and the people who tilled it was foremost in the minds of all the chiefs. "Do you think that Keoua will return? I say he will not. The gods have rejected him. You recall that many weeks ago, the mighty Pele flung forth her anger from her home of fire in the volcano of Kilauea. I was there to witness her awesome power. I was there to see the destruction of Keoua's army, buried under the rocks and lava of Pele's hatred. I say to you, Keoua has lost the blessing of the gods.

"Would you, my friends, defy them? Would you defy the greatest prophet of all Hawaii, the priest who communes with the gods? The kahuna who said: 'When Kamehameha finishes the great temple to Ku, he will conquer all of the islands of Hawaii.' At this moment, the greatest temple ever built is nearing completion. Already the heavens shout that Kamehameha, the chosen one of Ku, will be king of us all. Select Eleele your high chief. He is Kamehameha's friend and a favorite of the gods."

There was silence in the building when Kalani's speech ended. He did not know what would happen in the voting as the bowls of awa roots were passed to each of the chiefs. It was the custom, a sign of submission to the new leader, for each to chew his awa root and pass his expectoration to the chosen one.

The eldest chief would be the first to offer or to drink his spit. Kalani held his breath. The old man sat studying the contents of his bowl. He took the vessel in his hands, raising it high. He walked to Eleele and offered him his awa juice.

CHAPTER 51

KALANI STIRRED, HIS BODY PROTESTING his movement, but something hovered near him. He came slowly awake, lying for a moment rubbing his eyes, erasing the slumber that had been deep, dreamless. He felt thankful for that. For too many nights specters of Hauna, Hinalea, his father, and Minato had intruded into his sleep, speaking to him, persuading him, but what was said in the nightmares made no sense.

"Ah, my young koa, you are up. Come outside where we can talk."

Akaka stood at the threshold of the hale, cloaked and helmeted for war. Beyond the chief, Kalani saw a multitude of war canoes bobbing on the sea. He crawled slowly outside and stood, the sun burning his uncovered skin. He stretched his hands, yawned, clearing his head, realizing that Akaka had come to fight Keoua.

"Eleele tells me that he owes his election to you," Akaka said, admiration in his voice. "He also tells me that you helped win Hilo over to the cause of Kamehameha and defeated Hauna in battle."

Kalani twisted for some moments, stretching the muscles of his chest. As he worked he breathed deep, then blew out Pele's corruption that had scored his lungs. The air was clean, pure, not stinking like volcano gas. He noted Akaka impatiently shifting his weight, but he needed time to consider his answer. "Eleele gives me too much credit for what he could have done by himself. When did you come?" Kalani asked.

"Early this morning, at a time when the sun makes tiny rainbows in the dew on spider webs."

"I see boats. How many warriors are with you?"

"I have eight hundred men and sixty canoes. Kamehameha sent me to fight Keoua. I came here first, but I see that the district is secure. We will spend the day gathering food and warriors, then head for Kau to do battle in the enemy homeland. Keoua is weak. I need you. Eleele says you've been sick. Are you well enough to fight?"

The question stung his heart. When he first saw the fleet and Akaka he remembered the chief's proposal at Kawaihae: that he lead a strike force, hitting deep into Kau. *This is my chance for glory, but I no longer have stomach for war. What should I tell my mentor? I do not want to be thought a coward.* "I would like to join you in your adventure," Kalani said, hoping that Akaka would not sense the disingenuous tone in his voice, "but I would be a liability. I still need a staff to walk, and my lungs are not healed from the poisonous gasses of a vengeful Pele."

"That is unfortunate. I could use you in this venture. With a victory over Keoua, Kamehameha will reward those who bring him the man's body to be sacrificed in his new temple. Isaac Davis is with me. He has gunpowder and shot and additional soldiers. Send me your musketeers and any men you have to join us in the conquest of Kau."

The next day Kalani and Eleele stood at the embarkation beach. Canoes were already departing, hundreds of paddles rising and falling in a uniform cadence. Akaka strode up. "Thank you, High Chief, for your two hundred men, but you are not coming?"

"No, it is best I stay here, get my district under control, and make it a safe base for you if you need help," Eleele said.

Akaka laughed, "I think Keoua needs help. He must be reeling from all his losses. I will beat him easily."

His bravado stung. The man felt certain of victory. Kalani was unsure whether he was happy or sad not to join him. He thought the chief would win. Everyone who spoke of it believed that the volcano had torn the heart out of the Kau army, leaving only disorganized remnants to be eliminated.

Moki clapped him on the back. "Sorry you are going to miss out on all the fun, all the glory. Come with us, I'll take care of you."

There it was, even Moki thought I dodged the fight. Yet I still feel weak, hurting both inside and out, I need to heal, to learn from Mauloa. "You know I want to go, but I would be useless. It is best I stay here and mend. Do what I can for Eleele in Hilo."

"Yes," Akaka interjected. "A good decision. I think you've made your mark here. People respect you for what you said. Moki, we go."

Kalani watched sails cupping, and the paddles of a thousand men smashing into the sea. *Strange. Except for separation from Moki I am not sorry to see them leave. I remember a saying of Captain Russell when we discussed tactics: "A man has limited time for war." Maybe my time to do that is over.*

CHAPTER 52

Spring came and Kalani got well. Eleele visited, bringing news of events. Twice, Akaka had escaped disaster by taking to his canoes and fleeing along the coast. In Puna, the Kau chiefs, driven from Hilo, resolved the civil war between the factions and were gathering a small army to join Keoua.

Although enjoying his conversations with his blood brother, the most important meetings were with Mauloa. "Lono may be a slightly lesser god than the others but he is a peaceful god," the priest said. "He brings the rain, makes the crops grow, the beasts and women fertile. He does not oppress the commoners with fear of death and demanding sacrifice like Ku, the snatcher of islands. You can pray to him and he will not deny you. The people worship him because Lono does not preach repression."

"If he makes all things grow, then he is a god unified with the earth."

"You have it," Mauloa said. "Those who follow Lono believe that our *aina* is alive, that our god is within it helping things spring forth to nurture us to give us the means to live. That is why Lono desires peace, for war is a destroyer and farmers are not safe."

What a pragmatic man, Kalani thought. *Not fanatic like the kahuna nui of Kamehameha, the ugly savage who had killed Minato and so many more to please the war god.* "Davis tells me that if we keep people in fear of death and continue sacrificing to Ku, we will never progress and make our lives better."

"Your friend is wise. The chiefs repress using taboos to control us. Making rules that have no reason, forcing people to conform or die. There was a time when all were equal and loved by Lono. People lived without fear and tilled the land in freedom. But when the Tahitians..." Mauloa spat, screwed up his face and spat again. "When the Tahitians came from the southern islands they brought oppression. Their chiefs said: We are descendants of the gods. Obey us. Their priests said: Ku is our deity. He wants war and sacrifice."

The priest stopped his tirade, falling into a dreamlike state.

It gave Kalani moments to think of what he said. *My life has been controlled by inflexible edicts of the chiefs. It was like the common people had a rope around their neck held by a ruler who pulled, squeezed, or choked as he pleased. And women, they were especially restricted in what they could eat and do. I now begin to understand why my mother wanted me to go to war and become a chief. Those who claimed ancestry to the gods could bend the rules, live an easier life for themselves and their families. My love for Minato and my love for my mother had set me on the warrior path to find a way to end sacrifice and slavery. But should that be my quest? Or should I find another method for people to live free and without restrictions?*

Mauloa came out of his trance. "I dream a lot," he said.

"I've been dreaming too," Kalani agreed. "Teach me how to worship your god, the prayers, and rituals. Someday I want to build a City of Refuge where all people may come, worship Lono and live in freedom."

"I will teach you. But as to a City, you are not a chief nor do you have land. If you could get the power, I would help you."

"Don't you know better than to get out of the rain?" Eleele asked as he ran up to Kalani's shack.

Kalani didn't pause in his exercising. "It cools me. Watch this," he said, plunging his clenched fingers into a plank of wood. It splintered like a musket ball had blown through it, leaving a hole the size of a hand.

"Just like Waipio. You wanted to see me."

"Come inside," Kalani said, rubbing his body vigorously as he ducked through the threshold. Eleele followed. Kalani offered him a cloth when they squatted, taking one for himself, wiping his face. "You have to get me out of here."

"Why? I give you freedom to do as you please. Give you Nohea to work and take care of you." Eleele laughed, rubbing his thighs.

"That's the problem. Nohea wants to marry."

"What's wrong with that? But if you don't love her, then lie to her, string her along. Enjoy as long as you can, then kick her out, I'll send another."

Kalani winced. "I won't do that. I cheated in the past, deceived someone, and caused her death."

"The one you buried in Waipio," Eleele interjected. He had been puzzled by the time Kalani spent burying a female in the Hawaiian way. Three days of cleansing, shriveling, and mourning. Much too much effort, he thought, unless he loved her.

"Yeah, her name was Hinalea. I appreciate your lending me Nohea. She's a good woman. She helped me get well. But I don't love her and I'm not going to string her along. Give me an assignment where I can refuse to take her with me. Get me out of here."

Eleele split his sides laughing; his blood brother was running from a woman no better than opala. "Well, if that's the only way you can handle it, by running away, then I can send you to a military outpost I have on the border of Hilo and Puna."

Kalani winced. *I hadn't meant my request to seem so childish. However, I have wrestled with my guilt to the point that I would not lie to a woman to get her love. I had not considered the consequences when I impulsively asked for Eleele's help. Now I realize that in the world of men it is weakness to treat women fairly.*

"Just order me out of here," Kalani said, his voice firm, his fingers trembling.

At the border outpost, Kalani trained. He honed his warrior skills, practiced martial arts, and exercised, increasing his strength. By mid-June, he felt fit for combat.

Then Keoua struck. Early in the morning, with the sun burning away the cool air at sunrise, Puna and Kau warriors hit the outpost. Taken by surprise, defenders were killed in their sleep. Awakened by conch shells and the drums of the attackers, Kalani saved himself by wounding an onrushing attacker and escaping with survivors. In Hilo, he reported to Eleele, "We were still asleep when up to thirty men hit the camp. It is unusual for warriors to do that. Something big is happening in Puna."

"Sit down. Come eat. Hey, bring food," Eleele yelled, stuffing a chicken breast into his mouth.

"Forget about eating," Kalani said, exasperated that his blood brother spoke casually about the attack. Moki was out there, Akaka and other friends as well. "If you won't send someone to check things out, I'll go alone."

Eleele peered at him, licked his fingers, stuck his hand into a calabash of poi, twirled and came out with purple paste that he slurped like a sugar cane stick. "This four-day-old stuff is great. Try it with the cooked ahi head over there."

"We have a problem," Kalani exploded, his nerves frayed by concern. He couldn't understand why Eleele was so unhurried, but that's the way with older men, especially high chiefs. *I must learn the trick of ruling: be unconcerned, show you're in control even if you're quaking inside.*

The hale became silent. Eleele munched his food. Kalani hid his emotions and waited. Eleele cleaned his hand, fumbled with his loincloth and said, "I will send men into Puna. We will wait for their report."

Several days later Eleele summoned Kalani and three of his chiefs. "Keoua has left Kau and invaded Puna."

"A surprising move," one of the men said "It is a confession of weakness on Keoua's part."

"Yes, Akaka believes that is so," Eleele continued, ignoring the interruption. "He is marching with his army into Puna to bring Keoua to a final battle. He is confident of victory."

"What of his war fleet?" Kalani asked.

"They are returning to Hilo. The Puna coastline is rocky and the sea is powerful. It is difficult for canoes to land or wait offshore. After Akaka defeats Keoua, he will head overland to Hilo."

"That's a risky decision," Kalani said. "If Akaka doesn't win, he has only one line of retreat, by land. Is there anywhere along the coast that a fleet could rescue a defeated army?"

"We do not know where a battle will occur. If it is near Kalapana, there are black sand beaches. The currents are swift in that area. Removing an army from the shore would be difficult, but not impossible," Eleele answered.

Kalani shook his head, realizing that Akaka had to win on land. The odds of his army surviving if they retreated by sea were low. He studied the members of the council of war that had been summoned. Kalani knew his blood brother could be relied upon. He wasn't sure of the other three men.

Eleele continued, "Although Akaka is confident of victory, I fear that Keoua is stronger than we realize. We know that Puna is no longer in civil war, and minions of the Kau king have organized a force of warriors in that district. Why did they attack our outpost? I think it is to close our eyes to what is happening in Puna. Although I have very few men to spare, we must come to a decision. Do we send warriors into Puna to discover the strength of the enemy and aid Akaka if needed, or do we stay in Hilo awaiting the outcome of battle?"

"I say we stay in Hilo. Let Akaka fight alone," Nae, one of the chiefs, said. The other two nodded in agreement.

"And you, Kalani?" Eleele asked.

"The men of your war council are older and wiser than I. You know the temper of your people and the willingness of Puna farmers to fight. Maybe it is best to be like the turtle and hide within our shell. But what if Akaka loses? We will not know of it until the enemy descends upon us."

"What is the choice?" Nae demanded. "Charge blindly into Puna? You saw the army that attacked our outpost. What if they are waiting for us to advance? We would be destroyed."

"It is a risk that must be taken," Kalani answered. "If we fail to act and Akaka wins, we will be considered cowards. If he is losing, we may help him gain a victory, or at least prevent a disaster."

"I agree with my brother," Eleele said. "Sitting here in Hilo and doing nothing is not my choice. Go. Gather your men. We will attack."

The three chiefs scattered while Kalani and Eleele discussed strategy. They decided to march toward the point where the trail from Kau winds around Kilauea volcano and turns toward Hilo. There they would gather intelligence and, depending on what they learned, move southeast towards Pahoa, or follow the trail into Kau. Word was left for Akaka's fleet to return and marshal in four days at Kalapana.

CHAPTER 53

A SINKING SUN SPREAD SHADOWS across the woods and onto the trail leading into Puna. A hundred-and-twenty men with thirty female auxiliaries marched south in the dying light. Kalani noted their apprehension as their eyes searched into the ferns and broad-leafed shrubs lining the pathway. He knew from the scouts that soon they would break through the forest into a wide, treeless space covered by clumps of dry, hard, lava. He also knew that the land ahead was empty of enemy warriors.

Eleele brought his small force to a halt at the edge of the forest. They camped for the night within the trees. Fires were forbidden. The warriors munched their cakes of poi and sticks of dried fish in the dark, shivering in the cool air that whispered in from the snowcapped crown of Mauna Loa.

"This will be a hard night," Kalani said, striding over to Eleele, seated on a boulder.

Eleele nodded. "Yes. I can feel the icy breath of the great volcano clutching into my innards, but it is better to breathe its purity than the foul gases that filled our lungs six months ago."

Kalani remembered that time when he staggered like a drunk, tumbling as the earth waved beneath his feet. Tonight, everything was peaceful, not even smoke from Kilauea. "You're right. Better to smell clean air than Pele's stinking breath. The hundreds of deaths below Kilauea's fire pit still haunt me. I'm astonished that Keoua recovered from his losses and has fought Akaka to a standstill."

"Keoua has been clever up to now. But tomorrow, or the day after, could see his end. A few miles away, the path around the volcano descends into the lower lands of Puna. I suspect that the two forces will clash near Pahoa, where we fought months ago. Tomorrow we will know where the final battle will be."

Kalani lay down to sleep. He stared into a deep blue moonless sky. A few clouds colored the heavens with mist, not enough to blot out the multitude of stars gleaming above. He searched for Arcturus, the guiding star shining over Hawaii that had led ancient navigators from the Marquesas to this island.

He gazed at the brooding Kilauea in the distance, remembering the smoke and fire that had flowed from its deep crater. Kalani wondered: *were ancient sailors attracted to this land by fountains of orange-red fire and steaming columns of smoke when molten lava hit the sea? Or could it have been the snow-capped peak of Mauna Loa thrusting its pig-shaped snout through the clouds that guided those early voyagers to Hawaii? How had all these things happened*? Kalani wondered, falling asleep. His dreams did not disturb him. He slumbered in peace.

Morning came, the sky changing from blue to white, then orange as sunlight flooded over the horizon, turning dark clouds a muddy red. Men and women woke, ate, and then straggled south, Eleele herding them on. Kalani ran ahead, searching the land for enemies. He saw none. His worry mounted. He sensed that something was occurring. But where?

Rocks in a gully slowed his pace. The ground around him was smoke colored, flooded by eons of flowing lava that had cooled into pancakes of dark rock. Shrubs, parched flaxen brown by the sun, struggled through cracks in the frozen stone.

Kalani climbed to the summit of a low hill and went prone, studying the ground far below him. It was land no longer barren. Trees and grass grew in profusion among clumps of rock. In the distance, he saw the ocean shining blue in the sun, framed by palm trees fringing the shore with layers of white clouds above.

More than a mile away, in a grassy plain, he saw men forming up. Chiefs moved about in their cloaks and helmets. They mixed with warriors spreading out in a battle line. Beyond the deploying army, within a grove of dark brown trees, there stood another line of warriors in battle formation. White-clad priests moved between the two forces. Kalani knew they were calling on the gods for victory.

Soft sounds drew his gaze from the unfolding battle to the shrubbery below his hill. A force of warriors creeped toward the flank of one of the deploying armies. "These men are going to attack Akaka in the rear while Keoua hits him from the front," he muttered. Kalani scrambled down the hill, his head pounding as if it would burst. He reached the gully at the base and broke into a run. Far away, he heard the sharkskin drums and horned-shell trumpets heralding an attack.

Heedless of the sharp stones that poked his bare feet, the bruises when he fell, Kalani rushed along the dried rivers of lava searching for Eleele. After many minutes, he paused to rest and heard shuffling feet. Warriors were marching nearby. He crawled behind a boulder, his spear ready to strike. With a sigh, he saw his friends from Hilo.

A half hour later, Kalani stood on a hillcrest with Eleele and his chiefs studying the battlefield. "The army of Akaka is bent like a drawn bow. Those warriors are lost. The smart thing to do is return home while we can and save ourselves," Nae said.

Kalani's heart thumped against his chest, his pulse rising with worry for the imminence of Akaka's defeat. His anxiety brought vehemence to his words. "If we strike the rear of the enemy, yelling and screaming as we charge, it will bring fear to their hearts and force them to run."

"I agree with my brother," Eleele said. "There is still a chance for victory. We will divide into three groups of fifty and march to the battle. No drums or trumpets to warn them. There is plenty of cover below to conceal our advance. We will assemble at the edge of the plain. When I give the signal, yell, scream, call upon all the gods and attack. Nae, you take the left-hand column, I the center, Kalani will be on the right. Watch me."

Kalani joined his column, wondering about Nae. *The man's heart was not strong for this battle. Was he a coward, only fighting to gain status with Eleele? That was true on all sides, chiefs fought for prestige or advantage, but only when they were certain of winning. In this battle, the odds were against them. Akaka had been squeezed into a hopeless position, the pincers attack of Keoua had trapped him. I knew Eleele would fight, but what about Nae? It didn't matter. I am loyal to my friends. I will give my all to save them and if I die doing so, I would die with honor.*

The Hilo warriors poised themselves to strike the right horn of Keoua's army. Eleele yelled, "Charge." Trumpets blared. Drums beat. One-hundred-and-fifty warriors of Hilo attacked. By Kalani's side were two *pikoi* women. Their heads were shaved bald, their breasts bare. A dark wide belt girdled their stomachs and loins, tripping cords attached to it. Each woman twirled slings as they charged, hurling stones at an enemy unaware of their presence.

A startled warrior stung by a rock turned to fight. Kalani yelled to the pikoi, "Drop back. Fling over our men." He hurled his spear and the man crumpled, the haft of the weapon in his chest. He felt satisfied. Weeks of training had paid off. His actions were automatic, precise and immediate. He drew out his shark-toothed knife and cut the downed warrior open.

"Behind you," a man yelled. Kalani felt a shark tooth slice his back as a cudgel slid down it. He went low, turned and raked the warrior's face with his knife.

"Oh, Ku," the man moaned. His hands rose to his bloody cheeks as he stumbled from the fight.

Another warrior stabbed with a short spear. A pikoi woman flung her tripping cord around his neck and yanked it. The man pitched toward him. Kalani hit him with an elbow, then shoved the pommel of his knife deep into the warrior's stomach. The man grunted, bent his head. Kalani's fist smashed down on his exposed neck. He turned to thank the woman, but she had dropped back from the fight.

He heard Eleele screaming, "Kill, kill." He glanced at his blood brother swinging his cudgel left, right, smashing down men, making others retreat. He couldn't find Nae and hoped the man had not run away. A shout made Kalani look ahead. He saw a warrior charging, one half of his body covered with crisscrossing tattoos, his face masked by a gourd with strings of shark teeth dangling from it. "Die, Kamehameha man," he yelled, thrusting an eight-foot spear. With a quick move, Kalani stepped to the side, grabbed the haft, pulled, then used his leg to trip. The warrior tumbled to the ground. Three pikoi rushed up, pummeling him with stones. "A king's bodyguard. Take him prisoner," Kalani yelled.

Shadows were hurrying across the grass plain as half the sun blazed above the horizon. Heavy black clouds were moving toward the battlefield, dropping rain as they came. Eleele ran up, his face, chest, arms splattered with blood. "Kalani, we've smashed this horn of Keoua's army. I saw Davis ahead. Getting dark. Tell him to retreat with us."

"You're red all over, are you hurt?"

Eleele laughed. "No, blood from the ones I bashed. You know when you hit 'em how it all splashes up like a fountain."

"Yeah, I remember how hard you hit. Where's Davis?"

Eleele pointed and Kalani ordered his warriors to follow him. An eight-foot spear flew at him. He caught and tossed it to his blood brother. "Use this," he laughed, "and stay clean."

A club struck his shoulder, driving him backward, a jolt of pain running down his spine. The soldier swung again, but a pikoi guardian speared him. Ahead he heard Davis yelling, "Club with your guns." He couldn't find Moki and worried that he might be among the dead. He rushed to the gunner. "Where's Akaka? Where's Moki?"

Sweat striped Davis' powder-blackened face. His tattered white tunic was spotted red and black, and his eyes looked wild as he pointed. "Akaka is somewhere over there. I think he's a goner. Moki, I don't know."

"Eleele is holding a corridor open for your escape. Get your men. Withdraw. I'll help Akaka."

It seemed an impossible task. The battle still raged ahead of him, but dusk had come and rain fell. Kalani yelled, "Warriors, help Davis." Then he ran toward the sea. He sensed someone following and he glanced back. A slim, gangly pikoi woman, twirling her tripping cord, loped behind him. "I ordered you to go with Davis."

The pikoi glared. She swung her rock faster and said, "Eleele say guard you." She darted past him her eyes scanning the darkening ground. Light rain pattered her back, dripping over her and the small club bound to her waist.

"I don't need a baby sitter," Kalani muttered, resigning himself to the notion he would not be rid of her. A dog growled, nipping at his heels. He swerved to the side. The animal showed its teeth, then bit into a body, tearing out a chunk of flesh. He thought to stop, but knew Akaka needed him. He followed the path of the pikoi woman, trusting her instincts to avoid the heaps of dead and dying men littering the field.

CHAPTER 54

The hovering clouds slowly unfolded, letting stars cast weak light on dispirited men shuffling through the coco forest. Breezes, icy from glaciers that capped the massive twin volcanoes, roused Kalani. He willed his feet to walk faster, overcome his exhaustion, and catch up with Akaka. Within the grove of trees fringing the battlefield, fires sprang up, lit by the victorious army of Keoua. Somewhere to the north, Kalani hoped that Eleele and Moki were alive, retreating with Isaac Davis and other fugitives to Hilo.

He came up to Akaka, whose feet were dragging, his six-foot-six body bent low. His feather cape was torn, its underlying weave of sennit showing in patches. His war helmet, once as beautiful as that worn by Kamehameha, had been lost in the madness of the final melee. "We were doomed," Akaka said, humiliation in his voice. "My Alapa division saved us from defeat. Your news of the fleet returning may save us from annihilation."

His despondency shocked Kalani. The man had always been strong, sure of himself. He fumbled to find the right words to answer.

"It was not the Alapa that saved the army, it was you. I watched you fighting like a demon. Your inspiration kept men from surrendering. We are marching to the sea because of you."

A wan smile lit Akaka's face. His grim features relaxed and his eyes lost their faraway look. "Maybe I was brave to save my men, but I never should have walked into Keoua's trap and have to fight like fury to escape it. You said that Davis got away?" Kalani nodded.

"That's good. For us, we must seek refuge at the sea. It is the place we always go to fish, to be free, and to escape destruction. I hope the fleet will come. If they do not, then Keoua will have much food to sacrifice to the war god." Akaka fell silent and the two men plodded through the forest toward the beach of Kalapana.

Black sand crunched under his feet, a phenomenon peculiar to Hawaii Island, dark pebble beaches created when roaring hot lava strikes the sea and fragments into bits. Over time, the exploded pieces are ground fine by the restless actions of the waves. Kalani wondered whether the darkness would ever come clean like the beautiful yellow sand he had seen in Lahaina and Wailuku.

Waves smashed into his legs, splashing up to his belly. "Not good, the fleet could not land and if we swim out..." He stepped from the water striding toward Akaka, seated with a handful of chiefs in a stand of palm trees. On the horizon a crescent moon peeped, sending a shining silver ribbon reaching out to the meeting. "Ho, Akaka," Kalani said. "You sent for me."

The high chief studied the sea. He sighed. "I wish our army could mount that bright path and escape this horror that has struck us. But for you, Kalani, we would be no more, crushed by Keoua. The sacrifices would have already begun. At least some of us are alive. But tomorrow, if the fleet does not come, we are lost."

Akaka's gloomy mood saddened him. If captured, the high chief would be the first delivered to Ku. Others would come next. Kalani felt his temple pounding.

Would I die by the knife, or garroted until I choked, sacrificed like my father and grandfather to an insatiable god? Over the last few months, war and its consequences troubled him: death, destruction, the sacrifices of defeated warriors and slaves. Kalani knew that he could have remained in Hilo pursuing a course of peace, serving the god Lono in his temple. But I would never abandon my friends. "All men die, only a matter of when and how."

Akaka screwed his eyes onto him. "A philosopher. Tell me, how do you want to depart this world?"

"Die well. Brave, not cowardly. Silent, not shrieking. Thank the gods for giving me life."

He heard a murmur of voices. Restless movement. The word *maikai*, good. He smiled, the sour mood was changing.

"Well said, my koa, your words match your heroics. For your brave acts you are entitled to become a 'black land chief'. If we survive, I promise you that, despite your lack of royal blood line, I will petition Kamehameha to make you a 'black land chief' and be given land." The handful of men grouped around Akaka grunted their agreement.

"I am not worthy," Kalani protested. "There are others more deserving than I."

"End your foolish prattle. If the fleet comes to save us, you will be a chief."

Far too tired to argue further, and thrilled by the prospect, Kalani found a comfortable place on the ground and fell asleep.

The half-light of early morning washed the darkness away from a deep blue ocean. The sea frothed with whitecaps and a strong wind sent cresting waves crashing onto the black sand, then swept the shore in bubbles to the edge of the coconut grove. Kalani, naked and bruised, slipped out of his dream. He saw the roiling water and knew that even if the fleet came, embarkation would be dangerous. Yet escape by sea was the army's only hope.

He strode through the encampment. Warriors moved upland to serve as sentinels. Beyond the beach, the land was marred by heaps of sharp black rocks, jagged crevices steaming with the heat of underground fires. On a promontory, Kalani saw a pile of wood. He knew when the fleet was sighted it would be set afire signaling where Akaka hid.

The high chief sat in a discussion with a group of men. Kalani wrapped his loincloth around himself and hastened to the meeting. He heard Akaka say, "There are three entryways. We must block them with rocks and trees. Warriors will defend them until the fleet arrives. I and a reserve will be in the center, ready to be used where needed." Spotting Kalani he said, "You, to the far end. Take charge there."

His pikoi guardian ran beside him. She was silent. Tired, he thought, hungry. They all were. They had little to eat and only water from coconuts to drink. Men sucked their urine letting nothing be wasted. That's the way it had been in the days of long voyaging. Kalani stared ahead to where the black sand ended and the ground rose up in heaps of hardened stone. Mounds of lava, pocked with crevices, grassless and barren, rimmed the beach. Nature's quirks had snaked passageways through the dark stones to the sea.

They slowed at a passageway where warriors were blocking it up with rocks and felled logs. The two joined the workers. The pikoi did not complain, toiling as hard as any man building the defenses. Kalani's admiration rose. She had led him unerringly to Akaka, avoiding all confrontations. She had stepped aside when not needed but came forward when she was.

Someone shouted, "The fire is lit." Smoke mushroomed into the sky. Kalani climbed rocks. He saw canoes racing south, their crab claw sails spanking in the wind. He felt relief at the sighting, happy that his message to return had been given. Now if the fleet could get here before Keoua came they would escape. But everyone could see the sprouting black cloud. Within minutes the scouts returned, reporting marauding enemy warriors.

The sun was at its zenith. Waves of heat warmed the men huddled on the beach. Heavy surf from an incoming tide washed the shore. Inland, conch shells blew the call to battle. The pikoi woman came to him saying, "I brought you a spear." She handed the weapon to him. He felt embarrassed. In his excitement he had forgotten the tools of war.

At the barrier, enemy warriors hurled challenges, their spears thrusting like thorns over the rock wall. Missiles flew, striking indiscriminately friend and foe. The barrage of stones and spears had its effect, slicing a wedge into the defending men. The enemy climbed over the defenses, rushing toward the beach. From his reserve position Kalani shouted to his pikoi guardian, "Let's give it to them." The woman slung rocks as Kalani charged, skewering the first man through the barrier.

Keoua's warriors continued to pour in, defenders fell. The rocks hurt but did not kill. Kalani loved the fight. He stabbed with the spear. Reversed his hands and thrust the butt into a face or belly. Exhilaration flooded over him as he swung the spear like a club, striking a temple or an arm. Months of practice had honed his skills. Pride over his recovered abilities replaced common sense. He endangered himself constantly as he twisted, turned, and pivoted. A warrior slashed his chest with a shark-toothed knife. Then a man fell into him, pinning him to the ground. The warrior grinned and swept his knife down.

There was a blur, a slim body smashed into the attacker, blocking the hooking move with her body. The knife of the pikoi swept up, shredding the loincloth of the man. Blood spurted from the V between his thighs. He screamed, jumped about, and then ran howling over the barrier. Kalani said, "You're hurt, a knife is in your back."

"Worse injuries before," she said. "I pull you up. You pull it out."

A force from the reserve came running and drove the enemy over the makeshift wall. In the brief respite, Kalani glanced to the sea. The rescue fleet had entered the shallow bay. Enemy canoes were closing in. Warning trumpets sounded the retreat. Akaka's warriors abandoned their defense of the passageways and rushed to the sea.

The canoes could not land. The water's pull proved too powerful. Warriors struggled against the currents of the ocean, trying to reach the vessels. Waves smashed the fugitives, swirling around their bodies, threatening to suck them out to sea. Brave sailors fought to bring their bobbing canoes close to shore. Frightened men wrestled themselves from the water into the wave-whipped crafts.

Kalani joined Akaka, the pikoi woman by his side. Enemy warriors poured over the rock barriers, attacking the fleeing remnants of Akaka's army. A flotilla of Kau canoes fought with the rescue fleet. "Disaster, disaster," flashed through Kalani's mind. All about him, men screamed in fright.

Over the reeking smell of fear, above the wreckage of a lost battle, the trumpet of Akaka blew. His elite warriors flung their spears at the onrushing enemy, loosened their war clubs, and charged. Kalani with his pikoi woman joined them. He threw his spear into a mass of men, gripped his cudgel and swung it like a man berserk. His guardian was always by his side, silent and protective. The craziness of the charge destroyed the enemy morale. They ran.

Akaka blew his trumpet a second time, recalling his men. Kalani and a half-dozen warriors stood in swirling water, directing survivors onto canoes, sending loaded vessels to combat the Kau fleet. Kalani saw a giant standing on a plateau, caped by feathers. He shouted words that Kalani could not hear. His commands were unmistakable, the spear in his hand pointing at Akaka's small group.

Kau warriors poured over the barriers, pressing forward to attack the fleeing army. Akaka ordered his men to board the last canoe bobbing in the swell of crashing waves. Kalani waded into the water, the pikoi woman beside him. His feet stumbled on rocks rolling with the waves. Hands reached to help. "Get in the canoe!" He seized her buttocks, lifted her, and shoved her in, surprised at how light she was. As he reached for the jittering craft, something struck his head. He heard a woman scream, "Go back." He staggered, lost balance, and toppled like a felled tree into the ocean.

CHAPTER 55

MAKULA WATCHED HIS LUA TRAINEES perform kicks and leg sweeps. "You have done well," Namaka said, an Oahu chief standing by his side. "You have made these men expert in lua. Kahekili will be pleased. When we invade Hawaii, they will be the leaders of our army and end that upstart's rule."

"Yes, and then I will take back what is mine!" Makula's shout halted combat on the practice field. Twelve naked men ceased exercising and stared at their teacher. He waved them to continue and returned to the conversation. "You have developed a new tool of war, Namaka. I saw men training dogs in the compound next to this."

"Your eyes are sharp. We need new weapons to beat Kamehameha's guns. Kahekili believes swift attack dogs may be the answer."

Makula's face became rigid. He clenched his fists, stiffened his arms, the veins in his biceps rising like worms. "Kalani and his foreign fire weapons defeated me. At Hamakua, Keoua was beaten by Kamehameha's cannon. You cannot fight them in a solid wall of men, hemmed in. Dogs might be the answer. I have tried another tactic in Kau, hit fast and run."

Namaka reared back. "Run! That is not the way of a warrior."

"What are you doing with the dogs?" Makula exploded. "Quick attacks, then the animals move away, and attack again. That is my tactic, hit, run, when they follow, ambush. That is how I beat Akaka in Kau. That is how you must fight the guns. You can't stand there like a stone and be brought down! Only a fool invites death." Makula smashed a fist into his palm, emphasizing his words. He fixed his eyes on Namaka. For some moments the two men stared at each other until Namaka turned away. "I respect what you say, but there is only one way to fight, warrior against warrior. Follow me."

They came to a series of shacks. Makula saw tattooed men wrestling, staring at the sky, punching each other then laughing hysterically. "These men are crazy."

Namaka smiled, "They are, but they fight like fury and feel no pain. Let me show you." He strode to a man studying his palm. He jabbed a short knife into his side. Blood spurted from the wound. The man looked up, grinned, then shuffled away. Namaka turned. "Maybe you can use these warriors for your new way of fighting."

Makula wiped his hair with his palm. His brow furrowed, his finger stroked his lips. "Yes, I may have a use for them."

"Good. Ah, there is Kahekili's right-hand-man."

A giant strode toward them. Muscular, with tattoos on the right side of his face and body. The bizarre pattern of the design made the man frightening. He held a spear in his hand, which he drew back, and flung. Makula's eyes fastened on the missile. He bent back. His hand darted up and seized the weapon. In one smooth motion he brought it to his side, reversed the point, and hurled it back. The giant dodged, barely escaping being hit. The spear struck the ground, breaking the haft.

"Too bad. Good spear," the big warrior said. He pointed to Makula. "Kahekili wants you."

Makula studied the swaying, wiry, silver-haired man squatting in front of him. Drunk with awa, he thought, yet he is the craftiest ruler in Hawaii and its best general. He waited. The Oahu king must be the first to speak.

A trickle of drool seeped from Kahekili's lips. Eyes clouded with mucus, he peered at Makula. Kahekili started as if seeing him for the first time. "The chief of Kauai and I will attack Hawaii Island." The king sucked air then hissed, "Our raiders are striking the north shore. We will seize Waipio Valley. Destroy it! Kamehameha will starve." Kahekili fell silent. Before Makula could answer he added, "You were once a powerful chief in Kona, but defeated in battle. Have you anything to offer?"

Insulting. Bargain? That's what the man wants, to bargain as if he were nothing. As if he, Makula, is not enough. I who have trained his elite guards, his lua leaders, planned with his chiefs to end Kamehameha's quest for conquest. He should fawn at my feet. Give me what I want. Makula's anger mounted, rising as the king stared, his eyes rheumy, doubting him. Before he exploded he realized that he needed Kahekili's help to be revenged. "I have much to offer," Makula said, his tone shrill. "I have followers in Kona. I have fought with Keoua, defeated Akaka. The Kau king will give me warriors. But most of all—" Makula stood, flexed his muscles, breathed deeply raising his height to its full six-foot-four-inches "—you will have me to serve you."

"Good. You may have the pick of my soldiers."

"The crazy ones?" Makula interjected.

"You want them? They are my special secret, men immune from pain. Take them. Go to Kona. Our fleet is ready. I will sail in two weeks. Attack. Attack." The king rose. Steady, sure, he stared at Makula and hissed, "Attack, destroy Kamehameha."

CHAPTER 56

THE FOOTPATH WAS RUTTED, DIMLY visible in the weak light of kukui nut torches held by guards. Racked with pain, barely able to see, Kalani stumbled into a coco tree, bruising his side. He felt a sharp ache and worried that he had cracked a rib. A warrior struck him, and said, "Get up."

"Where are you taking us?" Kalani demanded. A prisoner in front of him moaned, "To our death." The guard prodded him with his spear point and rapped the haft into Kalani's ribs. Its sting choked the air from his lungs. He thought to strike the man, but that might mean the killing of prisoners would start here, in the coconut grove. Kalani settled into a sullen silence.

Firelight fingered through the trees. Kalani saw ahead a glade of koa and the silhouette of several huts scattered among them. The guards herded the captives into a low, walled compound. Gripped by two warriors, Kalani was manhandled to the threshold of a shack and kicked in. Vomit rose in his throat, the smell of the pigsty overwhelming. Sprawled in filth, his body covered with offal, his hands bound tight, Kalani dug his feet into the mush and waited.

Within minutes, he heard footsteps, voices. Two Kau warriors came into the hovel. "You dirty, smelly," one man said.

"No worse than your stinking breath," Kalani retorted, blowing through his nose and mouth to emphasize his point.

"What did you say?" The guard slapped Kalani on his head and punched him in the belly.

"Stop," the second man ordered. "The king wants to see him, alive."

"Yeah, not before I give it to this okole and make him remember me." A foot slammed into Kalani's legs, knocking him into the offal. "Go one on one with you any time," the brutal guard said.

Kalani grinned, thrust up his arms bound with ropes of sennit. "Cut them off and we go."

"Stop," the second man said. "Come and bathe."

Shoved to a trough, his bindings were removed. He washed, thankful that he was still alive, wondering if the king meant to torture him before he was sacrificed. A morbid thought crossed his mind: W*hat would he choose to eat? It would be his heart. It must be his heart. That is where his mana is stored, his spiritual power. Before he was knifed, he would ask the king to feast on nothing else.*

He wrapped a clean white loincloth around his waist and was led to a large shack set in a clearing beyond the trees. Bonfires filled the area with warm light, and an open pit of hot stones smelled of the sweet aroma of baked pig. His stomach growled. He was hungry, thirsty, tired, but he would not scurry to the king like a rat. He straightened himself and stepped into the palace.

Oil lamps lit the interior, their spiraling smoke disappearing into the darkness of the ceiling. Kalani saw a tall, well-muscled man, sitting at the far end of a mat filled with food. Dim light flickered over his bronzed skin, sleek with coconut oil. His hair was bound in a knot on top of his head with a colorful ribbon coiled around his forehead and temples. His loins were girded by a plain cloth, a black belt holding it tight to his waist. He dipped his fingers into a calabash, drawing out poi and letting the grey paste flow into his mouth. Spying Kalani he said, "Come. Eat," patting a place by his side.

Kalani prostrated. The king lifted his hand motioning him to rise and come to him. Wary, puzzled, Kalani searched the unmarked face of the man called the Red Cloak, cousin of Kamehameha, for signs of hostility. He saw none.

The king rose, his lips playing a slight smile on his face. "Let us exchange ha," he said.

Kalani breathed deeply, inclining his head to the shorter man. They exhaled together. Kalani breathed in the acrid air of rotted poi. He suppressed his vomit knowing that he was being honored, for words from the mouth are false but the breath is not. The exchange meant that the king intended the conversation to be truthful.

Kalani squatted and ate until he sated his hunger. Keoua remained silent. The only sound the swishing of fans held by servants. Kalani wanted to speak, to learn when he would die, but he did not. Protocol required that the king be first.

"You fought bravely," Keoua said.

Kalani acknowledged with a nod, waiting for the king to say more.

"You claimed in Hilo that I am not favored by the gods! That Pele is against me!"

Kalani paused, aware that these weighty issues could put him in serious danger. "Yes, I said that. I saw the bodies of your army frozen in death, covered with the dust of Pele's wrath."

"I saw them too. My warriors should never have angered the goddess by rolling stones into her hot bath. I am told you killed Hauna beneath the volcano. Why did you do that?"

"I did not kill Hauna. We fought by the bodies of the dead. He brought me down, tried to finish me with a final strike. Pele grabbed him with fingers of fire, drawing him into her bosom. I tried to save him. The smoke and fire were too strong."

Kalani paused, dropping his eyes. "Hauna tried to kill me many times. Why? I don't know. Maybe it is because I am not of royal blood. I know at the fatal meeting, I fought him to avenge my blood brother for Hauna's eating of his father's liver, like I must fight you for eating his heart."

"Who told you such a false tale? I sacrificed the Hilo high chief, that is certain. He was a traitor who had promised loyalty. When Kamehameha chose to invade Maui, the man joined his cause. He sent his sons, Hilo warriors, to aid in the venture. I never ate his heart, nor did I witness Hauna eating his liver. All that you heard of flesh eating is false."

Could the king be lying? But they had exchanged ha, breathing in each other's spirit. Kalani did not know the man, but deep in his heart he believed Keoua spoke the truth. What purpose could be served by deceiving him, someone without power? "I accept your word, but why do you fight Kamehameha?"

The king leaped up, towering over Kalani. "It is because he is vain and proud, wanting all of Hawaii for himself. I am the rightful king of Kau, a district granted to me by my father, King of Hawaii Island, Kamehameha's uncle. Your leader is an upstart. He refuses to let me rule what is mine. My people will rebel against anyone who is not their rightful king."

Keoua paused in his tirade, staring at the young man kneeling at his feet. Kalani swayed, overcome by the power of the king's anger. Though Keoua raged he was not mad. *His claim, that people will rebel against authority, startled Kalani. I have been taught to obey or die. Keoua was challenging the ages-old tradition of obedience to the chiefs, descendants of the gods.*

"My people fight for me because they hate the tyrant," Keoua continued. "How do you think I recovered from Pele's wrath and defeated Akaka in several battles?" The king leaned forward, eyes narrowed. "If you truly believe that Pele is against me and the gods favor Kamehameha, did you hear their voices? From your lips I want to know if what you say is true. The gods, did they speak to you or did you lie? Say the truth, your life depends on it."

"Keoua, I would not lie to you, even to cheat death, for I know that you can tell when words are false. I heard the voice of the greatest of the prophets say that Kamehameha would be king of all Hawaii. When I pursued Hauna into the roaring volcano's path, I found your warriors dusted with Pele's deadly powder, frozen in death. I believed you had lost favor with the gods. These are the truths on which I based my claims when I spoke in Hilo."

Keoua studied the ceiling, watching smoke escape through cracks in the thatching. He picked at his fingers, cleaning the skin, then said, "It is good that you have not lied. Your proofs I believe. Pele's wrath weighs on my heart. I am sick of war. Sick of the sacrifices made to a war god who is never appeased. Akaka should never have attacked me in Kau. He did so because he thought me weak. There is some truth in that, but my people love their independence and fought to maintain their freedom. Return to Kamehameha. Tell him I want our war to end. He may have all western Hawaii, Hamakua and Hilo, too. Leave me the lava-washed lands of Puna and Kau and let there be peace."

It was an unbelievable offer. Kalani knew that Akaka's army was whipped beyond repair. Eleele had lost so many fighting men that he had filled his ranks with women. There were rumors whispered of a war fleet being built by Kahekili that would fill the ocean from horizon to horizon. Kamehameha was surrounded by his enemies. If there was peace on Hawaii Island he could recover and stave off certain defeat.

Kalani felt overwhelmed by the mixture of political thoughts racing in his mind. He smoothed his hands over his hair to ease the pounding in his skull. He closed his eyes to think, to concentrate on what to say. "King Keoua, peace is what I want. But I have no standing in the court of Kamehameha. I am not a chief. At war councils my presence has been challenged for I cannot show royal blood. If permitted to attend, I must be silent. You need another, worthier than I."

Keoua reached to his shoulder. Instinctively, Kalani flinched. Kapu forbade contact with high chiefs lest their god-like spiritual power produced dire consequences to those who were touched. Keoua smiled. "My mana will not hurt you. Only those who are common or base should fear my hand." He seized Kalani's shoulder, gripping hard. "At Kalapana, my generals told me to watch for a special warrior, a koa. They said I would know you by your red belt and checkered loincloth. From high, I saw you fight, deadly and powerful." Keoua's eyes flicked to the mat, found a gourd, and spat. "Akaka should have fought me. Instead, he ran away, and you saved him. I knew at Kalapana that you were a special man. You shall take my message."

Finality rang in Keoua's voice, stilling his protests. Kalani nodded.

"Good. It is agreed. You will have safe passage to Hilo. Tell your king of my offer. If he is wise and does not seek absolute power, he will accept. Our people will have peace."

Keoua offered salt. Kalani took several grains, realizing that by this small gift, the king wanted to end war. He asked, "For eight years you and Kamehameha have fought, made sacrifices to Ku, but neither has more than the other. Is this why you seek peace to end this competition of death?"

The Kau king's eyes glistened. "My answer is yes. I have seen too much of death from Pele's wrath, from war, from human sacrifice. War brings only misery. It must end."

CHAPTER 57

ELEELE GRIMACED. "THERE ARE WHISPERS of rebellion to my rule. Akaka has sailed to Kawaihae. Kahekili and the king of Kauai have joined together and will attack Hawaii. Keoua is all powerful again. Kamehameha and I are doomed."

Kalani drew a circle in the dirt slashing a line through its center. "If Keoua does not attack, can you end any rebellion against you?"

"Why wouldn't he strike us? Our defenses are weak. He would beat us easily."

Kalani realized that Eleele had lost his will to fight. He needed to pull him from his gloom. "You should know this, I bear a message from Keoua, offering peace. He will not invade Hilo while he negotiates with Kamehameha. You have time to quell all who oppose you."

Eleele stood, paced in the sand, did a quick dance, pounded a fist into his palm, smiled, and said, "That is news to my liking. When I tell my people, it will quiet those who doubt me." Then his face turned gloomy. "But what if Kamehameha does not accept peace?"

"With all the enemies against him, he would be a fool if he did not."

"Agreed, but the man is ambitious, he wants to rule everybody. Be the king of all the islands. I think he will refuse." Eleele stopped walking, scuffing his feet in the sand.

"I hope that you are wrong about him. But take this time of truce between Kau and Hilo and regain your power. I'll deliver the message and see what happens. If war continues you can make a deal with Keoua to leave Hilo alone. I think you will find that he is tired of fighting. Does Moki live? Will you give me a canoe and paddlers to get to Kawaihae?"

"Yes, Moki left with Akaka. Do not travel by canoe. It is too dangerous. Take the overland route. Kahekili is raiding along the north shore. On the sea you would be taken."

The blood brothers walked to a path that led over the mountains to Kawaihae and Kamehameha. "This road twists and turns as it winds in and out of the cliffs," Eleele said. "But it is the safest route to take. There are good people who live along it and they will care for you." The two men embraced and Kalani started to climb.

For five days, he hiked the north shore. The land flowed from the gigantic heights of the dead volcano down to the sea in waves of rock. At the ocean, hardened lava dropped in stubs of sixty-to-hundred-foot fingers into the sea. Few lived in this barren land, but those he met provided him with food, shelter, and news. An elder warned him, "Stay far from the coast. Kamehameha's enemies are destroying canoes, raiding oceanside villages, killing everyone."

On the afternoon of the fifth day, Kalani turned toward Waipio. At a cleft in the rocks marking the entrance trail into the valley, rain fell, and he took shelter under a low-bending kiawe tree. A shriek pierced through the sounds of wind and pelting water mixing with a howling, more chilling than any Kalani had ever heard.

He released his spear and ran into the driving rain. A woman climbed through the cleft, her eyes wild, her face twitching. A baby screamed, she held him tight to her breast to quell the pounding of his fists. A boy slithered by her feet racing toward the kiawe tree. "Stop!" the woman yelled. She waddled after him, glanced back into the valley, and moaned. She hurried her pace, which proved her undoing as she slid on rain-slick stones, losing her grasp on her child who splashed into a trough of dirty water.

"Oh, Lono," Kalani said as he saw an ugly beast leaping from the cleft. Its pin-shaped eyes darted in wide sweeps. Its jaws open, its canines filed sharp for ripping. Drool lathered its fangs and lips. The animal's ears were pointed up like horns. The dog saw the screaming child thrashing in the mud. With a howl, it attacked.

The mother yelled. Kalani thrust his spear at the mouth of the beast and missed. The claws of the animal raked into the baby's belly, tearing flesh. He had only a moment to save the child. Kalani kicked the animal's side, rapping his spear haft on its head.

The creature skittered away. Barked, growled, bared its lips, showing discolored teeth. The baby screamed. Kalani thought for a moment to help the child, close up the wound in its stomach that seeped blood. Instead he stepped forward, jabbing his spear. "Run, you filthy cur." The animal pranced from side to side, darting in and out, avoiding his thrusts. Unusual, Kalani thought, a dog trained to fight and kill. Who could be so wicked as to create such an evil?

As if tiring of the game they were playing, the dog ran to Kalani's left and darted for the child in the mud. Its wailing had ceased and Kalani wondered if the baby was dead. He pivoted, driving his sharp stick into the dog's side. The animal's momentum snapped the spear. The thrust spoiled its lunge.

"Grab your child," Kalani yelled, drawing his knife and racing to the pond. The wounded dog struggled to its feet. Kalani swung, raking through the thick, wiry hair on the animal's back. Blood came. The beast yowled and yowled again, then skittered toward the entrance-way and slid through the cleft in the rock.

The woman cried, her tears mixing with the rain water that flowed over her. Kalani snatched the baby from the mud, a thin stream of blood pulsing from his belly. A movement caught his eye and he turned to see a tattooed man appearing through the cleft. They faced each other for some moments, the stranger's eyes glittering. Kalani tensed, holding the child close to his chest, waiting for the attack.

"Why do you hurt my dog?" the man challenged.

"Because it bit us," Kalani answered.

"He was only going for the woman and her children. Why did you stop him?"

Kalani's eyes opened wide. He could have escaped harm by letting the dog devour its intended victims. He fixed his eyes on the tattooed man. "I have never known such wickedness. Know this: I will defend those who are helpless against filth like you. Come, let us test your courage by a battle to the death."

The man grimaced, stuck out his tongue, pivoted, and fled.

He motioned the mother to follow him. "I'm going to Waimea. My name is Kalani."

"We are going there, too," the woman answered.

As they trudged on the trail, the rain splashing poison out of his wounds, sadness overcame him. He faced the heavens and called, "Why all this cruelty?"

The wind howled, the woman muttered, "No one cares for the weak." She fell silent.

CHAPTER 58

THE MORNING SUN WARMED HIS back, brightening the ocean ahead of him, a blue so sharp his eyes ached. Along the road to Kawaihae, farmers worked the dry ground, plunging sharp sticks into the earth, turning over loose rocks, scooping dirt with their hands. Beyond the workers were fields of sweet potatoes, green vines twining along the ground in neat rows. "Hey brother," Kalani hailed a farmer, motioning his hand over the tilled land, "these weren't here six months ago."

A thin, wiry man, full bearded, his hair mounded high on his head, struck his stick into the earth. "Chief tells us we need more food. Big trouble in Waipio." He pointed to a small fire. "Hungry? Come eat. Plenty potato."

Settling on a rock, Kalani fished out a steaming bulb, placed it on a leaf, and smiled at the farmer standing by the hot coals. The man said, "You need some drink? Here is beer."

"Beer?"

"The best in Kohala. The sweet potatoes ferment in two weeks and tastes good. Drink up. Where do you come from?"

"Hilo. I passed by Waipio, I was told by a woman I saved that Kahekili warriors are destroying the valley. Is that why your chief is creating these fields?"

The farmer looked at the ground, raised his eyes toward the foot-hills where a line of men marched toward the tilled ground carrying large gourds. "Chief tells us no more taro from the valley. We must work quickly and make food for Kamehameha's army. It is hard work. The ground is rock and there is little water. It's a good thing that potatoes grow in three months. Taro takes one year. If we had to wait that long, everybody would starve."

"What I see is a miracle, everything is green, but in this dry place where do you find water?"

The farmer pointed to the hills. "Caves in the mountains drip. We place gourds to catch them. Then men bring what we catch to the fields."

Kalani peeled his potato, bit into it, relishing its sweet flavor as he ate. The morning heat rose. He thought to go, but hesitated, wanting news. "The chiefess I helped in Waipio told me that her husband had come to Kawaihae to build a *luakini* temple for Kamehameha. Where is it? Is Kamehameha there? Is it finished?"

A sly smile flitted over the man's face. "We are only farmers. What do we know about those sacrificial places? But, if you go past Kawaihae, there is a small bay. On a hill above it called Puukohola, Whale Hill, Kamehameha has thousands piling up rocks. You will find him there placing every stone. The temple is almost finished."

The man's words knifed into him, opening memories Kalani had suppressed. He thought of the ceremony long ago and the waiting for death to come. He rifled his hair as if kneading his skull would wipe out dark thoughts. He shook his head like a hala tree whipped by the wind, then, gathering himself together, he said, "Once the ceremonies start you'll have to attend, and then you can rest."

The farmer laughed. "No way. If the priests want to eat, we have to keep working."

Kalani smiled. The man was simple and pragmatic. His knowledge of the land, the local conditions, were vital to the survival of everyone. "I guess the priests and chiefs need you to keep working. It's an advantage being a farmer, you don't have to stand for days watching someone get killed. Thanks for your help." Kalani waved goodbye. As he strode toward the coastal village, munching his sweet potato, dread crept over him. What would he find at Whale Hill? Could he convince Kamehameha to make peace?

At mid-morning he entered Kawaihae. A few old people scuttled between the huts casting frightened looks as he passed them. When he asked for his friends, they shook their heads and scurried away. When he asked of Kamehameha, they cringed, pointing to the south. Spying an open-air building used for construction, Kalani walked to it. Isaac Davis leaned over a cannon. "Chief, you're alive. You made it."

Davis reared up. Surprise, then a broad smile, spread over his face, "You're alive, too!" he yelled. He came to him, gripping Kalani to his chest.

"But I might not be for long, if you keep holding me so tight."

Davis let him go. "Akaka thought you were dead, sacrificed by Keoua. What happened after Kalapana?"

The two men settled onto a bench. "Not much to tell. Captured. Met Keoua. He gave me a mission."

"A mission. What kind of mission?"

"To talk Kamehameha into making peace."

Davis gazed into a cloudless sky, rocked back and forth and said, "God, make it happen. End this horror." Then he straightened himself. "I don't think he will listen. Kamehameha is intent on completing his temple to Ku. He will make sacrifices until he gains the war god's favor and believes he will be victorious."

Kalani saw sadness in his friend's face, heard it in his voice. Both men understood the ruler's obsession with the prophecy that he would never win unless he built this temple.

"Kamehameha, along with sixteen thousand men, are piling terraces of stone at Puukohola," Davis continued. "Every day, he kills another slave as his gift to that blood-thirsty god. The only reason I escaped working in that place is the fleet Kahekili is building to attack this island. Kamehameha wants ships with mounted guns to oppose him, and I'm the one who can do that."

"But Keoua wants peace. If Kamehameha agrees to peace, he no longer needs to worry about Kahekili."

Davis shook his head. "Kamehameha is obsessed with ruling Hawaii Island alone. He'll see any offer of peace from Keoua as a sign of weakness and will reject it."

"He would do this? Reject a peace offer?"

"As long as he believes that sacrifices to Ku will bring him victory over his enemies, yes."

Kalani looked away. "I promised Keoua that I'd bring his offer to Kamehameha."

"Then you must go where he is, at his temple to the god. Be careful. You could be forced to work on that mound of death. If you want to escape that fate, tell him I need you to build his war fleet."

A gentle wave swept toward a cupped, yellow sand beach, sweeping slowly to a stand of coco palms niched into a barren hill, pocked with ugly brown rocks. As he leaned against a hot boulder, Kalani watched the wave dancing to the trees. The warmth of the stone eased his chill, for above the green leaves of the nut trees, a long rectangle of rock grew on Whale Hill.

He rested his elbows, cupped his chin in his palms, and studied the long line of workers heaving rocks from one man to another. He thought most were exhausted. Many staggered under their loads or dropped stones to the ground that rolled and bounced down the hillside, crashing into the sea.

Oppressive, he thought, a place built for pain and fear. He remembered Mauloa's teaching that priests and chiefs used Ku and sacrifices to suppress. From Keoua's touch he had learned that, though royalty may be descended from the gods, contact did not burn. Could all the traditions he had been taught be false? It was a difficult question. He was not ready to answer it. He wiped sweat from his brow and trudged to the hill.

"Halt," a masked guard ordered. "Why are you not working? Come."

Malevolent eyes peered through slits in a gourd covering the burly man's face. He had an imposing physique, arm muscles well-toned, chest and abdomen rippling with hardness, his thighs and calves large and round as coconut trunks.

"But I'm not—"

"Obey or die!" the man threatened, emphasizing his order with his spear. Kalani resigned himself to obedience. He faced an elite warrior, masked to create terror and hide his identity. He could kill as he chose, without giving reasons and so practiced in fighting that Kalani might not beat him. He marched uphill reluctantly and joined the toiling men.

It was more grueling work than on the previous temple. A steeper hill, the rocks heavier. Kalani learned that thousands of men were stretched nine miles to a quarry. As he passed stones he searched for Kamehameha. He found him at the top of the pile, fitting each rock into place.

At dusk he and others were herded to a cluster of shacks built on a grass plain. Disheartened, aching, he searched for food and a place to rest. A cry from the hill jangled through the workers' compound, followed by screaming that weakened until the sound died away. No one paid attention to the calls of death. Workers kept shuffling toward the shacks.

Ahead, he spotted Moki. He waved, but his friend disappeared into a crowd. "Moki, wait up. It's me, Kalani," he called, and ran after him. A man struggled out of a mass of men, leaped, and tackled Kalani to the ground. The two brothers rolled, wrestled, and laughed in the dirt, relieving the pain of their separation.

It had shaded to dark when they finished their greeting and looked for food. "The screams," Kalani asked as they came to the eating shack, "have the ceremonies started?"

Moki shut his eyes. "No, just the evening sacrifices to Ku. Stay long enough, and you get used to them. Do not step out of line—you could be next."

Kalani stood silent for many moments. "Deaths every day? Why? Where do they get the sacrifices?"

Moki shuffled his feet and looked around to see if anyone was near. "Kamehameha is determined to win Ku's favor. The high priest keeps pushing him to kill more, to satisfy the god. Those who die are slaves, rule breakers, and anyone else the priest doesn't like. When the ceremonies start there will be a killing beyond any other that has gone before."

For two days, Kalani lifted stones, considering ways that he might escape and go to Kamehameha. But the guards were vigilant and he could not get by them. In the evening of the second day he slipped from the camp, heading to a compound he had spotted where he knew the chiefs lived. There he found Akaka. Kalani related his adventures since the fight at Kalapana and concluded with Keoua's offer of peace.

Akaka sighed. "There are rumors that Kahekili and the Kauai king have gathered a great fleet and are ready to attack. If Kau is no longer a threat, we could beat them."

Kalani nodded. "Isaac Davis believes that Kamehameha will not listen to peace offers. That he wants sole power over all Hawaii."

"I fear that he is right. Our leader has rushed the building of his temple and it is nearly finished except for the placement of idols and the building of structures. Though it seems useless, I will seek an audience with Kamehameha. Wait for my call."

By the evening of the third day all construction ceased. Within the workers' compound Kalani and Moki watched priests scurrying along the platforms of the temple, building sheds, erecting towers, and setting idols on the back wall.

"Eh," Moki said. "Did you ever notice Ku's penis?"

"No!" Kalani answered, startled by the question. "All I can remember is his huge head, twice the size of his body, a mouth gaping wide, rows of sharp white teeth, and mother of pearl eyes. Real ugly."

"If you look between his legs you'll see this little thing sticking out, no bigger than my thumbnail. But when you look at all of him, he's seven feet tall. His height does not fit his equipment."

The oddity of Ku pierced Kalani's thoughts as if a spear had been driven into his skull. *Gods were supposed to look human! Was the war god just a huge devouring mouth? An invented idol of wood meant to instill fear? As he sorted this through he realized that obedience to traditions instilled in him since birth might be false, designed by chiefs and priests to suppress.*

Two days passed and the temple with its structures and statues were complete. Rumors spread among the workers that Kahekili was attacking the north coast of Hawaii. Waipio Valley had been devastated, temples and ancient sites destroyed, fields trashed, and the people of the valley killed. The war had reached an unimaginable level of cruelty.

The day of the news, Akaka summoned Kalani to the royal compound. "Kamehameha is prepared to hear you. His advisors are present. You are not royal so there will be hostility. Observe protocol. Be humble. Do not brag. I have smoothed your entry as best I can." Akaka disappeared into the building, motioning Kalani to follow.

On his knees, his face to the ground, Kalani crawled into the palace. A dozen eyes played over him expressing the power of their collective anger. He inched to Kamehameha, his face touching the mat covering the floor. At the high chief's feet, he waited for permission to rise. An oppressive silence filled him with fear. He heard hurried breathing, clucks of disapproval, felt hatred in the room. His nervousness grew distracting, and he was startled when Akaka said, "Squat."

When he lifted himself, an impressive, beardless man without tattoos to mar his body or make him appear fiercer sat on a koa throne before him. His face was not handsome, but his features were noble and strong. His eyes shone with intelligence. His demeanor displayed great power. Kalani saw the lumps on his chest and the long scar on his abdomen inflicted in the legendary hand-to-hand combat at Pii-Holo Mountain.

Kamehameha spoke first. "You are the spear thrower who almost bested me a while ago. We must duel again. Akaka tells me you saved his army and you should be rewarded. You have news from Keoua?"

Kalani's throat felt paralyzed. Men and women around the king glowered, their flinty eyes messaging, "You are not of royal blood. What right do you have to speak to the king?" Only Kaahumanu smiled. Her warmth gave Kalani courage.

"Great king, lord of all the people. Keoua sends greetings and asks for peace. He says there has been eight years of war between the two of you. During that time, neither has gained more than the other. He proposes that you confirm him king of Kau and Puna, and he will confirm you king of all the other lands of Hawaii. He has promised not to make war until he knows your answer."

Kamehameha's expression did not change. He looked at his courtiers squatting around him. He returned his gaze to Kalani. "I am not ready to give my answer. My temple is finished and will be dedicated in a day. My chiefs and warriors must be at the ceremonies. Isaac Davis has requested your return to Kawaihae. Go and complete my fleet."

After leaving Kamehameha, Kalani passed by the slave pens. At least a hundred men sat or stood in the enclosures, the tattoo mark of the kauwa on their foreheads. He stopped for a moment to study them, but guards rushed up, yelling, "Stay clear of these filthy beasts. It is death to be near untouchables." He hurried away. He glanced back to see how many young boys, like Minato, would be sacrificed to Ku.

As he left the prisons of death, he shouted, "Make peace! Stop these sacrifices!" *That is what I should have done, forgotten protocol and said to the advisors, to Kamehameha: "Stop these sacrifices. Make peace." But courage had failed me. Tradition still grips me, and I could not speak plainly to those who claimed descendancy from the gods. He plodded on, scuffing up clouds of dirt as he walked. Lost in pain, he wandered like a leaf blown by gusting winds.*

CHAPTER 59

CLOUDS FLOWED OVER THE SEA trapping darkness, blotting out the daylight. Roiled by a strong wind, waves surged in heaping mounds of foam across the water, their rush ending in black cliffs that stretched along the north shore of the island. War canoes stabbed into the swells, flinging up shafts of water as they plunged into the waves.

The challenge of the sea roused Kalani from his dark mood. "One, two, three," he repeated. On each count he studied the drift of the vessel, keeping it on course with the main fleet. Intuitively, he kept a dynamic balance between his canoe and the natural forces attacking it. It was an art gained only by practice.

Kalani's thoughts wandered, thinking of the seven days of screaming from Whale Hill. While working with Davis, he had stuffed his ears to keep out the horrible shrieks. Though he concentrated on his tasks, his hands would shake when he heard the shouts of the dying.

Under Davis' supervision, gun platforms were constructed on ten war canoes. Brass swivel guns were centered upon them. Storage boxes had been built, and muskets, wrapped in tapa, stacked on the sides of the platform of each vessel.

Before they embarked for war, Kamehameha came to the bay where his gunships rode on the swells. "The sacrifices are over. Ku is happy. Go forward, my brothers, give us victory."

With this order the great fleet sailed. Kalani, in charge of one of the high chief's cannon canoes, directed his vessel into a stormy sea. "Push into the waves. Pull! Pull!" He cadenced a heart-stopping beat, his anger mounting over the rejection of peace and the sacrifices that had been made. Numb to reason, he pushed his men for more speed.

Within an hour of excessive effort, Moki vented, "What are you trying to do? Kill us?"

His harsh words stung Kalani from his lethargy. He saw his canoe rolling broadside to a wave. "Pull hard on the right." Twelve paddles thrust into the deep, turning the vessel into the swell, riding up, then cresting over it.

Once balance had been restored, Kalani answered his friend, "It makes no difference whether I die now or later. I'm angry about Kamehameha's rejection of peace. The sacrifices he has made to a false god created by priests and chiefs to limit our freedom infuriates me."

"Don't talk too loud. Somebody will hear you and there will be trouble. We in this canoe are your friends. Lead us wisely. Do your job right or give it up and get out."

"Sorry, I'm just stirred up by everything that's happened."

Moki nodded. "Yeah, too many days I heard the high priest scream 'Ku is not happy, he wants more'. I kept thinking, when the slaves run out, who would he choose next?"

Ahead of them, Kalani saw the white sails of the small schooner, *Fair American*. It struggled to make headway, its canvas flapping in the wind. "That ship, without paddles, is useless, not nimble like our double-hulled canoes," Kalani said.

"True. But Kamehameha loves the vessel. It goes with him whenever he travels by sea."

The gun canoes shot past the floundering schooner, heading under a canopy of clouds. Rain pelted them. The breeze freshened, speeding the war craft through the darkening sea. The fleet rounded the jutting thumb of Hawaii Island and raced southeast. "Something's coming from Waipio," Moki pointed ahead.

Rain sheeted into the sea. Kalani swiped his eyes, peered, searched into the mist. "I think I see crab claw sails."

A voice yelled, "Kahekili is coming."

Trumpets blared. "Pull," Kalani ordered. Others picked up his cry and a horde of canoes leaped into roiling waves racing to engage the enemy.

"Look, it's Kamehameha. Go. Go," Moki yelled, staring at a sixty-foot war canoe shooting through the waves, pennants whipping, crab claw sail cupping tight, black hull foaming spray high above the sea.

"The king," a thousand voices cheered.

"The king," Kalani joined them, anger and disillusionment swept away when he saw the man speeding past. Kamehameha stood at the prow, big, tall, and golden in feathers that caped his shoulders. A war spear in his hand pointed at the enemy. Beside him stood the high priest, a fluttering white toga draped around him. He thrust above his flowing hair a red-faced icon of Ku, eyes saucer wide, mouth gaping.

The two fleets rammed together, grinding, tearing, with shrieking sounds of wood breaking. Men grappled vessels, holding them together by grip alone. Kamehameha's canoe plunged into the midst of the Oahu fleet, the high priest jerking Ku to left and right. Whether from fear of the king or the threat of Ku, Kahekili's canoes turned aside, and Kamehameha, followed by his war fleet, clove into the heart of the enemy armada. In moments friend and foe were mixed, in an inextricable mass of boats and fighting men.

"Cannon won't fire. Moki, musketeers, grab weapons. Attack!" Kalani ordered, leaping from the gun platform of his double canoe onto the left-side hull of his boat.

"Die you bastard," a chief snarled, his cudgel smashing into the wale, missing Kalani's leg. The man raised his weapon again, his royal cape rippling in the wind. Kalani grasped its feathers, pulled, and hurled his opponent into the sea.

A knife slashed, drawing blood from his side. He glanced and saw the wielder stabbing again. Fast as lightning, he thrust his spear into the attacker's thigh, buckling him back into his canoe.

Waves smashed the two boats together, tore them apart, then crunched them together again. A paddle struck Kalani's shoulder driving him into the trough of his vessel. Like a frightened woman trying to swat a mouse, the attacker smashed his leaf-shaped stick against the right-side channel hooting, "Get you. Get you."

"Yeah, well, I got you," Moki shouted, shoving his spear into the man, then pulling it back. His opponent tottered, leaned, and collapsed against the side of his canoe. He draped over it for a moment, then slid into the sea. Moki bent down. "Brother, are you okay?"

Dazed, Kalani rubbed his head, tried to focus his eyes. A bedlam of noise wrapped around him. Warriors screamed, wood groaned, wind howled, sails whipped wildly. Dead fighters floated in a sea turned red, the roiling waves flinging their bodies, with loud thumps, against canoes. "Yeah, I'm all right," Kalani said, pulling himself up.

A monster wave struck the entwined canoes, flinging them toward the towering cliffs of Waimanu. He shook himself, gripped the wale, and rose from the trough. "Stop fighting. Grab paddles. Pull away from the rocks."

The canoes separated for a moment, then a wave lifted both vessels with fingers of angry foam and hurled them to the rocks. Huge boulders loomed. A great wave ahead smashed onto stone, cascaded, and swept up the cliff side.

"Pull, pull, pull, or we die," Kalani yelled, flinging his paddle into the foaming sea, pushing with all the strength he had, fighting the wave that shoved his vessel toward the rocks.

Twelve men motivated by a fear-driven ferocity paddled against the thrust of the surging water. Within moments of collision the canoe reached a balance between the force of the wave and efforts to escape its shove. The canoe crested the lip and plunged into the trough behind it. Momentum from the slide shoved its tapered bow into a wall of oncoming water that smothered the craft, tearing away its crab claw sail. With a sucking sound, the buoyant hardwood vessel popped above the heaving water with all men safe.

"Straighten the canoe. Paddle and bail. Head out to sea," Kalani ordered. He looked to the cliffs, searching for his opponent. A wave lifted the enemy canoe, flinging it into the rocks. The craft crashed, shaking men from it. Some thrashed among the unforgiving stone shore. Others were sucked back into the water, unable to fight the undertow.

Kalani shook his head, saddened by watching men die. "You bail," he pointed to two of his men. "Moki, cut away what's left of the sail. Steersman, turn the vessel toward the cliffs."

"We're going back into that!" a musketeer protested, pointing to the steep wall of rock.

"Yes, to save any who are still alive."

"But they are our enemy. We must save ourselves. Let them die."

"They are helpless men unable to fight. We will save whom we can."

Four of the sailors of Kahekili bobbed in the water, bruised but alive. Kalani rescued them and returned to the fleet. Broken canoes, splintered wood, floating corpses littered the sea. Shark fins sliced the water. Battered war vessels hovered near the *Fair American*, Kamehameha visible on its deck.

Disappearing into the dim night, Kalani saw crab claw sails heading toward Maui. Hailing Alapai-nui, whose royal double canoe bobbed near the forecastle of the *Fair American*, Kalani asked for news.

"Kahekili is retreating."

"Then we are victorious. Is Kamehameha going to chase the enemy and destroy their fleet?"

"No, our losses are severe. Kamehameha has decided to return to Kawaihae. He will declare victory, since the enemy has been turned away."

The news staggered Kalani*: Nothing had been gained by this battle. Kahekili was still alive. With his crony, the king of Kauai, they were in control of Niihau, Kauai, Oahu, Molokai, and Maui. Keoua was king of half of Hawaii Island. Waipio Valley and the north coast of Hawaii had been devastated. Untold numbers of men had died, sacrificed to Ku or killed in battle.*

"Hey, brother, it's over," Moki said. "Let's go home. I'm hungry."

With the sail post broken, the discouraged men paddled toward Kawaihae. A dejected Kalani Moku Tana, warrior and dreamer, knelt in the rear of his vessel, agonizing over his options for the future.

CHAPTER 60

IN HIS KONA HIDEOUT, MAKULA laced a shark tooth onto his *leiomano,* a short wooden paddle. He squinted at a hole and applied his drill to it, widening the opening. With practiced skill he sewed on two teeth to the board, then thrust the finished weapon out like a mirror, admiring his work. "Deadly, isn't it?" he bragged, showing the twelve neatly sewn teeth to Namaka, a stocky, medium height man next to him.

"Yes, it's beautiful," the chief answered, admiring the handiwork of shark fangs edging the oil-sleeked koa wood frame. "But did you hear what I said? Kahekili wants us back on Maui."

Makula scowled, slicing the long-handled knife through the air. "How can we leave? There are not enough canoes and I have not completed my revenge."

"What about Keoua? You said he would help you. Ask him."

"I did, but he promised that filth Kalani Tana not to make war while he is negotiating peace with Kamehameha. By all the gods, I will get that boy for interfering with my plans."

Namaka shook his head. "Keoua's refusal is unfortunate. Kahekili has lost many canoes. He has none to spare. It's not good for us."

Makula slashed his knife across a bamboo upright supporting the roof of his hale. The weapon cut a gash through the yellow wood, shredding the pili grass covering the frame of the building. "Good," he grunted. "The lacing holds the teeth firmly in place. As to leaving, I have a plan."

The cut grass lingered in the air, a light breeze blowing shards into Namaka's eyes. He wiped them away and in an irritated tone asked, "What is it?"

Makula smiled. He gazed with disgust at Kahekili's stooge sent with Maui warriors to fight in Kona and maintain control over him. But the chief was stupid. Not wise and strong like Makula. With sarcasm in his voice he said, "Under my leadership you have seen how successful we have been in raids on hill villages. I will change our tactics, harass Kealakekua, attack coastal settlements near Honaunau. Nothing major, just stings that hurt. We will spread the rumor that Keoua is sending canoes to attack the west coast of Hawaii. Alapai-nui will hasten with his fleet to stop me. I will ambush him, take his vessels, and we sail back to Maui."

"A risky plan. It depends on a foolish leader who will rush to stop us and somehow leave his fleet unguarded to be captured."

"Do you have a better idea? I know what I propose can fail. But what choice do we have? The fleet that Kahekili assembled from Kauai, Oahu, Maui, and Molokai has been defeated beneath the cliffs of Waimanu."

"The god is against us," Namaka lamented. "A thousand war canoes beaten by that evil man. People are calling it the 'Battle of the Red-Mouthed Cannon' because Kamehameha had the horror weapons that belched fire and iron at Kahekili's canoes."

"But didn't your master have similar weapons mounted on vessels of his fleet? Surely that should have been enough to win the battle along with the fearless warriors of Oahu!" Makula said with scorn in his voice.

Namaka reared back as if slapped on the face. "We men of Oahu are fighters. We are not afraid of any foe. I tell you it's that damned temple Kamehameha built. He made hundreds of sacrifices to fulfill the prophesy that he would rule over all of us if he pleased Ku, the Devourer of Islands. That is the reason our side lost the battle. The gods were against us."

Makula swept the leiomano against the side of his hale cutting through the leaves like a sharp blade through a field of grass. "That is what Keoua believes since the volcano killed his army. That is why he offers peace to Kamehameha through that insolent boy. He is wrong. You are wrong. The gods are not against us. I, Makula, promise you that. Let me have an army and I will destroy the upstart."

Namaka uttered a great sigh. "I want to believe what you say. If we can get back to Maui, I will beseech Kahekili to give you the forces needed to win. We must have boats to get there. I will gather my men. You rally your crazies who somehow in the dimness of their twisted minds follow your orders and we will put our plan into action."

Makula's face turned stony, his eyes blazed with malevolence. "And if Kalani should be with the high chief when he comes I will kill him and get my revenge. But if not, I know where his mother and sister live."

CHAPTER 61

KALANI WITH A DOZEN OF his men raised the war vessel from the water and carried it onto the beach. Once beyond the rolling surf, the warriors settled the brown-stained, double-hulled canoe to the sand.

"What do now?" asked Moki.

"Unload. Feed the men." Kalani strode toward the three-tiered temple squatting dark and ugly above them on Whale Hill.

"Hey. Where are you going? Eat first. We are hungry, you must be too," Moki said, stretching his arms, twisting his body to relieve the stiffness of days of paddling. A man beside him grumbled, "Yeah, we need food, only one fish in two days."

Kalani heard the complaint. Food and water had been lost as a great wave engulfed the canoe at the cliffs of Waimanu. Since then they had fished, eating raw bonito, sucking the marrow for moisture. He stopped. His eyes wandered to the *Fair American* waddling in the bay. "I'm going to find Kamehameha."

"That's a bad idea," Moki objected, punching his fist into the clear air, emphasizing his point.

"I have to talk to him. Get him to make peace." Kalani fixed his gaze on the anchored schooner.

"That's your trouble. You act before you think. You know Kamehameha won't listen. He just beat Kahekili. The man's going to keep fighting." Moki pressed a finger into his friend's skin, his lips firm, his eyes blazing.

The sharp jab stopped him from walking further. He tightened his loincloth, smoothed his hair, shook his head. "For two days I have thought how our priests use Ku to put fear in our hearts. How our chiefs say they are descended from gods, giving them the right to rule. We must believe or die. But Ku is just wood and not real. It is something we just imagine because we are told he exists. Mauloa taught me that Lono, who sends water from the sky to make the land fertile, loves peace, for with it everything grows without fear. Isn't it better to believe in Lono and not Ku?"

Moki rocked his head from side to side, rolled his shoulders, and cracked his knuckles. "Kamehameha will not change. Remember before these wars got started? The King of Hawaii died. He gave this island to his son, but control of the war god to Kamehameha."

"Everybody knows that story. Kamehameha got chiefs to revolt against the son and we have been fighting ever since. But why does possession of Ku mean our leader will reject Lono and peace?"

Moki shook his head. "You are smart in many things, but you don't know chiefs. Kamehameha's ambition is to rule all the islands. Once he got the war god, he knew that others would join him because people feared Ku."

"Maybe you're right. Kamehameha has used fear to his advantage. He builds this great temple above us, fights Kahekili, and wins. Take care of the men. I'm going to seek Akaka and Alapai-nui."

Directed to a village south of Whale Hill, Kalani saw Isaac Davis conferring with several men within a long open-air shack. He waved. Isaac Davis saw him and called, "Makula is on a rampage in Kona."

Worry gripped Kalani as memories of Aunt Lei's charred body flashed in his mind. In a voice suddenly parched, he said, "What news of my mother and sister? Are they safe?"

"Best to ask Alapai-nui, it's his district," Davis answered, pointing to the conferring men.

Without respecting protocol Kalani pushed his way into the group and asked, "Alapai-nui, do you know if my mother is safe in Kona?"

Irritated, the high chief fastened his eyes on Kalani. "I do not know. If they are by the sea, I am sure no harm will come to them. The attacks by Makula are in the hills."

"But he can strike the sea coast at any time. What are we doing to save my family, the people in Kona?"

"We are discussing what should be done," Alapai-nui said brusquely. "Kamehameha is involved with more important matters—"

"What could be more important than saving my mother and Kona?"

"Hush your tongue! The king is aware of the problem. We are here to solve it. You will help us. Isaac Davis has war canoes on this beach. Gather your men. Bring them here. Others are assembling. We plan to embark by nightfall. Go!"

Kalani raced to Kawaihae, found Moki, and asked whether arrangements had been made for escape.

Moki nodded.

"Good, take our men to the village beyond Whale Hill. Alapai-nui and Davis are gathering men to fight in Kona. The prisoners, where are they?"

"Over there," Moki pointed.

Kalani walked to four men huddling in a copse of coco trees. They stiffened when they saw him. Three prostrated, wailing, "You are coming to sacrifice us." The fourth warrior stood still, arms folded, watching.

Irritated by their begging, Kalani said in a harsh voice, "Get up. The war god has had enough blood." He looked at the standing prisoner, a tall man, face bearded, with tattoos across his forehead and on his right shoulder, "I will get you to Maui, if you promise not to harm those who help you."

The warrior's brow furrowed, a look of puzzlement crossing his face. "I am Iolani. Why do you help us?"

"Too many have died to Ku. Do you accept the offer?"

"Yes."

"Good, then come."

Kalani led them to a scrubby fishing hut at the sea. An elderly man worked on nets, his toes stretching out the mesh as he repaired it. Several children near his hut ran screaming into the ocean, smashing their small bodies against waves that swallowed them up and flung them onto shore.

Kalani walked to the old man, speaking to him in low tones. The children laughed in the surf, splashing water, throwing sand. With a loud grunt, the net maker rose, pointed to the four Kauai men, then gestured to the west. Kalani nodded. The old man shook his head. He yelled at the urchins to be quiet. They ignored him, running on the beach, giggling. The fisherman scuffed his feet into the sand, sighed, then said, "Yes, I will take them."

Kalani turned to Iolani. "The chief of Waipio owes me. I saved his wife from a wild dog of Kahekili. The old man is a trader. He acquires goods from Waipio and uses them to barter with people on Maui. Tomorrow, he will take you there."

Iolani studied the horizon, watching the sun pierce through clouds hovering above it. The children screamed. He smiled and turned to Kalani. "You are mad. We hurt the people of Waipio. We fought to kill you beneath the cliffs of Waimanu. Yet you let us go." Iolani prostrated, placing his lips on Kalani's toes. The three other warriors did the same.

As he walked away, Kalani watched the children. It made him happy that there could be innocent joy in the shadow of the oppressive temple.

CHAPTER 62

DRUMS BOOMED FROM THE TEMPLE, answered by trumpets blaring from the sea. In a fanfare of sound, Alapai-nui's war fleet landed beneath the walls of Hikiau. A wiry, white-haired priest, his voice thin, chanted from its top tier, thirty feet above the ocean. At the shore, local chiefs prostrated, presenting gifts and pledging their allegiance to Kamehameha.

Anxiety plagued Kalani, concerned for the safety of his mother and sister. Tension at Kealakekua Bay rose high. Rumors were rife of scattered raids along the coast and strange tattooed warriors marching toward the bay and then disappearing into the mists. Many who had come were armed and ready to fight.

He listened impatiently as the boastful speeches of bravery and a desire to fight went on and on. He wanted to rush to his mother, find her, and protect her. But he waited for permission to leave for Honaunau. The last speech ended and the high chief strode toward a nearby village accompanied by several men. "Moki, it's over. Let's get to Alapai-nui."

The two friends pushed into a throng of warriors strolling leisurely to the eating house. With elbows and hips, they shoved between men who cursed them for their rudeness and struck them in return. Soon they forced their way clear and came to Alapai-nui, who chatted amiably with some chiefs.

"Lord, may I leave for Honaunau?" Kalani begged, his tone anxious, his eyes pleading.

The smile that brightened Alapai-nui's face faded. "We are here to eat. Not to discuss leaving."

"But everyone is talking about attacks at Honaunau," Kalani answered, then continued without a pause, disregarding the disapproval writ on the chief's face. "My mother is there."

Irritated by the demand, Alapai-nui fixed a hard stare upon Kalani, saying, "Put aside petty concerns. You stay with the army. The gods will protect your mother."

"But gods may not be enough to save her," Kalani retorted, his tone sarcastic, insolent.

"Blasphemy," Alapai-nui answered, his brow furrowing. He pointed at the anxious boy. "Your place is here!" With a wave of dismissal, Alapai-nui stalked into the eating house. Men brushed against Kalani going in. He stood numb watching them. He turned to Moki. "I'm going to leave for Honaunau."

Moki gripped his shoulder with a firmness that made Kalani wince.

"What are you going to do by yourself? Beat Makula's army? No way. Stay with Alapai-nui. Do your duty." Kalani sighed, nodded, put his arm around Moki's shoulder, and the two men trudged into the eating house.

The delays were interminable: eat, sleep, and wait for warriors to assemble. Several times Kalani wanted to approach Alapai-nui and press him to go. Moki would say, "Cool head, that's the main thing. Wait." Today, as he listened to the chanter call for war, he knew the army would attack Makula.

"Gods give us a victory. All hail to Alapai-nui. All hail to Kamehameha," the chanter finished, his shrill voice piercing through the large hale. Alapai-nui spoke. "Makula is attacking the coast near Honaunau. Rumors have it that an enemy army is coming from Kau. Four hundred men will march overland. My canoes will sweep south to fight any fleet coming from the south. We meet at Honaunau."

"Kukae," Kalani swore, appalled at this splitting of the army, and rose to say that Keoua desired peace. He would not be coming from Kau. Moki scowled. Kalani settled back, realizing that he did not have the power to change the decision. Assignments were made for the next day's march. He left, worried that either Alapai-nui or the land army would be walking into a trap.

Before first light, the musketeers were up. Allied chiefs roused their sleeping men. By mid-morning, the sun beamed on an army marching to Honaunau.

"This is hot," Moki groused, trudging along the sloping western scarp of Mauna Loa. Kalani agreed, pausing to gaze around him. Above his vantage point great billowing clouds stretched upward for miles, drawn from the heated land. He knew when the sun eventually began its descent the clouds would flow downhill toward the cooling ground and colder sea. The mountain air would come with the creeping clouds and rain would fall upon the dry lowland.

For a thousand feet below the army, the earth slanted to a distant coastline marred by lava flows, jagged clumps of pock-marked rocks, black pebble beaches, and an occasional stretch of yellow sand.

Although he saw no evidence of the enemy, Kalani imagined them somewhere ahead, hidden by the mists or lurking behind rocks. Satisfied with his survey, he hurried to join his musketeers. Within minutes, someone yelled. Ahead of the moving column, a gesticulating man made an obscene gesture. He disappeared. Warriors in the lead hooted, rushing after him.

Kalani yelled, "Musketeers form battle line to the front." With precision, twenty- four men spread out, loaded muskets, and waited.

"Go forward. Keep alert," Kalani ordered.

Rocks crashed. Screams filled the air, followed by silence. The musketeers marched to a ridge beyond which a wild man had disappeared. Jagged rocks edged a ravine. Kalani peered in and saw three crushed men sprawled on stones. A hundred yards beyond the gully, a group of naked tattooed men leaped from hiding, hooting, taunting. Two survivors struggled out of the ravine. A warrior on the opposite edge popped up like a ball springing from water. Stones flew. For a moment Kalani considered ordering a volley, but the man disappeared.

Soldiers came to the edge of the gully, jabbering and pointing. The general in charge rushed to the ridge. Excited, swinging his club, he yelled, "Cross over. Get them."

"Wait," Kalani yelled. "It's a trap."

The general sneered. "Go on," he shouted to his milling men. He slid over the edge, unwilling warriors following. Kalani resigned himself to a disaster and as a precaution ordered, "Musketeers present arms. On my command, fire." He faced to the front, searching the rocks.

The general reached a rivulet at the bottom of the ravine, small stones and dirt showering him as his men slid down behind him. Frizzy-haired warriors popped up, hurling rocks. "Fire," Kalani yelled. Flame spit from a dozen muskets, smoke eddying into a clear sky. Screams echoed in the gully. A rock thrower mocked his victims, thrusting his middle fingers high. Blood dripped from a hole in his side. Despite the wound, the man picked up a stone and hurled it. "Moki, shoot him," Kalani yelled. The bullet creased the warrior's skull, yet he kept flinging stones. Puzzled by the man's foolhardy courage and his ability to control pain, Kalani yelled, "Hold fire." He released his sling and flung three pebbles. Two hit the man's body but he did not falter, continuing his barrage of rocks. The third almond-shaped stone smashed his temple, crumpling the crazed warrior to the ground.

Men groaned. "Musketeers be alert," Kalani cautioned, edging to the ravine searching for the general. Blood-smeared survivors climbed up. "Where's the chief?" Kalani demanded. A warrior pointed. Kalani slid into the gully and found the general. His forehead dripped blood over his eyes and face. He wrapped an arm around him and carried the man to safety.

The army halted at the gully's edge. Dispirited soldiers whispered of crazed tattooed warriors who felt no pain. The general squatted amid his chiefs, his face wiped clean of blood. "Blind charges will not kill men who hit and hide," he said.

"We can't just stay here doing nothing," a chief protested.

The general scowled. "You saw what happened when I attacked. Four men dead, four wounded. Constable Tana suggests we send a force uphill to the point where the ravine narrows, cross over and attack downhill. This is what we will do."

Once the flanking detachment moved out, tattooed men hidden in the rocks scurried away. "Moki, let's go," Kalani said, sliding into the deep hollow in the earth. He realized that speed was essential in case the enemy decided to return. He stepped past mangled bodies damming the rivulet, hiked up the side of the gulch, squirmed over the ridge, and went to the ground. There were no warriors in sight.

As the army crossed, Kalani pondered the enemy's tactic. Makula's warriors did not fight in the traditional way, standing in a mass taunting their opponents. Instead, they hit and ran away. He studied the clouds moving like an unrolling blanket descending the volcano's side. To the west, a circle of gold sparkled around the sun's bright mass as it slid into the horizon. He thought he saw movement on the sea. Was it clouds or a fleet of canoes? Memories came to him of Alapai-nui's victory a year ago, a central force defeating a larger, but divided foe. His breath came fast as he grasped Makula's plan.

Kalani searched for the general and found him among warriors preparing their evening meal. He hastened to him, "I think Makula is delaying us to attack Alapai-nui when he lands at Honaunau. Permission to leave tonight with my men."

"Go, we will follow at first light."

Kalani signaled to his musketeers already forewarned of his intentions. They hefted muskets, picked up their feet, and stepped at quick time for Honaunau.

"These rocks are sharp," Moki complained when Kalani caught up to him. "And I'm stumbling in the twilight. Why not wait for the moon to come up?"

"Every hour is important. My family is in danger. Alapai-nui is in danger. We must get to Honaunau before dawn."

"Yeah, but if we are all broken by falling, we'll be useless in a fight."

"The other men aren't complaining."

Moki settled into a sullen silence until the moon rose above the snow-covered peak of Mauna Loa. Clouds that threatened to blanket the land blew away in spiraling fingers of vapor. Moki clapped his hands. "We can see." He laughed.

The moon full, bright, shone from the heavens. "Pick up the pace," Kalani ordered. The musketeers shuffled faster, following a steep path leading downward.

For hours they marched. The shining ball of reflected light descended below the horizon. Men stumbled. Moki complained, "Brother, we must halt. Rest these guys. You keep pushing and they will be worthless in the morning."

Kalani breathed deeply, trying to ease the throbbing in his temples, the pounding of his heart. "Moki, we got to keep going. Get to my mother."

"Didn't you tell me that she is living near the City of Refuge?"

"Yes, Hinalea found her a home, told her to go to the refuge when in danger."

"Nobody violates the City without incurring the wrath of the gods. Your mother is there right now, safe. We have to rest."

Kalani realized his men were reeling with tiredness and reluctantly called a halt. His musketeers wrapped themselves in blankets, searched with their backs for flat spots in the rocks, and went to sleep. Kalani stood watch, a worm of worry burrowing into him, shaking his confidence: refuge cities had been violated in the past.

With the night sky graying, Moki shouted, "Up. Get up." Men grumbled, but fell into column and the small force resumed its rush to the sea.

"One, two, three, four," Kalani cadenced, quickening the steps of his men. "Chant," he called and the musketeers sang out, picking up the count, their bare feet slapping the rocks in unison, producing a single sound on each step.

"Hey," Moki yelled, "look at those warriors coming at us like Pele is chasing them with fire." Frightened men raced up the hill slope, some bent over, others limping. In the mid-morning breeze, Kalani heard the sounds of the ocean and the high-pitched screams of warriors fighting. Several of the fugitives yelled, "Alapai-nui is lost. Run!"

"Moki, take five and stop those deserters. Musketeers form a line and follow me."

As they advanced, Kalani recognized chiefs exhorting clumps of frightened men to fight. Strangely, beyond them, Makula's army held back from attacking. Instead, tattooed, frizzy-haired warriors jeered, stomped the ground in a disorganized dance, obscenely displaying their bodies.

"Halt. Front rank, kneel and fire." With a precision that made him proud, Kalani's musketeers executed the orders. A staccato of shots tore into the taunting warriors bringing several men down. Kalani ordered the second rank to advance and fire. This time the shots were uniform and tattooed men fell in heaps. Moki came with rallied warriors. Other chiefs brought men whose morale had been restored to join with the musketeers.

In the wreckage of the battlefield, he searched for Alapai-nui and found him dashing among heaps of bodies, fighting three tattooed men. Kalani yelled a war cry and charged.

An enemy warrior taunted a worn Alapai-nui, "I'm goin' to eat your heart raw. Suck out your spiritual power." He emphasized the threat with a stab of his spear. Stepping away, the high chief escaped the thrust, but stumbled on bodies stacked behind him. The attacker moved in for the kill, but Kalani rushed into him, thrusting his spear into the man. A knife sliced through the webbing of Alapai-nui's war cape, flinging feathers and fibers into the air. The chief groaned as a thin line of redness grew on his back. Kalani swung his musket, the butt slamming into the attacker's jaw. He howled, hopped away, holding his face.

The sharp sting of shark teeth cut him. Kalani twisted, sweeping his musket in a flat arc into the head of a tall, thin man. The tattooed warrior gasped and rolled onto the dirt. Kalani smashed him with a blow to the head, stomping him to be sure he stayed down.

He heard a deep sigh and found Alapai-nui lying on dead bodies, his face marred with pain. "Chief, are you okay?" Kalani asked, worried that his friend and mentor might be dying.

Before he could get an answer, the man that had been speared stumbled toward them, cakes of mixed dirt and blood mounding his chest.

He pointed at Kalani's side and its long shallow wound. He cackled, bent forward, and limped ahead, a dripping stream of red leaving a trail in the dirt. He thrust a thin dagger in quick jabs.

Kalani pivoted, sweeping the man's legs from under him. Unfazed by the fall, the insane creature rolled up and sank his teeth into a shoulder. Kalani jammed his palms into the man's jaw, flinging his head back. He put him to sleep with an elbow to the temple.

Alapai-nui hobbled up, his loincloth, once brown, now stained black with dried blood. His cape hung in shreds around his neck. His eyes filled with pain he said, "When we landed, there was no one on the beach. We spread out, marched upland searching. Makula ambushed us. He forced us away from our canoes. That is what he wants, the canoes."

The two men heard pahu drums coming from the mountain.

"Retreat to the sea," a voice boomed. A trumpet sounded a call.

"Stop Makula from escaping to Maui," Alapai-nui yelled.

"It will be tough." Kalani shook his head. "Your men look beaten."

Removing his helmet, the high chief waved it. "Warriors rally to me." Kalani joined in his call. Men came running and soon a mass of men formed around them. Alapai-nui thrust his helmet toward the beach. "Go forward, my brothers. Stop our enemies before they escape." Pahu drums boomed. Makula's warriors fled into the sea, swimming for canoes bobbing in the water.

Kalani raced after them. He climbed onto a low mound. A wave heaved over it, covering his feet with foam. He wiggled his toes, felt the coolness of the water. Salt burned his side where the shark tooth had laid his skin open. He ignored the sting, his eyes darting, searching for Makula.

He found him standing in Alapai-nui's royal double canoe, two dozen paddlers speeding the vessel toward his perch. Makula pumped a shark-toothed knife and screamed, "You cheated me of my victory." He swung back an arm and flung a spear swift, straight, and true.

So quick and accurate a throw, that only a sudden movement to the side saved Kalani as the spear brushed his chest, ricocheted off rocks, and disappeared into the sand. Makula's vessel passed by heading for a distant sea wall.

Alapai-nui stumbled to Kalani's side, anger lining his face. He fell to his knees, pounding his fists into the sand and moaned, "He's stolen my canoe."

Kalani wasn't sure what to answer. He watched Makula's vessel skim to the wall, a white fence bordering it. Tall gods loomed high above, their chests white, jaws gaping, their bared lips revealing rows of sharp teeth. Black pebble eyes, set into mother of pearl, stared out to sea.

Adjacent to the fenced area was a long rectangular wall of black stone enclosing the City of Refuge. Beyond the temple were towering palm trees, their size and number marking it as a special place.

City of Refuge

Kalani stiffened, his hand shook. Makula's canoe brushed to the wall of the Refuge. He leaped onto it, followed by two men. They disappeared into the city. For a moment Kalani thought that Makula might be seeking sanctuary. Yet the pulsing of his heart erased the foolish thought and he raced for the temple.

In moments, Makula emerged with a thin woman struggling in his grasp. Kalani's throat went dry. He screamed, "No! No!" He came to the edge of a sand beach that cupped around the ocean ending at the sea wall.

Makula pulled Ane up by the hair, stretching her out like a naked chicken. Her body twisted slowly in his grasp, her hands flailing. She beat the chief with her fists, reached her hands to break his grip. Kalani heard a sound like a nose flute hissing a discordant tune as Makula's knife slit Ane's throat. Her body jerked, convulsed, spasmed. Makula held her over the sea. He released his grip and she entered the water without a splash.

Kalani heard hoarse voices behind him, running feet slapping on stone. He did not turn, transfixed by the horror occurring a hundred feet away. Two warriors dragged Umi-ula to Makula. A white tapa garment rolled over her shoulders covering her chest. Makula ripped it away. Between wrinkled buds gleamed a royal white, whale toothed palaoa, its human hair binding curved firmly around her neck.

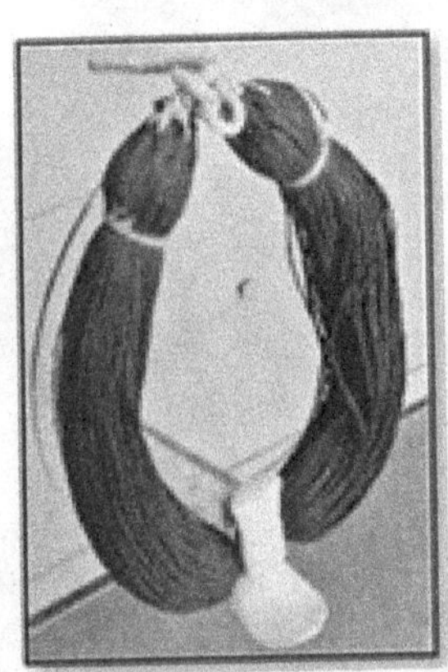

She stood proudly for a moment, then Makula pulled the woman into him and screamed, "You are not royalty. You slept with kauwa and produced him!" His hand stretched out pointing at Kalani.

"No! Kalani is royal—"

Makula twisted the whale tooth, stifling Umi-ula's cry. The human hair binding would not break, and he slashed his knife across her chest, cutting it away. In another quick move he sliced her stomach open. Umi-ula shrieked, her entrails spilling from her belly into the waves.

Kalani dove, swimming to his mother. When he surfaced, Makula waved his knife in a mocking salute, dropped the severed palaoa, and leapt into his canoe. Kalani dove again, crab crawling toward the temple. When he reached it, Makula was gone. Blood washed around him, fish nibbled on severed flesh. The bodies of his mother and sister bumped against the stone wall.

CHAPTER 63

HIS HEART SQUEEZED BY THE unimaginable savagery of the killing, Kalani performed the rituals and prayers that would save the souls of his mother and sister from being seized by an evil spirit. To preserve them, he cleansed their bodies of corrupting flesh and organs, salted their insides, and dried them in the sun. After three days, he folded each shriveled corpse into a ball, tenderly wrapped them in layers of tapa cloth, and bound them with cords of sennit.

Moki trundled a wagon up the slope of Mauna Kea. Its wheels screeched as he yanked it over rocks and onto level ground. The sharp noise roused Kalani from his sanding of a small koa block of wood. His eyes nearly puffed shut, he squinted and said, "Do you have to make so much noise?"

"You look like a drowning man," Moki said, ignoring the complaint. "Not sleeping?"

Kalani sighed. "I try, but I can't." His eyes flicked to mist that sifted through the forest bordering his campsite. *Like those white vapors, ugly thoughts creep into my head when I try to sleep. Should I have made love to Hinalea? Fought Makula in Kona? If I hadn't, would my family be alive today?* Kalani closed his eyes, shaking his head.

Moki began to unload his wagon and asked, "Where do you want these things?" "On that stack of wood over there," Kalani pointed. "You brought everything?"

"Yes," Moki answered, stacking goods on the pyre.

Kalani set fire to the personal items of his mother and sister. The two men watched the flames turn all the two women owned into a spiraling column of grey smoke. Sadness crept into his voice, "What they once owned is blowing away. Along with my mother's dream that I be heroic and become a chief. I have paid a huge price pursuing it, and now—"

"Brother," Moki interrupted, "what are you going to do? Bury your family in the earth, the sand of the beach. What?"

An angry look crossed Kalani's face. "How could you ask that? You saw my mother's palaoa, the symbol of royalty. She will not be in a common grave where others may desecrate her, use her bones for fish hooks or fashion arrowheads to shoot mice."

"You plan to hide the bodies in a cave," Moki interrupted again. "Bury them in secret like dead chiefs?"

"Yes, and you will help me."

The two men gathered the bundles and followed a trail up the side of Mauna Loa. In a shallow cave they placed Umi-ula and Ane. From a pouch, Kalani retrieved the palaoa. *I have taken my mother's hair and braided a new clasp around the whale's tooth. He tucked the necklace into the cloth wrapped around his mother's body. From his pouch he drew a koa statue of a man, the face friendly, the head, legs, arms, and body proportionate. The god's hands were cupped and rising from within was a tiny taro plant.* As he placed the image in the low cave Kalani said, "Oh Lono, help my mother and sister find peace." Then he began to beat his face.

Moki grabbed his hands. "I know you want to show respect, but don't knock out your teeth. Don't cut your body. Better that I shave your hair and place it over your mother and sister."

Kalani nodded. When the rituals were completed, cut hair spread within the crevice, the men sealed the cave and left.

A week after the burial a woman came bearing unexpected joy. "I lived with your sister and mother in the Temple of Refuge. When the battle started Ane came to me and related a dream of death coming to your family. She believed so fervently in it that she entrusted me with her most precious possession." With that, the woman unwrapped a bundle in her arms, giving Kalani a sleeping child. "This is your nephew. He is six months old." She looked into the baby's face. "I promised to care for him until Ane came back." Her voice fell. "Or I found you, if she did not."

Kalani held the child, felt the boy's breath on his chest. A tear trickled down his cheek. *This was his only living relative.*

"If it is your wish, I will care for him until you ask for his return."

"Yes, please," he said, placing a hand on the tiny head of his nephew, vowing as he did to make a home for the last of his family.

From sunup to sundown the next day, Kalani tilled the ground outside the shack where his mother and sister had lived. *The physical labor helped him sort out the conflicts swirling in his mind. "Revenge," he muttered, "I must have revenge." But how could I do it? I have no power or followers. I curse my inability to trace lineage to the gods as the ruling chiefs could. My mother had prodded me to go to war, gain recognition, and be rewarded with land. Yet promises made by Akaka are unfulfilled. With my mother dead, what should I do? Pursue war? Become a priest of Lono? Or find Makula and kill him?*

A sharp wind swirled twisters of dust into the darkening sky. Clouds banked against the mountain, inched down the cragged slope of the volcano. Through the whirling dirt, Alapai-nui limped toward Kalani, a brown garment around his loins, a cloth thrown casually across his chest and shoulders.

Kalani levered an embedded stone, raising his eyes as it came from the earth. Startled when he saw the high chief, he dropped his digging tool and went to the ground. In a stern voice, Alapai-nui said, "Do not place your nose on the earth. Stand and come to me."

Kalani stood, brushing dirt from his knees. He glanced at the tall, brown feather kahili towering above the high chief. On each side of the servants holding the emblems were armed warriors, their nudity covered by black cloth wound around each man's waist and held snug to the belly by a red belt. A crested black helmet cupped each man's head.

Alapai-nui clamped his hand onto Kalani's arm and drew him in, offering his breath. As he breathed in the acrid smell, Kalani wondered at the strange visit with its display of royal power, the dismissal of protocol, and the friendly touching as if he were royal.

With a grunt, the high chief held Kalani away and said, "I have not thanked you for saving my life. I waited until you buried your family."

Kalani stiffened. He bowed his head, hiding the anger blazing in his eyes. *He stilled his tongue from uttering the words that flared in his heart: had they sailed to Honaunau, had Alapai-nui released him, his mother and sister would be alive.* On an impulse, he went to his knees and said, "My chief, give me warriors and canoes so I can sail to Maui and revenge myself on Makula."

A frown spread over Alapai-nui's face. "I know that you have cause for revenge against the evil that has brought your family down, but this is not the time to make war. Negotiations are underway with Kahekili to cease fighting."

"If you will not help me, then I will go myself, seek out Makula, and kill him."

"I forbid you to do that." Alapai-nui struck his fist against Kalani's chest. "Let's see where peace efforts take us. Do I have your word that you will wait?"

There it was, the high chief giving me orders, preventing me from doing what I need to do. He did not speak, afraid that his words would sound surly. He nodded in submission.

Alapai-nui grunted his satisfaction. "That issue is settled. Now, I have important news. While negotiations are underway, Kamehameha is sending ambassadors to offer peace to Keoua."

Kalani shifted his gaze to the blue of the ocean sparkling in the western sun. "Then the wars of conquest are over. Peace with Keoua, peace with the kings of Maui, Oahu, and Kauai. That is good news for the common people."

Despite his words, Kalani felt cheated. *With peace a certainty, I am nothing more than a landless, unemployed warrior.* He mumbled his thanks and, expecting Alapai-nui to leave, prostrated himself.

"Stand up, Kamehameha wants you to accompany his ambassadors to Kau. He believes Keoua trusts you and will be assured by your presence of his peaceful intentions."

"Why me?" Kalani stuttered. "I am nothing. A nobody."

"It is a great honor to participate in bringing an end to hostilities. You must go and assure Keoua that Kamehameha wants peace. Who knows how one may be rewarded for doing so?"

Kalani cast his eyes on the wind-smoothed boulders that enclosed the compound of his mother's shack. *I have heard these vague promises before. They had never been fulfilled. But I realize that Kamehameha's request was a command. I cannot refuse.* "I will do as the king asks."

Alapai-nui nodded. "I have more news for you. You may use this land where your mother lived, and additional land enough to support you and your servants. But only Kamehameha can give you ownership of it. He has not made the divisions among his chiefs." Alapai-nui paused. "And only he can make you a chief."

"I am grateful for the use of land, but I have no servants."

"You may choose from my slaves in Kona who are not kauwa."

CHAPTER 64

SIX MEN SAT IN THEIR single-hulled craft, backs stretched forward and arms pulling paddles deep into the sea as they worked to maintain the distance between themselves and the double-hulled canoe ahead. "How come we didn't ride with the ambassadors?" Moki grunted, his breath coming in great gasps.

Behind him, Kalani answered, "Because they are royal emissaries, and we are just warriors keeping them company."

"Yeah, but Kamehameha sent you on this peace mission. How come we are not in the big canoe with the eighteen paddlers, instead of this creaky thing?"

"Because they are related to him and are uncles of Keoua. We are not of the same class. We have to be separate. Those are the rules."

"Maybe, but if you are not high class, why are you on this mission?"

"I think it's because Keoua once asked me to propose peace. If I return with the ambassadors, Kamehameha's promises of peace will be more believable."

"This thing smells. If the peace mission works, then the two uncles get the credit. If it fails, you get blamed and sacrificed to Ku. Besides, why does Kamehameha want peace?"

Kalani thought for many minutes about Moki's question. He studied the route they traveled. Huge swells smashed into the south point of Hawaii, flinging sheets of foaming water onto the black rocks of the headland. Above them, hidden in a ring of clouds, lay the towering snout of the great volcano. Streaks of green grass and shrubs, mixed with purple-black lava, grew unevenly beneath the hidden summit.

Far away, Kalani saw the caldera of Kilauea sending wisps of steam into the air. Memories of the horrors he has seen flooded into his thoughts. He flung the end of his paddle into the sea, pulled back, and then reached out to plunge it in yet again, seeking to bury the past with each concentrated effort. Through eyes stinging with sweat, he stared across the water at Kau, his former home. Moki's question disturbed him. What did this peace trip mean? If Kamehameha did not want peace, was there another reason for this journey?

Conch shells announced the arrival of the royal emissaries. The official chanter began the ritual, calling out the purpose of the mission, an offer of peace, and requested permission to land and present ambassadors to the king. On the shore, the warden questioned their intentions, suggesting their coming to be hostile. A series of pleas to land, and refusals to allow it, continued for some time until official word arrived that the emissaries could debark and come to Keoua's palace.

The ambassadors landed first, cloaked in intricately patterned feather garments. They were followed by their retinue of heralds and gift bearers. The two friends were the last in the column of dignitaries. Moki elbowed Kalani. "I'm not sure about Kau. Do you hear people shouting, 'Kill them'?"

"I don't like what I see along the roadway, either. There are lots of men with spears and clubs lurking around, but I think Keoua wants to hear what the ambassadors have to say. Until then, we're safe."

After a long march, Kamehameha's party came to the royal enclosure. The ambassadors and Kalani prostrated themselves before the entryway, calling in unison for permission to enter. After a short delay, a herald returned from Keoua and announced that the emissaries could come in.

They crawled into the royal presence, the three men came to Keoua on their knees. In turn, they clasped the royal feet, kissing them, and then wailed their good intentions. Keoua ordered cessation of their cries, demanding, "Why do you come?"

•

In unison, the two ambassadors answered, "We who are your uncles have come from Kamehameha, your cousin, to offer you peace. Let the war between the two of you end. He asks that you come to Kona to be reconciled with him so that each of you shall be kings of what you have."

The offer did not draw an immediate response from Keoua. Instead, Kalani watched a big man with a swarthy face and merciless eyes lean to the king and whisper, "Their words are false, kill them. Kamehameha will lose his closest supporters, and you will reign supreme."

Keoua nodded. Instead of ordering the death sentence, he said, "Kalani Moku Tana, we spoke in Puna. I gave you a message to deliver to my cousin, Kamehameha. Did you do so?"

His heart tripping, Kalani answered in even tones, "Great king, I did deliver your message of peace to Kamehameha."

"Then why has there been this delay of many months before I received an answer?"

Kalani knew that his life and the lives of the ambassadors depended on his response. "Oh Keoua, great king, you must know that Kahekili of Oahu and the king of Kauai, believing Kamehameha weak, attacked his Hawaii land. Great pillage and destruction did these two evil kings visit upon the common people of Hawaii. My master summoned all his resources, built a powerful navy, armed his war canoes with cannons and muskets, and sailed from the bay of Kawaihae to fight the invaders. Below the cliffs of Waimanu the two navies met, and Kamehameha's cannon and weapons of fire destroyed the enemy fleet. My king could not answer your offer until his enemies were defeated."

On a premonition, he concealed the fact that Kamehameha had spent most of his time and resources building a great sacrificial temple to Ku, only after its completion had he sent his ambassadors.

Keoua frowned, stroking his beard. "Young Tana, you are saying that my cousin needed to show his power before he offered peace. If Kahekili defeated him, it would prove that he did not have the blessings of the gods. Is that what you are saying?"

He raised himself high enough to fix his eyes upon Keoua, "Yes, my lord, you have understood correctly. Kamehameha offers peace at a time when he can show that he is blessed by the gods."

Keoua turned to the man next to him. "The gods have given Kamehameha great power, while we know that Pele has shown that I am no longer favored by them. It is best to make peace." Turning to his uncles, he announced, "I am agreed to end this war. I will come with you to Kona."

CHAPTER 65

IN DEEP WATER BEYOND THE beach, the two friends, united in brotherhood, watched the royal flotilla embark. Moki nudged Kalani's back. "Looks like the Kau king is heading for Kohala. But something strange about all this: Keoua's people tell him to stay in Kau, do not trust Kamehameha. But he put his royal cloaks, helmets, possessions in the canoe of the ambassadors. He is bringing Kamehameha's first son, Pauli, with him."

Kalani shuddered, remembering his premonition and his failure to mention to Keoua the completion of the new sacrificial temple on the Hill of the Whale. He swallowed several times, his throat dry. "Don't tell me your suspicions. Kamehameha told me he wants peace, Keoua wants peace. They are wise to end their war."

"Not suspicions," Moki snapped. "You're alive, that is important to me. But strange that Kamehameha wants Keoua to come to Kawaihae. Everybody should stay where they are, agreeing to peace. That's the way it has been done before."

"Kamehameha wants his cousin Keoua to embrace him in front of all the relatives and chiefs. Maybe it's to show that he's the stronger of the two. I don't know, but we better start paddling before the peace party gets too far ahead."

For two days, they sailed in the wake of the royal canoes. On the third day, the small flotilla pulled onto a beach, the last stop before Kawaihae. Kalani and Moki stood near the royal party and heard the chief counselor of Keoua urge the king not to trust Kamehameha and return to Kau. Other Kau chiefs came to him expressing their fear, saying they were walking into a trap and would be killed. They pleaded with Keoua to turn away.

The uncles, Kamehameha's ambassadors, assured him of their king's peaceful intentions. They said that he had nothing to fear for Kamehameha's eldest son, Pauli, was with them.

Keoua nodded and waved his followers away. Silence fell as he walked alone into a small temple near the beach and ordered servants to bring a knife and water. He unwound the royal cloth that girded his waist and washed his loins. He prayed to the god grimacing above the altar. Then, placing his penis upon the rock, he took the knife and, breathing deeply, severed it. Blood spurted from the wound. Keoua reeled away.

The two friends were silent, stunned. Finally, Kalani mumbled, "Why did he do that?"

"It must be the last act of surrender. Maybe he is saying he is no longer a man, Kamehameha is the stronger guy."

Kalani shook his head, trying to drive away a premonition of what lay ahead. "I don't know." He knew that when a chief is sacrificed to the god Ku, it is for the purpose of gaining his mana, his power. But what if a chief's penis is gone before he is killed?

The two men watched as Keoua, face contorted in excruciating pain, cleaned himself. A servant wound a cloth around the stump, staunching the flow of blood, then helped the king put on his royal clothes and helmet. Gingerly, Keoua boarded his double canoe and ordered his standard bearer to raise the royal emblem. The drummer began to beat and twenty-four paddlers pushed off for Kawaihae. In their wake came a second canoe carrying Keoua's chiefs, followed by the vessel of the two emissaries. Behind the royal party came another flotilla from Kau, this one led by Pauli, eldest son of Kamehameha. Kalani's canoe was last in line.

When the small fleet rounded the point of Kawaihae Bay, Kalani saw an astonishing sight: a great semi-circle of war canoes gliding toward them, the ends of this crescent closing like the pincers of a crab around the royal flotilla. On the shore stood chiefs wearing colorful feather capes, accompanied by thousands of armed warriors.

Magnificent in the glow of the mid-afternoon sun, Kamehameha stood on a large stone dressed in a full-length yellow feather cape and towering helmet, his 14-foot spear pointed to the massive rock temple at the top of Whale Hill.

Filled with apprehension by this display of power, Kalani's paddle froze in mid-air. His eyes ran quickly over the warriors on shore: is this to be a royal welcome or a betrayal? Surely, Kamehameha would be true to his word?

War canoes closed in around Keoua's craft, isolating it and preventing escape. As he approached the beach, the Kau King called to the golden figure standing below the massive luakini, "I am here."

Kamehameha's strong voice answered back, "Come, that we may know each other."

When Keoua leaped to the shore, a close advisor to Kamehameha screamed, stepped into him, and thrust his spear. Kalani's heart stopped as he saw Keoua dodge the strike, then stagger, as his assailant struck again, his weapon ripping into the Kau king's chest. Keoua dropped his head, clutching at the shaft. Blood spurted from his terrible wound, and he sank to his knees. His hands released their hold on the spear and he extended them to Kamehameha, beseeching. A club smashed Keoua to the ground. Tattooed warriors seized him. With his legs and arms twitching, they rushed him to the sacrificial temple.

At the same time, other warriors, emitting cries like wild animals in a feeding rage, smashed and stabbed at Kau chiefs and servants too bewildered to fend off the fusillade of blows. The attackers seized them, dragged them from the royal canoes, and passed the struggling men from warrior to warrior along a human chain that reached to the temple on Whale Hill.

Disbelief paralyzed Kalani, stunned by the betrayal. He watched in mounting horror the victims of Kamehameha's deceit being offered to Ku and felt helpless to stop the travesty. What had gone wrong? Had the demon god possessed his royal leader and demanded the deaths of Keoua and the chiefs of Kau? He had no answer. He could only clamp his hands onto his ears and blot out the shrieks of the dying.

He spied the vessel commanded by Pauli backing away from the slaughter as two canoes filled with howling warriors closed in. Ferociously, Kalani flung his paddle to left and right, yelling to his men to do the same. With prodigious heaves he rammed his boat into the intercepting canoes, disrupting them from their course.

Angry warriors screamed. Before they could counter his attack, a *conch shell blew, its shrill cry halting all combat. "Amnesty," Kamehameha commanded. "The Law of the Splintered Paddle is declared. No harm is to come to the weak, the defenseless, and those who are captives. My son, Pauli, and those with him, shall not die."*

Kalani gasped from the exertion of his efforts. He rested on his paddle, watching the parade of death coming to an end. The screams of the massacred no longer rent the air. Moki, silent throughout the attack, turned and stared at Kalani, anger blazing from his eyes. "You knew this treachery would occur?" His voice harsh, his fists clenched.

Stricken to his core Kalani said, "How could you say that? How could you believe that?" He choked, burying his face in his hands.

Moki spat into the water, a smile playing across his face. "So, you were fooled into getting Kamehameha what he wanted? If you are smart, brother, I wouldn't admit that. I would go to the temple and demand my reward."

"Shut up!" Kalani seethed. *"Don't you understand anything?" When he saw the hurt in Moki's eyes, his voice softened. "I will ask him for nothing." With that, he gripped his paddle and turned the canoe toward home.*

CHAPTER 66

When he returned to Honaunau, Kalani held Alapai-nui to his promise to give him slaves. He requested Minato's father, Mokihana, and his mother. On their suggestion he freed eighteen others from bondage. He brought them to the land he had been given control of in Kona and began to farm. Despite this peaceful endeavor, the desire for revenge burned within him. Alapai-nui commanded patience. *He suppressed his anger, developed the land, and prepared for whatever might come.*

On the slopes of the great volcano, he dug into the soil. Sweat beaded down his face, dripping onto the crushed lava at his feet. He worked with methodical strokes, driving a pointed shaft into broken stones as he excavated a hole in which to plant taro. Near him, freed slaves worked at the same task. Once the hole he dug became deep and wide enough, he added wet mulch, followed by a taro root, and then more wet mulch around the plant.

Once he completed his planting, Kalani rose, stretched, and studied his farm. It had been laid out according to Mokihana's wisdom. Hundreds of dry land taro sprouts thrust their leaves on the rock-strewn slope of Mauna Loa. Below them were terraces filled with green-and-orange-leafed vines. Moki, along with a few other warriors, were working among the plants, harvesting bulbs of red sweet potatoes.

He squinted at the sun glowing low on the western horizon. "Let's go," he called. Men put down their tools and walked to the training ground. There they exercised and practiced musket drills and martial arts combat until dark.

The evening breeze swept in from the snow-covered slopes of Mauna Loa, cooling the sweating men. With their training completed, they left the drill field, former slaves mixing with warriors, everyone laughing as they performed the night-time tasks.

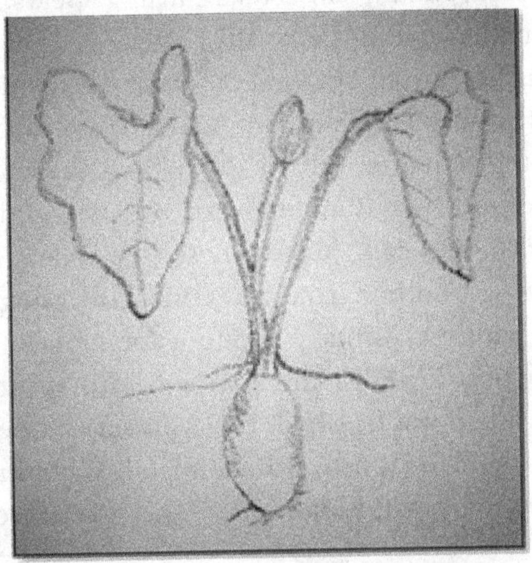

Taro

Kalani watched the happiness around him. He saw his nephew playing among the sprouting taro. He took the child and held him close, kissing his cheeks, breathing in his spirit as he rocked him. After a few moments, the boy squirmed to be free, and he set him down. He strode to where Moki and a stranger were in conversation.

"Hey, brother, this guy is from Akaka. He wants to talk to you."

"I have come with a message from the high chief. You are to come with me to Kealakekua."

Kalani scowled. *For four months since the death of Keoua, I have avoided all contact with Kamehameha and his advisors. In that time, I prepared an expedition to Maui to find Makula and kill him. I wonder if Akaka has learned of my plan and intends to stop me? He considered avoiding the request.*

Sensing his reluctance the messenger said, "Without delay, you are ordered to come with me."

A day later, the messenger beached their canoe near the royal compound at Kealakekua Bay. After climbing the bluff, they entered the enclosure. Warriors engaged in mock combat. Servants ran about performing errands. Women beat mulberry bark into cloth.

In an open area, Kalani saw Akaka hurling spears. When the high chief spotted him, he yelled, "Catch this!"

Without pausing, Kalani grabbed the descending spear and hurled it back, his quick throw so accurate that Akaka barely dodged the missile.

"You are better than ever, Kalani Moku Tana," a deep voice boomed.

Kalani turned and saw Kamehameha, wearing only a loincloth, a spear raised above his head. "Catch these," he yelled, hurling a spear and then snatching another from a retainer, throwing it in the same quick, powerful motion. Military training for months had honed his abilities to an expert level. Kalani plucked both spears from the air. But Kamehameha had not finished. From his servant he took two more spears, flinging them with astonishing speed. Catching the first and knocking aside the second, Kalani faced the man, three spears in his hands.

Kamehameha smiled. "Very good, but why do you wait? Hurl them back."

Kalani stood still. He did not raise a spear to throwing position. *His heart beat faster and faster as he fought his emotions, anger consuming him.*

"Why don't you throw?" Kamehameha demanded, his smile fading.

"I am trying to bury my rage. If I throw, it would be with the intention to harm you."

The action in the training area ceased. Faces turned, studying Kalani, and several warriors moved to disarm him.

Kamehameha waved them off. "You must learn to control your anger. If you fail to do so it will cause you to lose in battle. Throw your spears, then we may talk."

Kalani studied the man who stood without fear, a mixture of conflicting emotions seething within him. Is Kamehameha an evil, unscrupulous, bloody despot, or a man who has a broad vision of what is needed for his people? Watchers gasped as Kalani suddenly hurled one, two, then three spears with lightning quickness. Kamehameha grabbed two from the sky and brushed aside the third with a flick of his wrist. "You have improved since we last met. Here, catch this and follow me." Within a heartbeat, Kamehameha flung a spear with such low trajectory that Kalani fell to one knee to grasp it before it impaled him. Without a backward look, Kamehameha plunged across the threshold of a large hale.

CHAPTER 67

"WHAT TROUBLES YOU, KALANI MOKU Tana? Is it the death of Keoua?" Kamehameha demanded, sitting on a low platform covered by an intricately designed cloth. Below him, Akaka squatted. The only weapon in the building, the spear held in Kamehameha's hand. It pointed at the prostrate young man. "Rise up and answer me."

As he rose, Kalani thought of what he should say. *Should I offer flattery, falsehoods, or the truth?* "Yes, it is the death of Keoua that angers me. You used me to seduce him to come to Kawaihae, so that you might sacrifice him to that bloodthirsty god of yours. That was a treacherous act. For months, I have suffered for my part in this. If you dislike what I say, kill me now for telling you what is in my heart."

Twilight shadowed the interior of the hale, masking Kamehameha's face. In the dimness, his spear thrust close to Kalani's heart.

Kalani breathed deeply, calming himself. Resigned to my inevitable death. My only regret, that my mother and sister would not be avenged.

"When I sent you to bring Keoua to me, I had peace in my heart," Kamehameha said, honesty in his voice. "When he showed himself in Kawaihae, my advisors, who had suffered at his hands, were overcome with anger. Impelled by their hatred, they killed him and his chiefs. That explanation may not be acceptable to you but consider this: Keoua's death brings peace to Hawaii Island."

"And his death will bring peace to all Hawaii," a voice interrupted.

Kalani turned to see the chief counselor of Kamehameha, the same man who had speared Keoua, crawling into the hale.

"Know this," the counselor continued. "For a hundred years there has been endless war between the high chiefs of Hawaii. An ancient prophecy said that wars would not end until a special man moved the Naha stone. He would rule all the islands bringing lasting peace. Kamehameha is that man. He fulfilled the prophecy by lifting the stone and throwing it onto its side. He is chosen by the gods to be the king of kings. Furthermore, we—"

"Remember, too," Akaka interrupted. "That Keoua was allied to Kahekili and Makula. To end war and bring peace, some leaders must be eliminated. When the gods abandoned him, Keoua recognized his struggle with Kamehameha had come to an end. He came to Kawaihae knowing he must die to fulfill the ancient prophecy."

Servants entered the hale to light the kukui lamps, their yellow glow brushing away the darkness, revealing Kamehameha's face. Though set in stern lines, his face did not show anger. Instead, *Kalani thought he saw compassion and noted that the spear now lay by his side.* Emboldened, he said, "I will accept that Keoua's death was necessary to attain peace. Forgive me for my anger. If I must die for my poor judgment, then let me die in combat and not as a sacrifice to Ku. Chief Makula has committed sacrilege. He invaded the Temple of Refuge, stole my mother and sister from its protection, and in defiance of the gods, murdered them. Permit me to go to Maui and kill him."

Lamplight played over Kamehameha's features and exaggerated the natural curve of his cheeks into a grimace. Despite this, his eyes were free of hostility. The downward droop of his lips straightened slowly into a faint smile. With eyes glinting, he said, "You will not die. Go and revenge yourself on Makula, who has desecrated the Temple of Refuge."

Before Kalani could respond, Akaka said, "Kamehameha, I have a favor to ask. I promised Kalani that he would be rewarded for his bravery in battle. Even though he has no royal bloodline, let him become a 'black dirt chief' with a gift of land."

"I agree. This man has proven himself worthy, but there is no land to give him on Hawaii Island. My loyal chiefs must have their share of that land."

"Why not let him have land from the evil chiefs of Maui, where Makula is hiding?" the counselor suggested.

"A good solution," Akaka said "After the battle of Iao Valley, Alapainui gave Moku Tana control over some land in Kahului. Though you have lost Maui, Kalani can retake this Kahului land and you can confirm his right of ownership to it.

"I have also heard that Kahekili has made a terrible mistake, that he has allowed the Kauai king to give Maui land to his chiefs. This has made people angry at the oppression of these men and they would welcome a change, especially if the right person comes to free them." Akaka looked directly at Kalani.

The room settled into silence as Kamehameha studied the young man. At twenty, he was very handsome, and his physique rippled with well-defined muscles.

Kalani sensed an opportunity that might never come again. He said, "On that day four months ago when Keoua and his followers were brought down, you declared that 'The Law of the Splintered Paddle' would be in effect. The second group from Kau, led by your son Pauli, were given freedom from slavery and sacrifice. Will you grant me the benefit of that same law in the lands that I may control on Maui?"

The chief counselor spat. "My king, this is pure insolence. I have never heard of this 'Law of the Splintered Paddle' and I doubt it even exists!"

Kamehameha gazed into a dark corner of the building and said, "Years in the past, during a time we call *the bitter war,* a time when I never won a battle, I traveled the coast of Puna. On a reef, I espied fishermen and decided to seize their catch. When my canoe landed on the beach, they fled and I pursued them. My foot broke though hardened lava and I was trapped in a crevice. Two of the fishermen returned and beat me with their paddles, splintering one on my head. The steersman on my boat came to my aid. I managed to pull my foot from the crevice and escape to my canoe."

He paused so the men in the room could mark his words. "For years, I have thought of that incident and how nobles, like myself, oppress the weak, take what we want from them, kill them, or make them into slaves. On the day Keoua was sacrificed I saw my son Pauli helpless. I recalled that event and knew that I could not let my child be forced into slavery and sacrificed. On that day, I declared that the Law of the Splintered Paddle shall be the law of the land. That was the day I stopped the slaughter of my son and those with him.

Kalani looked around the room, noting the sullen faces of the chiefs. *I know that these men believe they are descended from the gods and could do as they wanted with commoners. Now, they were hearing their leader say that there would be limits to the exercise of their power.*

Kamehameha continued, "I was wrong when I attacked those fishermen with the intent to rob them. I now make this law for the safety of all people under my government:

> ***"If any man plunders or murders the defenseless or the innocent, he will be punished."***

"Kalani Moku Tana, your request is granted. Go with Akaka and prepare your attack."

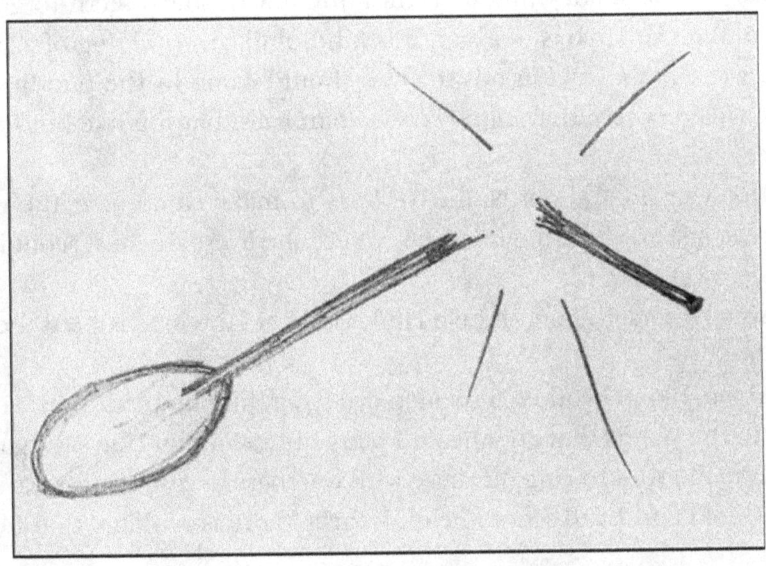

CHAPTER 68

A MONTH LATER, IN THE quiet before sunrise, a small army of three hundred men landed near Kahului, Maui. They were warriors from Hilo, Waipio, Kau, and volunteers from Kona, all seeking revenge for the desecration of the Temple of Refuge.

"We are near the fresh water ponds. Big trouble if a Mo'o lives in it," Moki protested as he marched from the beach toward spring-fed pools.

"You, the bravest of the brave afraid of a lizard!" Kalani laughed. "I can see you are frightened by legends that tell of evil, slithering beasts."

"Eh, brah, don't make fun of the Mo'o. That dragon can change how it looks. Maybe small thing to giant animal with sharp teeth to gobble you up. But the Mo'o is not bad. It is kind of like a watchdog of a place, protect it. That's why I'm not sure we should camp by the puddles. Go to the village where that high-class woman lives that you like but I don't like."

"Don't say that about Nani. We have to make camp near the water and can't just go charging inland to where she lives. We must scout it out first see what's what."

"Your orders, Kalani," Eleele High Chief of Hilo interrupted the two friends.

"Aloha, blood brother. The men are straggling up behind us. Direct them to the ponds that are ahead. Plenty of fresh water there. Organize the camp. Be sure to ring our base with watchers in case enemy warriors come. Moki and I will scout ahead. Nearby there is a village that I once controlled. We will investigate and see if it is friendly or not. I don't know. Kahekili retook Maui from Kamehameha. He divided up the land among Kauai chiefs for their help in the war. I have to find out what is ahead of us before the army moves further inland."

"I will do what you ask. But what is this talk of a Mo'o?"

"Moki is afraid of the spirits. This is a new place for him and he doesn't know about what kind of gods may be here. If there are lizards on this island they are on the west side. I wouldn't worry about them. Moki, we pick up some hoeing sticks and head to the village."

After an hour's march through scrub and low-growing trees they came to an open field with shacks scatted in it. Kalani took his shaft and began digging the ground. "Moki, bend over. Look like a farmer. Let's work toward the servants working over there," he signaled by moving his head. "Keep an eye on those guards at the compound playing a game."

As they came closer to the toiling men one of them asked, "Where you boys from?"

"We just came from Lahaina," Moki answered.

"What family?"

"Makanani."

"Don't know them."

"What's it like in Kahului?" Kalani asked. "Things are pretty bad in Lahaina. Those Kauai guys are sure bossy, they take everything for themselves. They are mean too. We just got here and they put us to work."

"I don't want to talk too loud, but I think it's worse here. Our overlord from Kauai, Ahi, killed our chief in a big fight over his daughter. Ahi makes us work sunup to sunset and takes everything for himself. None of our women are safe. Eh, we better stop talking, one of those Kauai guys is looking over here."

Kalani and Moki bent low in servile posture, eyes fastened to the ground, hoeing with their sticks. After many minutes of work, Kalani risked a glance toward the compound, noting that the curious guard had returned to his game.

The two men worked through the morning, Kalani studying the area and counting the number of warriors. Toward noon, he saw a familiar figure with a bag under her arm leave the compound and head for a line of bushes that marked a stream flowing to the ocean.

"Moki, if there is trouble, signal me with the *kee-oh* of the hawk," Kalani whispered. He began hoeing a furrow to bushes near the water. Going to his knees, he pretended to work on an imbedded rock. He checked the compound. Saw no one watching and slid into the shrubs, then down the bank into the stream. He searched for the woman and found her washing clothes. "Ho, Napua. Remember me, Kalani Tana? I helped your family in Iao Valley."

Startled, the woman seized her laundry, stumbling on rocks to escape.

"Please wait. I saved your husband. I visited your daughter. I am here to help."

Napua crumpled into the water, her laundry floating slowly downstream. Tears filled her eyes. "Oh, help us, Makula has murdered my husband. Ahi is raping…"

"Makula!" Kalani spat, gripped Napua, lifted her to his face. His eyes bored into hers. In a harsh voice he demanded, "Where is he? In your compound?"

Napua squirmed, her feet seeking footing in the bed of the stream. She twisted, trying to pull away from him. Kalani released his grip, realizing that his anger had frightened her. He said soothingly, "I'm sorry I hurt you. Makula killed my mother. I'm here to kill him."

Napua stumbled to the bank, moaned, and sagged to the ground. "Woe, woe, woe, he killed my husband, too. I have no one to save my Nani." She buried her face in her hands and cried.

Her agonized sobbing wrenched Kalani's heart. He sat beside her, reaching his hand to smooth her shoulder, reddening where he had gripped her. She shied from his touch. But he gently palmed her back, spoke soothingly in low tones. "Please forgive me. Is Makula nearby?"

Napua shook her head, swiped her eyes, and stared into the stream. The water eddied around her laundry that had snagged on submerged rocks. Kalani spoke softly. "Tell me of Nani."

Her hands shaking, Napua wiped her eyes, settled herself onto the bank, and said, "Kahekili gave our land to a Kauai chief named Ahi. He took from us and gave back nothing. We hid Nani from him for we heard the man was evil." Her voice dropped. She adjusted her garment, smoothing out wrinkles, gathering herself. Kalani remained quiet sensing that they were coming to the sadness of her story. He studied her face and saw the lines that marked her brow, the gathering of skin at her throat, the hair once black turning white. The woman had aged.

Napua clasped her hands, wringing them over and over again. With a sigh she said, "After months of Ahi's stealing Makula came and together they searched every village for weapons." Napua's voice faltered. She wept, gathered herself and said, "They came here and discovered my Nani. My husband tried to protect her, but Makula killed him and Ahi took Nani away." She wailed her last words.

A harsh voice yelled, "Hey, you! What are you doing, talking to that woman? How come you are not working? You're going to get a beating for being lazy, come up here."

Above them stood a warrior, a spear in one hand and a switch stick in the other. Kalani bent in a servile position, trying to conceal his face. He climbed the bank, his hoeing tool in his hand. The warrior flicked his switch, the cord of sennit biting into his flesh. When he reached level ground, the beating began in earnest.

"You lazy, no-good!" the warrior yelled. "Look at me so I can mark your face."

Kalani lifted his arm, letting the whip wrap around it, drawing blood. He smiled at the warrior and pulled. "Who are you—" the man's voice faltered as he stumbled into the digging tool that Kalani thrust into his belly. He brushed aside the warrior's spear and kicked his knee, then moved to the side, smashing the butt of his farming tool into the warrior's body

With a piercing yowl, the man fell to the dirt, dropping his spear. Kalani grabbed it and whispered to Napua, "Hide. I'll be back." He pulled a double-edged dagger from the guard's loincloth. The man clutched Kalani's feet. Kalani countered the attack by thrusting the butt end of the dagger deep into the warrior's belly. With a gasp, the man released his hold and Kalani kicked him over the bank and into the stream.

"*Kee-ho*," the shriek of the hawk drew Kalani's eyes to the compound. Enemy soldiers emerged from it. One warrior ahead of all the others whirled a tripping cord and flung it. At the same moment, Kalani threw his spear and dove to the ground. The man sprawled to the earth kicking up dust and stones, the spear embedded in his chest. Behind the wounded man, five warriors charged, howling like hounds.

Kalani rolled up and ran along the stream bank for a short distance, then angled in the direction of his base camp. Moki joined him, laughing and hooting "*kee-ho*." Farmers dropped their digging tools and scattered, some blocking the pursuing warriors, giving Kalani and Moki time to reach the path leading to the ponds. They raced onto it, with five enemies close behind.

A spear nicked his thigh, the sudden weakness in his leg sprawling Kalani to the grass. Moki stopped and turned to face the charging warriors with his farming stick. Kalani rolled upright, pulling the double-edged dagger from his loincloth. A spear wobbled toward him. He seized it and yelled, "Moki, catch this," tossing the weapon.

His eye caught the downward swing of a cudgel and he stepped to the side, pivoted, and sliced his dagger across the chest of a tattooed warrior. The man gasped, his face wrinkling, mouth gaping, showing teeth yellowed by olena root. Kalani smashed his fist into the man's belly and with a huge wheeze the soldier fell to the grass.

"Watch out," Moki yelled. The warning came too late as a club struck Kalani's shoulder, sending waves of pain down his neck and back. "Smash you to bits," grunted the attacker as he swung his cudgel again. Kalani shoved his knee between the man's legs. He bellowed, reaching down. Kalani smashed the palm of his uninjured hand into the attacker's jaw, breaking his nose. Coughing, spitting blood, the man stumbled backward, and fell into onrushing warriors.

For a moment all action ceased. A light breeze rustled the spiny twigs of the kiawe forest that shaded the path. The gnarled wood rubbing together emitted scratchy sounds that mixed in eerie discordance with the moans of the wounded men.

Blood pulsed from his thigh, his shoulder throbbed, but Kalani felt exhilarated. He was fighting again. He needed a spear. He studied the three enemies huddled twenty feet away. "You," he pointed at a scrawny warrior whose face twitched as he rapidly inhaled and exhaled, "Makula's rat. A coward, hiding behind his friends, afraid to fight."

The taunted man shuffled his feet, his body rocked from side to side. "You, filthy pig," he yelled as he swung back his arm, flinging his spear. With a quick move Kalani grasped it, reversed its point and taunted, "Thank you, eater of garbage. Come to me and die."

"Good catch," Moki laughed. "That opala is as stupid as he looks. But I think our troubles are just beginning, look at what's coming." Moki pointed to warriors racing toward them. One of the three men they faced smirked and said, "Give up. You cannot escape!"

Blood smearing his thigh and trickling down his leg, Kalani limped to the side of the path. "Ten men are coming. Moki, squeeze against me and back into that kiawe tree."

"We will be an easy target for their spears."

"Maybe, but at least we can watch what they throw, and our backs will be protected. Get ready, they are making their move."

A wide, toothy grin spread across the tattooed face of the scrawny warrior Kalani had called a rat. "I will enjoy watching you die. It will be slow, for we will poke you many times. Then when you have fallen, roast you like the pigs you are and eat your mana."

The pain from Kalani's wounds ached, but he ignored the pain and assumed a fighting stance. He nudged Moki's shoulder. "If we are going to die, let's make them eat kukae."

The charging enemy reinforcements slowed as they reached the battleground. One man who appeared in charge motioned his fellows to spread out, encircling the two friends. They clumped together watching, waiting for the moment that the enemy would make their final attack.

CHAPTER 69

MAKULA STOOD OUTSIDE THE PALACE of Kahekili, staring at the walls of a luakini temple snuggled against the side of Mount Leahi. Several priests were busy erecting an *opu* tower while others busied themselves with deities that were being placed along the back wall. From within the palace came the wailing of nose flutes that screeched to a high note sounding like roosters choking to death. The music ended and Makula was beckoned in.

The aged king sat on mats at the rear wall of the hale with several women serving him food and drink. Makula thought Kahekili drunk with awa and scowled at the thought that he must come begging to this man for land and warriors. He watched the flute players crawl out and, on a signal from Namaka, he prostrated, and with growing anger squirmed toward the king. Why should he, Makula, toady to a drunken old sot? But he knew the wily despot ruled Maui, Oahu, and Molokai, and people on those islands obeyed him.

When told to rise and face the king Makula modulated his voice to a friendly tone. "Great Lord, I come to seek land and warriors to help you defend Maui."

Kahekili rocked from side to side. He peered at Makula, slowly focusing his eyes upon him. "Defend! Why? Captain Vancouver is negotiating peace between Kamehameha and me. No fighting between us, he says. But then—"

"Kamehameha may attack while talks are ongoing," Makula interrupted. "He is consolidating his power on Hawaii Island. Once he is in control, he will invade Maui."

Kahekili grunted. "Maybe. For land and warriors, what do you offer me? You were defeated in Kona and fled."

With a supreme effort, Makula controlled his anger, "I beat Alapainui. Brought sixty war canoes to your cause. I have trained your tattooed wild ones so that they are good fighters, men without fear. I have—"

"He has two hundred warriors from Kona," Namaka interjected. "More are coming from Kau eager to fight the traitorous Kamehameha. Give him control of Kihei. With my forces in Lahaina, we will build an unstoppable army."

Kahekili stroked his chin and looked outside his palace, watching the afternoon sunlight brightening the dark rocks of the temple. "Kamehameha killed many of my warriors in Iao Valley. It has forced me to give Maui land to Kauai chiefs to fight the upstart. I grant you control of Kihei so long as you and Namaka destroy any invaders of my domain."

Makula smiled, took a thin dagger from his waist and made a figure eight in the sand, the lower circle bigger than the upper one. At the joinder he drew a line down the middle. "Here in Kahului, where the sand hills are, we will fight any invaders, and destroy them as you did, twenty years ago."

The king nodded. "The Alapa died, squeezed in my trap. Go to Maui and fulfill your promises."

CHAPTER 70

"I THINK WE ARE SURROUNDED," Moki said with a wry smile as he glanced at the enemy warriors who had completed their encirclement. "Will death be quick or slow?"

"You will die slowly," an enemy warrior sneered. "Pricked by a dozen spear points, your blood will water the ground until you are too weak to fight. Then we cook you and listen to your screams begging to die."

Kalani whispered, "Moki, let's die quick. When I yell *kee-ho,* charge."

As if sensing their intent, an enemy warrior yelled, "Draw back. Prepare to throw."

"Fire," Mokihana ordered. Muskets crackled, bringing four enemies to the ground. A mass of spears arched through the sky, striking down men turning to flee. Kalani's elite soldiers poured onto the battle-ground. The melee was loud, violent, and short.

Dead and dying warriors covered the pathway. One still quivered. Kalani spoke with the wounded man as Mokihana came alongside. Kalani asked, "Where are the rest of our men?"

"At base camp. You and Moki were gone for so long that I ordered our elite company forward to find you."

"Good that you did. This man says there are only six warriors in the enemy camp. Send a messenger to Eleele to come double-quick. Gather your men. We must press our attack while we have the element of surprise. Moki will lead you."

Kalani lagged, slowed by injuries. Moki took the musketeers to the enemy compound where their swift attack ended with the surrender of a half-dozen enemy. Kalani ordered a search for Napua, then questioned the prisoners. He learned that Makula had left for Oahu and Ahi had gone to Wailuku with Nani.

A healer cauterized Kalani's thigh and placed an herb-filled poultice around his shoulder. Toward evening, Napua was found and brought to him. The chiefess prostrated, begging, "Please, save my Nani. I fear for her."

He saw the mother's distress. *Her worry ached his heart and he closed his eyes, breathing slowly, trying to control its racing beat. He felt a sudden emptiness and realized that he no longer wanted to sleep alone. That the shaking of his body meant he loved Nani and if she was gone, the weight of her loss would be beyond measure.* In a whisper, he asked, "Where will we find your daughter?"

"I do not know, but there is a way to learn where she is."

"Good, you lead and I will follow."

At that moment, Eleele arrived with the rest of the army. Kalani explained his intentions, and Eleele agreed to bivouac the men for the night and await his return. Satisfied with his arrangements, Kalani limped out of the compound, followed by Moki, six men, and Napua.

Late in the evening a band of rescuers slipped into the outskirts of Wailuku. The town lay in shambles of squalor with huts and shacks indiscriminately scattered about. The only light came from the vast number of stars spread out across the heavens in twinkling pinpoints of white.

The silence was eerie – no voices, no barking dogs. Kalani guessed that the villagers were asleep or too frightened to be noisy. In this huge jumble of huts, he despaired of finding Nani.

As they neared the palms at the beach, the shacks became larger and better built. A few people hurried between them, heading to bright fires that burned within the grove of trees. At the edge of it, Napua asked the group to wait and left.

Many minutes went by and she did not return. Kalani decided to check for an alternative line of retreat. He sent two men to scrounge the shore for a canoe. A pale half-moon peeped through the clouds shrouding the great volcano of Haleakala. Its reflected light silhouetted saw-toothed mountains to the west.

Pointing to the dim outline of Iao Valley, Moki said, "Many men died there. When the breeze comes from those hills, it brings the screams of the dead. I can hear them calling."

Kalani chuckled. "You hear ghosts where there are none." In an instant, the smile vanished and he grew pensive. *I wish my mother was a ghost, so I could talk to her. Every night I pray to hear her voice, but it never comes. I hate Makula and all who are his allies.* He bent his head meditating on his loss.

A voice roused him. "You may have a chance to get his friend, Ahi," a woman said from the shadows. Startled by the words, six spears pointed into the darkness.

"Do not be alarmed," Napua whispered. "It is only a friend and me!" She and another woman slipped out of the shadows and into the uncertain light of the moon. Napua introduced her dead husband's cousin.

Eyes filled with hatred, the woman hissed, "Nani is imprisoned four shacks from here. The bastard Ahi is getting drunk at the bonfires. Soon, he will come to torture her and take what he wants."

"How many guards? How many entrances to her prison?" Kalani asked.

"Only one, but the door and the guard are lighted by the fires, and in full view of many. There may be servants inside the hut, I do not know."

"Show me where Nani is. The rest, wait here."

Guided by the woman, he limped to the back of a large grass shack with walls made of tight, interlaced leaves difficult to cut through. He put his ear to the woven fibers and heard voices but could not detect Nani. He knew there were at least two in the shack, possibly more. From his vantage point in the shadows, he saw a lone guard squatting at the threshold armed with a spear and club.

He hurried back to his men. The two he had sent to the ocean had returned with news: they had found a large canoe on the beach a hundred yards away. He explained his plan. When finished, Kalani's team moved into position.

Boisterous laughter filled the night as soldiers congregated around the beach fires, telling stories of manhood and bravery. Suddenly, there came a piercing cry from the far edge of the coconut grove, "Fire!" Men turned to see bright flames curling into the sky from a burning shack. At the threshold of the prison hut the guard stood to see. Napua tripped and fell in front of him, whimpering, "Help me, help me." The man reached for the distraught woman. Moki slipped from the shadows, swung his cudgel, and brought it down in a great arc against his head.

As the guard sagged to the sand, Kalani crawled into the shack. In the light of an oil lamp he made out the figures of nude women. One of them, Nani, huddled against two others. Welts lined her back.

Rage consumed him when he realized that she had been beaten. Kalani limped to the cowering females who whimpered as he approached. "I'm not here to hurt you. Nani, your mother is waiting for you. Come, I'll bring you to her."

Nani crouched closer to the two naked women, averting her eyes. Kalani sensed that her will had been broken, and he wondered how many times she had been beaten and abused to give Ahi pleasure. *He added the chief to his list of enemies and vowed to kill him.* He reached to the woman he loved, found her hand and drew her up. She was listless, unresisting. His heart pounded. He felt a pulsating desire for her but suppressed his growing feelings. He spoke soothing words as he helped her stand. She grasped a sarong from a heap of clothes and let him lead her outside.

Napua met them, both women wept as cloth wrapped around the naked girl. Kalani called into the shack, "If you want to escape, follow us. Everyone to the sea."

Two figures emerged from the darkness. Nani gasped.

"Friends, not enemies," Kalani whispered, taking a spear from one of his warriors. "There are two more inside the shack. Help them to the beach."

A man yelled, "Guard, what is happening?"

Other voices called out words lost in the wind. He knew they had only moments before they were discovered. Kalani hurried his group toward the shore. They had taken only a dozen steps when a voice challenged, "Who are you?"

"Keep moving," Kalani ordered. In the darkness, he made out the figure of an armed man.

"Stop!"

Another voice screamed. "The guard is dead! The women have escaped!"

Nani gasped.

Kalani whispered, "Napua, you and Nani go, quick." He fell to the sand as a dark shape lunged toward them. Moki reacted to the charge and drove his spear into the attacker. The man tripped. The wounded warrior tried to regain his footing, but Kalani rolled upright, kicked him to the ground, then finished him with a blow to the head.

Figures loomed in the darkness. The two women froze. Moki whistled and an answering whistle relieved the momentary tension. "Friends, pick up the pace, hurry," Kalani whispered.

Guided by the crash of waves, the small group stumbled toward the sea. Nani screamed. A man's voice shouted, "Got you!" Moonlight broke through the clouds, casting light onto the struggle between Nani, Napua, and a squat man. With a vicious backward blow of his arm, the attacker struck Napua to the sand. The man gripped Nani and began to drag her away.

Kalani cried, "No!", and limped toward the escaping pair. Two of the rescued women streaked by him and hurled themselves onto the man, pummeling his face and body. One of them hissed, "I'm going to kill you, Ahi."

The chief staggered under the force of their blows. Nani woke from her lethargy and bit his arm. Ahi released his hold and screamed, "They're here by the sea. Help!" Then he turned and fled.

"Come quick," Kalani said in a low voice. He gathered a bruised Napua from the sand, and asked, "Are you okay?" She ignored the question and spit out: "Did you kill the evil man?"

Kalani shook his head. "The coward ran away. I will kill him next time."

Napua clenched her fists, shook them in the darkness, “Next time I will kill him.”

Moki called, “Hey, get in before the opala finds us.” He stood next to the double canoe being shoved into the water by the remaining rescuers. Kalani helped push it into the waves. He admired the excellent workmanship that had gone into building it then realized the vessel had been stolen from Alapai-nui.

Voices screamed. Rocks plummeted into the sand or splashed into the shallow water at the shore. The double canoe breasted waves, crashing into them. Their surge pulled the vessel back to the beach. “Everyone get on,” Moki yelled.

Kalani helped Nani into the craft, seized the wale and hauled himself in. His forceful movements sent jolts of pain through his thigh and shoulder. He lay in the trough of the canoe, exhausted. With paddles raised Moki began the rowing beat, urging women and men to push the canoe out to sea. Clouds covered the moon. Kalani hoped that the darkness would hide them from pursuit. He noted that Napua had taken the helm, and he knew she would guide them safely to Kahului. Exhausted, he fell asleep.

CHAPTER 71

For three days, he lay in pain. His thigh throbbed. His neck and shoulder ached. A fever dazed him, he slipped in and out of a dreamlike state. He vaguely knew that Nani brought him food, water, and tended to his injuries. When she was near him, her sullen beauty brought an arousal. Despite his misery, he wanted to possess her. In a lucid moment, he asked about Ahi and Makula. She did not answer. Instead, her eyes welled with tears, and she left. He wondered what beatings she must have suffered that had stifled her arrogance.

On the fourth day, Kalani woke with his aches no longer throbbing. He left his shack and sought Mokihana. He learned that the former slave had gone to visit family in Wailuku. Near the compound, he discovered Mauloa, the priest from Hilo, working with several men and women in a small grove of trees. He strode to him and said, "You are starting our project?"

The holy man stood, stretching his limbs. "Yes, we're building the temple and altar to Lono that we discussed in Hilo. Once it's finished, we can consecrate this land to the god of peace."

His words brought a broad smile to Kalani's face. "Good, and then we will declare that Kamehameha's 'Law of the Splintered Paddle' is in effect. In the lands I control, there will be a haven for the weak, the poor, the enslaved, and the kauwa."

Mauloa nodded and returned to his work.

Kalani decided to find the princess and plead his love for her. At the stream, he found her mother beating soaked clothes. Near her, Nani washed garments. The older woman stood when she saw him, her face beaming a welcome. Nani glanced for a split moment, a wan smile lighting her face, then dropped her eyes and returned to her work. He sat on a smooth rock, dangling his feet into the cool water.

"Good to see that you are well enough to be up and about," Napua said.

"Many thanks to your daughter."

The young woman did not respond, averting her eyes, and continuing to wash her clothes. Kalani dipped his hands, stood, and smoothed his hair with wet palms. He stepped closer to Napua, towering over her.

The widow ceased her work and her feet searched for a secure perch among the stream-washed rocks. She looked at her daughter who remained bent low to the water, scrubbing clothes even harder against the stones.

Kalani stared at her back, then returned his gaze to Napua. He swallowed and with emotion in his voice said, "I love your daughter. I ask permission to marry her."

"No! Never, I am unclean, dirty," Nani sobbed, rising from the water that splashed high around her legs. She stumbled over the rocks toward the bank, her hands covering her eyes. Napua rushed after her and grasped her weeping daughter into her breast.

Kalani stammered a few words of apology, then added, "Nani, I love you, no matter what ugliness you have suffered."

With her daughter held close, Napua walked to a level place at the bank and they sat, rocking and crying together. Kalani remained silent, cool water swirling around his legs damping the passion that flamed his heart. He watched Napua dry tears from wet eyes. Nani, like a new-born child, huddled into her mother, her chest heaving with an agony that tore at his heart.

Kalani could stand it no longer and he rushed to where the women sat. "I have loved you since we met in Iao Valley. But I have held this love deep in my heart, because I was not worthy of you." He took Nani's hand. “Even with all the misery you have suffered, I love you with every part of my being and want you for my wife.”

Nani pulled her hand away. Napua kissed the tears from the eyes of her child and stood with Nani in her arms. The women climbed the bank together, Napua calling back, “Give her time, Kalani. She needs to heal.”

CHAPTER 72

MOKIHANA RETURNED FROM WAILUKU WITH mixed news. Chief Ahi had sought help to reclaim the land that Kalani occupied and had been able to convince some chiefs to join him in retaking Kahului. A major attack could be expected at any time. He ended his report, saying, "It is uncertain how loyal the Wailuku warriors will be to Ahi. Kahekili rewarded the king of Kauai with Maui land for his help in fighting Kamehameha. Ahi was given Kahului to rule. The man proved to be a tyrant, bullied the Maui people, took what he wanted and, with Makula, killed Nani's father. Only obedience to Kahekili keeps the Maui folks supportive of him, yet the balance between favor and disfavor is delicate."

With Eleele and Mokihana, Kalani laid out his plans for combat. Except for the hard core of his warriors—the musketeers, former slaves, and a sprinkling of men who had fought with him in several battles—Kalani could not depend on the rest of his forces to fight to the death. He had no land or slaves to offer them and they had no reason to fight and die for him. His plan would depend on his loyal troops. Soon, word came that an army approached.

Kalani stood beyond the stream marking the line between Kahului and Wailuku. At his side were Eleele and Mokihana, both dressed in the feather cape and helmet worn by chiefs. Behind them were a dozen musketeers and an equal number of skirmishers and spearmen. A hundred yards beyond Kalani's thin line a larger number of Wailuku men arranged themselves in traditional battle formation, a crescent of warriors with spear tips pointed forward. Between these two forces stood Mauloa and a priest from the Temple of Refuge in Honaunau. Both men held white stones.

Eleele leaned over to Kalani. "No one from the other side wants to talk. Maybe our small numbers make us appear weak and easily defeated."

"Be patient, the morale of the Maui warriors is low. They hate Ahi and it won't take much to turn them to our side. Kalani is wise to show peaceful intentions. If peace efforts fail, our battle plan will work," Mokihana answered.

Conch trumpets blew from the opposite side of the battleground. A brown-robed priest advanced, carrying a white stone.

Kalani strode to the center of the battlefield where the priests stood, followed by Eleele and Mokihana. From the Wailuku battle line, four chiefs advanced toward them, Ahi in the lead, swearing as he came. When the two factions faced each other, twenty feet apart, the priests stepped away.

Ahi eyed Kalani with narrowed eyes and sneered, "So you are the ugly bastard who stole my woman. Return her to me. Then, if you get on your knees and beg for mercy–I may let you live." He paused and laughed. "Of course, I will peel off your skin before I let you go."

Kalani ignored Ahi and spoke to the Wailuku chiefs. "I am here to talk peace. My quarrel is not with the Maui people. It is with Makula, who violated the Temple of Refuge and killed my mother and sister. It is with his ally, Ahi, who violated the most sacred of taboos by taking Princess Nani against her will and killing her father."

The Wailuku chiefs talked among themselves. Kalani heard words like *taboo* and *violation of the temple* being whispered.

"This is nonsense. This man is a liar and a thief of my woman. End this useless chatter. I want what belongs to me. Let there be war," Ahi screamed.

"It is not nonsense. You men know the truth, how Ahi and Makula stole the princess from her home, killed her father, a man loyal to our king and the rightful ruler of Kahului. That land does not belong to a foreign chief from Kauai. It belongs to Princess Nani, and her future husband, Chief Kalani Moku Tana," Mokihana yelled.

Stunned by the words, the three Maui chiefs drew closer together, conferring among themselves. Ahi screamed again, "I order you to kill these men!" His face ravaged with fury.

Weaponless, as required in peace negotiations, Eleele, Mokihana, and Kalani assumed a fighting stance for hand-to-hand combat, knees flexed, hands clenched by their side. All eyes focused on Ahi. He brandished a knife that had been concealed beneath his cloak. Pointing it at Kalani, he seethed, "Kill them."

One of the Wailuku men spoke, his words slow and sure. "We will not fight for you. The land of Kahului belongs to the princess, not foreign scum." The three chiefs walked back to their warriors.

Fear flashed across Ahi's face and he ran toward the crescent line of fighters and yelled, "They have violated the truce, attack, attack!"

A contingent of warriors moved forward at his call, but the bulk of the Wailuku army stood in place, waiting for a signal from their chiefs. Kalani, Eleele, and Mokihana retreated to the musketeers. Moki handed Kalani a loaded gun, a smile on his face. "What did you say to Ahi to make him run like a frightened chicken?"

"Look, the Wailuku army is leaving," Mokihana shouted.

Moki glanced ahead. "Yeah, but there are still a bunch of warriors pounding up dust and that crazy Ahi is stirring them up."

"Eleele, call the rest of our forces to this side of the stream," Kalani ordered.

Ahi finished exhorting his men. His warriors clashed their long spears, leveled them, and advanced on the thin line of musketeers.

"Present arms, fire!" Kalani ordered. He aimed at Ahi. His shot grazed the side of the chief's face. Blood streamed down his cheek. He screamed and ran from the fight. "Ho! Ho! The warriors are stopping. Shoot them again and they will run and catch up with Ahi." Eleele laughed.

"Fire!" A second volley of musket fire brought more men down. Leaderless and outnumbered, the remnants of Ahi's force fled.

Princess Nani strode to Kalani and looked him in the eyes. "I came to fight that man. Why didn't you kill him?"

A broad smile crossed his face. Her anger heightened her beauty, her flaming eyes excited him. "I saved him for you." He took her into his arms and kissed her. She did not resist, but instead embraced him. *Kalani paused in his passion, smelling her hair, filling his lungs with her fragrance, consuming her exquisite beauty with his eyes.* "Mokihana announced that we would marry? Did you tell him that you would?"

Nani pressed her palm against his chest moving them slightly apart, "No, I did not. But if you ask me properly, I might consider it."

CHAPTER 73

THE PRINCESS PACED NEAR THE altar of the newly constructed temple to Lono. "I cannot believe you would consecrate my land to the freedom of slaves and the despicable kauwa," she raged, her eyes flaring.

Kalani stood on the grass of the open-air temple, stunned by the violence of her outrage. *But then, I should not have been surprised, it had taken me months to break with tradition and overcome years of obedience to taboos. I should have realized that Nani would go crazy when anything involving slaves came up. He decided not to answer her, considering it best to be silent, and let her fury subside.*

Nani stopped her pacing and pointed at Kalani. "Kauwa are filthy beasts, deserving to live in reservations, outcasts from the rest of us who are of pure blood." She stomped her feet.

"They have the same blood as you or I. It is something I know, for I see their blood flowing from the altars of the sacrificial temple. It is the same color as the blood flowing from warriors on the battlefield."

Nani stamped her foot again. "You do not understand. They are darker than us, making it clear that they are of a different caste, untouchables. They have no soul, no spirit in their breath. They are evil, inhuman, deserving only to be—"

"Sacrificed! It's sacrifice that is evil, not the people. Is it the darkness of their skin that you fear? Kauwa are the same color as the farmers who work in the sun. Is it their breath? I tell you, it smells the same as yours and mine. No, my princess, you despise the kauwa only because of what you have been taught: that they are of the lowest class and should be kept landless, uneducated, and enslaved." He spoke plainly, challenging bigotry with truth. *I know that overcoming prejudice is not easy, and convincing a ruler that all people are equal is a task more dangerous than capturing a tiger shark with your hands.*

Nani stared at him, a crease forming in her brow. "Life would become unpredictable if we did not have class differences," she reasoned, her voice suddenly tremulous. "It is our ranking that makes life livable. There are those who are born to rule, while others are born to serve."

"Just like I was born to be inferior to you. Have you forgotten how you put Moki and me in our place the moment we first met? We came to rescue you, but you ordered us about like a ruler anointed by the gods. You were always far above us. You act superior to me now. Does this mean you will continue to feel high and mighty during our life together?"

"Those are harsh words. Perhaps they are deserved. Time has changed everything. Ahi brought me down and Kamehameha has made you a chief, we may be equal. But kauwa, they are not the same: they were born slaves and must always remain slaves."

"Kauwa were once free, the first to come to these islands. They built the fish ponds, created the terraces where taro is planted. They lived in harmony with each other. Centuries ago, high priest Pa ao came from Tahiti with bloodthirsty Ku. These Tahitians suppressed the people living here. They cast them from the good lands, called them untouchables, and used them for sacrifice to the war god. Why did these men from Tahiti do this? It was to put the fear of death into lesser people and keep them subservient. Men who want to rule created this class-filled society that you love. Let me help you find the truth, that all people are the same. That all people are equal in the eyes of Lono." Kalani gazed at the woman he loved. He hoped his words had been reasonable, his tone gentle and not savage. Yet he had a passion for freedom, a desire to fulfill the promises he had made.

Nani remained silent for a time before answering. "Your words are confusing me. I have been taught that ancestry means everything. Those who could not trace to the second son of the gods of earth and sky could not be leaders of our people. If you were without genealogy, you were common and meant to work for the higher class. Now you tell me that the people who came here first lived together as equals."

A great sorrow came over him. He trembled. His eyes became moist.

"Kalani, why do you shiver?"

"To ease my pain. My friend Minato, a slave boy, was murdered to satisfy Ku's lust for blood. He was kind to me and taught me many things: to be an expert slinger, to be tolerant, that slaves are good people, like you and me. Minato is dead, yet he will always live in my heart. If I do not end slavery and sacrifice, I will not be true to Minato, myself, or anyone else."

"This is horribly confusing. You love a ghost and reject the teachings of our ancestors. Your heart is set on helping bestial dark people, giving them a status equal to mine. To me, this is madness, something I cannot accept." Nani burst into tears and fled from the temple.

Later, Kalani exercised outside the compound, mulling over events. The day before, Mokihana had pulled a bold ploy when he announced to the Maui chiefs that Kalani and Nani would marry. There had been no such agreement.

Yet Ahi's defeat had swayed Nani and she had agreed to meet with Kalani at the new open-air temple. There, beneath the statue of the god Lono, they would talk of his proposal of marriage.

Initially, the meeting had gone well. Nani came to him smiling, cheerful. She told him that she and her mother had discussed his marriage proposal for many hours. As they talked she had come to realize that Kalani had always been kind and considerate. Unlike Ahi he never forced himself upon her. What was most convincing was his willingness to risk his army and his life to save her from the evil man. Yesterday, on the battlefield, seeing Ahi run, she decided to favorably consider his proposal. "Most important," she concluded, "Kamehameha has made you a chief. You now have status and I find you suitable to marry."

It was then that Kalani made his mistake. In his joy, he told her of the "Law of the Splintered Paddle" and how he intended to interpret it: consecrating their land as an enclave where all slaves could come and live in freedom. After he said this, there followed the ugly scene and Nani's angry departure.

Since then she had avoided him. *I don't know what I could do to heal the damage wrought by my eagerness. I should have realized that royalty would go mad at any suggestion that slaves be set free. Despite this I knew that I must not hide my intentions. Better to tell Nani the truth before we married. But what would I do if she refused to be persuaded?*

Mokihana came to him, interrupting his reverie. "Kalani, enemy forces are gathering in Lahaina and Kihei. We must talk."

"What enemy forces?"

"Word has come that Makula returned from Oahu last week."

"Makula, I wondered where that bastard was. Tell me, so I can find him and kill him."

"Patience, a warrior whom you helped, Iolani, confided in me that your enemy is in Kihei, raising an army. I'm sure Ahi will join him and when they are strong enough, I fear they will attack."

"What about the chiefs in Wailuku?"

"They have not taken sides, but who can tell what they will do?"

"Where is Iolani?"

"He returned to Kihei, promising to come back when there is news of an attack."

"Get Eleele, Moki, bring them to my hale. We must prepare for the avalanche that is coming."

When his friends had assembled, Kalani drew a circle in the dirt with an H on one end. "This is Haleakala, the volcano that built the eastern part of Maui." He drew a separate circle with a K in it, "This is Pu'u Kukui, the old volcano that created the west side of Maui. For many years a gap existed between the two parts, but the ocean cast up sand filling the divide at Kahului. Along the joinder, large mounds of sand have built up against the slopes of the two volcanoes. Any army marching from Kihei or Lahaina to attack Kahului must pass through the gap between the dunes." He pointed to the separation between the two circles. "Twenty years ago, the Alapa Division of the King of Hawaii attacked through this gap. From the sand hills, Kahekili's rock throwers and spearmen rained death upon them. In the time we have we will build two stone walls across the gap."

"You intend to fight from behind them, like you did at Pahoa," Eleele said.

"Yes, and with one other factor: rock throwers from the dunes will rain death from the sky as attackers try to cross the barriers."

CHAPTER 74

For a week, Kalani's army built two parallel walls of rock and coconut logs anchored on a low sand hill that sloped east onto the foothills of Haleakala. By the seventh evening, the defensive walls had not been completed. Kalani went to sleep worried that the attack would come before they were finished.

His slumber was shattered by loud shouts coming from outside. He grabbed his spear, rolling upright to face the door of his shack. A man crawled through the threshold, his body blotting out the morning light. "Who are you?" Kalani demanded, his spear pointing at the intruder.

"I am a sentinel stationed at the sand hills," he said. "From our vantage point, we saw warriors coming from Kihei. Eleele ordered me to report to you."

"How many?"

"As plentiful as rocks in a stream."

"A big stream or a small stream?" Kalani asked with a laugh, lowering his spear. "Let us go and determine the number of rocks."

He stepped outside and found men gathering, joking and shoving like children at play. A good sign, he thought, morale is high. He searched for Eleele and Mokihana and found them in council with several warriors who were strangers to him, except for one tall man whom he knew from the past.

"What news do you have?"

"The birds that feed on carrion are flying in to shit upon us," Eleele answered.

"You're as vague as your sentinel," Kalani laughed at his blood brother's dry wit.

"There are warriors marching to attack us." Mokihana interrupted. "Your friend Iolani has told me of their coming."

The Kauai chief bent to prostrate himself, but Kalani gripped him before he went to the ground, drawing him up. "You bring news from Kihei, Lahaina?"

Iolani nodded. "There are seven hundred warriors coming against you from the south, and possibly a hundred from Hana."

"And Makula, Ahi?"

"They are leading an army from Kihei. Makula swears to sacrifice you to Ku but claims he will not eat you since you are kauwa and rubbish. You should know that he has trained a pack of dogs to attack your musketeers. When they will strike during the battle I do not know."

Kalani stared at the horizon, watching the rays of the morning sun burning away the shadows that still cloaked the sky. "There are enemies coming from Hana to the east. Makula and Ahi are coming from the south. What news from Wailuku to the west?"

"Nothing yet, but we must be watchful," Mokihana warned. "So far, the chiefs have been content to let matters develop. They have no particular loyalty to us, nor to Makula or Ahi. But if we are losing, they could join with the winning side to feast on our corpses."

Kalani shifted his gaze to the sky, studied a large brown bird gliding aimlessly, then with a strident *kee-ho* it plummeted to the earth. He smiled as he said, "Io has made a kill. It is a good sign. Let us fill the streams of Kahului with the blood of our enemies."

"Well, that's a pretty speech," Eleele scoffed. "Just like Kamehameha before a battle, always talking about reddening the water. For me, I would shout: Shove our spears into the buttocks of the bastards when they run from the ferocity of our charge!"

Just then, Moki strode up. "Eh, what is this blood talk? I faint when I see it." He laughed, winking broadly, then saw Iolani and reached out to him with a clenched fist.

Kalani clapped his friend on the back. "We were talking about how fearless you are. I was telling them that while the rest of us are cringing when the enemy charges, you will be standing straight as a rod, pissing in your pants." Kalani laughed, dodging a playful swipe.

"Stop this foolishness," Mokihana scolded. "There is serious trouble coming from Kihei, Lahaina, and Hana. We must meet it, or we will all be sacrificed to the war god. Iolani, how much time do we have before Makula comes?"

The Kauai chief reached down and broke a tuft of pili grass. Chewing on it, he spat out a stream of green saliva, then took the bare stem and pointed to the south. "Maybe Makula and Ahi from Kihei will be here this evening. The warriors from Lahaina are slow. My guess is they will come in two days. The men from Hana must paddle around the volcano to get here. When they left I do not know," Iolani paused for a moment watching the hawk fly away with a rodent in its claws. He pointed his stem to the bird and then at Kalani. "Like the hawk who fixes its eyes on its prey and attacks it, Makula wants to kill you. Once he knows where you are, he will strike even if all his forces have not come. That may be your only chance."

Kalani fell quiet for a moment considering what Iolani said. His eyes swept across the gap between the sand dunes. "Then I will be the bait to cause him to attack. We'll follow the plan we agreed upon. You, Mokihana, will be on the right flank with a hundred men, covering that part of the ground not protected by walls. You must keep an eye on Wailuku and what may be coming from there. With fifty men, Eleele, you will hold the high ground on the sand hills to the south, where the temple to Ku overlooks the sea. Watch for enemy canoes coming from Hana. Moki and I will be in the center where the road from Kihei winds through the low sand hills. We will have two hundred men, half of them held in reserve."

"A thin line of warriors," Eleele said, worry etching his face. "Any word from Akaka about coming to help us?"

Kalani shrugged. "No, nothing. We'll have to make do with what we have and the defenses we have built."

"It is not to my liking to hide behind rock walls," Eleele announced. "A true warrior fights in the open field and does not conceal himself behind stone."

"If we were stronger, I might agree with what you suggest," Kalani said. "But we are outnumbered. Low stone walls have proved their worth in battle. It conceals our strength, has defensive value. Most important, it halts an enemy charge, giving us time to shoot them as they try to cross over.

"Remember: no individual combats. We follow the plan that Kahekili used to defeat the King of Hawaii many years ago. Iolani, can you fight with us, or will you return to Makula?"

"I will go back. I will not reveal your plan, nor will I fight for him. When I can, I will slip away."

"Thank you for your help. Someday if we survive, I will reward you." He looked at his friends, his face grim. "There is much to be done before the enemy comes. Get your men and go to your assigned positions."

CHAPTER 75

FROM HIS VANTAGE POINT FACING the throat of the isthmus of Maui, Kalani watched warriors marching toward the dunes. He judged the hour too late for battle, since shadows already covered the ground and only the distant mountain tops were in daylight. He looked to the west and shivered when he saw a mass of warriors moving toward Mokihana's position. Could the Wailuku chiefs be attacking his right flank? If they were, his small army was doomed.

He raced toward his reserve force where men were preparing their evening meal. He yelled, "Come with me. Quick time." He kept running toward Mokihana's bivouac, puzzled that an attack might be coming so late in the evening. He glanced behind and saw his warriors following him. They were enough, he thought, to deal with any threat from Wailuku, but should Makula attack tonight, he knew his center position would be crushed.

He was surprised when he came to Mokihana's camp to see warriors eating and bonfires blazing. Beyond their bright light he saw silhouettes of many figures approaching, but they were not in fighting formation. He slowed his pace, the scar on his thigh throbbing, protesting the speed of his run. He searched for Mokihana and saw a familiar figure walking through the gloom. "Nani," he whispered, his voice faltering with the excitement of seeing her. Then, to mask his joy, he said sternly, "What are you doing here? We will be in battle by morning."

Nani raised herself to her full height. She looked at Kalani with scorn on her face, fire in her eyes, "Do you think I will let that evil Ahi take me again? No! I will fight him or die!"

Kalani dropped his eyes, avoiding her glare. He did not want Nani hurt or dead, yet he admired her savage determination to fight the man who had humiliated her. In a low voice, he said, "You must return home where it is safe."

"There is no place that is safe from Ahi and Makula. If you lose, and I am told that you are outnumbered, what do you think will happen to my mother and me? No, Mr. Boss Man, I am staying here to fight for our land and I have brought help."

Her words flustered him. "Our land?"

"Yes, mother and I have discussed what you said in the temple. We have talked of your consideration for women and how you are unlike most men who only take without giving. Though I am not yet ready to break with all traditions, I will share your dream with you."

Kalani stared at the woman, her hair bound in a knot on her head, her breasts thrusting out, full, ripe, and provocative. A white cloth girdled her waist with a pikoi hanging from it. A sling and tripping cord wrapped around her belly.

"You brought help?" he said, suppressing his excitement at her promise.

"A hundred-fifty men and forty women, all from Wailuku. The women are magnificent slingers and great with the tripping cords. The men are warriors who served with my father when Kahekili fought to save Maui from invaders."

Kalani spied Mokihana and waved him over. "Take charge of these warriors. Tomorrow—"

"Tomorrow," Nani interrupted, "the women will come to the sand hill that is by the road leading to Kihei. It is a perfect place for slingers to fight. As for the men—"

Slightly irritated by her taking command, Kalani asserted himself. With an authoritative voice, he said, "Tomorrow, a hundred men will stay with Mokihana. The rest will come and defend the sand hill with the women." He looked sternly at Nani, who dropped her eyes avoiding his glare. Her sudden deference touched his heart. He realized she was no longer the imperious woman he had met at Iao Valley. Somehow Ahi's cruelty had changed her. He reached his hand, wondering if she would pull away, returning to the arrogance of class differences that had driven them apart.

She took it and murmured, "Let us walk together as we once did many months ago."

Kalani nodded. Her warm smooth skin felt like lightning bolting through his body. He twined his arm around her, pulling Nani to his side. He felt the rhythm of her breathing as her breasts rubbed against his chest. He took her from the firelight and into the darkness, their steps slow, languid. His passion rose. He wondered if he should take her. Yet despite the urging in his loins, he realized that if this is the woman he loved and wanted to make his wife, then he must wait until she willingly received him.

She sensed his tension. "Ahi was horrible," she said. Nani stopped, her chest heaving, tears flowing down her cheeks. He tried to embrace her, but she waved him off, breaking from his grasp. "Wait, let me finish what I need to say."

Nani stood from him. She wiped her eyes and folded her arms over her chest. Nearby, Mokihana's bonfires sent ridges of flame into the sky, the light flickering ambient on her face. Her eyes glistened from the wetness of her tears, "Many times I wanted to die, but stayed alive for my mother's sake. Then you risked your life to rescue me as you rescued my father from death. Your payment for two lives has been rejection."

"Don't say that," Kalani interrupted, uncertain where the conversation was bending but determined to assert his feelings. "I love you. That is all that matters."

A wan smile flitted across Nani's face. "That is what my mother told me you would say. She said that your gentle nature would help wash away the horrid stench of Ahi that made me feel unclean. It is my hatred of him that draws me to you. I felt it boiling within me when you shot him. I feel it now that you will help me kill him." Nani paused, pressing her hands against her heart. "I once had more than this to offer, but Ahi stole that special gift and I find myself conflicted between revenge and gratefulness for your saving of my family and me. If we die tomorrow, then these swirling emotions will end. If we live and Ahi is dead, my hatred will be over and I can learn to love again."

"Princess—"

"I am no longer a princess!" Nani shuddered. "My father is dead, our land given to others, my body despoiled. There is no royalty in what is unclean."

Kalani reached to take her, but she shied from his touch. He thought to soothe her by avoiding the truth, but he knew he could not deceive as he had done in the past. "I told you that I came to kill Makula. I did not tell you that Kamehameha has given me your land by right of conquest. No, do not speak," he placed a finger to Nani's lips as her throat quivered. "Let me finish. I will take my revenge tomorrow, but I will not take Kahului without our love becoming permanent and forever. No matter your final decision you will always be my princess."

She raised herself, pulling his face to hers. She breathed his ha. "I know you speak the truth. Give me time to heal from the awful demands of Ahi and the beatings he gave me. Once I have killed him, I can learn to truly love again."

CHAPTER 76

KALANI WATCHED MAKULA STRIDE TOWARD his battle line before the priests started their rituals to the gods and the pahu drums began their beat. His mother's killer stopped in the middle of the open area between the two armies and raised his face, painted with streaks of black and white. He lifted his arms, fists clenched, flexing his biceps. "Kalani Moku Tana, son of kauwa. Where are you? Come out, little boy, and fight so I can kill you."

Demons of hate swelled inside him as Makula roared. The evil man tested his courage. He looked at his musketeers crouching behind the stone wall concealing their presence from the enemy. His men watched him, saying nothing. He knew they had heard the challenge and he imagined that they wanted him to fight Makula to end the battle before it started, winner take all.

The posturing chief stuck out his tongue. Clasped hands in front of his chest ridging his shoulder muscles, bulging his chest, his quadriceps rippled as he tensed his legs. "Come out here, little boy and receive the same death that took your mother."

With that challenge, all reason left him. Despite his cautions to others to avoid individual combat, he leaped from hiding, spear in hand. Before he could advance, Moki tackled him to the ground. They wrestled among the rocks and scrub of the low ground within the gap between dunes. "Follow the plan," Moki gasped as Kalani shoved an elbow into his stomach. "No individual fights. Draw him and his army to you, not you to him. Akaka landed his army in the morning and is marching to join us. Delay the battle as long as we can. If you lose the individual combat our force's morale will melt away."

"I don't care," Kalani stood, trembling, breaking Moki's grip with a twist of his arms. He saw his warriors sitting among the rocks, their eyes fixed upon him, apprehension in their faces. None had moved to intervene, but he sensed they were uncertain as to what to do for many avoided his glare. When he saw their uncertainty, Kalani realized that they were wondering why he was disobeying his own orders. Discarding the plan that had been created as soon as it was known that Akaka had arrived with reinforcements.

Moki gasped, "Brother, you told us, no individual combats. Iolani said our only chance is to make Makula strike before all his men had come. That's what we must do. Bait him into attacking right now."

Kalani breathed deeply, fighting to control his emotions. He smiled at a musketeer and reached for his musket. "Is it loaded, primed and ready?"

The soldier nodded. Kalani stood, squaring his shoulders, resting his foot on the rocks of the stone wall. He studied the battleground, watching the enemy warriors lining into ranks. He looked toward Wailuku and saw that no threat came from that village. He looked to the sand hill on his left. He saw Nani standing, her hand waving. Women warriors were formed in a crescent below her. He looked to where Makula ranted and preened his body. He aimed low, knowing that at this distance the gun's jerk would fling the ball high. But he did not intend to kill, only gain the man's attention.

The bullet flew over Makula's head. The chief stopped his posturing, staring at Kalani, who brandished his smoking musket, and yelled, "Killer of helpless women. Violator of the temple of the gods. Eater of opala, come to me and receive death." Kalani raised his musket again, pretending to fire. Makula retreated to his army. From a distance he called, "We will come, and you will die."

Kalani lowered his musket. He looked at his men crouching behind a stone wall. His voice rose so that even the soldiers on the sand hill could hear. "Our day's work begins soon." He watched his warriors fingering the shell beads circling their necks or wrists, seeking the good luck that the objects might give them. He knew that he must cut though their nervousness and give them the spirit to fight. "We will give those Kauai boys, the traitor Makula, chief Ahi, a thrashing that they will not soon forget. We will make them run home to Kihei like frightened chickens. I can smell their fear of you, the best warriors in all Hawaii. Stand fast, my brothers, and slay our enemies."

He pulled Moki to his side. "Thank you for stopping me again from spoiling our carefully laid plans. It is hard for me to sit still when I am challenged. You, my brother, are my faithful guardian in battle. I am constantly in your debt.

"No one has been told of Akaka's landing. I know he must organize his men. It will take time. Go to him, tell him to march to our right flank. He is not to beat drums or make noise to warn the enemy of his coming. In the center we will slowly fall back drawing Makula's army in. When he is ready, Akaka is to charge into the flank of the enemy. Tell the high chief I do not know how long we can hold out against the superior numbers facing us. He must hurry. Go to him." Moki left.

Priests wandered in the open space exhorting the gods to grant victory to their side. Conch shells trumpeted. Pahu drums beat loud, their booming sound echoing through the hills. Enemy soldiers yelled insults. An hour passed as the taunting built to a huge crescendo of sound.

Kalani stood on the first rock wall listening to the long buildup of fear-inducing noise. Suddenly he saw enemy soldiers marching swiftly toward Mokihana's warriors. Flying spears darkened the sky and mowed down many in the charging enemy. More men moved forward to fill the gaps in the attacking line. Two walls of men came together in a horrendous crash of sound and screams. With dismay he saw his right wing falling back. "Fifty men from the reserve go and help Mokihana."

"Kukae, Makula is attacking our weakest point with his superior numbers. He will drain off the reserves, then hit hard in the center," Kalani complained to his musketeers who stood with him along the wall.

They were twenty superbly trained men, ready to fight. Flanking them were former slaves and lua mates. He prayed that they, his plan, and Akaka would swing the battle in his favor.

On the sand hill Nani and her women stood poised for combat. He wondered whether they and the assigned warriors could hold the high ground against a determined attack. Worried, he shook his head, then remembered his pikoi woman warrior, braver than most men. She had valiantly stayed at his side during the disastrous battle in Puna.

"They are coming," a warrior whispered. "I can hear the clash of spears. The stomping of feet."

Kalani heard the drum beats. "Musketeers, the enemy is attacking, kneel at the wall."

The thunder of running feet, the clash of spears, joined with the booming of shark-skin covered pahu drums, built up a cacophony of sound that filled the swale between hills. A horde of charging soldiers bore down on the defenders sheltering behind the rock wall.

"Fire," Kalani ordered. Flame and smoke erupted from twenty metal tubes. Musket balls hammered into the oncoming attackers, tearing holes in the enemy line. Yet they kept advancing, stumbling over the fallen bodies of their comrades. "Reload, fire!" Kallai yelled. Thirty feet away a line of men fell, some with legs shattered, others with blood oozing from their chests or bellies.

"Heave," he ordered, and eighty spears carpeted the sky. More enemy fell. From the dunes rocks flew arching high, some landing short, but others taking their toll on the attackers. Kalani searched for Makula. His heart sank, for he saw him attacking the hill, smiting down defenders opposing him. "Kukae, that man is strong," he cursed as he saw the chief shrugging off stones that slammed into his sennit armor.

"Retire to the second wall," Kalani ordered as the enemy advance faltered. With a precision honed by extended practice, his men fell back. Captain Russell had taught him that a retreat in the face of an enemy is the hardest military maneuver to pull off, but he was proud of the men that he had trained, for they retired in good order behind the second rock wall.

Moki returned with news that the reserves had stabilized the right end of the line. Also, Akaka had organized his army and begun his march to the battle. He laughed, pointing ahead. "Look at them. They're confused. They don't know how to climb over a wall."

"Their chiefs will sort them out. Moki, Makula is fighting at the foot of the sand dunes. He wants to take the high ground. Go with the last of the reserves and stop him."

"Brother, you will not have enough left to hold this line."

"We will manage until Akaka comes."

Moki grinned and yelled, "*Kee-ho.*" He called to the remainder of the reserve force, ordering them to follow him. Then he ran for the dunes crying over and over again, "*Kee-ho.*"

Kalani watched him go, keeping an eye on the enemy massing between the two walls. Only seventy of his men were still able to fight, hardly enough, he thought, to stop a determined attack.

From the high ground missiles catapulted into the enemy. Women swarmed downhill slinging rocks, then retreated as Makula led a counter-attack. His charge came to a halt as Moki and the reserves joined the fight.

"Fire!" Kalani ordered and fifteen muskets flamed, iron balls smashing into the enemy. "Hurl spears!" More soldiers fell. From the dunes, boulders rolled down channels that had been carved in the sun-hardened sand. They smashed into a confused enemy.

"Just like that day many years ago when Kahekili caught Hawaii warriors in a trap," Kalani bragged to a musketeer standing by his side. "He stood on that same hill," he pointed where Moki and the reserves fought to hold the high ground. "The Maui king watched the Alapa division come into the gap. At the right moment he said to his generals: 'The fish are in the channel, draw the net'."

"And the Alapa were destroyed," the musketeer answered. He placed his gun on the second wall and stared ahead. "The enemy is withdrawing. I think we have broken them."

"No, I see Makula rallying his men. They are charging the hill. The man is overwhelming," Kalani said, admiration in his voice.

"Shall we help them?"

Kalani did not answer. He studied his right flank, alarmed that Mokihana's line of warriors bent backward, a gap opening between them. The situation was desperate, but he had no reserves to send to stabilize the right flank. "Where are you, Akaka?" he muttered. He looked at his men and knew they were exhausted. Some nursed wounds, others munched sticks of dried fish, while still others were splayed on the ground trying to rest. Between the walls, he heard the groans of wounded men and closed his ears to their cries for water and help. He saw a warrior hopping, his leg shattered by a bullet, his face swiveling to left and right searching for an avenue of escape. The man stumbled and fell onto a heap of bodies. He struggled for some moments, trying to get up, but soon gave up the challenge, lying back onto the dead.

Kalani turned to the sand dunes seeking Nani. *He remembered last night, their tender touching, the breathing-in of her essence. A beautiful time together.* He thought to go to her, die on the hills, but then he heard a howling coming from beyond the first wall. He knew if he abandoned the center the defenses would collapse and his cause was lost. Whatever came at them must be stopped.

He turned his gaze to the musketeer next to him, a young lua student trained by Hepa. "Do you hear that howling? Something evil is coming." On his right he heard thunderous sounds, the screams of men and the booming noise of pahu drums. Could Akaka have arrived?

He dared not hope. Something never heard of in battle approached his line of men, ten musketeers and forty spearmen. "Fix bayonets, warriors make ready!" he shouted as the barking became louder. Over the first wall jumped dogs, spreading across the battle field, streaking like dozens of black sharks attacking prey.

"Fire." But his men were unprepared for such an attack, and their musketry did not hit a single dog.

"Use spears, knives, anything," Kalani yelled as the animals leaped across the second wall and into his men. They bit, clawed, and tore at limbs with teeth filed sharp as knives. His center position shattered, his men fighting to save themselves from mutilation or having their bodies shredded into strips of raw meat by the ferocious animals.

Knocked to the ground by a dog, he smashed his short club into the jaw of the beast as its toenails raked his chest. He hit again and it went down whimpering, a thin line of blood drooling from its jaws. He rolled up, and saw vicious hounds biting his men. Coming over the far wall were scores of tattooed warriors, hooting loud war cries as they came. He glanced to the top of the hill and saw Nani fighting with her women, then disappearing into a swarm of warriors. His heart sank, for he thought her dead.

He could not save her, for tattooed warriors were clubbing their way into his disintegrating battle line. They screamed wild cries, dogs howled, wounded soldiers moaned, a mixture of horrid sounds. Kalani flung himself into the attackers, thrusting his spear, swinging his club. A sharp point pricked his side, but he twisted away before being seriously hurt. He struck down the spearman. A club whizzed by his head, and he turned in time to bury the butt of his spear into the belly of a tattooed warrior. A rock struck his chest, bringing him to his knees. He could only watch as combat swirled around him and his men were killed. He felt broken. He despaired for his cause, fearing that Nani and all he cared for were lost.

Trumpets blew. A grinning tattooed warrior towered above him, a cudgel raised to strike. Before Kalani could react, a spear stabbed into the man's chest and he fell twitching at Kalani's feet. Other tattooed warriors were dying at the hands of men Kalani did not recognize. Then he saw the high chief marching forward, leading fresh soldiers into the battle.

He searched the shrub-filled slopes of the sand hill, seeking Nani. Enemy warriors fought halfway up the slope, screaming cries of victory, unaware of the reinforcements that had come to save Kalani's army. He spied her near the summit of the dunes flinging stones. He glanced around, saw Akaka's men pursuing a fleeing enemy. He looked to the wall and saw dead warriors and dogs coloring the dark stone red with their blood. Exhausted soldiers were slumped against it, seeking rest. He should let them be, but he yelled, "Warriors come, follow me." He ran for the sand hill yelling a war cry.

A rabid dog tearing at the flesh of a corpse growled as he raced up the dunes. He stabbed at the animal and it shied away, then returned to its grisly feast. Kalani leaped over bodies, swerved around rocks, heading for the swirling melee of warriors fighting for possession of the high ground. Behind him he could hear his men scrambling to keep up. But he refused to wait for them, for he felt a rage growing within him, enemy soldiers might be killing his Nani. With a cry, he plunged into the melee.

As if by magic, the enemy melted away. They screamed, "Kamehameha is coming. Run. Save yourself." These once victorious attackers fled for Kihei only to be met by a column of Akaka's warriors who smashed into them, smiting and thrusting.

Kalani had little time to watch the slaughter, for a knot of men fought near the crest of the hill. For a moment, he glimpsed Makula with Ahi cowering behind him. With another war cry he charged. A path to Ahi opened as enemy warriors fled. The chief turned to run with them. Kalani raised his cudgel.

"Leave him to me," Nani yelled. A tripping stone flew from her hand, its cord wrapping around Ahi's legs. She yanked, bringing her rapist to the ground. The man struggled to gain his feet, screaming, "Save me!"

Nani pulled again, toppling Ahi onto his back. She reached down, gathered a large stone and stumbled to him as he struggled to free himself from the bindings. Ahi saw her coming, raised his hands and cried, "I surrender. Don't kill…" Nani's stone smashed into his face. He spat out teeth and blood as he tried to scream. She picked up her stone and aimed at Ahi's head, now an ugly mass of bruises. He squirmed in the dirt, his hands flailing aimlessly above him.

Kalani stood transfixed, hypnotized by the warrior woman, her chest heaving, her dark hair whipping behind her. In a piercing voice filled with hatred Nani yelled, "Die, you bastard!" She pounded her rock into Ahi's skull over and over until his body stopped twitching and he lay still, blood and brains oozing into the sand.

For a long moment Nani studied the corpse, then raised her eyes and said, "Come. Makula is fleeing to the sea." Kalani gathered weapons strewn on the dunes, reached his hand to her and together they raced toward the sounds of battle beyond the crest of the hill.

Wailuku Heiau

They climbed over the top of the dunes and came to the terraced black stones of a sacrificial temple. A prayer tower reared ugly into the sky. Its torn cloth covers flapped in the wind. On the upper platform, Ku glared at them, his pearl shell eyes glittering in the sun, his grimacing mouth showing rows of white pointed teeth. *Kalani looked at the horror and vowed that never again in his lands would the war god drink human blood.*

Below the temple Eleele fought with Hana soldiers. Beyond him Makula smashed a war club into warriors. "Let's go," Kalani yelled, and together they attacked. A spear arced toward Nani, but Kalani snatched it and hurled it back at the thrower, impaling him before he could dodge away.

Nani unwound her sling and began peppering the enemy. Kalani rushed to help Eleele but could not stop a man from spearing his blood brother. "Bastard," he yelled, clubbing the arm of the attacker who howled, releasing his grip on the haft of his spear.

Eleele sank to the ground, a stick quivering in his body. "Take this," Kalani whispered as he ducked under a weak punch and slammed his clenched fingers into the warrior's belly. The man gasped and rolled to the ground, writhing in agony.

He knelt by Eleele, pulling the weapon from his side. "Easy, my brother," Kalani said, trying to staunch the blood with his palm. But instead of falling to the rocks, the Hilo chief rose and yelled, "Come on filthy scum from Hana, come and fight me!"

From beyond the crest of the sand hill war cries rose. Nani joined two men facing the enemy. Someone screamed, "Back to the sea. Retreat to the sea," and the Hana warriors fled.

"Look," Nani said, pointing to the far edge of the sacrificial temple. "Makula is getting away!"

"Makula! Stand and fight me!"

The chief turned, and with an insolent smile, beckoned Kalani to come and get him. He moved toward a knoll that sloped gently to the sea. Light from the setting sun burnished the flaxen grass on the plateau to gold and gleamed from Makula's muscular body. He stretched, cracked his knuckles, the tattoos crisscrossing his chest wrinkled in waves of purple and black as he exercised. He squatted, patted the ground, looked at Kalani and said, "Here is where you will sleep forever."

He hobbled over the rocks and faced his mortal enemy. The man stood six-feet-four inches tall with numerous scars of battle ridging his body. Grotesque tattoos crisscrossed his face, making him ugly and fierce. Kalani knew from the marks that marred him that the man had experienced many more battles than he and, judging from his size, Makula outweighed him by many pounds. He gauged his chances for victory over his family's killer were slim, but he would have his revenge or die.

As he cast aside his spear, Makula said, "We will fight with club and dagger, face to face, man against man. Spears are for children, only useful to throw and run away. But if you are afraid then hurl yours now and then run, for death is staring at you." Makula thrust out his lips, swung his club in wide sweeps, sliced his twelve-toothed dagger though the air and stepped forward.

Kalani tossed aside his spear, realizing that it would be useless against an expert catcher, and said, "Before I die, I must know why you killed my mother and sister." He asked partly to buy time to lessen the pounding of his heart and ease the pain in his body.

Makula stopped and peered at him, his eyes burning through dark bushy brows. "I killed them because you stole my wife. I killed them because you defeated my army by your tricks. I killed them because, for months, you forced me to hide in the hills." His voice rose to a howl and he bellowed, "I killed them because Hinalea died to save you! You who are trash! And now, I will kill you!" At that, he lunged forward, his club seeking flesh.

Kalani dodged but the weapon slid by his side and drove him to the ground. Makula swung again, but this time his cudgel slammed into the earth, its tip shattering with the power of his hit, as Kalani rolled away. "Cockroach, stand and fight."

He knew that Makula expected him to fight upright, facing him as customary at festival time when boxers faced each other toe-to-toe and threw punches until one man was broken. But on this plateau, there were no crowds to heckle him for avoiding hits, so he heeded Mokihana's advice, "In a fight to the death, it is not unmanly to dodge, weave, and block punches." He believed that his only chance against the giant man would be his quickness. Kalani rolled upright and slashed his club against Makula's calf, then danced away.

The hit angered the chief. He came at Kalani, swinging his cudgel in great arcs, his knife poised for darting movements. They fought in a natural arena. The plateau's edges were ridged with barren stone, its semi-round surface flat with tufts of grass poking through.

Kalani took advantage of its smoothness, dodging an avalanche of blows as he sought an opening. It came at a price, for as he twisted to the side, Makula's shark-toothed knife swept across his chest, drawing blood.

The move exposed the chief's stomach. Kalani swung his club into the belly. His opponent didn't flinch. Instead, he tried to wrap an arm around Kalani's head and smother him to his chest. Slithering like an eel through a hole in the reef, Kalani escaped the deadly headlock. Squatting, he sprang to the side and Makula kicked out, the blow smashing into his ribs. Kalani staggered back. Makula lumbered after him trying to crush him like an insect. He yelled, "Stand and fight, filthy roach. Die like a man."

Kalani dodged wild blows and found himself at the edge of the plateau. He moved back. Makula came up to the brink and stopped his attack. Two hundred feet below, the ocean surged onto the shore. From the water voices yelled, "Pull, pull." Canoes were rushing out to sea. On the beach were more canoes with warriors waiting. Kalani guessed they were Hana men fleeing for home.

Makula raised his hand and signaled. Kalani realized that the chief intended to join them as soon as he was killed. "I will not die easily." He knew his bravado to be false, for blood flowed from the slice on his chest, his ribs hurt when he breathed, and he ached from exhaustion.

Makula turned, stared, and hissed, "Time to die."

Kalani realized his enemy wanted to finish him quickly and escape. He feigned weakness as he stumbled. Makula scurried across the plateau like a crab. He swung his cudgel like an axe chopping into a tree. Kalani leapt beneath the blow and into his enemy, clenched fingers digging into Makula's gut in the short, killing blow that had never failed to bring an enemy to his knees.

Makula dropped his weapons and laughed, unfazed by the strike. "Is that your best, kauwa boy?" And then he began to pound him with fists, elbows, and knees.

Kalani winced with each blow, fending off the strikes as best he could. He tried jabbing his palm into the man's jaw, but Makula twisted away from the strike, smashing an elbow into his face. The punishment became unending, great blows landing on Kalani's chest and stomach. He felt a cracking of his ribs, weakness spread over him, his body hurting in every part. He no longer fought back, only blocking blows as best he could. He wondered if it would be easier to die. He was amazed that he could still stand and think.

Suddenly, he heard a howl, the sound like a wounded animal in distress. The blows stopped. Through puffed eyes Kalani saw Nani pushing a spear into Makula's side. She yelled, "Fight me, you cowardly mother killer." She slashed him with an iron knife, slicing a cut across his face and shoulder. With a sweep of his hand, Makula knocked her to the ground, and for a moment, his body came exposed.

Though blood poured down his face partially blinding him, Kalani saw his chance. His pain vanished as his hatred soared and he sprang with all the strength he could muster, driving his head into the belly of the evil man. This time Makula gasped with the shock of the blow. Kalani hooked a fist into his jaw, hit his face with a hard right cross and followed with an uppercut to the chin.

Makula clutched his face, blood spurting from his nose and lips, spreading over his fingers. More blood poured from the spear wound in his side, from the slice on his shoulder. He staggered to the edge of the plateau, balanced at the precipice, his belly naked, smeared with blood, and exposed. Kalani saw Aunt Lei's pitted corpse, the slashed throat of his sister, the terrible cut in his mother's stomach, and reason left him. Bent low, he ran and rammed his head into the belly of the dazed man. Makula's eyes opened wide, his hands grasped for Kalani, who had fallen to the ground, his head partially over the cliff. Makula's arms flailed as he fought for balance. For a long moment, he teetered on the edge and then, with a gasp, he toppled over the crest. Kalani watched him fall, his body bouncing off jutting stones as he dropped. Finally, the falling body landed into bushes and slid off onto the beach. Men at vessels by the sea stared upward, then at the fallen warrior. Several rushed over and hauled a lifeless Makula from the sand into a canoe.

Kalani felt himself slipping as stones beneath him dislodged by the struggle began to move in a small avalanche over the edge. “Nani, grab my feet and brace yourself,” he yelled.

He felt her hands grip his legs, but she could not stop his slide as his head and shoulders slipped over the precipice. He shoved his palms into the earth, but the ground crumbled in his hands.

“Let me go, or you will fall too.”

“Never!”

“Hold on!”

Firm hands grabbed his legs. Slowly his shoulders and face were pulled back from the edge.

Exhausted, hurting in every part of his body, Kalani felt himself pulled up and looked into Moki’s worried face.

“Eh, brother, next time do not play around like an acrobat.”

The two friends laughed, embraced, and then Kalani gathered Nani into his arms saying, “I love you.”

“I love you, too,” she answered.

CHAPTER 77

RELATIVES, FRIENDS, AND GUESTS OF the royal couple congregated before the altar dedicated to the gods Lono and Kane. They listened to the nose-flute tunes of love being exchanged by Nani and Kalani. Everyone knew that words from the mouth were false, but breath is always true.

The sound from Kalani's flute rose to the eighth note of the octave, while Nani's instrument reached that same pure note. Their love music mixed together in harmonious sound, ending in the highest note that nose flutes could reach. When they finished giving and receiving musical love, they walked toward each other, stopping before a grand wreath of flowers spread out before the altar. The priest Mauloa emerged from a hut, a white cloth binding his loins rose across his chest, and flung over his shoulder. In a vibrant voice, he chanted:

O Kane, god of power!
O Lono, god of peace!
Rulers of the heavens and earth!
We offer you swine, food, and drink of the awa,
Accept these sacrifices and shower your blessings
On our Chief Kalani and Princess Nani.
Give them long life, happy life, a life filled with love.
Bless them and keep them in love forever.

The priest turned to the altar and took from the food offerings the ears of a pig. He placed one in each of the gourds dangling below the gods.

Mauloa returned to the altar, took morsels of food and vessels of awa juice, and offered them to the gods in the same way. He returned to a wreath of flowers, motioning with his hands for the royal couple to enter and embrace.

From one side of the altar came Akaka and from the other, Napua, her hands holding an intricately designed cloth. Together they wrapped it around Nani and Kalani, binding them. With their bodies thus joined, man and woman breathed each other's spirit, while Mauloa uttered a prayer. Napua and Akaka then unwound the cloth. Nani and Kalani clasped hands, stepped from the circle of flowers, and followed the priest to a partially enclosed shelter. Mauloa directed them to the mats inside the nuptial bower and closed the couple inside by pulling down a beautifully patterned, delicate tapa cloth.

Family and guests chanted prayers of love and good fortune and their song, at first low, rose to a crescendo of joy. Napua and Akaka raised their hands for silence and spoke in unison: "May the union of this couple be fruitful, bringing forth a child who will be a leader of our people."

The blessing concluded, Napua and Akaka led the witnesses to the marriage feast, spread out on fine woven mats that lay beyond the open-air temple. The festivities continued until nightfall, when torches were lit. Toward mid-evening the cloth door on the wedding bower was thrown open and the couple emerged. A woman shouted, "Nani, your face is filled with happiness, the fishing must have been good!" Laughter erupted, followed by ribald hoots extolling the special beauty of a woman and the virility of a man.

Arms linked, the newly married approached the edge of the feast, flames from the torches reflected golden light onto their skin. They stood for several moments, waiting for the joking and laughter of relatives and friends to die away. Kalani studied the gathering, wondering how they would receive his message. He believed that, despite their prejudices, they would obey the decision of their chief and chiefess. Finally, in a strong voice befitting his position and rising with the passion of his beliefs, he said, "Nani and I thank you for honoring our wedding by your presence. We are blessed by your prayers and expressions of love.

"For many years, I have pursued the goal of freedom for slaves and the ending of sacrifice. Tonight, I announce to you that this goal has been achieved. Princess Nani and I agree that the *Law of the Splintered Paddle* will govern this land and the people over whom we rule. The weak, the poor, the enslaved will find safety and equality in our realm. They will find freedom, and they will no longer live in fear of persecution. There will be righteousness for all people who live here."

There was a heavy silence, many gasped, and then something intangible filled the air. Kalani looked around him, trying to determine this response. And then he knew it to be joy. Former slaves, his brave soldiers, were stomping their feet with joy. Their wives were sharing this joy with them, their faces wreathed in euphoric smiles. Akaka, Napua, and Mauloa beamed, their hands coming together in a rhythmic clapping that resonated in Kalani's heart.

He scanned the guests and his eyes found Minato's parents. They were smiling, tears streaming down their cheeks, eyes filled with happiness. *The pain that had torn at Kalani's heart since the slave boy's death washed away. In this place, lay hope for a new beginning in Hawaii.*

The guests increased their cheering, Moki leading the way. They stomped their feet and thrust their fists into the air. Kalani reached for Nani's hand and together they stared into the Hawaiian sky.

He searched for the star that had started him on this quest many years ago. He saw it, Arcturus, beaming above him. Its heavenly sparkle twinkled in his eyes, filling his heart with the knowledge that Minato's sacrifice had not been in vain.

AUTHOR'S NOTE

A REVOLUTION WAS OCCURRING IN North America at the time Captain Cook came to Hawaii. The turmoil would not be settled until the United States was established as a nation by its Constitution of 1787. France erupted in revolt two years later. There followed years of war and conquests in Europe instigated by Napoleon Bonaparte. During this period in world history, the monarchy of Hawaii was also in turmoil. Many chiefs, alii, contended for power. These wars of conquest were over control of land and people, the only resources of the islands.

At the time of the events of this book, 1790, the Hawaiian Islands were not united as one kingdom. Moi, a sovereign, with numerous chiefs owing allegiance to him, ruled on each island. As noted in the Prologue, Hawaii Island had split into three parts. Maui, Oahu, and Molokai Islands were loosely joined together under Kahekili who had to deal with rebellious chiefs on Oahu. Kauai and Niihau came under the leadership of Kaeo who had his own internal problems.

The titles of king or queen were introduced with western contact. Rulers were determined by heredity which meant genealogy decided a person's status. There was always an attempt to gain increased status within the hierarchy of chiefs. As an example, Kamehameha was in the fourth rank of alii. He desired that his legitimate heirs would gain the highest rank, the burning kapu. That is why he delayed seizing full control of Hawaii Island, to secure a future wife, Keopuolani, who had the highest rank, the burning kapu.

Kapu is a "thou shall not' command. Only high chiefs and priests could issue a kapu. A violation of such an order meant death which was enforced by a special group of koa, elite warriors. It was not unusual during the turbulent times of our story for innocent bystanders, women, children, aged, and slaves to be killed during the ongoing wars for breach of kapu or a whim. When Kamehameha declared the *Law of the Splintered Paddle,* he broke tradition by ordering his chiefs to keep the helpless free from harm. It was a unique event in Hawaiian and military history. No longer could the powerful kill commoners as they pleased. When Hawaii became a state, it adopted the law into its Constitution, Article 9, Section 10, and is the basis of the state social programs. Earlier, in 1840, slavery was banned in the islands by the first Hawaiian Constitution. According to missionary records, Kaahumanu overthrew the idols and kapu system in 1819, the year of Kamehameha's death, and before the arrival of the missionaries.

Hawaiian chiefs did not have standing armies. Instead, they maintained small forces of trained men called koa. These professionals learned martial arts training in the pa (lua school) maintained by high chiefs like Kamehameha. Since chiefly status depended on genealogy and the ability to trace to the gods, it was exceedingly rare for a person without heredity to attain that status. However, a heroic koa could become what is known as a "black land chief".

In 1790, Kamehameha acquired cannon and muskets. He kidnapped two British sailors, John Young and Isaac Davis, to train his people in their use. From that time on, Kamehameha began to win battles using his foreign firearms. The combats on Maui are based on actual events. The fighting with Keoua on Hawaii Island is partly true. Kilauea volcano did erupt as depicted, destroying some of Keoua's army. Kamehameha sent one of his high chiefs to fight in Puna and Kau, believing that those two districts could be easily conquered, but Keoua was able to defeat the invasion. At some point, Keoua came to Kawaihae at Kamehameha's invitation to talk peace, and was sacrificed as related. Kalani's fight at Kahului and the sand hills is fictional.

Because the Hawaiian language was oral and not written until the missionaries arrived in 1820, sources of history before then were oral history, and recordation of it after 1820.

Could a young Hawaiian like Kalani have broken with tradition and sought to end slavery and sacrifice? Early explorers and traders who arrived after 1778 were opposed to the indiscriminate sacrifice of human beings, and sea captains like Vancouver tried to end it. When Kaahumanu broke kapu, idols were destroyed, and temples abandoned.

The novel ends in 1793. Kamehameha would complete his conquest of Maui, Molokai, and Oahu by 1795. Kauai would resist two invasion attempts and not surrender to Kamehameha until 1810.

ABOUT THE AUTHOR

BILL FERNANDEZ, HALF NATIVE HAWAIIAN, was born in Kapaa, on the island of Kauai in the state of Hawaii, and is a graduate of Kamehameha Schools, Stanford University, and its Law School. He practiced law in Sunnyvale, California, the future home of Silicon Valley, served as its mayor, and was appointed to the Santa Clara County Courts. Married and retired, he and his wife returned home to Kauai where he began his writing career. He served on the board and as president of the Kauai Historical Society, is on the boards of Hale Opio, a social service agency on Kauai, and the Kauai Native Hawaiian Chamber of Commerce. The governor appointed him to the Juvenile Justice State Advisory Commission.

To learn more about Bill and his books, visit his web site and fcb page at www.kauaibillfernandez.com. fcb: Bill Fernandez Hawaiian Author Books available at local Hawaii stores and on Amazon

BIBLIOGRAPHY

Ancient Hawaiian Civilization. Lectures at the Kamehameha Schools. Honolulu: Mutual Publishing, 1999.

Daws, Gavan. *Shoal of Time: A History of the Hawaiian Islands.* New York: Macmillan, 1968.

Desha, Reverend Stephen. *Kamehameha and His Warrior Kekuhaupi'o.* Translated by Frances N. Frazier. Kamehameha Schools Press, 2000.

Dukas, Bernard Neil. *The Battle of Nu'uanu 1795.* Honolulu: Mutual Publishing, LLC, 2010.

Fornander, Abraham. *Ancient History of the Hawaiian People to the Time of Kamehameha I.* Honolulu: Mutual Publishing, 1999.

Kalakaua, David. *The Legends and Myths of Hawai'i.* Honolulu: Mutual Publishing, 2002.

Pagliawan, Eli, Kalauokalani, Walker. *Lua, Art of the Hawaiian Warrior.* Honolulu: Bishop Museum Press, 2006.

Malo, David. *Hawaiian Antiquites Mo'olelo Hawai'i.* Translated by Dr. Nathaniel B. Emerson.Honolulu: Bernice P. Bishop Museum Special Publication 2, 2nd Edition, 1951.

Tregaskis, Richard, *The Warrior King, Hawai'i's Kamehameha the Great.* New York: Macmillan Publishing Co, Inc., 1974.

CPSIA information can be obtained
at www.ICGtesting.com
Printed in the USA
LVHW030529131221
706034LV00004B/315

9 780999 032671